CAVE DWELLERS

CAVE DWELLERS

RICHARD GRANT

Alfred A. Knopf · New York · 2017

THIS IS A BORZOI BOOK
PUBLISHED BY ALFRED A. KNOPF

Copyright © 2017 by Richard Grant

www.aaknopf.com

Knopf, Borzoi Books, and the colophon are registered trademarks of
Penguin Random House LLC.

Library of Congress Cataloging-in-Publication Data
Names: Grant, Richard, [date]
Title: Cave dwellers : a novel / Richard Grant.
Description: First edition. | New York: Alfred A. Knopf, 2017. |
"This is a Borzoi book"—Verso title page.
Identifiers: LCCN 2016030611 (print) LCCN 2016037187 (ebook) |
ISBN 9780307270832 (hardback) | ISBN 9781101947944 (ebook)
Subjects: LCSH: Hitler, Adolf, 1889–1945—Fiction. | Government,
Resistance to—Germany—Fiction. | Intelligence officers—
Germany—Fiction. | Conspiracies—Germany—Fiction. |
Espionage—Fiction. | World War, 1939–1945—Fiction. | BISAC:
FICTION / Historical. | FICTION / Espionage. | FICTION /
Literary. | GSAFD: War stories. | Historical fiction.
Classification: LCC PS3557.R268 C38 2017 (print) |
LCC PS3557.R268 (ebook) | DDC 813/.54—dc23
LC record available at https://lccn.loc.gov/2016030611

Jacket photography by Kurt Hutton / Picture Post / Getty Images
Jacket design by Oliver Munday

Manufactured in the United States of America
First Edition

CHAPTERS

1. At Home with the Baroness von F—— 3

2. Crime in America 17

3. From the Kreuzberg to Hell 47

4. Librarians in Exile 56

5. Patriots of the Wrong Era 67

6. Strength Through Joy 77

7. Setback Theory 97

8. Bodies on the Second Floor 104

9. Netting Men Like Shoals of Cod 134

10. One Thinks of Dying Heroically 143

11. The Vampire Did Not Disappoint 153

12. Be Careful About Breathing 163

13. Golden Pheasants 175

14. Cousin Peter Is Ill 181

15. Trying to Count Bullets 200

16. The High Point of the Season 215

17. Do You Truly Want to Know? 223

{ CONTENTS }

18. Christ on a Rocking Horse   232

19. When Wars Start   246

20. The Naïveté of Youth   253

21. What Herr Boar Has to Say   261

22. Foolish and Dangerous   268

23. On the Road with the Baroness von F——   276

EPILOGUE

Several Lifetimes Later   335

CAVE DWELLERS

AT HOME WITH THE BARONESS VON F——

BERLIN, FASANENSTRASSE: NOVEMBER 1937

The tall east-facing windows would have given a splendid view of
sunrise over the Tiergarten were it not for a drapery of fringed and
weighted damask, drawn over them one morning in the spring of
1933 and never opened since. The Baroness missed the sunrise.
But not so much as she loathed the other lights that now regularly
played there. Torches, borne in endless columns by grown men in
short leather pants and foolish hats like drunken farmers on holiday.
Bonfires, encircled by boys with their hair cropped as if they were
little soldiers, voices raised in shrill *völkisch* anthems or pitched too
low for their throats and impossibly solemn, chanting oaths to the
Fatherland, to the Leader, to the "sacred brotherhood born of blood
and soil." Hand-held lanterns, bobbing and swaying in the sweaty
grip of policemen. Or maybe not policemen; they sometimes wore
long leather coats or uniforms the Baroness didn't recognize—who
knew what anybody was anymore? And once, before her own eyes,
a light she could not have mistaken: the muzzle flash of a rifle, like
the momentary striking of a match, burning a hole in her memory.

And so the Baroness had withdrawn behind her curtains, ced-
ing to the ruling mob its claim on the streets and the *Plätze*. Shake
your heads, believers in the magic of open views and the fortifying
properties of sunlight. The Baroness in her long life had collected
enough views to fill a vast private gallery. As for sunlight, well . . .

it fades the chintz and causes wrinkles and—don't you agree, *mein Herr?*—those things we can achieve without solar assistance.

A newcomer to the von F—— circle was advised, at such a moment, to neither demur nor agree but rather, in the old-fashioned style, to bow from the waist while holding the Baroness's gaze—a token of mute admiration, as it were. One might smile. One might, if an officer in uniform or a bona fide member of the aristocracy, clap one's heels. Above all, one would do well to hold one's tongue. Conversation with the Baroness had been likened by an old brigadier to advancing into unmapped territory held by Cossacks or Tatars. You just didn't know what sort of thing might come jumping out at you.

Fresh air was a different matter. The Baroness would not be denied her just portion of the famous *Berliner Luft.* And so each morning, even on a day like this when early snow threatened, an aged house "girl," whose service to the von F—— family predated the doorbell, was sent tunneling through chinks in the damask to throw open the heavy sashes and so admit the sounds and smells of the great, ugly, beloved city. Drapery puffed in and out, as if the old apartment were laboring for breath. A wood fire swelled in its finely carved, Gothically arched marble surround. Fine ash floated everywhere, and the so-called girl gave chase with a molting feather duster.

The Baroness had grown accustomed to moping in her boudoir until midafternoon, calling for the newspapers and then throwing them angrily to the floor, soaking for an hour in a hideous bathtub her late husband had dragged back from some château where his staff had wintered in 1916. She permitted herself three cigarettes a day. If the first came earlier than three p.m., the girl took this as an ill harbinger and sought refuge among the linens on the upper story.

Pünktlich at six, Sundays and Thursdays, the Baroness would appear, her wraithlike body lent substance by several yards of Parisian couture, in the archway of a long, dark and tomblike chamber she alone called the Grand Salon, and ceremoniously declare, "*Je suis à la maison,*" as though she quite expected the door to burst open with the press of friends and admirers and social comers and unappreciated artists and doe-eyed ingénues and musicians lugging battered instrument cases and banned novelists making straight for the bar, along with the customary handful of handsome Wehrmacht officers and discreetly murmuring diplomats and perhaps a strange boy with a doomed, Young Werther look, clutching the balcony rail as though debating whether to hurl himself over or wait and see if the music would be any good.

The amazing thing was, the Baroness was right—that's just what would happen, and soon. Exactly that sort of crowd flocked to her large, gloomy flat two evenings every week, come snow or rain or wrinkle-inducing sunshine. And the Baroness would breathe a deep sigh, nodding in the melancholy assurance that while that wretched Austrian cur might be dirtying the name of Germany among the nations of the world, he hadn't succeeded—not yet—in destroying the Berlin she'd always known, nor in driving *all* the interesting people into exile. If anything, the parties were better than ever.

"Would you permit me, Baroness," murmured a bent old gentleman at her elbow—he used to be something in the Bendlerstrasse, she thought—"to present my young friend . . ."

She would not remember the boy's name five minutes hence. But she raised her gloved hand to be kissed; it was vital for the sake of old and young alike that the forms be preserved. Let the heathens rage, loose the dogs of war, set truth and beauty to the torch—*ach*, the world is full of horrors, always has it been so. But surrender one's sense of decorum, forget the simple graces that set us apart from grunting beasts, and tell me, *mein Herr*, what is left?

The Baroness gave a slight shake of the head, willing such thoughts away. Her face felt oddly flushed, and she wondered for a moment if she'd actually spoken aloud. Perhaps not—the old gentleman was nodding happily at something his friend had said. Lowering her hand, she felt for a long, dizzy moment that she might burst into tears.

Naturally, she did no such thing. One didn't. But really, it was too horrid, all of it. The incessant marching. The banners, the beer-hall songs, the screaming on the radio. So much anger. So little ordinary kindness. Couldn't something—*anything*—be done? Wasn't it about time? The Baroness cast an eye over the Grand Salon, wondering vaguely who all these people were. Not their names or their titles. Who they *really* were.

The people one knows! That angular young man over there, haunting the corner near the piano: hadn't he given a recital at the Gedächtniskirche? She felt sure of it, though she retained no impression of the performance itself. Good or bad, it hardly recommended him for the grim requirements of the day. Nearby, gesturing theatrically with one hand while deftly balancing a plate of little sandwiches in the other, a White Russian princess, poor as a church mouse, essayed a canny imitation of her boss at the Foreign Ministry. Awfully impudent—yet the girl had that quality the British, God save them, call pluck. *She* might be good for something. Now, who was that frightful little man she was talking to? Short and dark, part Ottoman by the look of him, his naturally glum features twisted into a tortured smile at the Russian girl's antics. A dwarf, the Baroness thought, a mountain dwarf from the Tyrol.

Her spirits were rising again as the evening wound itself up, spinning faster and faster like a child's toy. She remembered the glass of aged cognac at her elbow and, turning for it, aimed a quip at the old fellow from the Bendlerstrasse—but he was gone, and his young friend with him. Yes, enjoy yourselves, my dears, she thought. Forget the ghastly world for a while. It will still be there tomorrow. And tomorrow and tomorrow, for the next thousand years.

Mendelssohn," said the Colonel with a chuckle. "She's got them playing Mendelssohn!"

Oskar, feeling stiff and graceless in his dinner-dress lieutenant's uniform and far out of his depth in this company, smiled politely even though he didn't see what the joke was. He peered around the library at the little crowd, a mixed lot—people from the ministries, soldiers like himself, Greimer the once-eminent journalist, a young count and an old one, a couple of drab-looking fellows whom Oskar suspected of being artists—while for several moments everyone listened dutifully to a trio for piano and strings that floated softly from the adjacent hall. The goings-on out there seemed far removed from this hushed, oak-paneled, high-ceilinged room, which he guessed had been the private sanctuary of the late Baron. *We mustn't disturb him, he's in the library.*

"Mendelssohn was a Jew," explained a quiet voice at his side.

He turned to find himself the target of an opaque, passionless gaze—from a man some years older than himself dressed all in black, affecting a cape and a curled lip and the approximate skin tone of a vampire, achieved with a dusting of facial powder over a complexion scarred from some childhood illness. An actor, possibly? A cabaret singer? Probably just another character, one of millions, out of the Berlin night.

"A Jew," the cloaked man repeated, in a voice now etched with sarcasm, "and thus forbidden in the New Order. Poisonous music, fatal to the German folk-soul!"

He made no effort to speak quietly and by now had attracted the notice of people nearby. The Colonel smiled, shaking his head, and the disheveled and startled-looking Greimer said, "Calm down, Stav, you're alarming a trained warrior, which can lead only to sorrow."

Oskar felt out of step, his reactions coming half a second late. A smile, signaling no offense taken. A nod, thanking the vampire for explaining what was funny about Mendelssohn. Though now he understood that it hadn't been a joke after all—the Colonel had laughed not in amusement but in admiration for the old lady's nerve. All these people . . . you had to expect a few of them would be having a chat later with the Gestapo, or the Ordnungspolizei, or the block warden, or some other defender of racial hygiene. At any rate, it was never safe to assume otherwise. To someone of Oskar's age and background, the habits of extreme discretion came as second nature. But he guessed that people like the Baroness had never needed to learn such things, or maybe simply didn't care to.

"Listen," someone said. "They've switched to Schubert."

Quiet again. An air of disappointment. Then a female voice, giggly with champagne, began trilling the Romantic lyrics of "Out of Old Fairy Tales." Laughter, a smattering of applause. Out in the hall, a man's voice shouted, "Brava, Cissy!"—then, in English, "Swing it, girl!"

"Heine," Stav murmured helpfully at his side. "This is based on a poem by Heine—another Jew by birth. Evidently, this will be our theme tonight."

Oskar found it odd that one was required, and again he felt, in this setting, self-conscious and stiff-backed, as though he'd just marched off the parade ground at Lichterfelde. Not for the first time, he wondered why the Colonel had invited him along—rather forcefully, in fact, as if it was a question of duty, one of those thousand subtle expectations, nowhere written down, that a German officer must satisfy. Especially an officer who, like Oskar, couldn't count on a famous name or high-ranking connections to smooth his career. His own father, a captain of artillery, had fought for several months without distinction in the Great War before being sent off by an opposite number on the French side. That hadn't kept Oskar from wanting to be a soldier; if anything, it made him feel obliged to carry on the family tradition, though more successfully this time. And so he stood now freshly commissioned in Berlin, the glittering *Hauptstadt*, in the fifth glorious year of the Millennial Reich, killing time as adjutant to a soon-to-retire operations specialist while awaiting his first real posting.

The song rambled a few stanzas further before losing itself among the clamor of other guests trying to sing along, until finally the tipsy diva lost her momentum. A violinist took up the melody, and things began to quiet down. Just then an elderly servant entered the library with a fresh tray of champagne, but something in the room—a charge in the atmosphere—caused her to reverse course and hastily shuffle back out. At which point the young count firmly shut the door. Oskar was able at last to eavesdrop on a conversation among a small group of men including his own Colonel who'd gathered beside a large, outdated globe mounted on a brass stand with complicated fittings like some arcane tool of augury.

"Didn't anyone object?" the Colonel wanted to know. Clearly riled by something. Indignant.

"Does anyone dare, these days?" said an old brigadier, his hair razed to a white bristle. "Talk back to Hitler, I mean. They've got themselves in a golden vice. Keep their mouths shut, he'll give them everything they've dreamed of. But raise so much as a whisper—"

"Not *everything*," the Colonel objected. "And not exactly *give* them."

The Brigadier smiled—benignant, patriarchal. His dinner-dress uniform had acquired a sheen from too many launderings but was resplendent with decorations, many dating from the previous century. "Naturally, they're worried about their careers," he said, with the detachment of someone for whom such worries were distant indeed. "Who *are* they, if they quit the army? What are they doing in this unholy mess?"

"What are any of us doing?" said a man in civilian clothes. Edgy, angular, leaning slightly forward as though prepared to make a dash for it, he flicked onyx eyes at those around him, catching Oskar too for just an instant. "Look at us—eating and drinking, listening to music, bantering with our pals as if everything's perfectly normal."

"What would you have us do, Hans-Bernd?" said the Brigadier, his tone still cordial, though now with a flinty edge. "Go around in sackcloth and ashes, moaning about the sorry state of the world? Hard times come and go. Rascals worm their way into high places but never last long there. Radical programs are self-defeating. Think of the Anabaptists in Münster."

"There's something to that," said Hans-Bernd. "We're seeing now the same level of fanaticism. And the same degree of wanton cruelty, masquerading as righteousness. But when you say 'self-defeating,' I'm afraid I can't agree with you. The Anabaptists didn't burn themselves out. They needed to be smashed to a bloody pulp."

"All right, but still—they brought their doom on themselves, didn't they? By their own excesses. The reaction was inevitable."

"I take it then, *Herr Brigadegeneral,* had you been around at the time, you'd have rallied to the banner of Westphalia?"

"Without a moment's hesitation."

"Well, then . . ." Hans-Bernd made a sweeping gesture with one hand. *Go right ahead, then.* Or maybe: *What the hell are you waiting for?*

The Brigadier's lips tightened. With the slightest of bodily adjustments, he turned a shoulder on this rude civilian, favoring instead a fourth party to the conversation—a gangling navy man, as long-faced and mournful as a hound, his Kriegsmarine uniform so ill-tailored it might have belonged to someone else. By reflex Oskar's eye flicked downward, counting the stripes on the blue-black sleeve. Three in all, two wide and one narrow: a *Kapitänleutnant.* Age, mid-thirties. As though sensing his gaze, the man lifted his head to look back at him. Oskar stiffened and gave him a brief, correct nod. A corner of the sailor's mouth twitched, but that was all.

"We interrupted you, I'm afraid," the Brigadier said to him. "You were talking about the conference with Hitler."

"Yes—the *Führerbetreff* of 5 November. I wasn't there—I've only read the minutes. The admiral has been discreetly passing them around. He's aghast, I can tell you."

"The war, damn it," said the Brigadier. "You'd just gotten to the war."

The navy man sighed. "The only question, the Führer says, is *when*. His tone reportedly was blunt—he wants to leave no doubt of his intentions. Our military preparations, he goes on to say, are more or less complete, our forces battle-ready. Our new armaments are superior to those of other nations. He doesn't *name* these nations, but later he speaks derisively of the British and the French—'two hate-inspired countries.' Then he changes tone. This favorable situation won't last forever, he says. Given time, our enemies will update their arsenals. So we have a definite but limited opening—a window of superiority. It closes, he thinks, no later than '43, but we mustn't wait till then. Providence has granted us this opportunity to solve our age-old problem of *Lebensraum*. So we must seize it, quickly and decisively. The first steps must come soon—next year if we can manage it. And so, my loyal commanders, as the scouts say: Be ready!"

The navy man paused. His voice had become high-pitched and strenuous, an unconscious imitation of the Führer's, and he dropped it to its normal register. "I've left out the details, of course. But that's the thrust of it."

The four men looked at one another, as though none wanted to be the first to react.

Finally, the brash Hans-Bernd slapped an open hand against his thigh. "Well, there you see the bloody insanity of the thing. *Lebensraum*—where does he plan to find that, I wonder? As far as I know, all the space on this continent is currently occupied. Does he plan to invade Antarctica?"

"The East," said Oskar, surprised by the sound of his own voice. Everyone in the room turned to stare.

"Gentlemen," said the Colonel wryly, "I present my adjutant, Leutnant Oskar Langweil. You were saying, Oskar—the East?"

"It's in his book," Oskar said, aware that he was talking too fast. "*Mein Kampf*—we were required to read it in *Gymnasium*. It's quite . . . difficult. All but impenetrable, actually. Most people only skimmed through. But you know, it's also quite informative. 'Our destiny lies in the East—only there can our *Volk* find the space it requires to breathe freely and increase in number.' "

"The East," fumed the Brigadier. "What the hell's he talking about? Poland? Czechoslovakia?"

"Russia," said Oskar. "He means Russia. Of course, the others too. But ultimately—"

Hans-Bernd shook his head. "It's madness."

"It's nonsense," said the Brigadier. "The army would never allow it. Not even Blomberg."

"Then he'll rid himself of Blomberg," Hans-Bernd said with a shrug. "There are other generals. Good, reliable National Socialist generals like Kluge or Reichenau."

The Brigadier seemed to be working up a sharp reply—Reichenau, indeed!—but Oskar's attention was deflected as the dog-faced *Kriegsmarine* officer stepped toward him with an apologetic smile.

"Pardon the intrusion," he said quietly, "but I wonder if you'd care to speak briefly about a matter of mutual concern? If so . . ." He motioned toward a shadowy recess that Oskar had taken for the entrance to a WC.

Oskar nodded uncertainly and followed him through a narrow doorway into a kind of sanctum sanctorum, a small writing chamber furnished with a leather-padded chair, a rickety escritoire and a lectern bearing a very old edition of Goethe's *Faust*. The navy man closed the door and turned back to him, his gaze now frank and devoid of social nicety.

"*Verlasst die Tempel fremder Götter,*" he said.

Oskar was startled, but his lips formed a reply without conscious direction: "*Glaubt nicht, was ihr nicht selbst erkannt.*"

It was the opening couplet of the Secret Anthem, a brisk and stirring tune that was sung in ritual fashion to open meetings of the Deutsche Jungenschaft vom 1 November, a progressive youth group banned in 1933 and then banned again, to little effect, at least twice since. *Leave the temple of the strange gods; believe nothing you haven't discovered for yourself.* A whole body of boyhood mythology surrounded this song, whose lyrics were forbidden to be written down or revealed to outsiders.

The man gave Oskar a fraternal nod. "I'm sorry, I guess that was unnecessary, but I hoped it might . . . reassure you. I'll be brief, then. I assume you're a patriot."

"Herr Kapitänleutnant—"

The other man made a gesture with one hand, waving military etiquette aside. "Call me Jaap, please—that was my Movement name. Yours, I believe, was Ossi. When I say 'patriot,' I don't mean a fool waving the swastika while kicking the shit out of some Jew on the sidewalk. I mean someone who understands what Germany means, someone with a sense of history who's upset by what's going on now in the name of the Fatherland. Crime masquerading as national pride. Contempt for knowledge, for culture, for books, for people who read books. Contempt for everyone who doesn't fit their picture of the New German Man. Look—you don't need to say anything right now, just listen. All right? Shall I go on?"

Oskar nodded. Whatever this was, it was happening fast. He'd never heard anyone speak like this—so openly, and to a stranger. But then they weren't really strangers, were they? As people in the Movement used to say, they'd circled the fire together. They'd made the same pledges, sung the *Geheimeslied.* Now they could trust each other. Or so Oskar hoped.

"You're expecting orders soon," Jaap said. "I imagine you're hoping for something challenging, something . . . away from all this." He cocked his head toward the party carrying on beyond the door. "As it happens, there may be a job that would be just the thing for you. A position somewhat out of the ordinary that requires a particular set of attributes, chief among them a certain . . . let's say, disregard of danger. You've got that, haven't you? I heard about your foray into Denmark."

Despite himself, Oskar laughed. "It was only milk paint. It wasn't meant to *permanently* deface the statue."

" 'Deface' is a curious verb, considering the body part in question. A job well managed, though. What I have in mind is a bit like that, only—please understand this—considerably more dangerous. You'll be going overseas, you'll be going alone, and you'll have absolutely no one to back you up if things turn out badly. You can't talk about it afterward, and very few people will know what you've done. The work is important, but the rewards are very *quiet*. So tell me, Ossi—does what I'm saying interest you?"

The question struck Oskar as faintly ridiculous. "Of course it does."

Jaap smiled. A look of relief? Oskar thought so.

"Very well, then." All business now. "This is how it will work. You'll be contacted presently through ordinary channels. Everything will appear strictly routine. An officer seconded to the Foreign Ministry will be seeking an individual, a courier, available on short notice. A number of candidates will be interviewed, and you'll be selected. From that point you'll be working for the Abwehr, military intelligence. We're outside the normal chain of command, and our boss is an admiral named Canaris who reports directly to the chief of the General Staff. There will follow a short period of training— you'll enjoy that, I think—and then you'll be given a very important, extremely delicate assignment. Do you have any questions?"

Oskar had so many that they seemed to crowd together in his throat, blocking his ability to pose any of them. He shook his head.

"Excellent!" Jaap nodded cheerfully. "I heard about Scotland too. Quick thinking there. I wonder, did you have any trouble with the language? With English in general?"

"No trouble. My English is—"

"Good. You might want to sharpen it up in the days to come. Go to the cinema. Practice on tourists. The German-American Friendship League has got something going this week, I believe. That might prove useful for you. Well—good evening, Ossi. And best of luck."

Oskar stood watching him lope in his rumpled uniform through the library and back into the cheerful mayhem of the main hall. He felt a growing sense of unreality. Had he really just—without pausing to think, without asking a single question—agreed to become a spy?

The short, dark man who'd put the Baroness in mind of a mountain dwarf (in truth a Munich-based art dealer whose business had more or less collapsed since 1933, as his clientele now lived mostly abroad) lowered his glass of wine. "It's quiet this evening," he said.

Cissy, the White Russian princess, touched his forearm. "Guido, dear, wasn't that Jaapi? Why do you suppose he's leaving so early? I haven't seen him in simply *ages.*"

Her voice sounded slow, something between a purr and a drawl. You might have guessed she'd been drinking, but not how much. Guido seriously believed that the poor girl—not really a girl anymore, but you couldn't help fretting about her—obtained the greater part of her caloric intake from liquor at gatherings like this one. He imagined her in the days between soirées, nibbling day-old bread sold cheap out of the bakery's back door. An aristocratic rodent. What were they paying her at the ministry? Secretary's wages, he supposed. A foreigner, after all. Worse: a blue blood. Lucky to be working at all. He strained to picture Cissy toiling in one of those mysterious offices in the Wilhelmstrasse, identified only by letters and numbers—Special Bureau IV-d-7 or some such.

"Where *is* everyone tonight?" she wondered, her tone plaintive. "Where's Ricky? And Dodo? Will there be dancing, do you think? Darling, ask them to play something for dancing."

Guido did not care to humor her. To be frank, he found her faintly annoying at times like this, fond of her though he was. She needed to toughen up, to grow a shell.

"Ah!" he exclaimed, spotting a well-known but officially non grata newspaperman wandering through the crowd like a hermit. "Greimer, how good that you're here! You know our Cissy, I believe."

Mechanically Greimer bowed, bringing his lips within an inch of the girl's hand. Close enough, Guido thought—there were crumbs in his beard. The man looked a shambles.

"It's all politics in there," the newspaperman said.

He waved absently over his shoulder toward the Baron's old library, still a refuge of sorts, though not one to Guido's liking. He preferred to keep his secrets out in the open: always the safest place to hide. *Look, there's Guido—an awful scoundrel, but harmless enough.*

"Politics," Greimer went on, "as understood by militarists. Rather like sex as understood by schoolboys." His voice became droll: " 'This can't go on! It's an outrage against German honor! We won't stand for it!' Well, then, gentlemen—*do* something about it. 'But oh my, whatever can we do? From whom shall we take our orders? They never taught us at General Staff College to think for ourselves!' The very idea!" Greimer snorted. "Right along they've wanted another war—now they're terrified he's going to give them one."

"Oh, war," said Cissy, "who could want that? There won't be a war, will there, darling?"

Guido's mouth was open with the ready lie—*Of course there won't, don't be silly*—but the journalist spoke first.

"Well, that's just the problem, isn't it, *Prinzessin*? Most people want peace. I mean in the broadest sense, in our daily lives—our dealings with neighbors, tradesmen, strangers on the S-Bahn. It's in our nature to placate the bastards, appeal to reason, bite our tongues—anything to avoid a fight. And that's all to the good. But it only works when you're dealing with civilized people. These ones we're talking about—"

Guido glanced around, worried about who might be listening, and Greimer caught him at it. He glared back but kept his mouth shut. Cissy—sensing his anger though perhaps not understanding it—looked dazed, and for an instant Guido feared she'd burst into sobs. Her mercurial temperament ran to such extremes. Instead she rallied herself, took firm hold of the journalist's forearm and shifted her weight with surprising steadiness.

"Let's find you a drink," she said, "something good and strong. And we'll ask them to play something more fun. Something for the saxophone! Look, darling, isn't that Dodo? *Kommst du, Herr Greimer.* Over here, Dodo! Look!"

Watching them weave across the floor, Guido let his lungs slowly empty. In relief or exhaustion? He couldn't decide which, but with Cissy off his hands, he felt at loose ends. She brought something, undeniably—a spark of gaiety. Now his eyes moved disconsolately across the room, from the musicians in the little nook under the balcony to the ancient and faintly ridiculous ormolu chair beside the hearth, from which the Baroness held court. The old gal was practically alone there, accompanied only by a tall fellow in a rumpled navy uniform who'd bent nearly double to hold a match near the tip of her cigarette. The flame rose dead steady while the cigarette, in its long meerschaum holder, bobbed crazily, as though the Baroness was . . . what? Beside herself with laughter? Quaking with grief?

Guido, now curious, strayed toward them, stopping once or twice to nick a canapé. At his approach, the Baroness raised her head and gave him a blank stare as if she had no earthly notion who he might be. Or because—this was probably it—her mind was somewhere else entirely. Some glamorous, long-vanished era. There followed a long silence whose awkwardness might have registered only in Guido's mind. He knew better than to break it.

"Isn't it time," the grande dame said at last, looking straight at Guido but perhaps not addressing him or anyone present, "for the talking to stop? Time to have done with it? Can't we just . . . get rid of them?"

Guido affected to have heard nothing: the only safe course.

But the navy man took her bony old gloved hand and gave it a reassuring squeeze. "God help us," he said, barely loud enough for Guido to hear, "God help us, we are going to try."

CRIME IN AMERICA

Come out, thought Oskar. Come out, damn you.

He stood on the glittering pavement outside the Argentine
embassy in weather that was neither warm nor cold enough. The air
was clammy as a wash rag, with a smell of rotting leaves and petrol.
In Berlin at this hour it would be coal black, but here in Washington a drab sort of twilight prevailed—the gloaming of cocktail
hour. Around him at intervals traipsed an assortment of ladies and
gentlemen in semiformal attire, and for the sake of distraction he
tried to guess who they might be, what nation or political faction
or social category they might represent. His training hadn't covered
any of this—hurriedly conducted at an Abwehr field station, given
the general theme of paranoia—so his guesses were uneducated and
probably wrong. This lady in a severe black waistcoat, for example,
might be a banker from Luxembourg—her smile calibrated to the
last decimal point of charm—or she might be an American secretary with an invitation passed along by a boss who was otherwise
engaged. And this gentleman with a top hat and a walking stick,
who was he? He looked so painfully British he must be Australian,
perhaps a chargé d'affaires, or an international criminal, or a newspaperman.

Oskar wondered how he himself must appear to these
distinguished-looking people in their evening clothes. Hopeless,
probably. His suit was well-made but drab, light wool dyed just to

the yellow side of tan, probably copied from a back issue of some American magazine with a view toward making him inconspicuous, whereas in practice it made him outstandingly unstylish. *Who is that man? Why, I believe it's the Polish industrial attaché.* To go with the suit, they'd given him a new identity, equally unbecoming: he was Erwin Kaspar, a low-ranking functionary in the Agriculture Ministry, dispatched to Washington to explore an upward revision of grain export quotas. They hadn't troubled to brief him on this. "The man you'll be talking to," they assured him, "won't know any more about it than you do."

The man I'll be talking to, he thought. And where is this man now, exactly?

It had taken some doing to run the target to ground. When Oskar had stepped off the Hamburg-America liner in New York two days ago, he'd had little to go on besides a name (Tobias Lugan), a job title (minority counsel, Senate German Affairs Subcommittee) and a profile patched together from Abwehr files (law degree from Boston University, friend of the Lindberghs', fond of parties, no known prior contact with German intelligence). The embassy staff had been of little help; they probably doubted Erwin Kaspar's bona fides, and good for them. The local Abwehr *Rezident*, who knew Oskar's real identity but not the nature of his mission, had only suggested, "Pick up the telephone. It's what people do here."

So Oskar had called Counselor Lugan's office and asked about arranging an appointment. The woman on the other end found something funny about this—he hoped it wasn't an embarrassing flaw in his dialect, the English they spoke here being unlike anything he'd heard in *Gymnasium*—but after that first bout of giggles, she became more helpful.

"Mr. Lugan doesn't really *make* appointments," she said. "His schedule is . . . always subject to change. You know the Hill—things come up." After a pause she added, "*Verstehen Sie?*"

"Yes, I think so," he said. Of course she speaks German, he told himself. It's German Affairs. It doesn't mean anything, so stop worrying so much. She doesn't think you're a spy.

"Well, look," she said, now with a note of sympathy in her voice. "If you want to catch up with Toby, you might try the diplomatic circuit. There's a reception tonight at Finland, and one tomorrow at, let's see—Argentina. He might be there, but I can't promise anything. Toby's all over town these days. *Ich wünsche Ihnen gutes Glück.*"

After he'd hung up, Oskar had found he was sweating under the tan wool suit. This strange game of being two people at once, speaking two languages in an alien land where important people didn't make appointments—it was all a bit absurd, but also exhilarating. He'd fretted over the logistics of arranging an invitation to an Embassy Row soirée, but that turned out to be no problem: such papers were kept in a file at the embassy; you just took one and signed for it, and if none was available, then the matter could be resolved, again, with a telephone call. It seemed to him a kind of magic.

And so by means of consular enchantment, Erwin Kaspar presented himself at the Embassy of Finland at six o'clock that same day. He was admitted with a courteous nod, after barely a glance at the heavy-stock card in his hand, and spent the next hour moving slowly around a large room with pale blue walls and remarkable chandeliers that seemed like a modernist evocation of reindeer horns. He forgot for a considerable time that he was a German intelligence officer and imagined himself instead an accredited member of this attractive, animated, champagne-sipping and ever-smiling crowd of . . . whoever they were. The diplomatic circuit. And the illusion was more compelling because at no point was it interrupted by the appearance of Toby Lugan—at least, no one who looked like the photo Oskar had stared at for hours before embarking on this American odyssey—so he was never obliged to stop being Erwin Kaspar and get down to the nonmagical business at hand.

The second evening—tonight—at the Embassy of Argentina, the spell had snapped. He'd arrived earlier this time, just after the guest of honor, a writer named Borges, had finished his reading. Lugan was there ahead of him. There was no mistaking the man, even from across the wide and glittering ballroom. He was Oskar's height but half again as massive, fair-haired, red-faced, a street brawler in a sharp blue suit. He'd parked himself in front of a buffet table, where he was chomping finger sandwiches two at a time while talking loudly to a Latin beauty young enough to be his daughter. He was drinking not champagne but something amber in a tall glass, filled too high and splashing out as he gestured expressively to enliven his monologue. The beautiful woman was laughing along with him, or at him, or just laughing. Oskar couldn't tell what was going on, precisely, but he sensed that Lugan in his boorish way had managed to charm her, and knew it, and was going to ride this as far as it would go. Oskar felt irrationally and irrevocably repulsed.

Trust your instincts, his trainers had instructed him at one point. At another point they'd told him the opposite: You can't trust instincts you've acquired in Germany, because they won't work in America, where people don't look at you as they do here and your enemies won't be so obliging as to show up in leather coats with an Opel idling at the curb. Now his instinct told him that Herr Lugan, minority counsel and man-about-town, was a dangerous brute, not just in a physical sense. There was something daunting about his *presence*, his power over a young woman who could be flirting with any man in the room. Should Oskar trust this instinct or not? Go ahead with the plan or change it in light of what his trainers had called exigent circumstances? But change it how, exactly—a different target? Or the same target but a new line of approach?

In the end, his feet decided this for him. The crowd in the ballroom was in constant flow, some occult social current seeming to nudge people in one direction or another. Clusters formed and dissolved around him, people hurrying across the marble floor to join or to avoid someone, and Oskar was borne along on this mysterious tide. He found himself drawing ever closer to Lugan, who remained anchored beside the buffet table. The young woman noticed him first and raised her glass in a vague, catholic salutation. Lugan turned, his upper body swiveling and the ruddy face reluctantly pulling away from the woman toward Oskar, his expression just shy of combative. At close range, his watery blue eyes were bloodshot yet penetrating, as though alcohol served to amplify his menacing qualities without blurring his focus. They seemed to demand that Oskar explain himself or get the hell out of here.

"Are you Mr. Tobias Lugan?" said the voice of Erwin Kaspar, Oskar now hearing it himself for the first time. It was about right, he thought: meek but self-important, the humble crewman who would rather be a budding captain.

"I am he," said Lugan, his own voice loud but modulated: the street brawler with a law degree. He raised an eyebrow: *And you are?*

"Erwin Kaspar, sir—I believe we met once, many years ago. You won't remember me; I was just a boy. At a Christmas party, I believe, in Charlottenburg. You were introduced to us by your friend Colonel Smith. You shared stories of Charles Lindbergh. It was a wonderful evening."

The party had really happened, so Oskar had been told. The long-serving U.S. military attaché Truman Smith had been there, and so had an Abwehr officer—probably an SD officer as well, and a Gestapo man, and someone from the Bendlerstrasse. No one liked to miss their slice of the pie when foreign dignitaries came to town.

Lugan seemed to spend a moment trying to recall this occasion and then to decide it wasn't worth it—it probably happened, or it didn't happen; it was all the same to him. "Well," he said, holding out a big hand, "it's nice to see you again, Herr Kaspar. And all grown up, too. What brings you to town?"

Oskar took the hand and allowed his fingers to be crushed. He reckoned it wouldn't be in poor Kaspar to squeeze back in his own defense. "I'm with the Agriculture Ministry now," he said. "I'm here to . . . but I'm sure this wouldn't interest you. Grain import quotas, boring stuff. Nothing like your own stories, or Colonel Smith's. Still, my father suggested I should look you up, were the opportunity to arise. He sends his greetings."

"Aha," Lugan said thoughtfully. Or maybe half-drunkenly. "Well. Why don't you stick around for a bit, then. Maybe we could go grab a beer afterward. Haven't been over there for a while, so you can fill me in on what's happening. How's that sound?"

It sounded like a dismissal, and indeed Lugan was already turning away, back to his lovely companion. Yet Oskar's instinct—trustworthy or not—told him he hadn't been dismissed altogether, that he'd gotten a hook in, that Lugan might be serious about going for a beer. Oskar rejoined the merry crowd, feeling mildly giddy. At the doorway he stopped and placed a palm against the jamb, sensing that he needed to steady himself. He looked back across the ballroom, and sure enough, Lugan was watching him. The man's expression was hard to read: speculative, perhaps. Hungry, perhaps.

Oskar stepped down onto the sidewalk, into the clammy Washington air. He posted himself there like a sentry and settled in to wait.

He was still waiting a considerable time later—he'd quit glancing at his watch an hour ago—when Lugan finally emerged from the ornate doorway. One of the final guests to depart, he did so alone and looked chagrined. So the beautiful woman had rejected him, after all that. Or maybe her father had arrived—her father the Generalissimo!—and Lugan had made a timely retreat, saving his body if not his honor, having eaten half his weight in finger sandwiches and tapped out the stores of Irish whiskey. He seemed surprised to see young Erwin Kaspar under a lamppost by the curb, at least to see him smiling. Lugan wouldn't take kindly to being left out of a joke if there was one going around. He strode over, swinging his arms and taking deep swills of air, as though purging his lungs of diplomacy.

"So you waited," he said.

Oskar shrugged.

"How about that beer?"

Lugan led Oskar onto a side street, a dark channel crimped on either side by narrow row houses and lined with ginkgo trees that rose above roof height and still clung to last autumn's crinkled, fan-shaped leaves. Oskar would have feared coming here alone, having heard about the crime in America, but the thought of someone trying to mug Toby Lugan was laughable. Look at him: marching down the center of the road as though he'd fought and won an ugly battle for the right to do so. Oskar had seen the same walk before, in German cities, usually executed with far less aplomb by younger men in tall boots.

They emerged after a few blocks onto a wide and well-lit avenue, eerily devoid of traffic. When a lone taxicab puttered past them—driven by a Negro, something unimaginable in Berlin—Lugan stepped out at mid-block and crossed the lanes at almost a trot, apparently indifferent to whether his guest was keeping up. He stopped, finally, in front of a row house with twin stairways, up and down, the first ending at a large door with a brass nameplate—

O'BRIEN & ASHBY, ATTYS AT LAW—and the second at a smaller door under a painted signboard showing an eighteenth-century musketeer and identifying the Hessian House.

Lugan swept a hand toward the concrete steps, deferring as one might to a lady, leaving Oskar to wonder what came next: conquest or mutual seduction? The tavern behind the narrow door would have lent itself to either, or to the sadder alternative of utter failure. One long side wall was given over to brooding landscapes, reproductions printed at poster size and mounted beneath tiny spotlights—every shade of forest green and mountain gray and earthy brown, shadows swirling around them, black-caped figures pausing in lonely contemplation, all the portentous trappings of *deutsche Romantik*.

Lugan chose a table next to *Knights Before a Charcoal Burner's Hut* and slumped down there, exhaling emphatically. Oskar joined him with such trepidation as befit his timid role, using the guise of nervousness to make a quick survey of the room. It was long and narrow, with a bar at the deep end camouflaged by failing greenery. There were few other patrons: a small man in a cheap suit reading a newspaper on a barstool, half a dozen sailors in uniform who'd dragged two tables together and sloshed beer over both of them, two other men, slightly older but still young, at a table nearby with their jackets draped over an empty chair and slouching postures that didn't quite match their catlike eyes, slitted yet attentive. For no reason in particular, Oskar marked these last two as German.

A waitress appeared, nails lacquered red and lips coated with impressive precision to match. A smile had settled permanently in the flesh around her mouth. Lugan ordered "a pair of tall ones, ma'am, and another in five minutes." The beer arrived flat and sweet, but by that time Lugan had lost interest.

"So," he said, leaning back in his chair, studying young Kaspar from this new perspective. "Colonel Smith. A friend of your father's, you say?"

Oskar shrugged. "Not a close friend. They knew each other through mutual colleagues, I believe. My father works in the armaments industry."

"Armaments! So he's not an, ah . . . public servant, then. Like yourself."

"He encouraged me to make my own choices."

"Smart man, I suppose." Lugan reached for his beer and took a long swallow that knocked the level down by a third. "My father told me to go to law school. Earn some money, get out of Southie, make the smiling bastards cry."

Oskar laughed, a bit uncertainly, wondering if *smiling bastards* was American slang for anyone in particular.

Lugan seemed to interpret this response correctly. His eyes were bleary, but they had attained a singular focus on this enigmatic young man across the table—a puzzle it would amuse and gratify him to solve. "The world is full of smiling bastards," he said. "Washington's got more per capita than any place I know of. But maybe it's not so different from Berlin. I don't know, I've only been over there a few times. Strictly business, not much time for socializing. I don't think I remember meeting your father, though. In fact, I don't recall this Christmas party at all. In, what was it? Charlottenburg."

Oskar wondered if this was a probe and, if so, if it required some kind of reply. *Perhaps I was mistaken, then.* Before he could decide, Lugan leaned forward in his chair, bringing his considerable weight to rest on elbows that suddenly crowded the table, dislodging the glassware. In clear phrasebook German he said:

"Wer sind Sie, Herr Kaspar? Was tun Sie wirklich hier?"

In a way, Oskar was relieved it had come to this so quickly— Lugan demanding to know who he was and what he was really doing. This was meant to happen eventually, with Lugan wondering and asking. He was the target but he should feel like the archer, aiming and loosing the questions at Oskar. So the answers, when they came, would seem reactive in nature, Oskar telling him what he wanted to know and Lugan feeling victorious, not like a man who'd been gulled. All these things were governed by a delicate protocol that Oskar's trainers had explained carefully, and Oskar had listened, though it had seemed needlessly complicated at times, too finely rationalized, too cerebral. But he was an army man. His trainers were members of the *Kriegsmarine*, and he supposed sailors in general had a lot of time to think.

"At the ministry that I represent," he said, looking straight in

Lugan's eyes and trying to sound, as Kaspar, as bland and affectless as possible, "there's a feeling that relations between our two countries have come recently under a good deal of strain. The feeling is that certain elements within your government, and certain elements in our own, may be at fault. These elements—which don't truly represent the feelings of the majority, on either side—they are set on a course of antagonism. But perhaps they can be sidestepped. Perhaps more reasonable elements on each side can determine to communicate directly."

Lugan listened to this, looking smug. "You're talking about grain exports now, I take it."

"Just so," said Oskar—cautiously hopeful, since despite his attitude, Lugan seemed to be playing along. "The hope is, in the ministry I represent, that if such a dialogue were to occur, both sides would find it greatly to their benefit, yours as well as ours. And toward that end the ministry is prepared to offer . . ." He paused for effect, pretending to search for a suitable phrase in English. In truth, he was reciting a script that had been written for him weeks ago, and he guessed Lugan was clever enough to realize that. But this was part of the shadow play: the target should draw his own conclusions, and feel smarter than the other fellow. "A demonstration of good faith," he concluded with a nod.

There: it was said, it was done. Oskar had just offered, in the language of his new trade, *das Baumeln*—the dangle. Now the target would either reach for it or not. While Lugan was making up his mind, or finishing his beer, or replaying his unrequited courtship of the Latin beauty, Oskar stood and walked past the bartender, who was pale and pudgy but surprisingly young, back to the men's room, where he stood looking at himself in the mirror under unkind light. Erwin Kaspar seemed to have aged a bit, but on the whole he looked pretty sound. The yellow-tan suit was an atrocity, though he might keep the tie as a memento. Too late he realized he was thinking beyond this moment, of the future, imagining himself back in Germany—and probably had just cursed himself and the mission, too. He left the bathroom to find Toby Lugan waiting placidly in the company of two fresh beers.

"You were just telling me," Lugan said, "about a demonstration of good faith. I wonder if you could give me some idea of what the hell you're talking about. Not much of an expert on grain exports, myself. You might need to spell it out for me."

Oskar didn't reply. Having already said what he'd come five thousand kilometers to say, he wasn't in a frame of mind to improvise. Wordlessly he reached into an inner pocket and pulled out an envelope, opened and bent and closed again, addressed to Hr. Erwin Kaspar in a rolling scrawl, just an envelope like any other, this one with a single sheet of paper inside. The paper likewise was unremarkable: plain bond with a typewritten list of names followed by curious abbreviations like *Ob d H* and *Chef HNV.* There was no title, but an informed reader would have recognized it quickly enough as a list of current posts held by senior members of the German General Staff. From an intelligence standpoint, the list had only modest value—nothing a foreign service couldn't piece together with its own resources—but by its existence, and by virtue of its being up-to-date as of the moment Oskar had boarded the ship in Hamburg, it served as a letter of reference, a telling signal of who he meant by *the ministry I represent.*

Lugan didn't open it—not here in the Hessian House. He stuffed it carelessly into a pocket and said, in an uncharacteristically soft voice, "Now, listen. I don't know what you're playing at and I'm not sure I even care. But I'll take a look at this. And *if* it looks interesting, I'll get back to you. Where you staying, the embassy? I'll drop you a note. Don't worry, it'll be all innocent—you met a lady at the reception and she's looking forward to seeing you again. Happens in this town all the time. Folks in the mail room open it up, see what's in there, get a laugh out of it—didn't know little Erwin had it in him. So the lady suggests a time and a place, and you *be* there. Got it? Sound all right?"

As before, in the ballroom, Lugan was announcing that he was done. He stood up, flapped dollar bills onto the table and left without saying another word, without even looking back.

Oskar felt light-headed, sweating in the muggy air of the tavern, steadfastly ignoring what he sensed were more than casual glances from the two men at the nearby table. He'd made the dangle, the target had grabbed it—the rest should be easy.

———

Toby Lugan headed north on Connecticut Avenue, his stride a bit slower than usual, staring at the next few yards of sidewalk with an attitude that might have passed for reflection. He was thinking of the envelope and the paper inside, which he'd merely glanced at because that one glance was enough; it told him all he needed to know and a bit more than he'd expected. He ignored the few other pedestrians, the passing motorcars, the traffic signal at Columbia Road. At California he turned left and crossed the street, scornful of drivers honking their displeasure. They weren't in all that much of a hurry. People in this town wouldn't know hurry if it ran up and bit them on the ass.

Toby had come down from Boston a few years back—make that more than a few, more than he felt like counting—and still loathed this drowsy little backwater, its summers and slowness of life, its food and the damn *smell*. For Toby's money, it was nothing but a sleepy southern town that lacked the genteel charm of Richmond or Savannah. Over the years, it's true, his contempt for the District and its inhabitants had taken on a worn-in, almost homey quality. You couldn't say he'd warmed to the place, only that he'd come to relish certain aspects: the ritual head bashing on the Hill; the visceral pleasure of gutting FDR's harebrained agenda in committee; the marathon, booze-fueled negotiations; the press wars; the parties. And you never knew—sometimes there was a little surprise.

Tonight, for example.

Toby slipped into the calming shadows of a neighborhood known formally as Kalorama, or simply the Caves. Rising like a walled fortress above Dupont Circle, its somber mini-castles stood buttress to buttress on small lots among magnolia and boxwood and holly, a favored roosting ground for the high and mighty who felt cramped in Georgetown but didn't care for the drive out Foxhall Road. Flanked by Embassy Row to the west, rolling down to Rock Creek in the north, it was a rarefied enclave where rumors of the Depression had scarcely penetrated. Lugan doubted that even all-out war would rattle these tall sashed windows. The ceaseless round of garden parties, dinner parties, after-theater suppers, Sunday brunches, extravagantly catered "teas," backyard cookouts, receptions and wakes and comings-out would, he was sure, roll along unabated. Forever and ever, amen.

He came in due course to a two-story brick Colonial squeezed tight by more prepossessing neighbors. Lights glowed handsomely through heavy maroon drapes, suggesting a cheery interior. Though he hadn't really thought this through, he mounted the steps and raised the preposterous knocker, a cornucopia in brass representing the bounty that sustained the good senator's midwestern constituency. It fell with a clunk loud enough to gavel half the District to order. From inside came a shout—"See who that is, damn it, would you?"—and after a few moments, the door swung heavily open. Toby cranked his head back so as to meet the gaze of young Clairborne Townsend, Clair to family and friends, the sole and strapping son of the Honorable Thomas DeWitt "Bull" Townsend, ranking Republican on the German Affairs Subcommittee.

Toby felt strangely nonplussed. Clair continued to hover in the doorway and seemed perfectly content to stare down at him, as though issuing a silent challenge: *Explain yourself or go away—you don't really belong in a place like this.* Which was true enough, but fuck it. Fuck the Townsend whelp, too. This snot, who might or might not have turned eighteen, had been handed the life of a soft-skinned, mollycoddled plutocrat's boy by none other than Tobias Lugan and men of his ilk—anonymous foot soldiers who carried out the unglamorous business of government while public figures like Townsend *père* were pleased to claim the credit, smiling for the cameras and signing their names to legislation that had been fought over so bitterly it ought to have been printed in hot blood on human skin. Clair might score top marks at a hoity-toity place like St. Albans, but let him try to survive even an afternoon in the schoolyard at Francis Xavier, Toby's alma mater up in Southie.

"I need to see your dad" was what he boiled this down to when pushing his way through the door.

The boy stepped back, barely in time. He smelled womanish, or maybe it was the florid air of the house itself—a mystery, inasmuch as you never saw the Mrs. about. Word was she spent most of her time back home (if that's what you'd call a drafty manor where the family camped out for a few weeks every summer) and the remainder on the top floor here, stone drunk.

"I'm sure my father will be delighted," Clair muttered.

The gathering, too loose to be termed a meeting, too quiet for a party, was in the back parlor, where French windows gave cheerlessly onto a moonlit patio. Toby recognized, besides the senator, one of his senior aides, a despondent-looking *Post* reporter and a woman named Maude who was said to be the mistress of a Supreme Court justice. There were others in armchairs whom Lugan ignored, though his gut suggested that a slender man with a crooked black tie, side-lit by a table lamp, bore keeping an eye on.

"Toby!" Townsend gushed, with the instantaneous ease of a modern bathroom fixture. "What's your poison? Jameson, I think?"

Toby drank anything; he seldom bothered to taste it anymore. Too much else to think about. He was half lost in thought even now, watching the senator enact with due solemnity the ritual of pouring a cocktail. No question, Bull cut a striking figure. He was a large man, nearly as tall as his son (who'd vanished from sight, though Toby didn't trust the brat to stray out of earshot), so featurelessly handsome that political cartoonists had little to work with. He was often accused—likely as not by a shill he'd planted in the audience—of being a thorn in Franklin Roosevelt's side. To which he'd reply, with an aw-shucks humility that played well back home, that he liked the word *barb*—one of those sharp things on cattle fences—because he felt more at ease on a ranch than in the Rose Garden. Thank you, ha-ha, next question, please?

"Here you go, Toby," he said, advancing toward him with a glass the size of a cannon shell. "What brings you around tonight?"

"A little something has come our way," Toby said—loudly, as he said all things, on the theory that people really take notice only if they catch you whispering. Nothing bellowed at painful volume could possibly be worth listening to, not in this town. "A little package from overseas."

"Wonderful!" Townsend exclaimed, as if he had the faintest fucking idea what Lugan was talking about. "That's just great—and you brought it here first!"

This was probably a question, though you couldn't tell from how

Bull was beaming at all his other guests. Belatedly, Toby wondered what was actually going on here. Was it anything at all, necessarily? Did Bull Townsend have an ordinary social life? Real human friends? The idea disappointed him. This man was only the *third*-ranking Republican on Foreign Relations, and his subcommittee assignments were nothing to retire on, German Affairs being roughly the Senate's equivalent of forty acres and a mule. He couldn't waste time on just plain friends—not yet.

Not that Toby worried much about that. What made Townsend of special interest wasn't his current standing in the pecking order—those things were apt to change—but, rather, his well-deserved reputation for knowing what, and whom, to come out against at a given moment. Immorality in the movies had been a good thing for Bull in '34—it was hard to find a Democrat with the temerity to defend it—but that had run its course, and resentment about freeloaders from the Dust Bowl wasn't showing any legs. Lately Townsend had gotten an inkling that German bashers (or maybe we should call them saber rattlers or warmongers—all perfectly respectable terms that voters would understand as synonymous with Jews) might be the next useful target.

Toby glanced around at the others in the room, most of whom were studying him with barely disguised avidity, hungering for some fresh morsel of Hill gossip. "Senator," he said, "would you, ah—maybe we could go somewhere and talk?"

"Oh, I don't know," Townsend said, exuding good will for all and sundry. "I'm sure we're among friends here."

Toby doubted that. The slender man with the crooked tie was avoiding his gaze. He looked disreputable, like an artist in town to ride the WPA gravy train. Or a writer—could Bull be friends with a writer? Picturing dime novels full of horses and gunplay and virile cowboys, Toby relaxed a little.

"Well, listen," said Townsend, dropping his voice. "I just need to wrap up a little business with Mr. Viereck here, then I'll meet you up in the study. You know where to find it, don't you?"

Toby was glad to be excused. En route to the staircase he passed young Clairborne again. The two exchanged looks but neither spoke. What, really, could they have to say to each other?

———

Oskar woke early the next morning and lay in his bed listening to unfamiliar bird calls outside the window. They'd given him a room in a back wing of the embassy that normally would have been occupied by a low-level diplomat, but the resident staff had been pared down this year as relations between the Third Reich and the United States had chilled and the two nations found fewer things to talk about. Recent arrivals tended to be young men of undiplomatic character who were listed in the directory under ambiguous titles, the most popular being "attaché" with no indication of an exact field of expertise. There apparently was no limit to the number of attachés without portfolio a German legation in a Western capital could employ. Oskar couldn't help wondering if he'd seen two of them in the tavern last night.

The room was monastic: a bed, a cabinet and a writing desk. A previous occupant had tried to enliven it with a travel poster, circa 1935, depicting "Motoring in the New Germany" with a three-color rendering of mountains, a ruined castle and the front half of a modern motorcar, strangely dispiriting in all. But the window opened onto back grounds that had been fashioned into a modest walled park—clipped yew hedges and strapping oaks and grass so perfectly groomed you imagined a gardener on his knees with a ruler and scissors. The birds must be up in the trees somewhere; Oskar couldn't see any, but their trills and peeps and polyphonous cross-chatter made a convincing case that it was spring and he should be out in it.

He was just passing through reception—a pleasant domain with tall, south-facing windows that might have graced the lobby of a prestigious law firm, except for the swastika banner and the imposing portrait of Adolf Hitler—when a matronly woman spotted him from her desk in a corner and waved for his attention.

"Herr Kaspar?" she called. "You are Herr Kaspar from Agriculture? A moment, please, sir. I believe we have something for you."

She rose from the desk and vanished into a smaller room just off the main chamber; a younger secretary at another desk lowered her pen to look at Oskar too intently for his liking, and now others were staring too. One of them was a round-faced man with tiny spectacles whose desk, near the front door, was utterly bare save for a German newspaper. Oskar had noticed him before; he sat there all day, and in the evening another man took his place, yet neither of them appeared to do any work at all. On the front page of the newspaper was a large photo of the Führer launching a battleship. There'd been no launches in the weeks before Oskar left, so the paper must be quite recent, probably flown over in the diplomatic pouch. And therefore this Nobody must be Somebody. Perhaps, as they said in the Abwehr, he was "from Prinz-Albrecht-Strasse"—that is, a member of the rival intelligence service, the Sicherheitsdienst, an arm of Himmler's sprawling SS.

The matron emerged from the back room bearing a small squarish envelope. She bustled over to Oskar and placed it rather delicately in his hand. It was pinkish beige and seemed to emit a faint scent of lilac.

"This was delivered for you last night," she told him, in a confidential whisper probably audible from the farthest corner of the room. "Delivered by a young woman—a quite *attractive* young woman, I'm told. Very *late* last night."

The secretary at her desk began to titter. Everyone was smiling except for the man with tiny spectacles, who seemed to have lost interest and had gone back to his newspaper. *Führer tauft Linienschiff "Gneisenau."*

Oskar exited the embassy at a pace that might have been taken for panicked flight but that he hoped would read as the natural excitement of young Herr Kaspar at having a received a communication from a quite attractive Fräulein. He stood on the sidewalk by Massachusetts Avenue, a wide and tree-lined boulevard oddly lacking in traffic, at least compared to Berlin, holding the envelope with his fingertips, as though without careful handling it might explode. From what he could see, it hadn't been opened—but if it had, how could he tell? He opened it now and pulled out a note card imprinted palely with yellow flowers and inscribed in a neat, presumably feminine hand:

> *Enjoyed our lovely talk. Can't wait for more, and . . . !*
> *Can we meet tomorrow? (Probably today for you!) Working*

*late, but I can make it by 10. Say the Q Street Bridge? (The one
with the buffaloes!) I know Germans are punctual, so I'll be right
on time. Cross from the east side, I'll meet you halfway!*
   'til then—V.

He slipped the note gently into a pocket. He wondered about the
V.—was that some kind of message? If so, coming from Lugan, it
was likely a crude one.

There'd be plenty of time to think about that later, too much
of it, really—he'd be going mad by ten o'clock. In the meanwhile,
there was business to get on with. The list he'd given Lugan at the
Hessian House had been more or less a teaser, with enough to make
Erwin Kaspar seem credible but also a hint of deeper, more tanta-
lizing secrets to come. Somewhere in this city was a package—he
imagined a box, battered at the edges, wrapped in brown paper and
stamped with the usual postal clearances—with an intelligence treasure inside it, something so precious that even the Americans in
their purblind neutrality would tremble to behold it. Oskar had no
clue what the treasure was or where it was hidden. But he knew how
to find it, or so he hoped.

Toward the end of his training, he'd been called in for an unusual
interview touching upon certain aspects of his past. There'd been
other conversations of this sort, quite a few of them, as his trainers sifted through the various stages of his life, his education, his
years as a cadet at Lichterfelde. It was a matter of truly understanding the operative, his unique strengths and possible vulnerabilities.
The questions were intimate yet oddly impersonal, as though his
trainers didn't really care about the answers; they merely needed
to hear them. But this time was different. For one thing, Jaap Saxo
was there, the man who'd recruited him in Berlin. For another, the
questions were more pointed than usual; these people were driving
at something, and this time his answers clearly mattered a great deal.

"Tell us, Oskar," one of them said—it wasn't Jaap, who was just
sitting there, staring out the window. "Do you know anybody in
Washington? Any friends of the family who thought it prudent to,
ah, seek employment abroad? Distant cousins, old pals from the
Movement, the nice Jewish doctor you saw as a child?"

Something in the man's voice unsettled him. And when Oskar didn't answer at once, he pressed harder.

"Ideally, this should be someone you feel you can trust. Someone who will trust you in return. The personal connection is key, for the other party's comfort as well as our own. Because we need to ask a favor of this person. Not a large or dangerous favor, but one that is important for Germany."

Jaap looked around at that point, his gaze brushing over Oskar before he again turned away, and in that moment Oskar understood.

"Think hard," said the other man. "Is there anyone?"

Well, yes—but they'd already known that. Oskar had felt it at the time, but he was certain now. The whole plan hinged on their knowing. But they had to hear it from him. They wanted to hear the whole story about Leo and its terrible ending—though it wasn't really an ending, was it?—in Oskar's own words.

Well, damn them. But they were simply doing their jobs, following the rules they'd written themselves. Oskar had been the target that day, and as with Toby Lugan, they'd wanted him to play the archer, aiming his bow across the Atlantic and loosing the arrow at Leo Gandelmann. And now—right now, this morning—he needed to track Leo down and find out how deeply his betrayal had struck.

Leo had been, once upon a time, the older boy next door, a musical prodigy, destined for greatness. But then came the *braune Pest* and, not long after, dark tidings from the Gandelmann household. The mother summoned for "questioning," returning two weeks later, ghostly pale. Her equally sudden death, a rumor of suicide. The hapless father, weeping at the dinner table. Finally it was Leo's turn. Grinning, yellow-shirted goons waiting outside the *Gymnasium*. Oskar ordered to empty Leo's desk and burn its contents, sheet music turned to ash, unheard notes blowing away on a sullen breeze. *Just a lousy bunch of paper*, Leo would say later. Then one summer morning, he and his father were suddenly gone—the house still standing empty when Oskar departed for Lichterfelde. By Christmas a new family had moved in, *Volksdeutsche* reemigrating from Uruguay.

A letter had come eventually. The father was living in New York;

Leo had quit school and found a job teaching music in Washington. *God must be laughing—a Gandelmann working at a place called St. Albans!* There'd been more letters back and forth, but they tapered off; there seemed to be no common language shared by people in the Reich and those in the unimaginable world beyond.

So that was what Oskar had to go on: a place called St. Albans. Which was (per the guidebook he'd bought upon arrival) a college preparatory school for boys in grades four through twelve, situated at the highest point in the District of Columbia, where it shared grounds with the Cathedral of St. Peter and St. Paul—an Anglican institution, mind you, not Roman Catholic. If God was laughing, He was doing so politely with a teacup in His hand. It was three-point-five kilometers from the German embassy and all uphill, a pleasant morning walk.

The weather had changed overnight as a cold front pushed through, clearing the sky and honing the wind to a nice edge that seemed to whittle away the blandness of Erwin Kaspar, revealing the Wehrmacht officer inside and the *Freideutsche Jugend* inside that. Oskar thought about practicing the tricks he'd learned for spotting people who might be tailing him, but he didn't feel like breaking stride, and it seemed pointless, anyway. Who would be tailing him, and why? At one point, passing a stretch of undeveloped woodland, he turned abruptly onto a footpath and halted a dozen paces in, affecting interest in a little sign indicating that this network of walking trails was a project undertaken by the Civilian Conservation Corps in 1935. No one turned after him, no silhouettes loomed tellingly at the trailhead—he was almost disappointed.

The grounds of the school and the cathedral were edged by a wall of mortared fieldstone, which he followed to a gate topped by an elaborate Gothic arch. It felt a bit like entering a castle, and he wondered if American boys also played at being knights, making swords and shields out of scrap wood and defending their realm. The ones he saw in the playground here were wearing blazers and ties—little knights in a new kind of order—but he walked past them to a small building with well-worn steps and a sign reading BURSAR. Though his English didn't register the word, the door handle was modern and designed for heavy use, so he turned it and stepped inside.

An elderly woman waited there at a large desk, apparently in hope that someone would arrive to annoy her; a suitable expression was already on her face. She listened with grim impassivity while Oskar explained the nature of his visit.

"You want to *see* Mr. Gandelmann?" she said finally, emphasizing the verb as though to confirm that his intention was not to *strike*, or *applaud*, or *murder* Mr. Gandelmann.

"Yes, only to see him," Oskar promised.

The woman sighed, then opened a drawer and consulted a typewritten document that appeared to be a schedule. "Mr. Gandelmann would be at *choir practice* now," she said. "That is in the nave. He prefers the *acoustics* there."

Evidently, she assumed that, being foreign, Oskar was also dull-witted. He saw no cause to disabuse her. She aimed a bony finger in what he took to be the direction of the cathedral.

"I shouldn't *interrupt* them," she warned. At last she favored him with a cold smile, like an act of Christian charity.

The cathedral was, it appeared, a work in progress. Its grounds were strewn in orderly fashion with chunks of limestone the size of steamer trunks. Oskar made his way past a crane, a crew of stonemasons shouting cheerfully in Italian and a phalanx of flying buttresses, before coming at last to the south transept, where a pair of huge doors hung open. There he left the sunlight for the cool depths of God's anteroom.

The place was dim, solemn and almost shockingly beautiful. The air smelled of burnt tapers, drying mortar and new-sawn wood. He saw no one about—but then the sound of high, clear voices floated down from the vaulted ceiling. The chant was Latin, the notes wavering and discordant, and after a moment came a tap of wood against wood, followed by a grown-up voice whose exact words were lost amid their own echoes but whose general tone—kindly, amused, exasperated—Oskar recognized at once.

Something overcame him then, rising up to engulf him. A wave of reality.

Until now, this journey had felt kind of like a dream. America was only half real, a place that existed in popular music, in the cinema, in boys' tales of Winnetou and Old Shatterhand, in lurid newspaper accounts of gangsters and hobos and crooked politicians living the life of Riley. Fairy-tale stuff, with Jewish bankers standing in for leering wolves. Nothing here could have the slightest connection with the mortally serious, blood-and-earth actuality of the Reich. Even Oskar's mission felt like something of a lark—another yarn for the campfire when he got home. Hadn't it started like all the rest, with the chanting of the Secret Anthem?

Only now, as he heard Leo's voice, did the reality of that other place seem to intrude here. Maybe it had clung to Leo's coattails when he'd fled into exile.

Oskar stepped deeper into the nave. Light entered from high above, through a row of clerestory windows awaiting their stained glass, covered now with paper that glowed amber where the sun burned through. To his right, behind an elevated pulpit, dark wood had been elaborately worked into pews and stalls, friezes, arches, a bishop's chair and a soaring enclosure for the pipe organ. At the center of it all stood Leo Gandelmann, poised heronlike before a dozen fidgety sixth graders. He was the same as ever, down to the finely cut black suit that inexplicably looked cheap on him. He'd stopped talking, perhaps because the boys weren't paying attention; a couple had noticed Oskar already, and others were turning to look. At any moment Leo would do likewise, and Oskar tried to prepare himself. But that was unnecessary. Leo looked around as though he'd known Oskar would be there and was expecting him. He gave Oskar a nod—a quick nod that said nothing but merely acknowledged the fact of his presence, Oskar in the cathedral, Oskar in America—and then turned back to his restless choristers. He gave a short cough, and they snapped to an unruly sort of attention. Whatever troubles Oskar was bringing would have to wait.

They sat close together out of necessity at a table in Leo's tiny flat. Outside it was growing dark, a few streetlights had come on and— adding a touch of drollery—some of the larger mammals at a nearby zoo were energetically resisting efforts to shoo them indoors for the night. That's how Leo explained the racket, and the idea must have amused him, because he stood up to crank the casement open wider.

"So I got your little package," he said, his back to Oskar. *Dein kleines Paket:* he made it sound chiming and childish.

"Ah," said Oskar. "That's good."

Leo stared out the window and said nothing else for a minute or longer. The zoo noises began to subside, though there were lingering roars and the piercing cry of what Oskar imagined to be a large predatory fowl.

"They're going to kill you." Leo turned finally to meet his eyes. There might have been a trace of melancholy in his expression, but if so, Oskar's approaching death didn't seem the primary cause of it. "Maybe not right away. But by the third reel, you're dead. Does that matter? I mean, does it make you wish you hadn't gotten involved? Because for all you know, maybe I destroyed the whole lot. Opened the box, saw what was in there and tossed it in the river. For your own good, my friend! And by the way, how dare you drag *me* into . . . whatever this is you're doing. What *are* you doing, anyway? Last I heard you'd joined the army."

Oskar remembered Leo too well to be caught off guard by any of this—or, to put it differently, to give him the sort of reaction he probably hoped for.

"I'm sorry, Leo," he said, all too aware that his paltry apology would mean next to nothing. "I know it was presumptuous to give them your name. You've made a new life here, and I had no right to intrude. But please understand, I'm trying to do what I believe—what I hope—is my duty as a German officer. No ironic comments, I beg you. Or go ahead, make them. I'm grateful for your help— truly I am. But it isn't just me you're helping."

"Oh, so it's what, then—Germany?" Leo's eyes were somewhat wild. "The glorious Fatherland? My own dear *Heimat*?"

Oskar feared this question, because the only answer he could give would strike Leo as naïve, or sentimental, or corny—probably all three at once. He gave it anyway, because it was the only one he had. "A nation is more than its government. Think of the tradition we've inherited, you and I. The culture of Beethoven and Goethe. The language. Our whole worldview. Or think of the bigger things, the greatest things, beyond all borders: science, art, philosophy. Human decency. The rule of law. For me it's not so complicated—it's a question of patriotism. A higher patriotism that looks beyond the current rulers to the soul of Germany itself."

"Patriotism? *Die ewige deutsche Seele?*" Leo shook his head. "Poor Oskar. This is so far beyond your depth. Joining the army . . . all right, that made a certain amount of sense. But this? Did they choose you on account of your lovely English?"

Oskar refused to answer. What could he say? *No, I think they might have chosen me because of you.*

Leo slipped into a grating American drawl. "You know, I did open that package of yours. Did you think I wouldn't? And then I closed it again. My God, where does all this stuff come from, Oskar? Do you even know who put it together? But hey, what a great read! So eye-opening. You have to marvel, really, at the purity of the thing. Most people, you know, they get cynical over time—they don't mean to, it just creeps up on them. But the Nazis! They've made it an art form." Then a stiff translation from the German, reciting from memory: " 'Military action is to commence no later than spring 1940, but only if—' "

Oskar tried to interrupt, but Leo kept talking, louder than before.

" '—*only* if a suitable pretext has been arranged on the political side. Above all, it is necessary that our actions be presented as purely defensive in character, coming in response to a definite threat.' " Then, in Americanese: "Ain't it grand? I can't help wondering, though—who's the audience here? Not the newspapers, I expect. Your masters won't think too highly of the Western press. Tell me if I'm off base, Oskar. Or should I call you something else now? Did they give you a new name? This is awfully damned exciting."

He spoke so fast that Oskar could barely follow. Some of the colloquialisms were unfamiliar—but no, he thought sadly, Leo probably isn't far *off base.*

Insofar as one could do so in such quarters, Leo began to pace. That cheap-looking suit made him resemble a marionette, his arms flapping as though tugged by invisible strings.

"Your bosses are probably thinking: We can't afford to deal with the Roosevelt crowd, they hate Germany, they've turned their backs on Christian values, they dance to jungle music and breed mulatto children, their New Deal is just Bolshevism wrapped in red, white and blue. No, we need to find someone more sympathetic, someone who shares our values, hardheaded realists who see things for what they are. In a word, Republicans."

Oskar rubbed his forehead. For all he knew, Leo was right. At least nothing he said was obviously wrong.

"I can see it all now." From the fixity of Leo's gaze, one might have thought this literally true. "Gentlemen with red stripes on their pants, heads bent over a good brandy. 'Is it not your opinion, *meine Herren*' "—he spoke now in a high-precision *Hochdeutsch* whose consonants could be used to etch glass—"that we ought to be talking to someone over there?' Though of course, Oskar, these fine gentlemen wouldn't dream of talking face-to-face. What, with Americans? A pack of upstarts with dubious ancestry and no understanding of how the Great Game is played? *Unvorstellbar!* No, let's send a messenger—no one important, someone who won't be missed if the whole operation blows up."

He turned with a malicious smile, as though the perfect scheme had just occurred to him. "Say—how about Langweil? He seems a game young lad. And while we're at it, let's not use our *own* channels of communication. Himmler's reading our mail, it might get traced to us—we might be held accountable! Maybe Langweil's got a friend. Someone in exile. A Jew, maybe. A *Socialist* Jew. A Socialist Jew *artist*—that's three nasty birds with one stone."

Oskar couldn't suppress the impulse to laugh. Despite everything, Leo was still Leo. "You're not in real danger, I don't think," he said. "No one followed me here. And I was told the documents would be posted from Switzerland. Once I'm gone, no one will trouble you."

Leo shook his head hard, back and forth. "Did I *say* I don't want to be troubled? Oskar, I'm *happy* you thought of me. I take it as a compliment that you just blithely assumed I'd want to join your little conspiracy. So yes, that's my answer, not that you bothered to ask. I'd do anything to get back at them. Of course this plan is stupid—I'm sorry, Oskar, that's the truth of it—but still, I'm happy to do what I can. It's been so . . ."

He took a couple of steps and turned, throwing his arms out.

"I can't tell you what it's been like being over here, where none of it seems to matter. These Americans—a perfectly nice people, but really, they have no idea. And it doesn't bother them! They have their baseball and their automobiles. They have movie stars getting divorced. They have a preacher who shouts on the radio, telling them they ought to be mad as hell at I don't know who, but there's always somebody. They have Lucky Lindy promising them Hitler only wants peace and Roosevelt's just trying to drag them into some European quarrel. Did you hear, Lindy's now talking about moving his family to Germany? It's true! So that his children can grow up 'in a more bracing moral atmosphere.' Who could make up such a thing, Oskar? There are times I can barely stand it over here."

He sat down, looking drained. The zoo noises had waned to an occasional desultory bellow.

"We could get some dinner," Oskar said. "I've got money. Any-place you like."

Leo seemed not to hear. "What I'm saying, Oskar, is I'm glad to be involved—glad just for the *chance* to be involved. All my energy, my talent, it's wasted here. I'm not even writing music anymore, do you know that? Korngold's tossing off scores for costume dramas, Weill's working in Tin Pan Alley, while Gandelmann is waving a baton at a bunch of squirming *Kerlchen.*"

"Bach was a *Kapellmeister.*"

"Bach had a fucking *Kapellenchor.* I'm allowed to babysit in the afternoons while the music director's napping, to give after-school lessons to older boys who fail to show a proper interest in sport. If I behave, someday I may conduct Evensong for nine old ladies and a queer priest." Unexpectedly, he smiled. "Though I admit there are advantages to being insignificant. If I make offensive remarks, it's because I don't speak the language properly. If I show up to teach hungover . . . well, poor Mr. Gandelmann, such a sad case, how he must have suffered over there, how noble we are to give him sanctuary! Because that's what this is, you know—not a real job. And I'm grateful, Oskar. I am. I'm living in heaven compared to the people over there. And the students aren't so bad, really. One of them actually shows a bit of promise."

Oskar nodded distractedly. A quirk of Leo's phrasing—"over there," *darüber,* connoting a sense of nearness, like a ball lying just beyond the neighbors' fence—struck him as oddly poignant. Home couldn't be so far away if it was only *darüber*. Did Leo feel safe here? Did he wake at night thinking he'd heard a knock at the door?

"His father's trying to pack him off to something called the International Youth Leadership Summit," Leo was saying, having evidently switched topics again. "The idea is to invite the sons of influential foreigners, pen them up together for a few weeks, fill their heads with National Socialist 'philosophy,' if you will, and send them home to tell everyone how swell things are in Nazi Germany. This kid's father—a senator, no less—thinks it would be just the thing for him. But he's frustrated because all the invitations are going to European boys whose fathers actually matter. What can a Yankee politician do for the Reich? So it seems my student will get a reprieve. But can you imagine?"

Oskar nodded, feigning interest and glancing at his watch, a gesture not lost on Leo.

"Running late, are we? Places to go, people to see, national secrets to barter? Don't let me detain you."

"No, Leo, it's not—"

But he'd spun around and was opening a cabinet in the little alcove that made do for a kitchen. There was a clatter as flimsy metal cookware was dislodged; then he extracted what looked like an extra-large box of chocolates wrapped in gleaming gold foil and tied with a large red bow. If he'd actually opened the package, he'd done a neat job of resealing it. He handed it to Oskar with an air of reluctance, as though he'd grown fond of this souvenir of his terrifying homeland.

"If they do kill you," he said, looking Oskar straight in the eye, "I'm happy I got to see you again. If they don't, let's have that dinner sometime. But after the war!"

It was the first time Oskar had heard anybody say *after the war*. It rang strangely in his ears because of both things it implied: that war would come and that you could dream of surviving it.

Only in America.

The Q Street Bridge was neither long nor grand. What it was chiefly was dark, despite twin streetlamps at the midway point. Yes, there were buffaloes. Four of them, in bronze, further declarations of an artistic theme carried over from the main structure, which featured iconic images of the American West—arrows, eagle feathers, Indian braves—carved in limestone. Like most German boys of his generation, Oskar had grown up reading Karl May and had spent a certain mandatory phase of his childhood creeping through the woods in makeshift buckskins, smeared with war paint, whooping ecstatically as he menaced his friends with a homemade tomahawk. He wondered what sort of game he was playing now and, in particular, who was coming to this rendezvous: Lugan again, the unknown V. or someone else entirely?

He'd arrived early—not too early, he hoped, though he felt ridiculous standing around with the flashy box in his hand—because he wanted to get a sense of the location. His guidebook informed him that the bridge had been built in 1914–15 to connect two neighborhoods, Georgetown and Dupont Circle. The map showed it spanning a narrow green strip identified as Rock Creek Park. From here the park looked insignificant, more like a gorge whose shoulders were too steep to build on, and the neighborhoods were hidden behind mature trees, making the bridge feel quite isolated and muting the noise of the city to a level at which he could hear water gurgling below. Supposing that would be Rock Creek, with time on his hands, he decided to go down to it.

He found a little path through the undergrowth tight against the bridge and slipped and clambered down the embankment. The bridge now hulked above him, four stories tall. The creek was high with the spring runoff; even so it was a tiny thing, no more than fifteen meters wide, stray boulders carving the flow into narrower channels. He tossed a couple rocks into the water, hoping to gauge the depth, and one of them struck the channel with a satisfying *ploosh*. Maybe deep enough to swim in, maybe not.

He climbed back up feeling oddly satisfied, the exertion having taken the edge off his nerves. It was just shy of ten now: time for the last stage of his assignment.

Oskar took his position at the eastern end of the bridge and waited no more than half a minute. *I'll be right on time*, the note had promised, and with Teutonic precision a pair of headlamps appeared at the opposite end, slowly moving forward. Oskar could make out a long, low-slung automobile, its roof a lighter color than its body. He stepped onto the bridge, trying to match his own speed to that of the driver, who evidently was highly cautious. Maybe this was how things normally happened in matters of international intrigue, but somehow Oskar didn't think so. Something about the car, the fact of there being a car instead of a person, the headlamps blazing in his face and flashing off the foil box in his hand—all of it made him consider his next few steps very carefully.

Your enemies won't be so obliging as to show up in leather coats with an Opel idling at the curb. No, he thought, this is America, regarding the dark green sedan and holding the box out in front of himself, letting the red ribbon flap in the cool breeze from the gorge, calculating his distance from the streetlamp. The car pulled abreast of him and at last he glimpsed the driver, a slight-figured man in ordinary evening clothes set off with a narrow tie. Car doors were opening— one on the passenger side, another in the rear—and there was an odd, unhurried quality to how stiffly the two men moved, as if they couldn't ever truly relax over here, even when pretending to slouch in a murky tavern. Oskar actually felt annoyed with them for making him wait, closing on him as slowly as wrestlers, every motion calibrated, like they were working from a checklist.

He found time in those final moments to wonder if this was, after all, how it was meant to end—if these were indeed the people for whom the treasure in the box was intended, if Oskar himself had been written off from the start. He tossed the box up high in the air, roughly in the direction of the closest man, and it seemed to float there in the penumbra of the headlamps. All eyes were on the gleaming foil, the waving ribbon, and not on Oskar as he vaulted cleanly over the opposite sidewall, vanishing in blackness.

Clairborne!" Bull Townsend called. "You get down here right now. We need to have a little talk." He was about to stomp upstairs— for which his son would be sorry, you can bet on that—when the boy materialized in the doorway, backlit by the hall fixture, his hair, as usual, too long. He was holding his damned flute, or piccolo, or whatever the hell it was. "Come in here, son. Take a seat."

The boy loped in like some wild, long-legged animal, a fawn or an antelope, that needed to be either housebroken or hung up on the wall, take your pick. Bull loved him, of course—that was what you did with children—but there was something a little abstract or theoretical about this love; it didn't always seem to connect with the ungainly presence of Clairborne himself. About ninety-eight percent of the time, the sight of him just pissed his father off.

"Come in, sit down," he said, motioning to a chair, already impatient. *Act like a man* was what he felt like saying. *Square your shoulders, look the other fellow straight in the eye.*

Clair dragged himself sullenly over the carpet with his whole upper body in a slump, dropping finally into the lozenge-shaped love seat favored by his mother on those rare evenings when she ventured downstairs. Bull gritted his teeth. The boy's limbs fell every which way. He twiddled his piccolo like a baton. He was wearing, God alone knew why, a thick, green-and-white striped scarf—not St. Albans colors—draped twice, loosely, around his neck.

Like that goddamn Cole Porter, Bull thought, despite having only the vaguest idea what Porter looked like and only one clue as to who he was (viz., the fellow who wrote those pornographic lyrics that got the Women's Decency League all hot and bothered). Forcing a smile, he said, "How *are* you, Clairborne?" His tone was hearty, he hoped, his manner paternal. "How are things going at school?"

The boy said nothing, only stared—his latest infuriating habit, sitting there with wide, empty eyes and his mouth clamped shut like some deaf-mute. Just watching you, waiting you out. Well, let him wait, Bull thought, till he craps in his pants. If he's not careful, this little game will end with somebody—maybe his old man—slapping an expression onto his face. And that'd be the end of the Helen Keller act. But then he'd probably (it came to Bull in a rush of horrible clarity) just move on to the next fucking thing, which was sure to be even worse. So let's put the kibosh on that right now.

"Clairborne," he said, watching the boy carefully, alert to any change in his demeanor, "I want to talk to you about your plans for the summer."

At first it seemed he wouldn't deign to answer, but then he said quietly, "I have no plans, Father."

Bull hated that voice. Flat and world-weary, like he'd come down with the vapors or some such thing. "Now that's where you're wrong, son." These words gave him considerable pleasure. "You do have plans for the summer. Yessiree—big plans."

There was a change now, though not exactly the one Bull had hoped for. The boy's eyes opened a bit wider, and he seemed for the first time to take an interest in the fact of his father's existence. Then he managed a very slight, almost secretive smile. "Do tell," he said, dropping the monotone and speaking in the fruity voice of a Hollywood "personality."

This was more than Bull could take. He felt himself getting hot, his face reddening. On the whole, he was more comfortable like that. He'd built a career on anger, and it had carried him pretty far. You could say—as Toby Lugan did now and then—that Bull Townsend knew how to make anger work for him. He stared hard and silently for half a minute, maybe longer, at his only son. You could see the boy growing uncomfortable, though he made a fair show of hiding it. But in the end it was Clair who broke, of course. He would never be Bull.

"Might one inquire," he said, picking up the words and placing them down just so, like somebody wearing fancy gloves, "what precisely these summer plans of mine are? Also, did you actually say *Yessiree?*"

Bull gave him an honest grin, letting the happiness of the moment, the triumph, just hang there, gathering force. "Tell me, Clairborne," he said finally. "Is there anybody at that fancy school of yours that can teach you a little German? You won't need much. Just some useful phrases like 'Please, sir, where is the laundry room, my uniform needs washing' or 'Pardon me, sir, I've got to use the shitter, that Bavarian horse cock we had for dinner didn't agree with me.' Because where you're going, son, that kind of thing ought to come in mighty handy."

The boy's expression was reward enough, almost.

FROM THE KREUZBERG TO HELL

BERLIN: APRIL 1938

Stav, feeling more than ever like the vampire he resembled, gazed pensively from the dark sanctuary of a stage wing at the audience packed hip to hip beyond the footlights at the Cabaret Trigilaw. The crowd swayed and throbbed like a monstrous, multiheaded jellyfish tossed by waves of blaring jazz—the permissible Nazi equivalent of jazz, containing no more than twenty percent "swing" and ten percent syncopation; it had reached maximum frenzy after midnight, then abated steadily, stuporously, in the hours since. The loud arrival around two a.m. of a party of dignitaries—what a laughably inapt term for the likes of Heydrich, head of the Security Service and a fixture of the Berlin demimonde—had only thickened the air of sinister lechery that pervaded the Trigilaw and was, indeed, its principal drawing card. People flocked here like so many carrion birds hoping for something delicious and horrible. It was Stav's personal belief that most of the legends about the place— young women found with dresses over their heads and throats slashed in the WC, drains blocked with congealing blood—had been concocted by Glewitz himself, the owner, though one couldn't be sure.

This was, after all, as Stav never ceased to marvel, a city that had managed both to surrender to the direst sort of thralldom and at the same time to throw off every kind of social and moral restraint. Thus, a novel business opportunity for those with *die Schnauze*, the

Berliners would say, "the nose," as in something you stick where it isn't wanted. God knew Glewitz had that.

The Trigilaw took its name from a three-headed pagan deity in whose honor, roughly a millennium ago and not far from the current premises, a rude statue had been erected by Slavic raiders jubilant over the sacking of Marienburg, the razing of its Ottonian cathedral and the butchering of its priests. Heydrich, if he'd heard that story, could only approve. For the SS (of which his own service was an aggressively metastasizing part) had made great strides in rolling back the intervening centuries of Christianity. So give Glewitz his due: the man knew his audience.

Stav lit a cigarette but after a couple puffs lost interest. He tossed it deeper into the shadows backstage and watched the glowing ember roll over the floorboards, settling finally to a dull red glow like a demon's eye. What if the place caught fire? Would even that drive the celebrants away? Or would the screaming and the licking flames and the stench of burning tempera be met with wild applause— another titillating spectacle and, when you thought about it, perfectly in keeping with the Trigilaw's landmark status on the broad, dark *Strasse* running from the Kreuzberg to hell? Stav's own act, coming up soon, after the "Grecian dancers" finished their routine of simulated (though sometimes actual) polymorphous copulation, should be a case in point.

From the audience came raucous cheering. Scattered cries of "*Noch mehr!*" from gentlemen straining the seams of mustard uniforms. A lady's high-pitched, demented laughter, which might be heard as a prolonged keening of despair. The crowd was, as they say, warmed up. It would fall to Stav to chill them down again. Freeze their blood and give them yet another reason not to think of going home so soon. Why, it's barely three o'clock! The sun won't be up for *hours*.

One by one, sweaty limbs gleaming, smiles flashing gamely in the spotlight, the dancers filed offstage. Out front, the MC, a bald little fellow known professionally as Der Aal, made uncouth jokes about members of the audience in a sneering voice amplified by the PA to a kind of electrified, reptilian snicker. He was a man of whom you might think, Well, but of course it's just an act—except in the Eel's case it wasn't. He was a sadist and a misanthrope. *Where'd you find the dame, my friend—on the bargain table at Wertheim's? Last year's merchandise, not even a Jew could sell it!* Just an act. Are the Jews still running Wertheim's, Stav wondered. Surely all the big department stores must have been Aryanized by now. But no matter—good for a laugh.

Now the Eel launched into the run-up to Stav's routine, dropping his voice the better part of an octave while the pit orchestra struck up an eerie sostenuto, indebted about equally to *Peter and the Wolf* and to decadent atonalists like Webern, banned from the concert hall but welcome here along the infernal S-Bahn.

"And now soon, ladies and gentlemen," hissed the Eel, "you will meet an individual with a foot in both worlds: the Now and the Hereafter. A personage thought by many to be . . . *something other than human.* So please, honored guests, I implore you, heed my words: *I make no guarantee as to your personal safety.* Not while our, ah . . . our guest stands among us. Not while his gaze falls upon this one or that one—upon you, *gnädige Frau*, or you, *Herr Oberst*. And so I urge all individuals of a sensitive disposition, and especially women of childbearing years, to please move a prudent distance from the stage. Move now, before—my God, there's no time, he comes, he comes! I must . . . you'll forgive me . . ." Trailing off with a whimper, the Eel scurried offstage while the orchestra flew into a dirge of dissonant horns and screeching strings. At last the beefy percussionist, lately employed by the Philharmonic, brought down a mallet to shatter a pane of glass—flying shards glittering briefly against black curtains, stage rear, before falling harmlessly into a cloth-lined crate—and the music ceased.

Into the stillness Stav glided soundlessly. Literally glided, on a mechanic's trolley pulled by a rope from the opposite wing. His back was to the audience and his cape drawn tight around his neck, so when he finally stepped off the trolley and turned, throwing his arms wide, baring teeth between dark-painted lips in a face from which all blood seemed to have drained—soaking, perhaps, into the cape's crimson lining—two members of the audience screamed, which meant that one of the screams was real. Stav smiled. It was a smile of genuine amusement, but the sorcery of stage lights and greasepaint changed it to a frightful leer.

Stav blinked and stared, as though unaccustomed to the light. "What is this place?" Pacing, groping, shading his eyes. "To what realm have I been summoned? Which of you devils called me here? Was it *you, Mein Herr*? Or you—or *you*? What do you want from me?"

He spoke in the dialect of his working-class childhood, as distinctive and rudely flavored as the thickest Cockney. This was something of a joke, and the audience got it—the Dark Prince himself is a native Berliner!

Now people began shouting. Many of them had caught the act before; they knew what was expected. "How's my old friend Gunter doing down there? Warm enough for him, is it?" "Please, sir—could you give a message to my *Mutti*? Tell her I forgot to wear my rubbers and now my big toe's all red and swollen!"

Stav affected difficulty comprehending. He narrowed his eyes, fluttered his cape, moved this way and that, as though disoriented by the cacophony of voices. Then he paused when a lone voice seemed to detach itself from the rest and to ring out in a room suddenly grown silent.

"Where has Jakob gone? Can you tell me that? Have you seen him, where you come from? Where is Jakob, please—it's important that I know."

Stav could see the speaker clearly. A young man, university age, clear-eyed and blond. Not a local, he thought. Up to the city for spring holiday, perhaps. You weren't supposed to call it Easter anymore; it was something different now, allegedly Germanic, a rediscovered planting festival. The boy stared at him from a dozen paces back, beyond the table of VIPs, his eyes imploring, his neck craned forward, reaching hard for this foolish hope. Ignoring, or trying to, the unkind laughter around him.

It was just an act, this was true. But what kind of act? Stav wasn't always sure. There was a feeling he sometimes got, and was getting now—as though a secret were passing between himself and this boy, streaming like the thin yellow paper from a teletype machine—a delicate connection, take care not to rip it. Read it out slowly, one word at a time.

"Your friend is alive," he said. Then, more firmly, declaring it to the room: "Jakob is alive!"

The audience was quiet now, perceiving, blearily, a change in mood.

"But in pain," Stav continued. "Constant—a kind of ache. The back, I think. The legs. He's been beaten. Yet he must get up and work. And hungry, always hungry. They don't give him enough food."

"Will he come back?" the boy asked. No need to shout this, just an ordinary question.

He will not come back. Stav felt it right away, a certainty. *In the end, they'll kill him. You'll never see Jakob again.* He couldn't bring himself to say it, but there was no need. Tears welled in the boy's eyes.

Then Stav felt something new. A different set of eyes, staring. A fresh summons. *Look at me.* He resisted for several moments, as long as he dared. At last he allowed his eyes to pass over the table immediately before the stage, there meeting the cool, passionless gaze of Reinhard Heydrich.

"And what about me, *mein böser Herr*?" the tall officer said, speaking calmly but at parade-ground volume. His features were small, as though the skin had been stretched too tightly around his skull. Tonight he sported the sort of long white gloves one wears at the opera. "What message have you brought for *me* out of the infernal depths?"

Stav willed himself to go blank, to feel nothing. Heydrich had come here before, was almost a regular, but this was the first time he'd taken an overt interest in the show. Ordinarily his attention was occupied by the "entertainers" employed by Glewitz (who liked the English term) to join certain preferred customers at their tables and evince an unquenchable thirst for champagne. He held his lock on Stav's eyes for quite a while, and the audience stared too, thrilled by this unexpected sideshow. At last Heydrich broke the silence.

"That was quite good, just now. Very convincing. How does it work, I wonder. Perhaps you'll tell me sometime." Smiling mirthlessly, he turned his head away. *All right, if that's how it is, then I'm done with you.* One member of his party, not in uniform but in smart civilian attire, rose from the table and approached the stage, where he produced a small white rectangle, recognizably a calling card, and laid it primly by a footlight.

Stav feigned indifference. Earthly affairs—so petty, so sordid. He swept his cape sideways, swooping with high melodrama from one wing to the other. But it was forced now; he'd been knocked off his rhythm. The crowd, too, sensed that the vital spark was missing. After ten more painful minutes, the Eel yanked him off, signaling the orchestra to strike up the exit music, something from Orff, a brownshirt favorite. Stav allowed himself one parting glance at Heydrich, who caught and returned it with a slight raising of the brow. And now, of all times, the connection came alive again.

We'll be seeing you, said the cold blue eyes.

Stav looked away. Just an act, he reminded himself. And so there was no danger that the chief of the Security Service might have sensed his unspoken reply. *Go fuck yourself, Nazi shit-hound.*

Heydrich's companion, the man in civilian clothes, was waiting outside the stage door, just standing in the alley reading a newspaper by the day's first light. He wasn't such an ominous figure; the threat lay in the fact of his being there. Stav lowered his shoulders and glanced up and down the alley. He saw no one else, no black motorcar idling on the street. But what of that? There was nowhere to run, no place in all of Germany where these men couldn't find you. So he turned north, as always, and began walking home.

The man fell into step beside him. Neither spoke. They emerged together into a residential street running parallel to the Oranienstrasse, where Stav turned east, the man pivoting beside him, sharp as a soldier at morning drill. He knows the route, Stav thought. Well, of course—they know everything.

The new morning light fell like a fine powder on dirty sidewalks, placard-bearing kiosks, seedy apartment façades. Somehow the urban renaissance that had transformed Berlin into a gleaming world metropolis had not penetrated the Kreuzberg, despite its lying just south of the thriving Mitte. Stav guessed that men like this one, men of the shadows, friends of Heydrich's, had need of a place like the Kreuzberg so they'd kept it as a sort of protected habitat—somewhere they could breathe freely, loosen their limbs, bare their fangs and take down their prey without upsetting the ladies at tea on Unter den Linden.

Stav turned right and left again, as usual, aware that every step took him deeper into the maze of narrow streets and dark housing blocks, *Hinterhöfe,* on the wrong side of the river Spree. His own habitat, come to that, though his niche was a humble one. *Don't kill me, Herr Wolf, I'm an unsavory fellow, there's nothing on these bones worth eating.*

The man reached over and touched Stav's arm. Gently, almost. The simple gesture brought him to a halt. He returned the man's gaze, which was focused, intelligent, even respectful. One civilized being to another. "I won't importune you for long, my good sir," the man said. "I merely hope we can talk for a little while. Why don't you let me buy you breakfast? Isn't there a place just ahead?"

This was a neighborhood café called the Black Shoe, though no sign marked it as such; the name was known only to locals and was a kind of historical allusion, commemorating a particular customer and a serving of liver and onions. It was the kind of place where you could order a glass of vodka with your *Blutwurst* and eggs. And it was already crowded at not even six in the morning, with the late shift covered in coal dust and sweat, rubbing shoulders with the early shift still half-drunk from the night before. And now an exhausted cabaret performer, traces of black greasepaint showing around his eyes, and an immaculate gentleman who looked like—in the careful expression people used nowadays—*someone from the ministries.*

"You have a remarkable talent," the man told him, smiling broadly, while they stood at a small raised table waiting for coffee. "I'm sorry, I must properly introduce myself. Kohlwasser is my name. Helmut Kohlwasser." He held out a hand.

No title, Stav thought. No ceremonial rank. A puzzlement, but he deemed it worth a handshake.

"Your talent," Kohlwasser went on, "would seem to consist in knowing things. Please correct me if I'm mistaken. But in knowing by means that are not at all apparent. That boy, his unfortunate friend—you managed that quite discreetly; it was clear you could have said more but chose to spare his feelings. This sort of fine judgment, this restraint, is not expected at a place like the Trigilaw, is it? Nor in many places, truthfully." He leaned closer. "I won't insult you by asking how is it done. But if I may, sir, without causing offense, ask instead: Do you *know* how it is done? Or does it come as a surprise? To you as to the audience? I confess, sir, this was my impression."

Stav, taken off guard, opened his mouth, then closed it again. A haggard waitress left coffee in two small cups. A splotch of liquid, black as oil, had spilled into the saucers.

Kohlwasser backed off—literally pulled away and sipped thoughtfully at his coffee. His expression betrayed nothing of how he felt about it. Stav thought it tasted terrible.

"But you know," the man said, his voice now cheerful, avuncular, "this is what I found so striking. As I believe the General did as well. This mysterious awareness. The information"—snapping his fingers—"just there! No one knows how, not even yourself. And that's better, isn't it? Because to know the *how*, the *from where*, this would be a distraction. All that matters, all one cares about, is the information itself. The answer coming exactly at the right time. Amazing the audience. Ensuring one's continued employment. Don't you agree, my good sir?"

Stav felt himself nod.

This cheered Kohlwasser. "Yes, yes, I thought so. And this is why I so much wanted to speak with you. Because you see, it occurs to me—as I'm sure it occurred to the General—that you and I are in very much the same business, we're paid to perform the same trick. To be aware, by dark and mysterious means. To have the answer to a question at just the moment it's wanted." His manner grew animated. "No one cares how! No one cares from where! These things are distractions. The General doesn't care about those. Nor do those to whom the General must report."

Stav got it, finally. *The General*—he'd let the title pass without thought. Everyone in Berlin had a title, and everyone delighted in proclaiming it. But not Kohlwasser. He'd been using the old-fashioned army term, *General*, in preference to the clumsy, up-to-date SS terminology when talking about Reinhard Heydrich. Stav waited, feeling sick at the pit of his stomach, for the rest of it. The invitation one could not refuse. Come work for us, give us the answers when we need them. Did you know Reichsführer Himmler is a devotee of the dark sciences? He'll recognize your great talent for what it is.

But the pitch never came. Maybe the words were too crude to pass Kohlwasser's lips. He patted them now with a monogrammed handkerchief, which he then replaced in his breast pocket with the corners showing, like an English film star. Contenting himself, in the end, at their amiable parting under a sooty Kreuzberg sun, with repeating a single motif, this time with a slight variation.

"Nobody ever needs to know how," he said, shaking and briefly holding on to Stav's hand. "Nobody ever needs to know from whom. We don't care about that. But you understand. You and we—in this respect, we're really very much alike."

LIBRARIANS IN EXILE

A crowd was screaming on the radio.

Oskar winced, an ingrained habit—but the voice shouting over the cheers wasn't that of a foaming Jew-hater, it was a sportscaster with a southern drawl, enthused beyond all understanding by a *great* play, a *super* play, quick thinking there by Buddy Myer at second, that'll send 'em *packing* back to Philly.

Six weeks in America, holed up in a fleabag Leo had found for him—"Just keep quiet, Oskar, they'll take your cash and ask no questions"—yet still it was strange to him. More than strange, *fantastisch*, something out of a new kind of fairy tale.

"You'll be fine, Oskar," Leo had told him. "You're *alive*—isn't that enough for you?"

It was and it wasn't. He was alive, yes. The hotel, for all its shortcomings, had proved a safe haven, tucked into a dark street north of the train station. Oskar was on friendly terms with the Negro woman who changed his sheets and the one-armed white man who sat after hours at the front desk, studying the *Daily Racing Form* and perpetually shaking from delirium tremens. In daylight hours he kept to his room, staring out over a railroad switching yard.

As to "You'll be fine," that also was true to an extent. His shoulder still hurt but he could walk now without limping. Erwin Kaspar's ugly suit had been ruined, but Leo had brought him a set of workmen's clothes: blue denim pants, a checkered shirt and a secondhand jacket more than adequate for these warm nights. But he was alive, so yes—he *was* lucky.

Only it wasn't enough. He'd failed in his mission. He was out of contact with his superiors and could not think how to get in touch except by walking into the German embassy and, thus, directly into the line of fire of whatever enemies he might have there—a swarming host, he imagined. He'd been betrayed; that much was clear. Perhaps by the two young men from the tavern, perhaps by Toby Lugan, perhaps by some flaw in his cover. That didn't matter, but this did: he was on the wrong side of the ocean, far from the struggle being waged for the soul of his homeland. Now that his injuries were mended, and the weeks were slipping by, and his money running out, he needed to "get back in the game," as Leo would say. But what a perplexing game it was—worse than baseball and a good deal rougher.

He'd tried impressing this on Leo at one of their dinners together, at an establishment called the Dixie Pig. Had such a place existed in Germany, Oskar would have been loath to set foot in it. But Leo breezed through the door and past the glowing jukebox to a booth jammed into a corner, equipped with a lever-action dispenser of paper napkins and a bottle of scarlet pepper sauce, sliding over the grease-stained bench as though he'd been coming here for decades. The place was narrow and noisy, an unseen radio pumped out Tommy Dorsey, "Satan Takes a Holiday," and the patrons shouted happily above it. A nation of uncouth innocents. Leo, who'd swapped his black suit for a proletarian outfit like Oskar's, ordered for both of them.

"You know, I've been thinking about your situation," Leo said once the waitress brought their beers and left, "and there are things that make no sense to me. But they have to make sense, there must be something we're not seeing, because things happened exactly *this* way, not some other way. You really were sent over here—that's the first thing. Your masters concocted this stupid plan, so we have to assume they had their reasons."

Oskar glanced over his shoulder, though he supposed there was scant likelihood that anyone here understood German, and even less that they could hear over this racket.

"So I ask myself, What is it that makes these anal-retentive General Staff types so eager to spill national secrets? And to a decadent Western power. Yet the fact remains: they did it."

"They want to avoid another war," Oskar suggested.

"Maybe they do. Or maybe they just want to avoid the *wrong* war. But there are other means of doing that, surely. Why don't they all resign? Go to the Führer and say, Sorry, old boy, if you want this war so badly, get your pal Himmler to fight it for you. I mean, he could scarcely hang the lot of them, could he?"

"Officers are normally shot," said Oskar dryly. "Hanging is for the lower ranks."

"Duly noted." Leo rewarded him with a smile. "Shall I tell you what I think?"

But then the food arrived, something identified as barbecue—the portions huge and odorous, sauce dripping from the edges of sturdy jade-green plates.

"Anything else for you boys?" the waitress asked, her gaze moving incuriously between them.

"Two more Nationals," Leo told her, then glanced at Oskar. "We'll need them."

"You were saying," Oskar prompted.

"Try this first. It's a local specialty. The epitome of Washington cuisine."

"What is this meat?"

"You won't be able to tell, but I think it's pork. I know"—an overdone shrug, the Yiddish comedian plying his trade—"a Jew eating pork. But this is America! At least it's *one* America.

After a few bites Oskar was blinking through tears, gulping mouthfuls of bad but very cold beer.

"Wonderful, isn't it? And cheap, too. They must breed pigs here like rabbits. No, Oskar. There can be only one explanation. They're lining up allies. They think if they show the world what Hitler's really up to, they'll have backing from abroad when they make their move."

What move, Oskar wanted to know, but his throat seemed to have locked down. He feared the reception of this food in his intestines.

Leo nodded, apparently taking his expression for a sign of understanding. "You see it, don't you? Your masters are planning a coup."

Oskar managed to swallow. "A coup? No, I don't think so."

"It's the only thing that makes sense. I've been thinking about this quite a lot."

"I can see you have. But listen, Leo. Coup or no coup—I need to get back over there. You've got to help me."

Leo shook his head. "They'll only kill you."

"You told me that before."

"Did I? Well, at least you listened." Leo regarded him shrewdly for a long moment. "A soldier's place is at the front—is that it?"

"Well, of course there's that. But suppose what you say *is* true—then they'll just keep trying. They'll send another messenger. So it's important I get back and tell them what happened—so maybe they can figure out where it went wrong. As it stands, all they know is that I've vanished. I might be dead, I might've defected. I could even be under interrogation by the FBI. I'm serious, Leo. You must know somebody. Don't the Socialists have some kind of underground?"

Leo shrugged like the innocent man he was not. "How would I know?" he said, in the voice of someone who knew very well indeed.

Promptly at eight o'clock on the night of the next baseball game—a home-team triumph, Oskar heard later, Washington beating Philadelphia nine runs to two—Leo came to fetch him in a taxi. Oskar enjoyed cab rides in America, since the drivers were never in a hurry and there was often good music on the radio.

"Where are we going?" he asked as the cab pulled away.

"Silver Spring," Leo said, to the driver as much as Oskar. "A little after-dinner soirée. Cheese and brandy, cigars for the gentlemen—you know how it goes."

Oskar hoped he was kidding. He had only these clothes, and they were hardly proper for an evening out. Leo was in his black suit again. Well, there was nothing to be done about it now, so he settled back into the generous American upholstery and watched New York Avenue flash by.

His attention was briefly caught by a new streamlined building in the Bauhaus style announcing itself as THE HECHT CO. in lighted vertical lettering. Something you'd see in Germany. Even a German name. Jewish German, probably. Despised immigrants who'd brought a little of the Fatherland with them, if only by way of their surnames and their taste in architecture. Ironic, really—Jews wearing their Germanness so proudly. Though of course they were right to be proud. The land of *Dichter und Denker,* poets and thinkers. And lately of stormtroopers, snitches, "mercy killers." Where every boy dreams, as Oskar had, of growing up to be a soldier.

The city turned to woodland—Rock Creek Park again, wider and greener up here—and then to a comfortable suburb with tidy bungalows, a modest town center, more modernist architecture, a movie house showing *Robin Hood* with Errol Flynn. Leo read an address from a piece of paper and the cab maneuvered though neighborhood streets, stopping at last before a small house that wouldn't have been out of place in Saxony: pitched roof, mullioned windows, half-timbered façade.

The front door swung open at their first, tentative knock, and a round-faced, eager-looking man beckoned them to enter.

"I'm Gregor," he told them, speaking the German of the north, Schleswig-Holstein, a hint of Scandinavia behind it. "Please, come in, we've just opened a bottle of Riesling. You are Herr Gandelmann, yes? With whom I spoke on the telephone? And so this must be Leutnant Langweil."

Oskar was startled to hear his own name spoken aloud. He'd left his real identity so far behind that now it hardly seemed to fit him anymore. Gregor led them down a hall to an informal sitting room where a young couple waited, expecting them—or, at second glance, maybe not a couple, just a man and a woman who happened to be sharing the sofa.

Introductions all around. The young man was Stefan Sinclair—the second name a gift of his American father, who'd left his mother years ago but not before bestowing upon Stefan the gift of dual citizenship. The woman was Lena Hamel, red-haired and striking, a touch of the wild East in her cheekbones. Both looked slightly older than Oskar, about Leo's age, in the mid-twenties somewhere. Their stories intertwined, and they told them simultaneously over glasses of wine, interrupting each other and apologizing, then laughing, everyone settling down as the atmosphere changed to something these people must have grown familiar with over here—Germans in a room together, enjoying their native tongue.

"We worked in the library at Weimar," Lena told him. "The grand old library, a marvelous building. The light in the reading room—people would come and sit there, maybe with a newspaper but not really reading, just to be in that wonderful light. I worked at the main desk—"

"I was in Literature." Stefan spoke over her. His voice had a bitter edge. "Not a bad collection. Particularly strong in the older texts. Many fine original editions, quite rare in some cases. We had a separate room for these; one needed special permission—"

"You saw every kind of person there. Old people, boys from *Gymnasium*, mothers with their children—"

"Jews," said Stefan pointedly. "It didn't matter—we welcomed everyone."

Politely Oskar said, "Yes, that's very good." He thought he shouldn't be feeling so impatient, and yet he was.

Stefan shrugged. "Very good, yes. It was a place of knowledge, a public treasure—we worked hard to make it so. We were professionals, you understand? Professionals doing our job. We were not political."

"Some of us," Lena said gently, not quite contradicting him, "a few of us were political. I was a Social Democrat. A matter of personal conviction. I went to meetings but only in my free time, in the evenings. I spoke about such things only to my friends. At work I kept my opinions to myself. It's what I'd always wanted, this work. What I'd studied for."

"Of course, they didn't care about that," said Stefan. "The Nazis don't care about studying, really. It's too tedious for them, too time-consuming. 'Germany cannot move slowly at the present time!' "

Oskar recognized this as a quotation and was happy to be able to place it. "Stefan George."

"Yes!" Lena said, slightly rolling her eyes, flashing Oskar a brief, mischievous smile. "These troublesome nationalist poets. Quite a demand we had for them, right along. People always asking, the same names over and over. You felt like saying, Look, there are hundreds—"

"George isn't *that* kind of nationalist," Stefan said crossly. "Not if you actually read him. Of course, the Nazis aren't interested in reading, either. Has anyone actually read *Mein Kampf*? I mean, for the love of God—"

"I did," said Oskar. "It was—well, it was terrible, but I read it. We were required to."

Stefan smirked. "So *you're* the one. But George, anyway, turned down the honor of being the Reich's first poet laureate. Did you know that?" He looked at Lena, a challenge. "He sent a member of his circle—a Jew, in fact—to give Dr. Goebbels his regrets. And then he died."

"I guess *that* showed them," she tittered.

"Why'd you leave?" said Leo. "Did you get in trouble?"

Stefan and Lena exchanged glances. "Not trouble, exactly," she said. "It never quite came to that. But there was tension. Always there was a struggle, confusing directives: first this author can stay on the shelf but not that one, then it changes and *that* one must go, too. And nothing ever gets put back. Once it's gone, it never existed. Heine goes but Mendel stays, because Mendel's a scientist, and you know, science is science, it doesn't care who your father is. But then Mendel becomes a *Jewish* scientist, in other words no scientist at all, and definitely no German, so that's it for him."

Stefan shook his head. "With the Jews, though—well, of course you expect this. Everyone knows you can't have Freud, you can't have Adler, that's a given. But how about Jung, can you have him? One bureau says yes, because he's a proper Aryan. Another says no, because he's still a psychoanalyst, and psychoanalysis is a Jewish invention. You don't know which bureau to—"

"And there were *seventeen* different bureaus, can you believe that? Seventeen different authorities telling you what to do, all competing to be the most zealous, the most pure. But it was even worse than that. There was an 'asphalt' list—these were simply banned, discarded—but also there was a 'poison' list. Anyone requesting these titles must be reported."

"It reached a point," said Stefan, "at which only one policy was safe: get rid of everything. Clear the shelves until nothing's left but approved authors. Any doubtful case becomes a no. Proust? He's French and queer, so he's gone. Alain-Fournier? He's not queer but he's French, so maybe he knows Proust—I'm not joking, this is how people thought. What serious professional can work like this?"

"What decent human being?" said Lena, looking from Oskar to Leo imploringly.

"Anyway," said Stefan, slapping his knee, "that's just how it was. And so we left."

"You came over together?" Leo asked.

Lena smiled. "I pretended to be his wife. We had papers drawn up. Under German law, we're actually married."

Stefan said nothing. This, apparently, wasn't something he cared to talk about. He turned away to pour himself another glass of wine; the Riesling was good, high-toned and crisp. Oskar knew a little about wine from his training at Lichterfelde, those evenings you were required to spend at staged and stuffy gatherings, learning how a German officer comported himself in society.

"But you know," Lena said, "the funny thing is, we weren't even really friends. Stefan and I, we were just . . . we knew each other from work. We got along fine as colleagues, but we never spoke about anything. Not the poison list, not the Nazis, not the little men from the agencies who came in to verify compliance. Nothing, really. Yet somehow—"

"You just *know*," said Stefan, angry now. "You know who is *what*. You can tell by looking at them. The way their eyes move, the things they laugh at, how they watch people."

Oskar remembered. "That's true."

Lena went on: "One day Stefan just asked me. This was only a few months ago. He's going to America, do I want to come along? He explained how it would work. The make-believe marriage, everything. I was so surprised and . . . grateful." She gave Stefan a tender look, which he ignored. "And so now here we are. The state of Maryland. Librarians in exile. Who could possibly imagine such a thing?"

In a sane world, she meant. In this room, everyone could imagine it very easily.

"Excuse me," said Leo loudly. "This is all really interesting but . . . am I to understand that you people can get our Oskar back to Germany?"

Boom—out with it. Leo's forte. There was a moment of silence, an invisible regrouping; then their host, Gregor, said, "We're willing to help. All of us. But under strict conditions. First, you must be completely truthful with us. There are risks involved—I don't need to tell you that. We need to be certain whom we're dealing with."

"I'll be truthful," Oskar assured him. "I give you my word."

"As an officer and a gentleman?" Stefan asked rather mincingly.

"As a German. The same as you."

Leo asked Gregor, "Who's this *we*?"

He started to answer, but Stefan cut in: "I'm sorry, perhaps I gave you the wrong impression. I told you that in Weimar, as a librarian, I wasn't political. Over here, it's different."

"We're all political now," said Lena. "To the extent we can be, so far away. Perhaps you've heard, *Herr Leutnant*, of the SOPADE?"

Sozialdemokratische Partei Deutschlands im Exil. The principal left-wing opposition party, operating now from abroad. Oskar knew a little, as everyone did. Now these people told him more, though probably not everything.

They told him about the headquarters in Prague, the offices in other cities, and cells everywhere, even in Germany. The newspaper *Neuer Vorwärts*, distributed to the exile community and smuggled bravely into the Reich. And—to Oskar the most interesting part— the "Blue Papers," a series of reports on conditions inside Germany, compiled from data provided by thousands of informants, some of them well-placed, most just ordinary people taking notes on what they saw and heard around them.

"And what do these Blue Papers tell you?" Leo asked. "How exactly are the conditions inside Germany?"

"They still love him," said Stefan. "After everything that's happened, the people still support the regime, and Hitler himself remains overwhelmingly popular. You have to wonder just how stupid people are."

"You can't blame the people," said Lena. "Not the ordinary workers. They only know what they read in the papers, or what they—"

Leo cut in: "What about the Jews? Do your reports talk about the Jews?"

"They do," said Gregor, his expression turning grim. "Things are getting worse all the time, and yet so many remain. It's not easy to get out, of course—but many don't even try. They're waiting for all this to pass, I suppose. Bad things have happened before. Terrible times come and go. They don't believe the Nazi time is really so different."

"You see?" said Stefan, straight at Leo. "People are stupid. Even Jews are stupid."

Leo started to reply but in the end only gave him a sad smile. "I suppose you're right."

"You can't believe that," said Lena. "Not really. Not as a true Socialist."

"So I guess I'm not a true Socialist anymore."

"What, then?" said Stefan. "A Communist?"

Leo gave them his comedian's shrug. "I'm an American."

Only Oskar laughed, struck by the absurdity of Leo Gandelmann, sitting in a stranger's house with a bad-fitting jacket bunched up around his scarecrow shoulders, proclaiming a new nationality. Though maybe he was simply speaking the truth. He could no longer be German but needed to be something, wanting so badly to belong somewhere. An American, then—what else?

"You said there were conditions," Oskar said, speaking to Gregor now. "What are the others?"

"The others. Well—"

"I'm going with you," Lena blurted. "Back over there. As soon as arrangements can be made. This may take a little while; it's complicated. But we can start tonight with the passport. You'll need a new photo."

"The passport." He hadn't thought of this. But of course it was necessary to have one. "You'll be giving me a new identity, then?"

"An old one, actually," Stefan said. "Mine, to be exact. You'll be going as Stefan Sinclair. It's an odd name, I'm told, but you'll get used to it."

Oskar tried to absorb this, and the effort must have shown on his face.

"It's quite safe," Stefan told him, sounding annoyed, "in case you're worried about that. I never got in any trouble. I kept my thoughts to myself, I never spoke against the government, I did my job. Quite well, in point of fact. I never even officially emigrated—it wasn't necessary. As I'm an American citizen, it was just a matter of booking a ticket and getting my visa stamped. I gave them a story about an illness in the family, a paternal uncle . . . but the point is, I can return at any time. You know how it goes—'the call of the homeland.' You'll be welcomed, *Herr Leutnant*, as a patriot."

Oskar nodded in acceptance—a new mission, a new cover identity. He looked at Lena. "And you'll be going too? As my . . . escort? My contact with the underground?"

She smiled at him oddly. He glanced around to find the others also smiling, as though he alone had missed something.

"What?" he said, frowning, resisting embarrassment.

"As your wife," Lena said.

PATRIOTS OF THE WRONG ERA

BERLIN, PRINZ-ALBRECHT-STRASSE: MAY 1938

Nostalgic music on the phonograph: "Irgendwo auf der Welt," a tune made vastly popular by the Comedian Harmonists back in the twenties, dripping with the schmaltz of that era as well as the despair.

> *Somewhere in the world*
> *My road to heaven begins;*
> *Somewhere, somehow, sometime.*

The singing group had disbanded, its two Jewish members fleeing abroad—but the *Schlager*, the hits, played on, in a misty German twilight of dance halls and wedding receptions and, most curiously, this tall-windowed third-floor office at the RSHA, the Reich Security Headquarters, demesne of Reinhard Heydrich, a hive of black-coated scholars and lawyers and analysts and filing clerks. "Desk murderers," Berliners called them.

While the phonograph spun, the naval officer known to his friends as Jaap wondered again, as he had all week, just what he was doing here, why they'd summoned him—though perhaps that was overstating it. The invitation had been lightly proffered, as though on a whim, over drinks at the Yugoslav embassy, one senior intelligence officer to another. The other man—name Kohlwasser, rank colonel, though Jaap had never seen him in uniform—had said, "You must drop by my office someday soon," adding slyly, "I'd love to compare notes with you. I think we may have a case or two in common; what a shame if we were to duplicate our efforts."

Jaap dutifully reported the encounter. His superiors spent a couple of days deciding that, yes, it did rise to the level of an "approach," and therefore he must respond to it; because coming from the SD, this was quite peculiar.

What wasn't, though? The whole outfit was odd, a stark contrast with its sister service, the *Geheime Staatspolizei*. With the Gestapo you knew where you stood and took it for granted that your name was in a file somewhere. With the SD you knew nothing, not even what they were about, fundamentally. "Security Service"—that could mean anything at all. One branch conspired to undermine hostile governments while another compiled data on the number of people shirking traffic fines. There was a *Büro* called the Race Ancestry Office that funded archaeological digs of proto-German settlements and vetted long-dead poets for weak, effeminate tendencies. Another, devoted to "German Christianity," redacted the Bible to eliminate traces of Hebrew poison. And somewhere in this building—Jaap had it on good authority—a full *Brigadegeneral* called Weisstor concerned himself single-mindedly with restoring the lost Wotanic priesthood. *That* was national security for you, in this sixth year of the eternal Reich.

The big, loping, phlegmatic sort, Jaap sat quite still on the leather sofa that took up a whole wall of Kohlwasser's office while his host kept up a thin pretense of being occupied on the telephone. "Yes, I know, Schmundt, the fool has been badgering me all week about this idiotic paper. You can tell him we'll send it as soon as it's ready—gift-wrapped, by special delivery! What's that, Schmundt? Please speak up, I've got a gentleman waiting here." It was all for show, but it gave Jaap time to glance over the periodicals arranged with seeming artlessness over a wide coffee table, the international touch heavily on display: *Paris-Soir*, a couple of Swiss dailies, *Life* magazine, *The Times Literary Supplement* and, tucked not quite out of sight, the real catch: *Neuer Vorwärts*, the journal of the exiled Social Democrats.

This was so heavy-handed that Jaap had to restrain himself from smiling. Look what a liberal fellow I am! See all these Western magazines! And this lovely music—they don't write songs like that anymore!

He looked up to find that Kohlwasser had rung off at last and was watching him with an expression that was perhaps too open-eyed, too amenable. This wasn't a social occasion. *I think we may have a case or two in common.*

"Do you smoke?" Kohlwasser asked, pushing a silver cigarette case across a desk that was otherwise bare except for a few papers in a single neat stack. The top sheet, apparently a routing slip, was printed on blue stock and bore a series of scrawled initials in small square boxes. All in order.

Smoke or don't smoke: the important thing was not to hesitate or betray any uncertainty. "Thank you," Jaap said, a gentleman's way of declining. Kohlwasser nodded but left the cigarettes lying there, as one might do at the start of an interrogation. You'll want to later, the gesture signified.

A delicate protocol governed meetings like this. There was no official rivalry between the SD and the Abwehr, the intelligence arm of the General Staff. At the same time, there was scant direct liaison and even less collegiality. In theory, their respective missions didn't overlap—each served the Reich in its own special realm, civilian on this side, military on the other. No one believed it, but all agreed on the utility of maintaining the pretense. That was point one. Point two was reciprocity. You had to assume, in these circumstances, that the other party was trawling for information—of a very particular sort—so your goal was to yield it as sparingly as possible while extracting the maximum payment in kind.

On the phonograph, the needle reached the end of its spiral, and by some clever mechanism the playing arm lifted itself from the platter and a switch turned the drive motor off. Ingenious! Kohlwasser gave it an appreciative glance and, waxing expansive, spread his palms wide and leaned back in his chair. "It is a sadness, isn't it," he said, "that so many of our most gifted citizens should choose to place themselves on the wrong side of history? In these great days, the German *Volk* should move forward as one."

"If you mean this singing group," Jaap said, "I should think it's more a question of placing themselves on the safe side of the border."

Kohlwasser deflected this provocation with a faint smile. A man confident enough to display *Neuer Vorwärts* on his coffee table could afford to be indulgent. Still, the message appeared to have gotten through: Jaap, too, was confident, and didn't plan to speak in slogans. Kohlwasser was happy to continue in the same vein. "That's not really what disheartens me. A few popular singers more or less, who even notices? Though my wife, you know, she was fond of them. 'Veronika,' 'Schlaf, mein Liebling'—she would hum them around the house. And why not? It's harmless stuff. You'd need a trained ear to detect the racial element there. Certainly it's no Mahler, with corruption oozing from every note. Anyway, you can't blame a Jew for being a Jew, wouldn't you agree? You just acknowledge the fact and treat him accordingly. No, what disheartens me—quite saddens me, really—is when a German chooses not to be German. When one of our own racial comrades refuses to think and feel and act according to the natural dictates of the blood. I don't care which side of the border he's on. But of course it's only *our* side of the border I'm concerned with. Professionally speaking."

Jaap kept quiet for a few moments, wondering if there was more. "You're the expert, I guess," he said finally. He meant it as a question of sorts. He was curious about exactly what Kohlwasser's position was here. The brass tag on the office door had been uninformative, and if there was any kind of internal SD phone book, the Abwehr didn't have a copy.

"Oh, no," the man said, "no expert, certainly not. A patriot. And an interested observer." Modest words from an immodest man, served with a patronizing smile. He changed the subject though not the tone: "I believe you're on friendly terms with the circle in the Fasanenstrasse."

Jaap considered this formulation: the circle. Connoting an association, a closed society, a cabal. Such a thing, if it existed, would be viewed with suspicion by the authorities. National Socialism recognized only one rightful association: the unified body politic, the *Volksgemeinschaft*. He said, "I'm unaware of any such circle."

"Unaware? That surprises me. I should have thought you'd be a highly observant fellow." His nod completed the thought: *in your line of work.*

Jaap shrugged. "Sometimes there's nothing much to observe."

"Ah!" Kohlwasser seemed to find this a very original thought. "Well, of course we're not speaking of tanks and planes, enemy formations."

Jaap wondered what in hell they *were* speaking of.

"Quite a crowd of luminaries," Kohlwasser pressed on, "there in the Fasanenstrasse. Poets, aristocrats, diplomats, high-ranking officers—and real musicians, not the cheap radio hacks. Anyone would feel honored to have a place among them. Is that not so, *Kapitänleutnant?*"

Jaap acknowledged the use of his formal rank with a faint bow of the head. An easy enough trick, but more than he'd been able to manage on his end. "I'm always surprised when a hostess lets me through the door. They seldom make that mistake twice."

Kohlwasser nodded, as though Jaap had said something quite different. His gaze moved out over an imagined view, as vast and glittering as a ballroom. "They say the Baroness is an amazing woman. A grande dame of the old school. She must be ninety if she's a day, yet so . . . incisive, so opinionated. And altogether fearless, I'm told. Says exactly what's on her mind. And if you take offense, well—" He flipped one hand as though dismissing an annoying person of no significance. "What does she care? Her mind is on greater things. On the arts. On culture, on history—all the great events she's witnessed. And those occurring this very day. A truly Olympian *Weltanschauung*, one must imagine."

He paused as though expecting a reply. Jaap aimed to appear placid, to keep his expression neutral. He feared he'd somehow opened a door and now wondered what might slip through it.

Kohlwasser warmed to his theme. "Naturally, around such a personage, a like-minded coterie would gather. People who also have strong opinions, perhaps not quite so bold, not quite so fearless, yet willing to be outspoken in sympathetic company. I'd love to be a little bird perched on those splendid railings, listening to the music and the conversation floating through those windows. I'd love to know—I'm being quite frank with you—what those brilliant people are talking about. It's my job, actually. My job, and my duty as a patriot. To learn what people are saying, what people are feeling, what people really think."

Jaap took it for granted that Kohlwasser, like anyone who boasted of *being quite frank with you*, was lying to his face. But the lie was a subtle one, wrapped, it seemed, in a layer of truth. He gave him a doleful, commiserative smile. "Not the easiest job in the world."

"These days—is that what you mean? This day and age? Or in our particular kind of society?"

Jaap let it pass. Kohlwasser waved a hand, dispelling the momentary tension.

"No, you're right. It's never easy. In our profession, a man is only as good as his informants, isn't that so? Now, I happen to think my informants are better than most. Well-placed, at any rate—that I can say. But how does one really know? Informants play their little games; we all do. They tell their tales, they point their fingers, but always there's uncertainty. They may be telling only part of the story. Or they may have gotten hold of something but they don't know what it is; they can't see the whole picture, so they fill in the gaps with inferences that seem plausible yet turn out to be quite wrong. They interpret when they ought to be reporting. They insist on making connections when in fact there's only coincidence. Yet we don't want to discourage them, do we? Because sometimes, you know, they turn out to be right."

Jaap stared at the wall behind Kohlwasser's desk—the obligatory display of certificates and commendations, a group portrait autographed by some party eminence, a gilt-framed diploma whose Latin text was printed incongruously in an imposing Gothic typeface. He sensed the other man's pent-up, maleficent energy as one feels the approach of a storm. Nothing to do but wait for it. "I'm more of a technical man," he said mildly. "Tanks and planes."

Kohlwasser exhaled strongly, like a venting of steam. "So would we all be, if we could. Reduce everything to numbers and diagrams. This piece goes here, that one goes there. Add and subtract, study the charts, and just so, you've got the answer. Clean and unambiguous. But where do the numbers come from? Who draws the charts?

Human beings, ultimately. And so we're back to the first question: whom is one really to trust? Here, let me give you an example."

He opened a drawer. No need to search—the manila envelope must've been right on top. It was closed with a string, and Kohlwasser made a ceremony of unwinding it, tilting the open end downward to spill the contents onto the shiny wood of the desk. Photographs, a dozen or more, alike in their amber-gray blurriness. They appeared to have been captured by a tiny lens, the type you could conceal in a buttonhole, but the prints had been blown up to the dimensions of a business letter. Courtroom size. Efficiently, like a chess player setting up the board, the man's tapered fingers moved them into two neat rows, interior scenes on top, followed by a sequence of street shots. Ambient light only—candles blazed like flares on a battlefield, passing headlamps left bright smears. Jaap guessed the order was chronological.

"Two *separate* informants," Kohlwasser said, his tone now clinical, "have confirmed independently that the subject *here*"—tap tap, with a pale, slender finger—"was present at a gathering in the Fasanenstrasse. They give different dates, but sometime last autumn, perhaps as late as December. It's possible he attended more than once. Not a regular member of the circle, though. Nor a casual guest, either. Someone specially invited. A curiosity—young for that crowd. Someone's paramour, one might surmise. Or someone's protégé."

Jaap tried to look without seeing. Failing that, to see without feeling. His eyes moved dutifully from one shot to the next.

"Another curious thing," Kohlwasser went on, watching him carefully, "is that *these* photos were taken not in Berlin nor even in Germany but in America—in Washington, back in March."

"America?"

Kohlwasser made a clicking sound, drawing air sharply between his teeth. "This is someone you know?"

He managed, in asking, to imply that Jaap himself had suggested the possibility. A nice interrogator's trick. Jaap knew that one and knew also the correct response: a slight frown, quickly and politely withdrawn, calling into question the mental soundness of the questioner.

"Is he someone I ought to know? A navy man?"

"No."

"No? Well, then." Jaap shook his head. "I'm sorry I can't help you."

Kohlwasser watched him a few seconds longer and then looked down at the photographs. He chose one and lifted it for closer examination, careful not to disturb those on either side. It was an indoor shot: Oskar slightly to the left of the frame, a second figure partly visible across a small round table, the background in deep shadow. Jaap fought the urge to project himself into the scene, to imagine the sweat, the stuffy air, the tension of a *Treff* in a foreign capital. Idly he wondered how close the photographer had been sitting. Close enough to listen in? To read the address on the envelope being handed to the large man on the right?

"An act of treason is being committed here," Kohlwasser said. He seemed to be trying for a tone of proper outrage, but his pleasure seeped through. "It's not often, in this business, we manage to catch anyone so cleanly in flagrante. A live drop in a public restaurant. Which makes one ask, Can it possibly be real? Might this be one of those little games covert operatives like to play? Spies and their masters—one in plain sight, the other safely hidden, pulling the strings. What do you think, *Herr Kapitänleutnant?*"

Jaap spent a few moments inspecting the photograph while wondering what the SD man was getting at. Was he accusing Jaap of cowardice or heartlessness in sending an agent to his doom from the safety of a desk in Bremen? Did he divine that this very notion had been rattling like a ghost for weeks now in Jaap's innermost thoughts? In the end Jaap supposed it was merely a goad, meant to provoke a reaction—nothing more.

"From these," he said, dismissing the pictures with a brush of the hand, "it's impossible to tell. I'd have to know the contents of the envelope. I'd have to know the identities of the two men. Maybe they're friends. Maybe they're involved in a business venture. Maybe, as the Americans would say, they're freelancing."

"I was rather hoping you could help me on that score."

Jaap stared back opaquely. It was easy enough; his feelings were strangely remote. He'd long ago accepted the probability that

Oskar was either dead or banged up in a cell somewhere, German or American. He'd long ago acknowledged his own responsibility. Such things were part of the kind of war they were fighting. He wanted now only to be certain of Oskar's fate. Military custom demanded that, at least. "You've learned nothing, then, from your own investigation?"

Kohlwasser looked faintly surprised. Not the reaction he'd been hoping for. He made one last thrust, eyeing Jaap coolly. "Well . . . there was one other detail, something rather odd." He opened the drawer again. As before, the very one he wanted was waiting right on top. Another photograph, this one in color and sharply detailed. He laid it down emphatically, covering those already there. It showed a box wrapped in gold foil, rectangular, thick enough to hold a ponderous typescript, tied off with a crimson bow. "This object," he said primly, "was recovered later, from the scene of an aborted rendezvous, having been delivered there by the young man in question. And no, it's not a box of chocolates. It's a gift of an entirely different nature. But that needn't concern us now. It's the package itself I find so interesting. Not the sort of thing one often sees, is it, in this business of ours?"

Jaap allowed himself a shrug, mostly to release the tension in his shoulders. "I'm afraid it's out of my line."

"Mine as well, until now. But, you know, it strikes me there's a certain type of criminal who leaves what might be called a signature. A distinctive pattern that reveals something of who he is, how he operates. He thinks it means nothing, just a little flourish, maybe a private joke. But such a little thing may prove to be his undoing."

"Then perhaps you're in luck, sir. I gather your interrogation of this young man has been . . . unproductive?"

A clean thrust there: Kohlwasser looked momentarily stung. "I'm afraid," he said tersely, "there was no opportunity for interrogation. Our representatives on the scene found it necessary to bring this little game to a halt. A definitive halt."

So—dead, then. Kohlwasser held the stronger hand, but in the end he'd revealed the only card Jaap cared to see. In that respect, from the Abwehr's point of view, the meeting had been a notable success.

"I'm sorry," said Kohlwasser, "if this news causes you any distress."

Jaap studied the man for a moment. He reckoned it was too early to start hating him. There would be time later to indulge that sentiment. "I'm a patriot too," he said. "If this man was a traitor, well—"

"Yes, a patriot," Kohlwasser said irritably. "Of course you are. Everyone, it seems, feels patriotic nowadays. Even this one, probably." Flicking one of the photographs with a finger, spoiling the arrangement. "Even he may have felt himself to be motivated by some twisted form of love for the Fatherland. What is needed, however, is to recognize that some of these fine men, these officers and gentlemen from the best families, are patriots of the wrong era. The wrong end of history. That's a lesson many people, unfortunately, have yet to learn."

Jaap regarded him calmly, without expression. The gleam of his eyes, the tawdry sheen of his "Parisian-style" suit. No Frenchman would wear that outfit to a dogfight, but it was the height of fashion in Goebbels's Berlin. "You've won a victory, then, comrade," he said. "The war goes on. For now, you should celebrate." He gestured to the gleaming silver case at the edge of the desk. "Have a cigarette."

STRENGTH THROUGH JOY

NORTH ATLANTIC: MID-MAY 1938

The German liner *Robert Ley* made turns for twenty-one knots in a choppy sea nearly the color of a Wehrmacht field uniform. Oskar stood holding a rail with the northerly wind in his face and the porridge he'd eaten for breakfast shifting in his stomach like ballast left improperly secured. Despite the uncongenial weather, there were other people on deck, quite a lot of them—young men and women of sturdy build and bronze complexion and hale, confident manner, all of them wearing the wool-and-denim uniform of the DAF, the German Labor Front.

Leo's friends in the Socialist underground had agreed to help Oskar, along with his notional wife, Lena, secure passage back to Germany, and so they had. On a ship full of Nazis.

This cruise—that's how it was billed, a cruise, not a pitching-and-rolling purgatory lasting six days—was a propaganda stunt on a grand scale. Oskar figured it must have been conceived by someone in the arid reaches of the Wilhelmstrasse, but it was being effected through the good offices of a morale-boosting enterprise called *Kraft durch Freude*—Strength Through Joy—that offered cheap holidays to ordinary citizens, normally chosen by lottery. Why not extend this happy German pastime (the Wilhelmstrasse person must have thought) to the people of America? We have friends over there; look at what a fine job the German American Bund is doing. And there's Gau-USA, Americans Against Rearmament, the Free Society of Teutonia—the people are rising up against Roosevelt and his warmongers, so we only need to give them a little encouragement. They'd settled eventually on a group called Friends of the New Germany, its membership said to run to tens of thousands. Tickets printed in both English and German had been shipped over around Christmastime. Expectations were high. The *Robert Ley* was chosen for the historic voyage by virtue of its being recently commissioned and therefore up-to-date in every detail; the ship's plumbing was especially fine, something the Yanks would appreciate.

Oddly, when the ship sailed from New York on May 15, there were many unfilled berths, clearly the fault of the American organizers. And so there'd been room for late bookings, Herr and Frau Stefan Sinclair among them. The crew had welcomed them effusively— nothing raised their spirits more than expatriated citizens answering *der Ruf der Heimat*, the call of the homeland, unless it was passengers able to carry their own luggage. Most of the Americans who'd boarded up to that point had been somewhat older and—shall we be kind?—not at the peak of physical prowess.

Oskar, moving cautiously around the deck while Lena took refuge in the stateroom, bewildered and possibly terrified, found the Yanks to be a jumbled lot: pallid couples from the heartland, proprietors of small businesses, salesmen with straining belts and immaculately polished shoes, bellicose shirkers of military service who admired the martial culture of the Reich, disappointed pensioners who railed against the New Deal and the Jews who ran the papers and the filth coming out of Hollywood. And their wives—a Greek chorus of pinched-looking women who stayed largely in the background, working hard at "letting their hair down" and having a little fun. On the whole, Oskar guessed the overarching principles of Strength Through Joy must elude them. There were certain things they liked—cheap tickets, clean staterooms, free servings at the bar—but who wants to be dragged out of bed at six in the morning for calisthenics? Why on earth would civilized people engage in communal showering? Why is so much deck space given over to volleyball courts? Why is there no shade? Why is the menu so inflexible, and does it have to include so much porridge? Oskar suspected the Reich was losing more friends than it gained here.

The Labor Front people were a different story. The DAF was a queer beast to start with: a paramilitary corps in the guise of a national trade union. The young men and women assigned to this voyage had apparently been chosen for their fitness, language skills, outgoing personalities and political reliability. Their job was to mingle with the American guests, serving as proctors, translators and—it went without saying—informers. Every one of them was friendly to a fault. They were eager to talk to you, fascinated by whatever you had to say. The Americans were susceptible to such treatment and loved the attention, not knowing any better. Oskar felt like he was trapped on a ship with a pack of gregarious wolves.

Maybe Lena had the right idea: stay bunkered down in the cabin. But Oskar's training militated against that. The first task of an undercover operative was to live your cover, to be the person you were pretending to be. He was Stefan Sinclair, a German librarian recently married and now returning home. He should be out and about with his countrymen, taking the air, stretching his limbs, savoring the pale northern sunlight. He should be seen doing it. And so here he was at the rail, slightly nauseous, smiling through chattering teeth, repenting that second helping of boiled oats.

At last some Americans appeared on deck, half a dozen men carrying bottles of beer, the early hour notwithstanding. One of the DAF wolves pounced on them. How about a game of football? What do you say, gentlemen? The DAF man opened a gear locker and pulled a ball out. He bounced it off his knee, then tapped it lightly into the shins of one of the Yankees—a bald-headed individual whom Oskar deemed, on no grounds at all, to be a bricklayer. A bricklayer from Indiana. This fellow looked at the DAF man as though he had no idea what he was talking about or what kind of game you would play with a ball like this. The German kept at it, knocking the ball against one set of shins after another; the Yanks couldn't seem to decide if he was making a joke or asking for trouble.

The scene was becoming too awkward. Oskar strolled over into it, intercepting the ball and holding it in both hands as if he intended to launch it toward a basket. Show some cultural empathy, he thought.

"Let's pick teams," he said. "I'll take this guy. He looks pretty strong—I bet he was a star back at school."

"I lettered in football," the bricklayer admitted. "Never played soccer, though."

"That's swell! We'll show them how it's done. Who else here is good?"

"Hold on a minute!" The DAF man grinned; he relished a challenge, and winked at Oskar like a conspirator. "My side gets the next pick! We pick . . . this fellow here, the tall one."

"Don't worry," the bricklayer teased, "he's not so great. He may look big, but he's awkward as hell. Sammy here, that's who we want. What do you say, Sammy? You and me and—"

"Stefan."

"Stefan." The bricklayer stuck a hand out, adding in schoolboy *Deutsch*, "*Ich freue mich, Sie kennen zu lernen.*"

"*Mir auch.*" They shook. "Your turn."

The DAF man looked happy and a bit surprised. His experience with Americans evidently hadn't led him to expect very much.

Teams chosen, four to a side, they moved to the aft deck, where a miniature field had been marked out in yellow paint with goalposts bolted port and starboard, nets strung behind them. With any luck, they'd soon lose the ball overboard and be done with international sporting for the day.

The air out here, away from the ship's protective superstructure, was a physical presence, hard and blue and unalloyed. Even the sun felt cold. Lifeboats suspended from davits did nothing to block the wind, which must have just swept down from Greenland. The Americans looked around as if surprised to find themselves in the middle of the Atlantic. But the notion of playing ball here seemed to agree with them. No doubt the beer helped.

There was uncertainty over the rules: where to begin, how to explain something so familiar. The better course seemed just to play, shouting instructions as needed. That worked out all right, and once engaged, the Yanks proved tougher than one might have predicted. The bricklayer in particular showed an impressive degree of animal cunning. These men put Oskar in mind of the aging alumni of a student dueling club—red-faced gentlemen who turned out for yearly reunions, draining tankards and bellowing the old club songs. Though seldom taking up a sword, when they did, they fought with guile and brutality, often overwhelming younger, more agile opponents. These Yanks were a bit like that. They were just starting to tire when a modest clamor arose at the forward end of the deck, below the pilothouse.

Oskar turned to see an odd procession clambering though an open hatch. First came a senior ship's officer, his blue-black uniform draped with gold braid, followed by half a dozen gentlemen of middle years in gray, well-tailored suits. Behind them lagged a train of hangers-on, assistants with leather briefcases, reporters with notepads, a pair of ship's stewards in white jackets trailing like footmen. Last to emerge, in notable contrast to the others—indeed, to anyone on board—was a young man, Oskar's junior by a few years, tall and wispy in an overlarge coat that billowed like a cape, hair unkempt, neck wrapped twice around by a green-and-white scarf. Oskar guessed this boy could only be American, though until a few years ago you might have seen him prowling the streets of Leipzig or Heidelberg, a disconsolate reader of Hesse, blinking in the sunlight. The boy managed to look at once bored, angry, exhausted and aloof—all the familiar symptoms of *Weltschmerz*, world pain.

No one but Oskar seemed to notice him. All eyes instead were on the large, imposing man at the center of the crowd. He was speaking—orating, rather—with his words whipped off by the wind, leaving only a vague aural trail; he reminded Oskar of one of those blustering characters in a Hollywood western: the wealthy rancher, the powerful oil baron. All around him cameras clicked and reporters jotted, his fellow eminences nodding sagaciously, the ship's officer standing locked in ceremonial courtesy. Meanwhile, the tall boy looked angrier by the moment. Oskar hazarded a guess that the orator was his father.

On the aft deck, the football match sputtered to a halt. It was like the advent of Gypsies in a quiet town: everyone obeyed the common instinct to stop in their tracks and watch the show. They might not approve of it but were transfixed all the same. The soccer players drifted over, craning to catch the big man's words. Oskar was about to join them when a hand grabbed his sweater and tugged him back.

He turned to see Lena—and what a sight she was. She stood bundled in the kind of robe you pull on after swimming, tufted blue cotton pulled tight and a hood drawn over her head, with enormous sunglasses that left exposed only her lips, narrow chin and upturned, freckled nose. She must have felt this rendered her invisible.

"Come," she whispered dramatically, drawing him into the gap between two lifeboats. "Do you know who that is?"

Oskar shook his head. It wasn't smart, this furtiveness.

"That's a United States senator," she said. "I heard people talking at breakfast. He's making an official visit to Germany, a 'fact-finding mission.' I thought I should warn you."

"Warn me of what?" Oskar felt uncharitably cross.

She frowned. She had no clear notion, evidently—just felt in her bones that a warning was called for. Social Democrats, he'd come to think, were temperamentally unsuited to clandestine affairs. They lacked a talent for duplicity. He took her firmly by the arm and said, "Look, you should go sit on the sundeck for a while. Blend in. Let people see you. If they don't see you, they start to wonder."

"But this is . . ." She tugged herself free. "We need to report on this. We should learn as much as we can."

Oskar sighed—she was beyond his power of reason. He had a mission and she apparently had her own, a private and nonsensical one. At 1435 hours: Senator So-and-so observed on deck surrounded by admirers. At 1442: Senator So-and-so takes out a cigar; a light is provided by Ensign X.

"You're getting yourself worked up over nothing," he told her. "There's nothing here you need to worry about."

She tossed her head, defiant. "I'm *not* worried. And I'm not worked up. And you don't know it's nothing. You don't know what it is."

He felt sorry then. He wasn't mad; it was endearing really, this capacity for excitement. But before he could apologize, the tall boy in his billowing coat detached himself from the group and began drifting toward them. He moved disjointedly, a step this way and a step that, like he'd come unfastened and was being pushed along by the wind. Lena tightened her grip on Oskar's arm. The boy halted a few paces away, his eyes all over them in a frank display of Yankee curiosity.

"Hello!" Lena said, too forcefully.

The boy smiled but didn't speak.

Lena took a step forward, extending an arm. "I am Lena, here is my husband, Stefan. You are American? This is your first trip to Germany?"

The boy stared blankly for a moment, as if he'd not quite understood. Oskar wondered if there was something *not right* about him.

But then the boy shook his head. "I've been to Germany before. I've been all over the place. It's important to *see the world, to understand how good we have it at home.*" He gave them a joyless grin. "You could say this is my first *mandatory* visit to Germany. And my first on a ship with a portrait of Adolf Hitler in the dining compartment. A very *large* portrait. Of Adolf Hitler *on a horse.* Oh, I'm sorry—am I offending you? My name is Clairborne, but people call me Clair."

He held out a hand to shake theirs, Lena's first. His grip was firm and his gaze unblinking—a lesson from his father, Oskar supposed. Clairborne dropped the handshake and looked out over the empty ocean, his chest rising in a sigh. Something—perhaps life itself—seemed to disappoint him.

"You're not with the Arbeitsfront," Clair informed them. He didn't look around, having evidently seen all he needed to. "You're not students. You're not businesspeople. Civil servants? On your honeymoon?" He gave them a glance and a sly, diffident smile. "I'm sorry if I seem rude—it's a social disease, endemic to Washington. Of course, there they just come out and ask. Where do you work— you do *work*, don't you, Stefan? And where do you live, what church do you go to, where do you stand on the Neutrality Act? It's horrible, but that's how they are. Have you been to Washington? Are you"—his voice quickened at this new idea—"*diplomats?*"

"I am a librarian," said Lena, making the truth sound like a ridiculous cover story. "My husband also. In Weimar, the Anna Amalia Library—you must see it if you can."

Worse and worse. Tossing out details like a trail of crumbs.

"Librarians!" said Clair, sounding delighted. He studied them for several moments, back and forth. He seemed to come more fully to life, the world pain momentarily dissipated. His greenish eyes sparkled slyly, and he turned them on Lena. "Now tell me, is there any place on board where I can hide for a while? Stow myself away?" A quick glance in the direction of his father said all that was needed about what he wanted to hide from.

Oskar reacted too slowly. He might have suggested a lower-deck gallery, filled with billiard tables and dartboards and noise.

"Of course," Lela was already saying, "you can come to our stateroom! Wouldn't that be nice, Os—" She caught herself, maybe in time, and slid over the consonant into "Stefan?"

Before Oskar could reply, he heard his name—the latest of his names—shouted across the deck. The football game was starting back up. The distinguished passengers, moving on with their tour, were being led to the foredeck. If any noticed that young Clair had gone missing, they raised no alarm.

"Hurry, Stefan! We've had our rest, now it's time for some action."

Oskar watched helplessly as Lena and Clair, laughing like truant schoolchildren, made for the nearest ladder. What could he do? Quitting the game would require some excuse, and party types didn't take excuses kindly, particularly on a field of battle. And for such men, all the world is a battlefield, every known human activity a stand-in for the one true and eternal calling of German manhood. The ball came blasting toward him like a cannon shot, a whirl of black and white against the ocean's Wehrmacht gray.

Oskar's reaction, immediate and perfect, sent the ball back at redoubled velocity toward the enemy goal. I am, he thought, as deadly a warrior as any of them.

How much damage Lena had done—to their safety, their cover, the tenuous fiction of expatriate sheep returning to the fold—Oskar could not begin to gauge until much later. After his side lost the match, 7–3, he returned breathless to the little cabin three decks down to find it empty. A note on ship's stationery, laid carefully on the lower bunk, read in English, "We've gone out for drinks. See you at dinner!" The hand was Lena's, but he suspected the words were Clair's. The tone as well, hinting at blithe and reckless mis-adventure. Lena had spent two days afraid to leave the room and now she'd run off God knew where, "out for drinks," with the son of an American senator. On a ship crammed forepeak to fantail with enthusiastic National Socialists, for whom reporting unusual behavior to persons of authority came as naturally as saying hello to an old chum on the sidewalk.

Oskar pondered his next move. The governing principle, as always, was to live your cover. So: we have a young husband crossing the ocean with his bride. He returns from a football match to find his wife having left, her destination unrevealed, to have drinks with another man. Well, no—a boy. *But* a tall and confident boy, an American, the son of a powerful political figure. Is the husband jealous? A little, probably. But there might be a reasonable explanation. Yes, he would think that's the case. After all, my wife, my new wife, loves me. And I love her. I'm somewhat blinded by this love. And so I feel agitated yet also hopeful. Worried, yes, and puzzled, but also trusting. And so I, the husband, will just go out and find her and learn what this is about, what a fool I was to worry, and we'll all have a good laugh.

It took Oskar a few minutes to think this through, longer to make himself feel it. Longer still to open the cabin door.

The afternoon had taken on a vivid and surreal quality, a hint of Kafka, a few strokes of Max Ernst. Oskar walked down the expansive, hotel-like corridor, swaying lightly with the roll of the ship and self-conscious about his movements, which felt awkward and forced, as if he were concealing an injury. He reached a bank of elevators and stepped into one, joining two women in pastel dresses of a style no longer worn in Germany (or in Washington either, from what he'd seen), beneath sun hats tied under the chin with ribbons. One of them smiled, not warmly but inquiringly, as he imagined her greeting half strangers on the steps outside her church.

He wondered about these women, their lives, what they were doing here. Had they attended bund rallies with their husbands at the county fairground? He'd seen these rallies in the newsreels: American men in homemade uniforms listening to speeches, waving placards, exchanging the Hitler salute. They looked just as foolish and just as harmless as the SA bullies in Saxony had seemed a few years ago, before they took over the streets, then the cities, finally the nation. Offscreen, the announcer had shouted frantically, in imitation of Goebbels: *Our racial comrades overseas stand united in support of the Führer!* Then shots of a bonfire, women in dirndls folk-dancing, little girls weaving garlands of flowers. You had to imagine spring colors; in the movies, the flowers were gray.

The promenade deck, forward of the ship's superstructure, had grown busy. At this hour, with the last of the pallid daylight, the wind had slackened and a festive atmosphere prevailed. Oskar peered through the crowd, looking for Lena in her Mata Hari costume, Clair in his scarf and billowing jacket. The idea seized him that everyone on deck was moving too slowly, making a subtle but concerted effort to block his view. Knowing it was irrational didn't dispel it. He shoved off from the rail and edged around a kiosk dispensing glasses of warm, honeyed *Glühwein*. Nearby, a small audience had gathered to watch a DAF man juggling what appeared to be tennis balls wrapped in yellow handkerchiefs. The tied-off corners of silk flapped like tiny pennants as the juggler threw the balls higher, snatched them overhand, changed his pattern and spun in place, drawing applause and laughter from the onlookers.

Through all that clapping, among all those voices, Oskar heard a voice he knew—its distinct flavor of giddiness with a soupçon of panic. Lena, wherever she was, sounded happy but also anxious. That reassured him. He looked around for her, turning in every direction; it was impossible to tell where the sound had come from, and he saw only unfamiliar faces, stupid American grins, a hundred middle-aged children playing Follow the Leader. Lena's laughter came again.

Oskar turned. Far up in the bow, where the deck narrowed into a blunt spearhead, a temporary platform had been erected: metal scaffolding with a floor of wooden planks surmounted by a wide canvas awning like a party tent, made festive by scarlet banners bearing the swastika, black on a white background. There was a bandstand and bistro tables and a team of stewards in white jackets—an entire ad hoc café for very important passengers only, and there among them sat Lena at a table with *two* male companions now. Poor Stefan Sinclair must have been hot under the collar; Oskar felt only a deepening chill. Lena waved at him, affecting gaiety. Clairborne smiled wanly. The somewhat older man stared without expression. Leading up to the platform was a little stair of five risers with no handrail, and Oskar ascended them like a prisoner mounting the gallows.

The band—four instrumentalists and a singer of uncertain age, lashed into a gown of decent length but a size too small in the upper body—struck up a medley of cabaret tunes, leading off with "If Only Elisabeth Didn't Have Such Pretty Legs." They played like they meant business. The platform was cramped, nearly every seat taken; Oskar was obliged to squeeze between people as he made his way over to Lena's table, where a single chair sat empty between her and the boy. The other man gestured politely for him to take it. As he did so, Oskar realized that this fellow wasn't as old as he'd looked from a distance—barely older than himself, twenty-five or so, with prematurely thinning hair so blond it was almost white.

Lena smiled at him but seemed too nervous to speak. She'd traded the blue robe for a white cotton sweater and pulled her hair back with Yankee nonchalance, allowing several strands to come loose in the shipboard breeze. Oskar found it becoming. He leaned forward, took her hands and kissed her lightly on the cheek.

"Darling," she said, clutching a bit too hard, pulling him closer, "I'm so happy you found us!" She didn't sound happy so much as rather like the bundist wives, determined to enjoy herself. Perfect, really.

"We're having champagne," Clair said. "You'll join us, won't you?"

The second man tightened his lips at this breach of decorum. In Germany, introductions would have been made before the talk turned to drink. Oskar understood then—why should it come as a surprise?—that he was German.

"Stefan," said Lena, "may I introduce Hagen . . . Hagen von—"

"—von Ewigholz," the man said, making a slight bow from his seat.

Lena rattled on, still in English, fixing Oskar with a meaningful stare: "Hagen is in the SS. The cavalry! Isn't that interesting?"

As usual, overdoing it. But it *was* interesting. An Aryan superman in a Bond Street suit.

Von Ewigholz shook his head, smiling as though in regret. He spoke in the careful manner of someone using a language he hadn't yet mastered. "I am not here in . . . any official situation."

"Hagen is my *minder*," said Clair. "That's something, isn't it—my own personal minder. I suppose I've always needed one."

Oskar disregarded him. "Are you an officer, then?"

Hagen shrugged. "My grade is *Obersturmführer*."

"That means *senior storm leader*," said Clair, sardonic.

What it really meant was first lieutenant—only one rank higher than Oskar's own. He couldn't help staring at the man with professional interest, an officer sizing up a peer from a rival service. He quickly wiped the look off Sinclair's courteous face—but in just that instant, he got the feeling that the SS man had also experienced a flash of recognition. If so, he covered it quickly as well.

A fresh bottle of champagne arrived, then another. The band struck up "If You're Ever in Hawaii," followed by "Dreams of the South Seas," wistful, vaguely exotic tunes that expressed that strange Teutonic longing for tropical climes, warm breezes, waving palms. A race of sun worshippers, confined to a gray and chilly corner of northern Europe. Though not, historically speaking, always content to remain there.

Lena now seemed to feel it her duty, as the woman at the table, to play hostess. "Well, Clair, it appears that you've got a fascinating summer ahead."

"No doubt," he said, sounding doleful and at least partly drunk. "Yes, I imagine it'll be great fun. Lots of marching, I'm told. Long guided hikes through the countryside. *Und ziss flower vee call ze three-pronged zombie tongue.* Athletic competition to foster a healthful taste for physical combat. A chance to form lasting bonds with *young men just like myself from all over Europe*, apparently by sharing the same toilet. And I'll finally learn how to give a proper *Hitlergruss*—you know, whenever I try it, my whole hand seems to droop, like this."

He thrust out his arm in a parody of the Nazi salute, allowing the wrist to go limp and the long, tapered fingers to dangle, his lips curled in a smirk.

It was, in such a context, the most shocking thing Oskar could imagine. Mocking the Nazis in front of an SS officer, aboard a vessel that was in essence a tiny floating province of the Reich? But maybe that was what Clair intended; maybe he was angling to get sent back home in disgrace.

For a couple of seconds, no one said anything. Then Lena, succumbing to the accumulated tension, gave a short, anxious laugh that was sharp as a bark. Too late, she lifted a hand to her mouth. Clair raised his eyebrows and smiled, accepting this as due recognition.

Von Ewigholz reached over calmly and laid a hand on Clair's forearm. He didn't grab it, simply allowed the hand to rest there, like a man comforting his wife. "You are nervous," he said. "You are frightened to be going there alone, to the Ordensburg—frightened of what will happen, how you will feel, what people will think of you. After everything you've heard. But it will be all right. I don't say you'll have fun, like a vacation. I just suggest it won't be so terrible. And you won't be alone."

His voice was patient, almost gentle, and Clair must have been as surprised as Oskar, for he only stared back as if this SS man was a being from another universe. Hagen's eyes were like drops of northern sky, frozen and set in his skull. Placid, beautiful, opaque. Oskar found it impossible to tell or even to guess what he was thinking. Which made von Ewigholz, he supposed, ideally suited for his job. And now those empty eyes turned on Oskar.

Once already, he'd sensed that von Ewigholz was peeking though his cover—seeing him, for a moment, not as Stefan Sinclair but as someone a little closer to himself, a proper opponent. That feeling now returned as the Nazi officer studied him unhurriedly, dispassionate as a scientist contemplating a specimen that had turned up unexpectedly in the field. What do you say, gentlemen—shall we pop this one in a bottle and have a closer look at it?

Well, that was the SS. Oskar was a Wehrmacht man, and the German army had its own methods of sorting things out.

"So . . . you're his minder?" he said, in Sinclair's mincing style, and gestured toward Clair, who'd slumped once more into a sulk. "What does that mean, please?"

The question irritated von Ewigholz, so much so that he responded in German. "That's a foolish term, 'minder.' I've been chosen this year to be a *Sippenleiter.* You belonged to the Movement?"

The half-lie came easily: "The Young Lutheran Bund."

"So then you know the term."

Oskar did. A *Sippenleiter,* in the old days, was the senior member of a "kin group," a band of brothers. Not a minder. Not a teacher. Not even a leader, in the ordinary sense. Probably nothing Clair had a word for—an elder brother not in blood but in spirit. How strange that such an outmoded, Romantic concept should live on in Himmler's SS.

Von Ewigholz nodded; he was glad Stefan understood. "Our young Mr. Townsend has been accepted into a special program for ethnic Germans and other . . . sympathetic foreigners. It's an honor to be invited. We use the facilities of an Adolf Hitler School—the newest one, Ordensburg Vogelsang. An amazing place, like a private castle for the boys. A magnificent settling in the Eifel, with a lake below where we can swim every day. And of course an outstanding faculty, the most highly regarded experts in every field. There's more than just hiking and sport involved, you must understand that. Over a hundred thousand of our German boys apply for these schools every year. Those few selected are truly the elite, the leaders of tomorrow. It's not usual to get someone who . . . doesn't want very much to be there."

He glanced at Clair, not unkindly. Oskar could read nothing more sinister there than zeal, the kind you expect from true believers. Von Ewigholz bore watching, he decided, but seemed to pose no immediate threat.

Clair had meanwhile taken an interest in the musical program; he'd refilled his champagne flute and now busied himself scribbling requests on a linen napkin. The ink from his fountain pen bled into the fabric, but Oskar made out "Minnie the Moocher," "The Man from Harlem," "One O'Clock Jump."

"I'm sorry, boys," said Lena, rising from her seat, "but I need to freshen up before dinner. Thank you all so much for your company."

The men stood—even Clair, into whom the social niceties had clearly been hammered.

"I'll go also, with my wife," Oskar said. "It was a pleasure meeting you," he told von Ewigholz. This time he got a handshake and one last probing glance. You could practically hear it bounce off, like a sonar ping. "That was excellent," he murmured to Lena as they crossed the platform. "Absolutely perfect timing."

She might not have heard—something had distracted her. Pausing by the stairs, she said very quietly, "Who is that man? The one in the awful blue suit, over there by the band."

Not whispering—that was good. Whispering drew attention. Oskar slapped his pockets as though missing something, a wallet, a watch, then finally shot a glance toward the bandstand. "I must have left it in the stateroom," he said, turning away. They went down the stairs. The lift and plunge of the ship, the sound of crashing water, gave him a feeling of vertigo.

Lena slipped her arm through his. "Come, darling. We'll have a little rest before dinner."

Oskar barely heard, his thoughts swirling as he allowed himself to be led onto a narrow deck running outboard of the dining compartment.

Lena halted there, turned to look at him. "What's the matter?" Her voice was gentle, but there was something hard beneath it. "Who is that man? Someone you know?"

Her hair was redder in this light. The wind played with the loose strands, and Oskar felt like pushing them back into place. "That man is called Toby Lugan," he said. "I met him in Washington, just the once. He'd been drinking. He might not have recognized me."

"He was staring at you the whole time. That's the only reason I noticed." She grasped his wrists, firmly, as if planning to give him a shake. "Stefan"—protecting their cover, even now—"tell me, Stefan, are we in trouble? What do we need to do?"

"The same as before. Get back to Germany. Then disappear."

She seemed to consider this. At the far end of the passage, a party of Americans was noisily crowding the walkway. Oskar turned to leave, to go on to the cabin. But Lena held his wrists, and he was more or less obliged, by a kind of tactile inertia, to turn back, to face her again.

"I've never seen you rattled before," she said. "I thought . . . but now, like this, you seem more normal."

Rattled? He opened his mouth, but the Americans were here, pushing to get by. Lena pulled him closer, making room. An expensively dressed plump woman—a banker's wife, perhaps—bumped into Oskar from behind. He felt the length of Lena's warm body as the two of them were pressed against the bulkhead.

"Pardon *me*!" the banker's wife said jovially, catching his eye, giving him a horrible, knowing wink.

He found himself staring into Lena's face, inches away. There was really nowhere else to look. The freckles on her nose seemed very large, very near. He felt her breath, softly, on his chin. Maybe it was a question of cover. She raised her face to his and kissed him. Right there on the side deck, as though they truly were newlyweds or had been rehearsing this for months.

For Oskar, it was new. But as with many new things, it wasn't hard to pick up. Her tongue was narrow, like her chin. It made him, for no good reason, want to laugh.

Then the Americans were gone and the kiss was over. There followed an interval of shyness, like a cloud that appeared without warning in an open sky. They stepped apart. Wordlessly they strolled back to the cabin. By unspoken agreement, for appearance's sake, they continued to hold hands, but now this point of contact seemed to draw all of Oskar's attention. He felt that his palm was sweaty and he was doing it wrong and everybody on board would notice. From what he could tell, though, they did not.

Lena sat on the lower bunk, her usual place. Oskar stood by the door with his fingers on the burnished handle, as if physically unable to let go. He couldn't figure out how to break this ludicrous impasse. The room was too small for pacing. There was nothing he could plausibly busy himself doing. They needed to talk, that was certain—on operational grounds alone, they should debrief each other—but he wasn't sure that tactics was what he wanted to talk about.

"You know," Lena said, "Stefan and I . . ." She paused, looked up at him. "I mean the other Stefan, the real one."

She didn't go on. Oskar realized then that he'd been wondering about this, without really thinking about it. Another empty slot in his understanding of the world. How a gasoline engine works. What the food is like in China. Whether Lena and Stefan were, in bodily fact, husband and wife. Just one more thing he didn't know. Only now he knew that unlike gasoline engines, this particular topic had been wriggling there, just out of thought, for some time.

"It's none of my business," he said.

She narrowed her eyes—maybe it was, maybe it wasn't; that depended. "I've had lovers," she told him matter-of-factly. Sitting up straight, as though this had become a business meeting. "I'm a modern person. Don't feel you have to treat me like a . . ."

What *had* he been treating her like? A colleague? A co-conspirator? A cabinmate? He couldn't think beyond that, though he guessed there were other possibilities.

She sighed. "Well yes, all right, we did, Stefan and I, a few times. It was just—I don't know. We were together, we were *married*, for God's sake. And having an adventure, going to America. Making love, that was another part of it. After a while we just . . . stopped. I don't know why. The adventure was over." She paused, completely unembarrassed. A modern person. "What about you, then?"

"What?"

She didn't laugh, for which he would long be grateful. "Here, come sit with me. Please. Otherwise this is getting awkward."

Strangely enough, it didn't feel awkward. It felt almost natural to slide onto the bunk beside her, no more than an extension of the role he'd been playing for days, a role he'd internalized. It was as though their make-believe intimacy had turned real, at least in a limited way, without ever passing a milestone to mark the change. She smiled at him, and he laid a hand on hers. She squeezed it, lightly. They'd come to the edge of something and now paused there, holding on. The feeling was surprisingly comfortable.

"What about you?" she asked again.

What about Oskar? Well. "There were a few times . . . when I was at the academy. Once before that, at *Gymnasium*. A bunch of us would go out together, you know, drinking, and—"

"Oh, God." She held up a hand, shaking her head, her eyes closed. "I don't want to hear. Drunken schoolboys and what, prostitutes? Somebody's sister's older friend? A party in the woods somewhere? That's all it was, something like that? You can keep your secrets, then."

Oskar was relieved—one more thing to thank her for.

"So no lady friends. No real lovers." There was a methodical quality to her voice, as though she were placing objects in a certain order. "But anyway you're not . . . all new."

Oskar felt pretty new. He could barely remember any of those furtive, grappling encounters. "I guess not."

"That's good, don't you think?"

He had no idea what she was asking. "Is this how you all are?" he said. "Is this a point of Socialist doctrine? 'All party comrades shall be open and free in their expression of physical desire.' "

She tittered. "Maybe. Something like that. You should have seen our camps—or come to the Leuchtenburg, you know, before—but you were probably some kind of straight-arrow type, a Pathfinder."

"Deutsche Jungenschaft," he corrected her.

"Oh God. Are you queer, then? We thought you all were queer. And very beautiful."

"Not all of us," Oskar said dryly.

She laughed. She gave his hand another squeeze, then released it. And just like that, it was over. Now back to business—the whole tangled and frightful business of resistance and spying and reinfiltrating the Reich under the eyes of the SS. Why it should fall to Lena to decide such a thing—how Oskar even understood that this was so—remained altogether mysterious.

"Tell me about your Mr. Toby Lugan," she said, "and I'll tell you what I learned about Senator Bull Townsend. Maybe together the stories will make sense."

———

And so it was not until hours later—after dinner and a prolonged joint appearance at one of the nightly folk-singing sessions (Oskar had insisted on this, believing it was important to seem relaxed and unconcerned, to play newlyweds for all it was worth), with no further sightings of Clair, his father, Lugan or von Ewigholz—that they were able to pick up a certain dropped thread. Moving down the quiet ship's corridors, they finally reached the door of their cabin and briefly stopped there. But it was only a door, the same door, and the familiar cramped quarters within.

Oskar switched on the tiny desk lamp, and Lena began to undress. Previously he'd averted his gaze while she did so, reckoning that's what an officer and gentleman ought to do. Tonight he found himself looking away again but with less conviction. For Lena, the sight of a young man in his underclothes seemed to neither alarm nor especially interest her. Oskar guessed there was some Socialist doctrine about that, too. All limbs being equal, perhaps. Folding his trousers—a military habit, protecting the crease—he caught her watching, and her expression made him smile.

He crawled up into the top bunk and willed himself to go to sleep. He felt time passing, heard Lena's breath, wondered if she was sleeping or instead pretending to sleep or not even bothering with that. He thought for a while about her lying there, imagining her body in this or that position. Then his thoughts turned upon himself. What was he doing here? Was he expecting anything? Waiting for something? It was a muddle. But the same was true most of the time. This, in fact, had been part of his training at Lichterfelde: Everything in war is a muddle. Your intelligence is never adequate, the terrain never matches the map, too much is happening at once, and anyway it's not as if you have the field to yourself. There's another party out there, intentions unknown, slinking around like a weasel. You need to take that into account, but you can't, not properly, so in the end you must simply decide. Advance, retreat, hold your ground, open fire—just do it and hope for the best, because you'll never be any more certain than you are right now.

He climbed down into the lower bunk and found that Lena had made room for him. It was remarkably warm under the covers, and the feeling of her pressing against him was not likely something he'd ever forget. He found her mouth with his and she moved around him somehow, not quite embracing, sliding over and under him, as though trying to touch every part of him with every part of her. Their nightclothes became superfluous. He marveled at the texture of her breasts. Had he ever felt a breast before? Not that he could remember, certainly not like this. There were many places, up and down her, that seemed important for him to kiss, and urgently, but she drew him back up to her mouth and looked deep into him and held his cock in her hand, guiding it, pressing herself down, adjusting, pressing harder. The room was dark, but enough light passed through the crack beneath the door for him to make out her expression, which was almost funny: her jaw clenched, her lips held tightly together, her brow furrowed in concentration, as if she couldn't get enough of him inside her all at once yet had resolved to try. Suddenly he couldn't bear it anymore. He flooded her once, breathed hard for a while, found himself erect again and still inside her, and the second time went on much longer. The third—waking at some hour for which no number suitably magical has been thought of—lasted longer still, deep, deep into the night.

In the morning, he skipped calisthenics, as they seemed unnecessary. He'd learned everything he needed to know about strength through joy.

SETBACK THEORY

BERLIN, FASANENSTRASSE: LATE MAY

The crowd at the von F—— salon had dwindled noticeably, its numbers thinned by emigration, by the transfer of several officers to the Czech frontier, by a growing reluctance among certain public officials to be seen with certain others, by typical inconveniences, including the protracted "interrogation" of a young cleric—*How terrible! He had such a lovely countertenor, like a choirboy!*—and the rumored but unsurprising arrest of the cabaret artist Stav, who was said to have gotten up the nose of Reinhard Heydrich. And so it was a smaller and rather more sober group that occupied the old leather armchairs of the late Baron's private study.

"Have you noticed that our friend Greimer is working again?" said a Kriegsmarine officer known to his friends as Jaap, widely thought to be close to Admiral Canaris, head of military intelligence. "They're printing his stuff in the *Morgenpost*. Fluff pieces, mostly. But apparently he got a voyage to New York out of it."

"He went to *New York*?" exclaimed Cissy, the White Russian princess, as though the man had robbed her of her dreams. "And he came *back*?"

"Why not?" said Guido, the former art dealer. "It sounds like he's in with the right people now."

"Hard to fault him, really," said an elderly brigadier, a holdover from the long-defunct Prussian army. "Nothing sadder than a writer not allowed to write."

"I don't know," Jaap said, smiling ruefully. "Erich Kästner seems to be doing all right."

The princess gave a mirthless laugh. "Erich's got enough money to wait it out. The royalties from *Emil und die Detektive* alone—"

"It's not about money," Guido insisted. "It's about your calling, your gift."

"Greimer has a gift?"

"It *is* about money," said the princess sadly, "if you haven't got any."

Only one man in the room took no interest in the conversation: the slight, dark-haired and intense Hans-Bernd, who stood beside the desk slowly turning the Baron's giant globe in its complicated mounting, as though attempting to correct a misaligned Earth. The green patch that was Germany, as its borders had stood in the Kaiser's heyday, rotated slowly to the top. Hans-Bernd stopped it there, looking down on it from his Jovian perspective.

"I hold out," he announced, as though his fellow guests and the world itself had been waiting for this, "little hope for our esteemed *Generaloberst.*"

Conversation came to a full stop. No one needed to ask who or what he was talking about. Ludwig Beck, a four-star general of unquestioned brilliance and integrity, had served since 1935 as chief of the General Staff. While he commanded not a single combat division, his post made him, in effect, the senior member of the world's most illustrious officer corps. As such, he was the focus of a great deal of hope on the part of the nascent Resistance. He represented— so it was widely felt—both a moral and practical counterweight to Adolf Hitler. The army, surely, wouldn't act in defiance of its *Chef des Generalstabs.* And Beck, hardly a pacifist, had made it known that Germany, in his view, would on no account be ready to undertake major armed conflict before 1940, at the earliest. So let Hitler huff and puff over Czechoslovakia. Beck would keep the army in its barracks long enough for the Resistance to achieve—in the jargon of that season—a "political solution."

The old Brigadier scoffed. "What are you on about? Beck's absolutely top-drawer. A first-rate intellect. And shrewd. More than a match for that Austrian cur."

Jaap watched Hans-Bernd with interest. "Do you know some-thing? Has anything happened?"

Hans-Bernd shook his head. "No—and that's the problem, isn't it? Beck's *saying* the right things; at any rate, he's saying them to *us*. To Hitler he says, Give me more time. To the other generals he says, Just wait and see what happens. To the British—"

Jaap cleared his throat.

Hans-Bernd continued heedlessly: "I'm not divulging any secrets now, am I? Naturally, he's talking to the British. Our nations aren't at war; it's part of his job. To the French too, of course, and the Poles, maybe the Russians—why not to everybody? Of course that's just at an official level. No doubt he's running some back-channel operation with you Abwehr chaps. You needn't bother denying it, we're not stupid. I'm only asking, What's the point? The Brits are hardly going to lend him an SIS assassination squad to do his dirty work, are they? The French—they love nothing better than seeing the German General Staff brought down a peg. And Beck's not the sort to want blood on his own hands."

"The Americans," declared the Brigadier, "that's who he ought to be talking to. That's who settled things the last go-round."

Jaap gave a pained sort of smile. "We've tried that, actually, *Herr Brigadegeneral*. A couple of months ago. A special operation. We made a very substantial demonstration of good faith. But there were, well, unforeseen problems."

"Unforeseen because nobody in the Abwehr has ever read a for-eign newspaper," said Hans-Bernd abrasively.

Jaap tightened his lips. "Not the easiest thing to get hold of these days."

"Yet somehow the Foreign Ministry manages to. And the Propa-ganda Ministry, and the Economics Ministry. Even at Interior we get the occasional peek. What in God's name is the business of an intelligence service if not to gather pertinent information overseas and disseminate—"

"Now, look here," rumbled the old Brigadier, "you're rather pushing it, aren't you?"

Hans-Bernd continued unabashed: "You've got agents all over the globe! But apparently there's no one who can tell you, as any reader of, say, the Washington *Evening Star* could, that the Nazis have friends, as they say over there, 'from coast to coast.' They call it neutrality. It's practically the entire platform of the Republican Party, as well as the dominant position in the Congress. Roosevelt has got his hands tied."

"Thank you," Jaap said dryly. "I think we've learned that lesson now."

"Better late than never," said Hans-Bernd, "if rather beside the point. Suppose you did find somebody in Washington to talk to—somebody who wouldn't respond with a lecture about, you know, *not judging a man like Hitler by our standards here in America.* What then? You whisper a few secrets, hand over a few incriminating documents—in exchange for what? Does Beck really think he can persuade the Americans, or the British, or anyone, to stand up to Hitler when he doesn't have the courage to do it himself?"

This was too much for the Brigadier. "Now, just you look here—"

Hans-Bernd waved him off. "Or maybe . . . I suppose Beck might only be seeking some kind of assurance. An exchange of undertakings, as the diplomats say. *We* promise to get rid of the Nazis, *they* agree to recognize whatever government we install in their place. But who in his right mind—in any sane country in the world, let alone a band of cutthroats like the British—would sign off on something like that? With respect, gentlemen, you chaps in uniform would do better to leave off playing Bismarck and go back to what you're so good at. Three or four divisions marching on Berlin would make short work of the Brown Plague. The problem then becomes managing popular opinion—but give me two hours in Gestapo headquarters and I'll give you enough evidence of criminal activity to indict the lot of them. Of course, it goes without saying that the Führer must be shot."

Cissy laughed, and there was something pure, open and honest about her laughter that dispelled the tension filling the room. "My goodness," she exclaimed, "it's so nice to hear people talk like this! I've gotten so used to whispering, and speaking in code, and never coming right out with what I mean. Thank you, gentlemen." She raised a glass in which a dram of murky liquid swirled.

"To plain speaking," proposed Guido.

"While it lasts," said the Brigadier glumly. Despondent now, he stared down half-seeing at a stack of the day's newspapers—the Baroness still took most of them, excepting only the most rabid party organs—and finally chose the *Tageblatt* as perhaps the least unsound.

"Barring the possibility you suggest," Jaap said, his gaze thoughtfully directed at Hans-Bernd, "absent the Wehrmacht marching on the capital . . . what would you say is our best chance?" He paused for a moment, then added, "Realistically."

"Realistically?" Hans-Bernd twined his fingers and cracked his knuckles. "Well, one hears the word *setback* a lot these days. Reportedly among the General Staff, and also in certain sections of the Foreign Ministry, and for some of my own colleagues it's become a matter of faith that Hitler will eventually commit some kind of blunder. He reaches too far, he loses his balance, Germany looks foolish, the world reacts—this is what is meant by *setback*. And the thinking is, you see, that *then* we'll have the opportunity to move against him. Then and only then. Because we'll be able to present ourselves as acting on behalf of Germany, intervening surgically, so to speak, to avert further harm."

"But that would still be true, wouldn't it," said the princess, frowning, "even if you were to act tonight? What else is there to act *for*, if not the sake of Germany, and to avert further harm? Why must we wait around for some . . . excuse, a pretext? That's the Nazi style, isn't it?"

"Naturally, you are correct." Hans-Bernd's curt little bow scarcely concealed his impatience. "And this is exactly the case I've tried to put forward, time and again. But to this argument, the *Generaloberst* and his inner circle remain completely deaf. Deaf by choice, I hazard to say. They cling to this idée fixe of the inevitable setback. Which I'm coming to think amounts to nothing more than an excuse *not* to act. Because no matter what happens, as long as the regime isn't brought right to its knees, you can always say, Well, that was a stumble, but we'll find our footing again."

"But if something suitable *could* be arranged . . ." Guido stood twirling the tip of his mustache like a silent-film villain. "Some dreadful embarrassment for the regime. With an international dimension, if possible. A diplomatic scandal—all the talk of Paris and London, even Washington. If such a thing *could* be managed . . . well, wouldn't the *Generaloberst* be forced to act? By the logic of his own setback theory? To preserve German honor, or something of the sort?"

"Why, darling, how frightful!" the princess declared, taking Guido's arm in hers. "What *kind* of scandal, though? Something . . . *geschlechtlich?*"

The Brigadier grimaced. "Perhaps I'm speaking only for myself, but I'd say the public appetite for erotic scandal has been sufficiently slaked of late."

He was referring, as everyone present understood, to the outrageous events of the past winter, when one high-ranking officer and then another became snared in a Gestapo-spun web of blackmail and innuendo. The room fell quiet again.

Jaap sighed. "It does seem as though all the setbacks recently have been to our own cause."

"That's because we're sitting still," said Hans-Bernd, "and making ourselves easy targets. They pick us off one by one." He turned to Guido. "I think you're exactly right, *mein Herr.* It's time we engineered some scandal of our own."

"Easy enough to say," Jaap noted with a frown. "Have you got anything in mind?" He spoke rhetorically, scarcely expecting a reply.

It therefore came as a surprise when the old Brigadier tossed down the newspaper he'd been browsing—spun it deftly, so that it ended up pointing across the table at his younger colleague. "There's something you might start with. Look right there—some Yankee bigwig. 'Most senior member of the U.S. Congress yet to make an official visit to the Reich.' Maybe your Amt II fellows could work with that."

The others drew their heads closer around the table, staring down at the jowly, ebullient face of Senator Thomas D. Townsend, photographed amid an evidently admiring entourage on board a gleaming white cruise liner. Something about the image caught Jaap's attention . . . an indistinct figure in the background. He sensed a drawer opening somewhere in his mental filing cabinet, but which one?

"What a horrible-looking man," said Cissy, with a level of contempt difficult to attain without an aristocratic pedigree. "He looks like one of those sausage makers who joined the Party in '21 and now is Gauleiter of Saxony."

Hans-Bernd laughed. "He does, rather. I believe the real Gauleiter of Saxony has a firmer jaw."

"What are you suggesting?" asked Jaap sharply.

"Why, nothing at all," said the Brigadier, giving the younger man a pat on the arm. "Not my line of work, is it? Never had the sort of mind for it. Strictly an infantry man."

The silence crept back in. The afternoon was growing old but the sun remained high, making a bright gash in the seam of the heavy damask drapes.

"*Himmelfahrt* is late this year," said Guido, referring to Ascension Day and making it sound as though he suspected the Nazis of having rigged the calendar.

Hans-Bernd's fingers played nervously at the top of the old globe, setting it back in motion.

Cissy put down her empty glass, her expression now something of a pout. "Where is Dodo these days?" she wondered petulantly. "What's happened to Ricky? I haven't seen anyone for ages." She glanced at Jaap, as if anyone close to Canaris would *know* where everyone was. "And poor Stav! My goodness—what will become of us all?"

The old Brigadier smiled at her sadly. "More setbacks, I'd expect."

BODIES ON THE SECOND FLOOR

BREMERHAVEN AND BREMEN: 23 MAY

You'd hardly have thought it was almost summer. Or have guessed there was a sun in the sky.

The "new" port at Bremerhaven—founded just over a century ago at the mouth of the Weser to provide deep-water access for the ancient Free Hanseatic City of Bremen, which languished among silt beds fifty kilometers upriver—lay motionless in fog as thick as smoke and as clammy as Oskar's palms. The *Robert Ley* juddered unsteadily, nudged onward by a pair of harbor tugs whose motions were imperfectly coordinated, as if the two captains couldn't agree on a proper speed at which to approach the wharf that stood ready—you had to take this on faith—somewhere in the netherland ahead. At intervals the ship's great horn sounded prolonged blasts, as required by international maritime law. The noise was so tremendous that it cleared the decks except for members of the crew and a handful of Americans apparently deaf already; passengers filled the observation galleries and the second-deck promenade, crowding against the glass like so many fish gaping from their bowl and seeing nothing, or at most a blurry movement in the haze. Through the bulkheads the great horn moaned again, and again.

Oskar found it odd to think that the same law that governed ships on the high sea—a prudent and sensible one adopted, so he imagined, after long deliberation by a committee of white-bearded mariners, convened in a paneled chamber in The Hague, let's say—held sway even in Hitler's Reich. Or that an eagle taking flight from Great Yarmouth could plausibly soar on a favorable wind to the beach at Norden. Or that a weather report for Copenhagen would give you a fair idea of conditions in Lübeck. Such things reminded you that Germany was not, after all, a world unto itself; it was connected at every point to the greater world, and in fact the merger was often seamless. There'd been no change in the motion of the ship, no alarm, no darkening of the sky, when the *Robert Ley* crossed into the Reich's territorial waters. Oskar himself had not suddenly reverted to the person he'd been a few months ago. Everything moved along exactly as before—maintaining course and speed, in the language of ships' logbooks—with perhaps the lone exception of Lena.

She'd been jumpy all morning, this final day of the crossing. Just yesterday she'd been fine and they'd kept punctiliously to their normal shipboard routine, Oskar alert for any sign of heightened scrutiny—Was the waiter unusually attentive? Had their cabin been too scrupulously cleaned?—but seeing nothing out of the ordinary. A great relief. Though instead of sharing it, Lena seemed only to grow more restive. They'd agreed to spend the morning in the cabin—hunker down and wait for the ship to tie up—but this proved beyond her reach. Around noon, still four hours before docking, she announced that she was going to the library.

"Don't worry." She said this in a warning tone, before he could speak. "I know what's expected. But who could be in the library at a time like this?"

Oskar wasn't going to argue. What must it be like, he wondered, to escape the Reich and then, out of some mysterious conviction, come back again? For himself, his army training had left him quite capable of savoring these last few hours at sea. He stretched out on the warm bunk and, one final time, ran through every detail of his cover biography: the facts of Stefan Sinclair's life as far as he knew them and the alterations he'd made so as to bring that curriculum vitae into closer alignment with his own. The effort soon tired him, and he drifted into a dream-free nap.

Lena didn't return until much later, when the low, dun-green swells of the Frisian Islands stood off the starboard bow, windswept and stark yet strangely beautiful, a first glimpse of home. From the cabin window, the fog bank shrouding the mainland seemed an ominous, drifting mass. Lena was hugging herself, shivering—perhaps she'd ventured outside after all. Oskar let it go. She gave him a quick embrace, then slipped away before he could return it.

"I ran into Clairborne," she said, avoiding his eye.

"We agreed—"

"Oh, *we* agreed, did we? Look, it's just—when I got to the library, he was there."

"Waiting for you."

"Don't be ridiculous. He was making a scene over *The Saturday Evening Post*, why hadn't they got it, what kind of library is this—in terrible German, of course. Then he asked for Tintin. *J'adore Tintin!* As it happens, Clair speaks a beautiful French. I wanted to tell the poor librarian, Don't you see, he's just playing, he doesn't really want any Tintin, he's only looking for attention."

"Why didn't you?"

"Well. It *was* rather funny. By the end he was asking for *Death in Venice*. That's banned, you know. I thought I should get him out of there before she called someone."

"So you've spent all this time babysitting Clair? Where was his minder?"

"Who knows? Not in the library, thank God. After that, we hid for a while under a lifeboat. Listen, let's not argue, all right? We had an interesting talk—maybe even useful, I don't know."

Oskar waited.

She glanced around the cabin. "Maybe we should go up on deck," she said. "It's nice, the view. Lonely but nice."

This was something he'd taught her: always safer to talk outdoors. He plucked his jacket off the hook and they stepped into the passageway. The upper decks were still crowded—the foghorn hadn't yet started to blow—but they found a spot on the port quarter, which was empty as there was nothing to see from there, aside from a few gulls swooping optimistically in the vessel's wake.

"It's about that man who was staring at you."

"Toby Lugan."

"Right. When I was talking to Clair, I happened to ask who that fellow was I'd seen his father with, the one who looked like an old prizefighter. Clair knew *exactly* who I meant. He rolled his eyes and he said, 'That's the worst man in the world. He represents everything I despise about Washington.' "

Oskar allowed himself a very faint smile.

"Then he said he'd *begged* his father not to let him tag along. But he said, 'Are you kidding? Toby's the genius behind this whole boondoggle.' "

"What did he mean by that?"

"You're rushing me. I didn't understand, so I asked him to explain. He told me how his father, the senator, was fixated on the idea of enrolling him in some Nazi summer camp. They're running a special program this year for the children of foreign VIPs, though evidently the senator wasn't important enough. He was mad about that and started calling people, writing letters, having German diplomats over for dinner—all with no results. Then one night Lugan showed up and handed him an envelope, saying something to the effect that there's more where this came from."

"He did?" Oskar's heart thumped almost audibly. "Does he know what was in it?"

"No, it was just an ordinary envelope. Clair wasn't close enough to get a good look—he was spying from the hall. But he says that after Lugan left, his father gave it to a man called Viereck. Clair doesn't know who he is, exactly, only that he's German and quite creepy and shows up anywhere there's a party. But not long after that, the official invitations arrived—Clair's to the camp, the senator on this fact-finding tour. So he blames Lugan—he *hates* him—but it sounds to me like it's this other man, Viereck, who's really responsible. We should find out who he is. We should—"

Oskar held a hand up, needing quiet and time to think. This envelope had to be the one Erwin Kaspar had passed to Toby Lugan, then Lugan to Townsend, then Townsend to some creepy German called Viereck. The next morning, quite early, another envelope had been given to Kaspar by the embassy mailroom, a request for a rendezvous on a bridge. Where he was met by three men, probably German and decidedly creepy.

Taking a step back, he looked at Lena with a new sort of clarity. She'd just solved, in one breezy conversation, a mystery that had bedeviled him for months. And now it was more important than ever that he contact his case officer about this weak spot in the Abwehr's planning. It had a name and an approximate location. It was connected to someone with the authority to invite a U.S. senator for a state visit and, incidentally, condemn his son to a summer in hell. Oskar didn't know what to make of all this, but he imagined his superiors would.

A voice came over the ship's loudspeakers, advising passengers in that curiously monotonic style—the words being read verbatim from the *Watch Officer's Guide*, Oskar supposed—that the ship would presently begin sounding low-visibility signals. The point of this warning didn't become fully apparent until the damn horn actually blew, with a sonic force scarcely below that of artillery fire. The deck vibrated sympathetically.

"Maybe we should go back in," Oskar said when it was over.

"Go if you like," Lena said, turning her shoulder on him.

He realized that in his excitement he'd neglected to give her the praise she deserved. He would have done so then but the horn sounded a second blast, and it wouldn't be stopping anytime soon— the first tendrils of fog were creeping over the gunwales like the feelers of a gray monster. Oskar paused at the hatch for one look back at his surprising lover, her shoulders squared and feet planted defiantly as though against some notional gale. While he watched, she dug into her pockets and found a crumpled napkin, which she twisted into earplugs. Not so crazy after all, as Socialists go.

The *Robert Ley* got its bowline over at 1620 hours, twenty minutes behind schedule — not bad under such conditions.

Oskar knew Bremerhaven in passing. It lay just an hour's drive from the Bremen *Nebenstelle*—a satellite location, a "nest" in service jargon—where he'd been hurriedly inducted into the fraternity of espionage. Nest Bremen was a substation of the larger *Abwehrstelle* in Hamburg, traditionally commanded by a naval captain, who, in turn, appointed other naval officers to run the outposts at Flensburg, Bremen, Wilhelmshaven and Kiel. The primary task at Nest Bremen was intelligence activity directed at the United States. There were twenty-odd such Abwehr stations scattered around Germany, each with its own cadre of field officers and a wide latitude of operation. So it was possible that another agent dispatched from, say, Nest Cologne, whose specialty was economic warfare, had been operating in Washington at the same time Oskar was there. Or another from Münster, snooping into aircraft designs. None of these agents would have known of the others; nor would their masters in Germany have been aware of the parallel, often competing, operations. Admiral Canaris liked to encourage a spirit of clandestine entrepreneurship, and he preferred to keep the messy aspects of the job as far as possible from his base in Berlin.

So much Oskar had been told, and he'd also been told to keep it to himself. There'd been no more fuss than that: no blood oath to swear or Official Secrets Act to sign. Security in the Abwehr was less a question of institutional secrecy than of personal character. You were brought in, generally, by someone you knew and who trusted you. Out of loyalty to that person, and to the tradition of the officer corps, you acquitted yourself honorably—if need be, to the last breath. It was a straightforward system and a very German one. Oskar wondered whether things worked differently on the SS side. Perhaps one day in a fit of madness he'd ask his new acquaintance, Hagen von Ewigholz, about this.

Just now, feeling no madness coming on, Oskar looked down from the rail of an upper deck as the customary dockside ritual proceeded on the shore. The inner harbor at Bremerhaven closely resembled every other German seaport he'd seen: bristling with giant cranes, walled off from the city at large by red-brick warehouses and newer, metal-clad buildings with high rows of sooted windows, loud with the beeping of horns and grinding of cargo lifts and revving of transport engines, swarmed over by a platoon of stevedores. Somewhere a train whistle blew. A foreman shouted. Northerly gusts brought drier air and the acrid smell of an ironworks, scouring the wharves of fog but doing little to relieve the oppressive grayness of the afternoon.

Oskar watched a pair of black, late-model Opel sedans pull up at the head of the pier. They had a certain look about them, even as they sat idling, like scarabs taking stock of a large, interesting corpse. At last the doors opened and out climbed four, five, six men in nondescript civilian clothes. In modern Germany, the lack of a uniform was often a kind of uniform, and Oskar surmised that these men were Gestapo. Two of them sauntered in opposite directions along the wharf, which ran parallel to the shoreline, taking up positions from which they could watch the berthed liner along different sight lines—thus able to spot, for instance, someone trying to elude passport control by lowering himself into the water. Another pair, meanwhile, opened the trunk of one car and began pulling out the unremarkable tools of their trade: a portable card table, a folding chair, a pair of brown leather cases. Parceling out their equipment, the men strolled down the pier toward the spot where a team of dockworkers had just finished rigging the ship's gangway.

Oskar went down to the main deck, bumping shoulders with fellow passengers who had crowded there. A team of stewards, good-natured by profession, struggled to maintain a degree of order, asking the Americans again and again to please remain standing behind this rope line—*Yes, madam, just there, thank you. Excuse me, sir, please do not*—but they were accustomed, of course, to dealing with Germans, who would stay put where you told them to. The Gestapo team came aboard and began setting up shop at the brow of the gangway.

Where was Lena? Oskar wasn't worried, but he did want to know.

As soon as the control point was manned and ready, the American dignitaries were ushered through. The captain himself oversaw this, walking with Senator Townsend to the card table, effecting rapid introductions and looking on while the great man's passport was given a cursory glance, stamped with an entry permit and politely returned. The rest of the party—a few lesser members of Congress and the mayor of a steel town on the Great Lakes, with their sundry aides and sword-bearers—were waved through with equal alacrity. At the sight of Toby Lugan, Oskar drew back into the crowd and watched him, jostled from behind by crewmen toting luggage. While his papers were stamped, he paused to light a cigarette and, amid a venting of smoke, engaged one of the Gestapo agents in what seemed a pleasant if insistent chat. Then he chuckled and clapped the bewildered-looking man on the back, hard enough to make him wince, and finally clambered obstreperously down the gangway.

The agent turned to murmur to a colleague, a short, stocky fellow who stood a couple paces back and whom Oskar took to be the officer in charge. This man pulled out a small notepad and made a brief entry, no more than a couple of words.

It occurred to Oskar that Clair hadn't been among his father's entourage. No sign of von Ewigholz, either.

Now the routine at the control point changed. The security team rearranged itself so that each departing passenger could be scrutinized from a couple of angles. Meanwhile, down on the pier, a Hitler Youth group marched out and assembled in two neat rows facing the ship. The boys were from about twelve to fifteen years in age, their commander was only a couple of years older, and they all wore crisply ironed yellow shirts with colorful shoulder patches and short brown woolen pants. Two at a time, they came running up to the quarterdeck, where—panting and beaming like well-trained puppies—they offered to help the American visitors with their luggage. They must have been vetted for English-speaking skills, because each proved capable of engaging in the rudimentary banter of a tourist phrasebook. The Yanks were charmed—especially the women, who shared an insuperable urge to stroke this or that shock of sun-bleached hair. The boys bore it all in good grace, apparently having been vetted as well for cuteness and docility. Oskar felt mildly disgusted.

Lena materialized as the last passengers were processed through security. Still no sign of Clair. She was dragging rather than carrying her sturdy portmanteau. Oskar's plain canvas duffle was already waiting on the quarterdeck in the care of a friendly steward. Together they bumped forward in the dwindling line until it was their turn to present themselves to the officious man behind the table, with his companions looking on from either side. Oskar stepped up first.

The man stared back and forth between Oskar and his passport photo, then with no particular expression raised the passport head-high, where it could be examined from behind by his superior. This meant nothing, necessarily. Oskar had watched the same routine carried out half a dozen times.

The officer in charge flicked an eye over his papers and asked mildly, "The purpose of your extended stay overseas, Herr Sinclair?"

"An illness in the family," said Oskar, playing back the story given by Stefan Sinclair upon departing Germany several months before. A note would have been made then; somewhere, a record existed. "My uncle, my father's brother . . . who has since, regrettably, passed."

"*Es tut mir leid,*" said the officer dispassionately.

"*Danke.*"

"And this is Frau Sinclair?"

Lena stepped forward, pressing her own papers into the officer's hand. He declined to examine them, merely cocking his head toward the man seated at the desk.

"Welcome home," he said, unsmiling.

In a nod toward beautification, the civic authorities had made a little park fronting the wharf, with a trapezoid of clipped grass enlivened by beds of salvia and tubs of alpine geraniums, given vertical interest by two rows of fastigiate beeches and a heroic statue of the city's founder, Johann Smidt. At the center, a three-masted pole displayed the flags of the Reich, the Free City of Bremen and the Kingdom of Hanover. A modest ceremony was under way in a small proscenium nearby. Oskar watched from some fifty meters off, where he stood with Lena by a massive bollard at the edge of the wharf, as Senator Townsend and his party were welcomed with the correct degree of official enthusiasm by a thin man in an old-fashioned morning suit. Toby Lugan was just visible over his shoulder. In the middle ground, plump-cheeked girls from the Bund Deutscher Mädel presented flowers while a small wind ensemble tried to coax a fanfare from the throats of their clarinets and flügelhorns. Oskar didn't recognize the music and guessed it must be something by one of the new "patriotic" composers whose work had been deemed free of unhealthy Jewish and Negro influences—stylistically, somewhere between *Also sprach Zarathustra* and the "Horst Wessel Lied." They were interrupted twice by a film crew seeking better camera angles. Nobody seemed to mind. Propaganda was the true art form of the New Germany, and the weekly newsreel *Die Deutsche Wochenschau* among its purest expressions. Everyone, including the senator, wished to be seen at their best.

"Oskar, look!" said Lena, supplying punctuation with a sharp elbow.

He glanced back at the *Robert Ley;* and here at last came Clairborne, clattering down to the wharf, green-and-white scarf flying like a pennant, trailed by a pair of overladen stewards and, at a discreet distance, Obersturmführer von Ewigholz. No one was waiting to receive them, and Oskar wondered if the SS man hadn't purposely held Clair back until there was no possibility of his creating an awkward scene. Well played, he thought. He touched a finger to his hat.

"What are you doing?" said Lena.

"Nothing. Watching the show."

Von Ewigholz was in uniform today—resplendent, if that was the word, in coal-black and gleaming silver, wearing a peaked officer's cap and sporting at his belt something that looked quite like a riding crop. A cavalry officer, Oskar remembered. Then he saw that Lena was waving to Clair, trying to catch his attention.

"Stop that," he hissed.

Too late—Clair had spotted them. He stopped walking and then started again, a comical bit of artlessness, limbs tangling and untangling as he changed course. The acrid breeze caught his long hair and threw it over to one side.

"Lena!" he shouted. "And Stefan—thank God! Friendly faces at last! I've been under lock and key."

Behind him the stewards hauling his luggage exchanged looks of amusement. They liked him, you could tell, in spite of everything. Von Ewigholz they did not. In fact, Oskar thought the stewards might actually have flinched as the SS officer marched past them, boots clomping on the pavement like hoofbeats.

In the little square, the ceremony went on. Senator Townsend pumped his arms like bellows driving air through his larynx, and the cameraman moved back, as though anxious not to miss some nuance involving a clenched fist or the slightly terrified expression of the *Bürgermeister.*

Clair hove up beside Lena. "I wonder if I should go over there," he said, "and give my father a hand."

Lena shot him a quick look. "I'm not so sure—"

With a laugh, the boy laid a hand on her arm as if they were conspirators. "At least let's get closer, shall we? I love to watch people's reactions."

The two of them stepped forward to what Lena evidently felt was a safe distance. Von Ewigholz posted himself like a sentry at Oskar's elbow. They looked on in silence, as though studying some avant-garde performance, a play within a play.

"She keeps him happy," the SS man said after a while. "She keeps him under control."

He spoke quietly, though Oskar doubted Clair would have minded being spoken of this way, as a problem to be handled. Oskar guessed he'd be used to it by now and might even have come to enjoy it.

"She does," he agreed—or, rather, Stefan did: the affectionate husband, showing tolerance for his wife's harmless flirtation. He could feel the SS man's attention moving onto him like a shadow.

"Where do you go from here?" von Ewigholz asked. "Back home now? To Weimar, is that right?"

"First to Bremen. Lena has family there, an elderly aunt I've never met. We're hoping to stay a night or two, but first we've got to find a telephone—in a hotel, I thought—so Lena can let her know we've arrived."

"Then you must let me give you a ride," von Ewigholz said. Something in his voice made it sound like a command. "At least as far as Bremen. We'll be driving right past there on the new highway."

For a moment Oskar almost wondered if he'd actually heard this, or if it was something his fevered imagination had conjured up. Thankfully Stefan was out in front, already making a polite demurral. "Why, you are so kind, sir, but we couldn't possibly—Lena and I are frightfully disorganized, we'd only delay you . . ."

Von Ewigholz turned to him—face-to-face, one man to another. "Please. It would be a favor to me. This American boy . . . I've come to like him, actually, and therefore I'm worried. His little tricks, his antics, may have been harmless on the ship, but here in the Reich? He doesn't understand, he has no concept of proper limits, and so there's no telling how he might behave. But your wife, your Lena—

you see how it is with them. And please believe me, Herr Sinclair, this is not the kind of man you need to be concerned about. Please do come with us to Bremen. At least that far. First, we'll find you a telephone; then I need to requisition a car. Something big, I think. He's got a lot of luggage himself."

The man's eyes had a curious quality of being frozen yet gleaming with life, sharp with alertness and curiosity, while the rest of his face remained impassive and expressionless. It was difficult to stand fixed in that gaze without fidgeting. In the end, even Stefan was no match for it.

"That's very kind of you, sir," he said. "That would save us . . ." He gestured with an arm—a wordless summary of all the things it would spare them, this ride in a big car with an SS *Obersturmführer.* Random security checks. The expense of travel. Negotiation with ticket agents. The ritual of presenting one's papers at every turn.

"Indeed," said von Ewigholz, nodding curtly, acknowledging all the things that need not be said.

They turned to watch the wrapping up of formalities in the square. Bull Townsend, faintly ridiculous with a clutch of daisies in his fist, yielded the podium to another American, this one elderly and genial and sporting a blue sash under his shiny sports jacket. He spoke about enduring bonds and cultural affinities and the burdens of history we all must bear. Finally there was polite applause and a palpable air of restlessness, the crowd ready to move on to the next thing, whatever that might be.

At this point—while the *Bürgermeister* intoned some kind of benediction and the camera crew started breaking down its equipment—Clair stepped forward at last, approaching his father but halting a few paces away. The senator spotted him, delivered a parting handshake and a couple of slaps on nearby shoulders, then pressed through the crowd like a football player exiting the field. Father and son regarded each other for a moment as though trying to decide whether there was something, anything, they ought to say. Clair offered a hand to be clasped, but then Bull Townsend surprised them all by taking the boy into a full, vigorous embrace. You could practically hear the bones crunching. Clair endured this for a second or two before pulling back, looking flustered yet also gratified. He brushed the long hair away from his face and said something too quiet to overhear. "That's the spirit!" said Bull. "Go out there and show 'em what you're made of!"

Then he marched off, making for a Mercedes limousine that had pulled up on the far side of the square. One of the doors hung open and Toby Lugan stood next to it, clutching his papers and glancing at his watch. Just before Oskar turned to go, Lugan raised his head and looked over, meeting his gaze for the first time since he'd walked out of the tavern in Washington, DC. He might have grimaced, though it was hard to be sure. Then he climbed into the car and was off, Oskar supposed, to commence fact-finding.

At twenty-three, Oskar was old enough to remember a time when Germany hadn't been so obsessed with uniforms. He'd been obliged, in the course of adolescence, to take up the habit of scanning lapels for gold-and-scarlet pins, deciphering the insignia on badges and epaulets, recognizing subtle markers of rank and position from across the room. But it hadn't always been so, and he could recall when a coal-black uniform trimmed out in silver wouldn't have commanded the immediate, nervous, even servile deference that greeted von Ewigholz when he stepped off Schillerstrasse into the lobby of the City Hotel. By the time the other three followed him inside, a hush had already fallen on the reception area and was spreading into the adjacent parlor, where a group of businessmen around a tea table paused with their schnapps glasses in the air, caught in mid-toast. The day manager, hurrying out from an office, gave the party an officious bow and inquired how he might be of assistance.

"I should like to have the use of a telephone," said von Ewigholz. "This lady also. In privacy, if that is possible."

"Of course." The manager ushered them down a corridor to a smaller and more spartan sitting area, a few chairs of indistinctly modernist style arranged before a fireplace over which hung the true glory of the room and perhaps of the City Hotel: an oversized photograph of Karl Kaufmann, Gauleiter of Hamburg, surrounded by what Oskar took to be the entire hotel staff. Near the center, at the elbow of the great man himself, beamed the day manager in his tuxedo, tiny and self-important. "Here," he said, stepping aside like a master of ceremonies and indicating a closet with a chair and lamp table visible inside, "you find the telephone."

"Thank you," said von Ewigholz. Something in his voice sent the manager bowing and trotting away. "I will go first, if you don't mind. This matter of the car may be . . . The situation has become more complicated."

When he'd shut himself in, the others spread themselves across the furniture.

"You think anyone will steal our luggage?" Clair wondered aloud, twirling a tasseled scarf end. His tone was faintly hopeful.

Lena seemed to consider a response, and Oskar was relieved when she held back on it.

"I'm sure the wharf is well policed," he said. The hotels, too, he thought of adding—but Lena surely realized that.

Clair said, "I suppose that's meant to be reassuring."

Von Ewigholz was right, Oskar thought: this boy could easily become a danger to himself, hence to all of them. "Your aunt," he said to Lena. "She'll be happy to hear from you, I imagine."

"Well, I *hope* so. I imagine my parents will have told her the ship was due in today. But she may not be expecting a call like this, out of the blue."

Clair perked up, taking an interest. "What's she like, this aunt? Another book person, like you two? Or no—I bet she's a bit of a wild one. A rebel. Does she like Americans? Or does she think we're all cowboys and G-men?"

Oskar smiled. He was curious himself about this notional relative. Lena had been tight-lipped, saying only that the woman was "an old comrade," one hundred percent reliable. It was his personal belief that the two of them had never met.

"Oh, Aunt Tilde," said Lena. "She does have a mind of her own, I can tell you that. You know, people used to say I'd turn out just like her. That may have been a warning—I'm not sure."

She was, Oskar realized, enjoying the spy game. He glanced at the door of the telephone closet, pulled shut with a stripe of amber light at the transom. He could hear von Ewigholz, speaking and then falling quiet, his voice just a murmur yet firm and steady even so. A voice confident of being heeded and indifferent to being over-heard. With no precursory good-bye, the telephone earpiece struck its cradle and the door popped open like the lid of a jack-in-the-box. Von Ewigholz stood there for a moment, backlit, looking annoyed but triumphant.

"They're sending a car," he said, stepping out and choosing a chair for himself. "So, it's your turn," he told Lena. "Take as long as you like. And don't worry if the switchboard girl sounds upset. That would be my doing."

"Come, Stefan," Lena said, glancing coquettishly over a shoulder. "Tilde will want to hear your voice, too—I'm not sure she believes you're quite real."

The automobile waiting on the Schillerstrasse was no gleaming black Mercedes. It was blue, and its paint had weathered in the North Sea air to a pocked and blistered matte. The growl of its once-powerful engine was interrupted every few seconds by the cough of a misfiring cylinder. The canvas top had been furled and lashed down like a sail, revealing bench seats covered in cracked, silvery leather. Its most durable and striking feature was its chrome-work, which was elaborate and, by present-day standards, excessive, extending to spotlights and mirrors and bulging headlamps and a trio of long, trumpetlike horns protruding from a monumental grille. At the brow of the hood, a bird of prey leaned into the wind, looking a bit too fat for actual flight.

By the driver's door, beaming proprietarily, stood a paunchy man in the mustard-brown uniform of the Sturmabteilung. He blanched noticeably as von Ewigholz bore down on him.

"What is this?" was his demand.

"It's a Gatsby car!" said Clair.

"I think it's a Horch," said Oskar, who, like most German boys, had been enamored of automobiles. "Maybe a '28 or '29."

The chauffeur, mildly terrified, looked from one to the other. "It's . . . it's from the Deputy *Kreisleiter*'s own garage. There was . . . at such short notice . . . it was the best we could manage. The best!" Seeing that no one challenged this assertion, he puffed himself up and went on: "And look at her—a splendid old girl, when all's said and done. Get her out on the autobahn and she'll fly, she will. Believe me, I know how to talk to her. Just let me—"

"That won't be necessary," said von Ewigholz. "If this is the best you can offer, then it will have to do. Give the Deputy *Kreisleiter* our thanks." He climbed into the driver's seat, bumping the SA man aside.

"But . . . this is—"

"That will be all." Von Ewigholz, not bothering even to glance at him, concerned himself now with the confusing array of levers and knobs on the dashboard, sliding his gloved hands experimentally around the steering wheel. "All right, this should be no problem. Get in, everyone."

Only then—after the old motorcar was coaxed and bullied into motion and their luggage was retrieved and they were finally out on the newly completed highway linking Bremerhaven to its mother city like a smoothly curving umbilicus—did Oskar finally feel himself to be back home. The land on either side had the raw-shaved and brutalized look of recent road building, but it gave an unimpeded view of the river Weser and the marshy, windswept countryside. If not a gentle landscape, it was a strongly German one: a stubborn place that after centuries of being drained and plowed and replanted still had an air of wildness about it. The wind smelled of salt and new grass and gasoline. The engine grew louder as von Ewigholz thrust it into higher gears, and for the first few miles they rode along without speaking, apart from one brief exchange, von Ewigholz to Oskar:

"Have you come here before?"

"Just once. Lena and I, on our honeymoon. And yourself?"

"Never. I prefer the mountains."

They'd seated themselves according to the unwritten conventions of road travel: the lady in back with Clair, Oskar in the passenger seat up front next to von Ewigholz, the chauffeur having been abandoned at the wharf. Oskar felt he should be holding a map, even though there was no need for one—the road ran straight to Bremen, and the drive should take less than an hour.

"You know, Clair," Lena said after a time, her voice unnaturally strident so as to be heard above the wind and the engine noise, "there's an old story about four travelers on the road to Bremen. Maybe you've heard it. Over here it's called 'Die Bremer Stadtmusikanten.' "

Clair laughed, for no reason Oskar could understand. "I don't believe I know that one."

"Yes, well." Lena turned sideways in the seat, bending closer to his ear. "They were a donkey, a dog, a cat and a rooster. It's complicated, but each of them was about to be killed for one reason or another, so they set out to become street musicians in Bremen."

"Sounds perfectly logical."

"Well, in a way it was. You see, Bremen was a Free City, not under the rule of some aristocrat, so it was a refuge for . . . for anyone, really."

"Even animals."

"Even musicians!" said von Ewigholz, loudly—which surprised Oskar so much that he gave an involuntary laugh. The two men exchanged looks and for that instant were something like companions. Oskar glanced quickly away.

"Okay," said Clair, "so what happens?"

"They come upon some robbers," said Lena. "This is the scary part if you're a child. These robbers have taken over a nice little house, and they're inside there with heaps of food and all the nice things they've stolen. The donkey and the dog and the cat and the rooster are very hungry, of course, after walking all day, so they make a plan for how to get the robbers out. I can't remember how it went. But anyway, they end up singing or, rather, making their animal noises, which for them *is* singing. And this frightens the robbers into running away from the house."

"They climb one atop another," von Ewigholz said pedantically. "They stand just outside the window, and the dog hops up on the donkey, the cat crawls up on the dog, and the rooster flies up on the cat. When they start singing, the donkey puts his hooves up on the windowsill and they all crash through the glass. *That's* what scares the robbers."

"Got it," said Clair.

"But the robbers come back," Oskar pointed out.

"*After* the animals are asleep," said Lena. "But everything goes wrong for them."

Von Ewigholz surprised them with an Americanism, delivered with comical precision: "All hell breaks loose."

"*Exactly,*" said Lena. "The robbers get kicked and bitten and clawed and pecked at, but they don't understand why and think they've been attacked by an evil witch. So they run away and are never seen again."

"And the musicians never make it to Bremen," said von Ewigholz.

"They don't have to, because they've got this nice little house."

"No, but—well, that's right, but doesn't this bother you?" He twisted around in the driver's seat, dangerously so in Oskar's view. "The story is called 'Die Bremer Stadtmusikanten,' but where is Bremen?"

"Straight ahead," said Oskar, "up the road."

Von Ewigholz turned his attention back to driving but added, "It always bothered me, as a boy. I wanted to hear more about this magical place where animals sing in the streets."

Lena looked fleetingly sorry—for the disappointed child this black-clad SS man had been? It was too ridiculous.

"Is there a moral to this story?" Clair asked after a few moments. "Is it supposed to teach you some lesson?"

"It's just a story," said Oskar, now annoyed.

"I always thought . . ." Lena glanced at him, sensing his mood. "I always thought it was saying, Be true to yourself, whatever you are. Use whatever gifts God's given you. If you've got claws, use them to scratch the robbers. If you've only got hooves, kick with them."

"I like that," said Clair. "But I was thinking maybe something about strange bedfellows. Joining up with other people even if they're different. Like cats and dogs."

"And the donkey!" said Lena. "He was the funniest."

"What do *you* think, Hagen?" Clair asked. Oskar couldn't tell if it was meant to be a goad.

"It's a simple folktale. You read it to children at bedtime. They laugh at the pictures. I don't know why we're talking about it."

Oskar agreed, which further annoyed him.

They hadn't encountered much motor traffic, and the landscape had been pleasing but monotonous. As they drove on, the highway curved gently eastward, away from the river and onto firmer and higher ground. They sped through pockets of woodland that yielded to well-ordered fields and at last a couple of tiny villages, the first signs of the idealized German country life that featured so prominently on government posters and in sentimental movies and other approved expressions of the national *Volksgeist*. And here there finally were other motorcars, on little farm roads beside the autobahn and then on the highway itself. None of the other cars were as ornate as the Horch and few were as old; mostly they were late-model DKWs or Opels or Fords, the last having been given a kind of dispensation on account of the Führer's special regard for Henry Ford, whose portrait (so they said) hung on his wall. Altogether Oskar got a sense of forward motion and modest prosperity, with none of the startling affluence of Washington or the furious bustle of Berlin.

It was not long after—indeed, much too soon—that Oskar began to recognize local landmarks, a tower here and a steeple there, an old fortification rising improbably from the tidal moraine, sights he remembered from his brief and somewhat perfunctory training only a few months ago. He'd come straight from the Christmas holiday with his family to find this landscape swathed in fog, so now his memories had a blurred and dreamlike quality. He'd made a pro forma appearance at Kriegsmarine headquarters, then been spirited to an overgrown manor with sizable grounds north of the city. He remembered looking out in the morning over the fields—these same fields, or ones very like them—and marveling at the spiky tips of larches where the mist had frozen overnight, glittering like a million tiny daggers in the sunrise. The sun was getting lower now, falling behind them as the highway swept east and Bremen proper rose to meet them on the right, a collection of dark shapes arranged along the riverfront like a child's wooden blocks.

"Your aunt lives where?" said von Ewigholz.

It was the first time anyone had spoken in a while, and Lena seemed startled by the question. Answer, thought Oskar, for God's sake. It's not something you'd need to think about.

"The Eastern Vorstadt," said Lena, probably soon enough. "Here, I've copied down the address."

She made a little business out of finding a piece of paper in her handbag and passing it up front, where Oskar made a similar show of reading it. All unnecessary—both of them had memorized the street number and the directions that came with it—but the practice of taking notes, of being seen to consult them, was a bit of fieldcraft the Abwehr drilled into you. It had never been explained, so Oskar was left to his own surmises: that it made you seem forgetful and therefore unthreatening; that it provided a physical distraction, like a film actress lighting a cigarette. These might have been true, but as with any game, you only needed to learn the rules, not understand them.

"Celler Strasse 49," Oskar read. "Near the St.-Jürgen Hospital. Enter off Lüneburger Strasse. She suggests you approach from the Breitenweg, which will take you to the Bismarckstrasse, and turn when you see the hospital on your right."

"Well, it can't be too hard."

The afternoon was turning into evening by the time the old Horch left the autobahn and began snorting and lurching along the streets of Bremen, which narrowed as the travelers progressed from the leafy northern suburbs to the crowded Altstadt. They passed a complex of athletic fields where boys in brightly colored jerseys ran or huddled or marched, holding sticks for rifles, their chants competing with the growl of the unhappy engine and the sounds of city life. Oskar felt a touch of sadness, though whether it was for those boys and whatever doom awaited them or for his own vanished youth, he couldn't have said. Beyond the fields lay waste ground, then warehouses, then a sprawling railway yard whose many tracks they sped over on a bridge, and at last they entered the old Free City, a medieval thicket of heavy-timbered buildings enlivened with gilt signs and flower boxes and red banners showing the swastika.

The traffic slowed to a walker's pace. Oskar scanned kiosks posted with show bills, advertisements, civic notices in Gothic type and the latest news headlines: Porsche unveils its newest model, a "People's Car" for just RM 990. Sweden affirms her neutrality. The Kriegsmarine launches a new battle cruiser, the *Prinz Eugen*. Switzerland slams England, 2–1.

They reached a busy intersection, blocked by foot traffic, and by the time Oskar spotted the Breitenweg street sign, it was too late to make the turn. Irritated, von Ewigholz stomped the gas pedal and released the clutch too quickly, the car lurching and stalling and rolling slowly into the crossing. He then stomped angrily and seemingly at random on the various pedals at his feet. By now the engine was flooded. A traffic policeman approached, spotted the SS uniform and stiffened into a pose of either martial attention or mortal fear.

"Here!" Oskar called, waving to a small group of university students, probably, dressed in the sort of bright-hued, cheerfully shabby clothing you never saw in Berlin. "Help us, would you? Come give us a push."

The youngsters—there were just four—took counsel among themselves and seemed to decide the fun on offer outweighed the risk. Or perhaps, in their naïveté, they thought an entanglement with the Black Knighthood was not at all alarming. They weren't Jews, were they? So they loped over, grinning, and took up positions around the flanks of the old car.

"Now!" Oskar said, and they started to push.

At first the old Horch barely rocked forward a notch, but after a couple of tries they managed to get it rolling; it cleared the intersection so the traffic on the Breitenweg could flow through. The students cheered and the traffic policeman saluted, then pulled out a handkerchief and mopped his brow.

"*Wohin geht's du?*" one of the boys asked Clair, who'd climbed onto the seatback for a better view of the unfolding embarrassment.

He seemed to understand, if not the words, at least the general spirit of the question. "I haven't the foggiest notion!" he said cheerfully.

This seemed to amuse them. "American?" one of them asked.

"That's enough," snapped von Ewigholz. His pallor had flushed to a dangerous red, as though some chemical reaction were occurring beneath it. "Thank you—your help is appreciated. Now go on with what you were doing."

The students looked surprised, but they managed to stroll back to the sidewalk casually, even a tad defiantly—not enough to get called on it, or so their instincts told them. Oskar shook his head, thinking, You can't trust those instincts anymore.

It was a full ten minutes before the carburetor cleared and the engine would restart. The sky continued to darken, and the lights came on in shop windows and in upper-story apartments and on the marquee of a theater that was showing, of all things, "The first full-evening cartoon-film by Walt Disney, *Schneewittchen und die sieben Zwerge.*"

Von Ewigholz drove cautiously after that, circling the block and turning east, parallel to the river. After a few blocks they left behind the theaters and restaurants and wine bars, entering a more somber, dignified quarter that was recognizably the government district. Oskar had prepared himself and yet felt an inner jolt at the sight of the largest and ugliest building in that district: the Haus des Reichs, a decade-old limestone monstrosity that looked like something between a jail and a mausoleum. Six stories tall, it flashed a bit of decorative carving and other traditional features near street level, but as it rose it cast those off in favor of a stony Brutalist façade up to the roof fascia. It occupied a full, irregularly shaped city block, its four unequal limbs bent around a courtyard that (as Oskar remembered it) was empty and joyless except for a lone clock tower visible from every inward-facing window. The top floor had been claimed by the district leader of the NSDAP, and the remaining floors were shared by a miscellany of other agencies, offices, boards and services, including the Kriegsmarine, under whose protective cover the Abwehr ran its nest. Oskar counted the stories up to four and scanned to see if there were any lights on at this hour. Of course there were.

Celler Strasse was quieter and darker than the city around it, on account of lindens planted on either side late in the last century when these large, impressive town homes were built, shoulder to shoulder and set back from the road, allowing each a generous front garden. Oskar was reminded of Washington, with its similar neighborhoods full of drawn curtains, the same yellow light seeping through, the inhabitants living their *bürgerlich* lives in comfort and secrecy. The Horch rumbled down the middle of the street in the only permissible direction, toward the riverfront, which you could sense was close now. Few of the houses had visible street numbers, but their destination, number 49, was marked by a tasteful signpost bearing the name Dr. Kuno Ruhmann and a courteous warning: BY APPOINTMENT ONLY, PLEASE.

"Is this right?" said von Ewigholz, as the car braked to a halt with a piercing squeak. "This is where your aunt lives? Who is Dr. Ruhmann?"

They were all staring at the sign and waiting for Lena to respond. Say something, damn it, thought Oskar. Trust Socialists to screw up such a simple thing.

"Yes, I—" Lena didn't quite stammer, but very nearly. Her face was completely blank.

"So *that's* the tenant she was talking about," Oskar said, then forced a chuckle. "A doctor, no less! Well, that's certainly stylish. I trust he's old and bent over, or else tongues will be wagging. Such goings-on in a respectable neighborhood!" He paused, giving Lena time to catch up. "Well, then, I'll go fetch the luggage."

He opened the passenger door and clambered out with what he deemed a suitable degree of fumbling and awkwardness. Lena offered von Ewigholz her hand, thanking him in half a dozen ways for the kindness of giving them a ride.

"It was my honor and my pleasure," he assured her. Then, against Oskar's silent prayers, he opened the door on his side, stepped down to the road and brushed the wrinkles out of his tunic. "I'll help carry your bags in."

Oskar started to say there was no need, but von Ewigholz knew perfectly well that there wasn't. He'd decided for some reason of his own, maybe no more sinister than ordinary human curiosity, to have a look inside this house and to meet the famous Aunt Tilde. *Lena has told us all so much . . .* There was nothing Oskar could do. Only stick to his cover, trust Lena to do likewise and hope the SOPADE, which had managed to survive the Thousand-Year Reich for this long, could hang on a few minutes longer.

"I'm coming too," said Clair. "I *must* meet your aunt! The wild one in the family in a house like this? Well, you never know." He climbed out of the car, not bothering with the door, just hoisting one long leg and then the other over the side and sliding down like a child on a playground.

This could be good, Oskar thought, and perhaps helpful, a wayward American violating social conventions he wasn't even aware of. Distracting his minder. Drawing attention away from any lapses in performance by Lena, or Tilde, or whoever else might be involved—and Oskar dearly hoped these people had the sense to keep the dramatis personae to as few as possible.

They approached the house, Lena leading the way. The front walk ran dead straight, paved with flagstones and lined on one side by clipped boxwood, on the other by a tiny medicinal garden whose patches of herbs bore neat copper labels. The stoop was three steps high, surfaced in granite and splashed with light from electric lanterns that framed the carved-oak door. Thanks to the raucous Horch, there was no chance of surprise—the door swung back while Lena was reaching for the knocker. And there, effusing, stood their contact in the Socialist underground, a sprightly sexagenarian with cropped silver hair, shy of five feet by a good two fingers, wearing a patterned silk dress that fell from her shoulders to her knees in the style of the twenties. This woman, thought Oskar, had been a middle-aged flapper.

"Lena!" Aunt Tilde exclaimed with both hands out. "Do come in. Please, everyone, let me get a better look at you! My eyes aren't so good anymore in the dark."

She stood aside as they trooped past, Clair on Lena's heels, then Oskar with their luggage, von Ewigholz trailing nonchalantly, keeping the lot of them in his field of sight. Tilde shooed them into a room off the front hall where a fire crackled needlessly in a large grate and a gentleman in old-fashioned at-home attire—a vest over a high-collared shirt—rose from a chair, holding a newspaper, to greet the new arrivals. Probably a decade older than the woman, he'd folded the paper so its name was clearly legible: the *Hamburger Abendblatt*, a safely nondescript regional organ. Well played if maybe too obvious, in Oskar's professional judgment.

"I present Herr Doktor Ruhmann," Tilde announced, lightening the formality with her buoyant delivery and a mischievous smile.

"And here, *Herr Doktor,* you see my dear niece Lena with, if I am not mistaken, her husband, whom for the very first time I am meeting now, so naughty a girl! She tells me his name is Stefan."

"I'm sorry, Aunt—" Lena began, but Tilde waved it aside and held out a hand for the new in-law to . . . clasp, he decided. A flapper wouldn't go in for the kiss.

"You are welcome to our family," she told him, "even if I am a trifle late in saying so."

"It's an honor to meet you," he said. This wasn't going badly at all.

"And here, Aunt, are the others I told you about. Obersturm-führer von Ewigholz, who was so kind as to drive us all this way in his motorcar, and Mr. Clairborne Townsend, who comes from America."

Tilde had a flair for this. She admired the SS man's uniform as though it were an ordinary, if possibly extravagant, business suit. Clairborne she favored with a demonstration of her excellent, finishing-school English. "You poor young man—I am certain our Old World manners must seem quite stuffy to you. I beg you to indulge us. So many visitors, all at once—the doctor and I are quite unused to such goings and comings."

Clair's smile looked real enough, lacking its usual irony. He was evidently charmed, or at least entertained. Every bit the senator's son, he began praising the house, speaking clearly and slowly in case either her hearing or her bilingualism might require special consideration.

"It's an old place," said Tilde, "but all the working parts are fully modernized. The doctor requires that, you know. In fact, just down the hall"—she pointed to an inner door—"we have a full water closet, in case anyone should like to freshen up."

It seemed to Oskar that this was directed especially at Lena and that a further suggestion was implied. If so, she missed it by making small talk with the doctor, with von Ewigholz looking on impassively, and when Oskar managed to catch her eye, she only smiled at him. He glanced back toward Tilde, who, without a break in her discourse to Clair about ornamental molding, managed to tilt an eye in the general direction of the door. That was enough for Oskar.

"If you'll pardon me," he said to no one in particular. Taking care not to hurry, he crossed the room and turned the handle and found himself staring down a narrow passageway, evidently meant for servants, leading back to a distant, well-lit room he guessed would be the kitchen. There was indeed a water closet en route, and a pantry, but Oskar kept going until finally stepping out into the sort of all-purpose domestic work area you find only in houses dating from an era when the presence of household staff was taken for granted. The room ran the width of the house and was outfitted for cooking, laundering, pet bathing, harvest processing, livestock slaughtering and God knew what else. Probably the architect hadn't foreseen the need to accommodate a party of armed resistance fighters, but that is what Oskar found gathered there around a chopping table in the center of the room: two men and a woman, all about Lena's age. One of the men aimed an antique pistol approximately at Oskar's left eye. The gun looked heavy, and the fellow's hand weak.

"Ah, good," said Oskar, approaching him with only a minor break in his stride. "It's Gunter, isn't it? We were told to expect you." He stuck out his arm as though to offer a handshake.

"No," the armed man said uncertainly, "it's Alex. Stop—"

Oskar swept his arm sideways, knocking the gun to the left, where he grabbed it and easily pried it out of the man's grip. The maneuver took all of two seconds if you did it properly. They'd taught Oskar this trick in his first week of training, and he was amazed how well it worked.

He dangled the pistol by the trigger guard with one finger, demonstrating that he had no plans to use it. "What the devil's going on here? There's an SS officer out in the sitting room. Whoever you are, keep absolutely quiet and stay the hell out of sight. Do you understand?"

He looked at each of them in turn, hard in the eyes. Only the woman seemed to be considering a reply, but in the end she simply stared between the gun and Oskar's furious expression.

"All right." He switched on the safety catch and handed the pistol carefully back to the one who'd called himself Alex. "You won't need this. I'll get rid of the SS, and then we can all sit down and talk, yes?"

Alex nodded, his brow running with sweat and his hand trembling visibly as he took the gun. Oskar turned and stepped as softly as he could back up the servants' hall to the bathroom door, which he opened and then shut with a bang louder than he'd intended.

Back in the overheated sitting room, something was amiss. Lena had sat down near the fire, where she seemed to be in conversation with Dr. Ruhmann. Only they weren't speaking just now; both looked expectantly at Oskar, and the doctor was grasping the newspaper so tightly it had crumpled in his fist. Von Ewigholz stood in the doorway through which they'd entered the room, seeming to contemplate the banisters of the wide formal staircase. Aunt Tilde, left on her own, stood there in the middle looking befuddled, as though she'd failed in her hostess duties but couldn't work out just how.

At last Oskar understood what was wrong. "Where's Clair?" he said, trying to sound jovial. "Not up to his usual mischief, I hope."

"He's gone *exploring*," Lena said. She glanced toward the SS man, though his mind seemed to be elsewhere.

"I was just telling him about the library," said Tilde. "It rises two full stories, shelves all around, with a balcony and ladders. Perhaps I—my English—"

"Your English is lovely, madam," von Ewigholz said. He stepped back into the room, and his courteous bow to Tilde only served to make him look taller when he straightened again. He continued in German: "I'm afraid my young friend is prone to, shall we say, a certain excess of spontaneity. He doesn't mean to be rude." He smiled ironically, not unlike Clair, which Oskar read as meaning: *not this time, at least*.

Should he go looking for Clair, then, on the pretext of seeing this remarkable library for himself? But no—there'd be plenty of time for that, their stated story being to stay for the night. Maybe Lena could go instead? Presumably familiar with the house, she might plausibly intervene as a kind of deputy hostess. Or maybe the best thing was to just wait. Why behave as though anything was wrong? Clair would get bored soon enough. *Ach!* Oskar thought. This sort of improvisation shouldn't be necessary.

Then they heard the sound of voices.

"Quiet!" von Ewigholz commanded—quite unnecessarily, as they were all straining their ears.

The voices came from some indistinct place overhead but were loudest near the stairwell, which Oskar discovered by drifting toward the SS man into the front hall, where together they stared up the shadowy staircase. Oskar could make out at least two voices, maybe more, interspersed with ripples of laughter, so giddy or nervous it might've been a projection of his own mental state, which was roughly akin to how he'd felt before crawling out of a trench during live-fire exercises at Lichterfelde. It was all right to panic, they'd told him; that's a normal reaction to bullets flying inches above your head. But some part of your mind must remain calm, and you must condition your limbs to obey that part. Now the calm part of Oskar's mind was telling him that the situation could be salvaged, that he would figure out how to manage it.

Then, a shriek.

Not a shriek of terror, probably—only surprise. Probably that. Yet a shriek nonetheless. And von Ewigholz was not a man to stand dumbly in the dark while someone was shrieking at the top of the stairs; nor, for that matter, was Oskar. So the two of them advanced cautiously in quiet, deliberate steps upward.

"Stay behind me," von Ewigholz ordered softly, and Oskar realized the man had pulled from somewhere a small sidearm of the type issued to officers of his service, a lightweight Walther, not a combat weapon but efficient at close quarters and easy to slip into a pocket. He fell a step behind with one eye on the gun.

The two them paused on the landing and listened intently for several moments. At first it seemed the voices had stopped, but in fact they'd only dropped in volume; you could just make them out, and now there were three of them, including a woman's. Frowning, von Ewigholz crossed the landing to a spot from which he could peer down the hall, running back to front the length of the house, with three rooms on each side. The doors were shut but light was spreading from the sill beneath one of them. Abandoning stealth, von Ewigholz strode to it directly and placed his free hand on the knob. Oskar hurried to catch up but was one step too slow.

The door swung open, the effect akin to yanking a stage curtain up before the actors have reached their marks. There were four people inside, two perched on a bed, two others standing beside it. But what drew the eye wasn't the people, it was the large pistol held by one of them: Clair, on the bed, who appeared to be inspecting it, turning it carefully like a pawnbroker estimating its value.

The person seated beside him—the young man called Alex—stared at the armed SS officer in the doorway with a look of pure terror. A third man hovering nearby made a grab for the pistol, and that's what Oskar saw in the instant he reached the doorway.

Had he been that one step faster, he might have disarmed von Ewigholz or at least deflected the shot. In the event, the bullet went precisely where it was aimed, into the man's forehead. The old pistol clattered to the floor, the victim collapsing beside it. Alex made a frantic grab for the weapon as von Ewigholz took aim again.

"Stop there," the SS man said, almost conversationally. "Keep your hands—"

Clair interrupted with another shriek, this one more plangent than before. "What have you *done*? We were only—"

"Be quiet. Move away, please."

Oskar stood inches from von Ewigholz with every muscle taut, trying to game this out. The possibilities were too numerous and none of them good. He punched hard at the officer's wrist, reaching in with the other hand to pull the gun away. This time the trick didn't work. Von Ewigholz, his grip still tight on the Walther, rammed an elbow into Oskar's ribs. The world turned bright and red for a moment, but it seemed to Oskar that on the edge of his vision the woman made some rapid move, and then there were two gunshots at nearly the same time. Von Ewigholz lurched backward but stayed on his feet. In the room, something thumped to the floor. Oskar threw his body into the SS man, grabbing the gun and twisting it loose. His hand, when he pulled it away, was sticky with blood. Von Ewigholz gave a low, vocalized sigh and lowered himself to the hallway floor, leaning back against the stair rail. He looked up at Oskar and nodded—meaning what?

And now Clair shoved himself through the bedroom door, all disorganized limbs and flying hair and pink, tear-stained face, making straight for von Ewigholz, whom he stared down at for a moment before folding up next to him like a puppet whose strings had been cut, holding out one trembling hand as though he wanted but feared to touch him.

"It's all right," the SS man said, then lifted the arm with the bloody gun hand to reveal a dark spreading stain on that side, roughly at the level of his diaphragm. "A small wound, I think. Nothing to worry about."

Clair turned so as to look up at Oskar, bewildered and furious. "What just happened? Why are people *shooting* each other? Is there some kind of war going on I haven't heard about?" His eyes grew more focused. Maybe he was starting to realize that the question was not, in fact, rhetorical.

Suddenly, or so it seemed to Oskar, other people were all around. The woman stood in the doorway behind him, gripping the old pistol in both hands and training it, dead steady, on von Ewigholz. Meanwhile, Lena had reached the top of the stairs with Tilde behind her, a few steps down, so only her head was visible through the banister. Her face registered terror, confusion, helplessness.

This is what happens, Oskar felt like telling her. You agree to do a favor for some old friends in the SDP. Next thing you know, you've got bodies on the second floor.

"You should go in there," the Resistance woman told him, her voice surprisingly calm; she sounded, if anything, resigned. "Peter, I'm pretty sure, is dead. Alex, I can't tell. Perhaps you have more experience. I'll keep an eye on your friend."

Oskar nodded. He looked at the gun in his hand, still slick with blood, and wondered pointlessly what he could wipe it off with. Then he turned grimly toward the bedroom but noticed the old man, Ruhmann, emerging from the shadows at the far end of the hallway. He'd come up the service stairs, Oskar guessed, discreetly tucked behind one of these doors—the same route the Socialists must have taken, which had brought them face-to-face with Clair. One small mystery solved. Ruhmann came forward slowly, lugging a Gladstone bag that looked as full and substantial as he himself seemed frail and spent.

"I imagine you'll be needing a doctor," he said.

NETTING MEN LIKE SHOALS OF COD

BREMEN, ALTSTADT: 23 MAY

Jaap Saxo's navy-issue shoes, in need of polishing, left tracks in the dew that had collected overnight on the marble paving slabs around the statue. He'd begun his day in Bremen, as a matter of preference grown into superstitious habit, with a stroll through the Old City. It was early, but already a gaggle of tourists—could they be American?—had assembled on one side of the famous monument, clutching their cameras and Baedekers and dictionaries while a young man in an Arbeitsfront uniform lectured them about Roland, his heroic deeds in the service of Karl der Grosse, his sword Durendal, his status as protector of the Free Cities and the legend that the Bremen town fathers kept a duplicate statue hidden in a cellar, in case the original should be toppled and the city left thereby defenseless. When Jaap drew near, the young man snapped to attention and offered him a Hitler salute.

"Good morning, *Herr Kapitänleutnant!*"

Jaap returned an ordinary naval salute and kept walking. It was imprudent, he guessed, but these Nazi boys annoyed him and he was in a gray mood to begin with—and had been for weeks now. Perhaps that's why Bremen suited him. The northwest always suited him, with its salt air, its easygoing spirit and its distance from Berlin.

His destination was the Aussenhandelsstelle, the Foreign Trade Office, which occupied an old guesthouse off the main square and was the final stopping point for businessmen traveling overseas—

this despite the fact that nowadays no oceangoing vessels departed from here, all such traffic having moved downriver to the daughter city's deep-draft harbor. Such is the German civil service when it's dug its claws in. Jaap couldn't fault them. They'd grown comfortable in Bremen and so, if he wasn't careful, might he.

The clerk at the reception desk knew him by sight as a "special client," an officer whose professional interest in certain aspects of their operation was understood to lie outside the bounds of normal scrutiny. *If the* Kapitänleutnant *needs to look at a file, Fräulein, just be sure it gets put back properly.* Jaap's business today required access not to files but, rather, to stories, personal recollections. He passed through an inner door and up an ancient, narrow flight of stairs to the former guest rooms on the topmost floor. Squeezed into a corner and lit from overhead by a murky skylight, a secretary acknowledged him by lowering her half-glasses and waving him past her tiny desk to where a blackened door sagged half-open.

"The assistant director is expecting you," she said, a note of play in her voice. "They called up from downstairs. You know they don't like it when you won't stop to chat. They've got certain theories about you, but they need more information. You should wear a wedding ring someday. That'll keep them going for a week."

Jaap favored her with his best smile. "Thank you, Heidi. How's your little brother—have you heard from him?"

The secretary, who couldn't have been much over twenty, lifted a framed picture from her desk: a blond boy too young to shave in a crisp white tunic, its sleeve showing the lone stripe of a seaman recruit. "He volunteered for the U-boats," she said. "He says there's special training involved."

Her eyes, raised to meet Jaap's, seemed to be asking for something: a reaction, encouragement of some kind.

"That's very exciting," he told her, smiling again. "I'm sure he'll do well."

He held the smile until he stopped to tap lightly on the open doorway.

"Yes, all right, you can see I'm here," said a heavy man in a fine but yellowed shirt, from a swivel chair he'd rolled over to a bank of diamond-mullioned windows. His broad desk, stacked with papers in several colors, was several paces off, as though its mooring lines had been cut. "Give me more notice next time and I'll find some reason to be out. Then you can have the run of the place. Have the run of—" He winked, tossing his head in the direction of the anteroom.

"Herr Kretschmann," said Jaap. He closed the door behind himself and settled into an empty chair. "How is your memory these days? Sharp as ever?"

"*Ach!*" The big man concealed his pleasure by jutting his chin out and shaking his jowls. "Too many things stashed away up there." A tap on the forehead. "Never find the one you're looking for. Ask me the last port of call of some leaky coastal freighter fifteen years ago, I can rattle it right off. Ask me what I ate for lunch yesterday, your guess is as good as mine."

"My guess would be blood sausage," said Jaap. "In plum sauce with a splash of sherry, to cut the grease."

Kretschmann laughed, an event in which most of his body participated. "Not a bad guess. But I think that was Tuesday. What can I do for you, my good sir?"

"Erwin Kaspar," said Jaap. "Early twenties. Trade mission, late last winter. Dispatched by the Agriculture Ministry, but I suspect he might have trailed through here to present his credentials, maybe left his name in a ledger. Strictly by the book, young Herr Kaspar."

Kretschmann sat for a while impassively, his head angled toward the bank of windows. God alone knew what went on inside that great round cranium. In his own good time, he swiveled his chair to face Jaap straight on. "I know the name," he said.

"Ah." Jaap knitted his fingers, waiting for the story that must be gaining force just over the horizon.

"In point of fact," said Kretschmann, "you're not the first one who's come in here, to this office, asking about this Kaspar fellow. A young man who seems very much in demand. What'd he do, knock up some *Kreisleiter*'s daughter? Pilfer the Winter Aid box? Make off with secret documents?"

Jaap chose not to react, though the last question was too pointed for his taste. "It's rather what he didn't do. He never came back. I'm trying to trace him."

"Never came back!" Kretschmann raised his eyebrows, but not, thought Jaap, in surprise. "Well. That's not so unusual these days, is it? Fellow sails off to America. On a government ticket, no less! And we never see him again. Not a new story. And hardly much of a mystery, *Kapitänleutnant*, I shouldn't think."

Perhaps not—yet Jaap hadn't mentioned America. Kretschmann seemed to realize this as well. Still seated, he rolled across the creaky floorboards to his desk, pumping the chair along like a paddle boat. He opened a drawer and pulled out a bottle of schnapps and two dubious-looking glasses.

"You mentioned," said Jaap, "that I'm not the first who's been asking about Erwin Kaspar."

"I'm coming to that!" said Kretschmann, pouring the drinks. "Here, don't make me get up. I was just *coming* to that. I'll show you something. It's here somewhere, God knows where."

Jaap took a glass while Kretschmann pawed through one drawer and then another, knocking things loose that rattled against the old wood. The man had begun to sweat. Finally he pulled his hand out, holding it up to display a business card that was printed on oversized stock and pinched between his fat thumb and forefinger. He waved this briefly, like a fan, then handed it to Jaap, who stared at it for a moment before giving it back.

"That's the one," said Kretschmann, energetic now. "Here, raise a glass with me. *Zum Wohl!*"

They drank. The schnapps was fierce and peppery: a tonic for the nerves.

"Helmut Kohlwasser," said Kretschmann, reading from the card. "*SS-Standartenführer.* Reich Security Main Office. That's all. A big shot—no phone number, no street address. And no office hours, the lucky chap!" He poured himself another glass and waved the bottle at Jaap, who shook his head.

"These men don't have office hours," Jaap said, "because they're on the job all the time. Day and night."

Kretschmann seemed not to be listening. "I didn't like him," he said, lowering his voice. "Between you and me, *Kapitänleutnant*, the way he marched in here, demanded to examine my files—*examine* them, like some kind of doctor."

"And asking about Kaspar."

"Kaspar? Oh, your young, ah, traveler. No. Not Kaspar in particular. He was looking for names, anyone who'd booked passage to America in a trade-related capacity, either privately or officially, between certain dates in . . . I believe it was March. Yes, March. And there was Kaspar, right in his window. Not the only one, but for some reason, given how this big shot behaved, you got a feeling: *This is the one I'm looking for.*"

Jaap smiled; the man was good with accents. "You're very observant, Herr Kretschmann. That's really quite a remarkable memory."

"Well . . ." Kretschmann glowed at the compliment, his face now even redder.

"Listen," Jaap said, "this is not an official visit—just a personal call, yes? I'm in Bremen on navy business and dropped by in passing to say hello. But in case anything else arises—"

"With Kaspar?"

"Or with Kohlwasser. Should there be any further developments, anything at—"

"I shall contact you," said Kretschmann, barely above a whisper. It was a conspiracy, just the two of them, and he loved it. "I shall be very discreet. 'A discrepancy in tonnage figures'—how's that for a signal?"

"It's perfect, Herr Kretschmann. But I must go now."

"*Zum Wohl!*" said the big man, raising an empty glass in imitation of a farewell toast.

To your health. Well, that was apt, thought Jaap. "And to yours," he said.

The Haus des Reichs was as ghastly as he remembered it. His uniform got him through the front door and into the wing occupied by the Kriegsmarine. The place seemed busier than usual today— messengers scurrying past with sealed envelopes tucked under their elbows, huddled conversations that fell silent when he approached. Here and there, desks and cabinets had been set up in the broad hallways, suggesting that certain aspects of the operation were expanding faster than had been envisioned a couple of years ago when the office space had been allotted. He glanced at door plates in passing. Munitions. Logistics. Communications (Secure). This sort of information would be very useful to a hostile agent, and here it was, right out in plain sight, available for the price of a sailor suit. You never thought a spy would dare, or bother, to stroll into a place like this, but the same could be said for most places, and Jaap himself had cabinets filled with things obtained just as unimaginatively. None of that especially concerned him today.

Abwehr Nest Bremen had a floor to itself on the north side of the building, away from the river, and to enter it Jaap needed to present his identification twice. At the second checkpoint his clothing and his letter case were pawed through with reassuring vigor. When at last he was granted admittance, he found the atmosphere curiously charged. There was excitement in the air, but it seemed of a nervous sort, as in a newsroom with a big story in the works whose ending was still in doubt. There was none of the bustle of the hallways below. People were in their offices, speaking quietly into telephones or flipping attentively through documents with classifications stamped in red.

Jaap walked slowly, expecting to be greeted or challenged or at least recognized by someone. He was no stranger here, having come over to Intelligence in '35 with Admiral Canaris and his cadre; in navy parlance, he was a plank owner. Yet the faces in these offices were unfamiliar to him. Times were changing, the bureau was growing and Jaap felt out of touch. Such feelings were to be expected when you'd been out in the field, working and living undercover. You came in and resumed your true identity, but it could take weeks, or months, to really feel like yourself again. Except the field Jaap had come in from was Berlin, where the dangers he'd faced were on the order of loose chatter at cocktail parties. The worst moment had been his meeting with Kohlwasser, and that had amounted to a comparison of cock sizes. It wasn't Jaap who was out of touch; it was these people here, running their agents and training their saboteurs and plotting their infiltrations of American shipyards, while the real war—or, rather, the question of whether there was going to be one or not—was being decided by gentlemen in well-appointed rooms in the Wilhelmstrasse, the Élysée, Whitehall, Capitol Hill.

Canaris understood this. So did Beck, Weizsäcker, Oster, Gisevius. Even von Kleist, that firebrand, knew when to sheathe his sword and pop in a boutonniere and go calling on his friends at MI6. The smartest thing Nest Bremen could be doing right now was to stop yammering about "the American target" and start cultivating useful contacts there. Jaap had made one stab at that, and from what he could ascertain—precious little—it had come to grief. But he would try again, if he could.

Promptly at eleven o'clock, he was ushered into the Holy of Holies: an oversized room filled with potted jungle plants, a conference table, two large nautical charts (one of major Atlantic shipping channels, the other of the eastern seaboard of the United States) and a desk designed for use from a standing, not sitting, position. Here he found Dr. Erich Pfeiffer in his element: monocle in place, cigar smoldering in a brass tray, cognac in a cut-class decanter and a secretary at each elbow as he riffled through a sheaf of classified documents like a rummy player checking for marked cards.

Jaap came smartly to attention. "Commander," he said.

"What? Who is it?" Pfeiffer removed his monocle, blinking. "Ah, Saxo, good. Just the man. Fräulein, if you'll— Thank you. And the door, please. For God's sake stand at ease, man. You know we don't go in for all that fuss here."

Jaap thought better of smiling. Fuss was exactly what Pfeiffer went in for. The commander—his actual rank was *Fregattenkapitän*, but he preferred its Royal Navy equivalent—was known to be a rabid colonialist, and if he couldn't have his globe-spanning empire, he would have all the trappings anyway.

"Thank you for your letter, Commander," Jaap said. "I'm glad you found my report satisfactory. I was hoping today to request your counsel on the possibility of mounting another operation along similar lines. In fact, as luck would have it, an American delegation has just—"

"You know, Saxo, I was up in Hamburg the other day. Kapitän Wichmann asked after you. Sorry, I had to tell him, haven't seen hide nor hair of him since he trotted off to Berlin."

Jaap did smile now. He'd just won a bet with himself—a wager that he couldn't get through all four of the sentences he'd prepared as an opening salvo. "My time in Berlin was quite fruitful, I believe, Commander. Especially with regard to our friend at the Interior Ministry."

"Interior Ministry." Pfeiffer chewed the words like a chunk of bone he'd found in his sauerbraten. "Intriguers. Whisperers. Conspirators. Slippery two-faced bastards in evening jackets, the lot of them."

It was no use suggesting that in Intelligence, intrigue and conspiracy were roughly like soil and water, basic elements from which all else grew. Pfeiffer had his own style of doing things, and it was hard to argue (though Jaap would have done so) that his methods weren't fabulously successful. Nest Bremen was the largest and most active of the Abwehr's several dozen outposts. It had the biggest staff and the greatest number of field agents. Though it was nominally a suboffice run out of Hamburg, the two station chiefs, Wichmann and Pfeiffer, barely spoke a common tongue, and so a de facto division of responsibility had evolved: Hamburg would keep its eye on the traditional enemy, Great Britain, while Bremen could throw history to the wind and go after—that loathsome phrase again—the American target.

But the real difference, in Jaap's view, was that Wichmann was too much of an old-blood conservative to feel much real animus toward the Brits, with their royalty and lovely harbors and schoolboy honor. Pfeiffer, in contrast, was a fanatic—not a Nazi but strictly nationalistic. He despised the Yanks and wanted them to know it. And so he dispatched agents in waves, practically recruiting them off the streets and sending them over the wire with a few weeks' training, an English phrasebook and orders to blow up the White House. The whole thing was a fiasco—there were probably FBI agents building their careers on it, netting Pfeiffer's men like shoals of cod—but nobody noticed this, because outside of Nest Bremen no one took the American target seriously.

"According to information I've recently received, Commander . . ." Jaap let this float for a moment like a fly over water, fishing imagery having somehow gotten into his head. "The American delegation that just landed includes a senator who is in support of healthy relations with Germany. And he's brought at least one member of his staff, a gentleman known to be fond of drink. As well as a son, an eighteen-year-old."

"Honey trap!" Pfeiffer exclaimed, slapping the tall desk. "That's what you're thinking, isn't it?"

"Not necessarily, Commander. Though I do believe it's possible these people might have useful knowledge to impart, given the proper . . . enticement. In particular, I hope they might be able to shed some light on the fate of our earlier operation, the one involving a young Wehrmacht officer. But beyond that, and seeing that the other operation may not have achieved its objectives, I was contemplating, so to speak, a different sort of dangle. This one aimed at the senator personally. Our friend at Interior will make the approach, while we provide the *Blattmusik*. Better us than the Tirpitzufer, I think."

He'd rigged this with every hook he could think of. The dark hint of failure. The chance to upstage the command center in Berlin. A dash of clandestine flavoring with "sheet music," the trade term for documents, especially fake ones, to be fed deliberately to an enemy. As it turned out, none of that may have been necessary.

"I don't much care for honey traps," Pfeiffer mused, as though his attention had run aground on that point and gone no further. "But there's no denying they can yield solid intelligence. I'd leave the boy out of it. Well, unless there's no luck with the others. Keep me posted. I should say, keep me *current* on this one. I won't be waiting months for your report this time."

"Understood, Commander. Thank you, sir." He considered snapping to attention and offering a salute, but Pfeiffer was already waving him out. He made for the doorway.

"Oh, Jaap?"

He halted at this unexpected use of his Christian name. Pfeiffer wasn't normally given to informality.

"I'm sorry about your man, the young officer you sent to Washington. We'll find out what happened to him; then we'll do something about it. Field agents are one thing, but this was a colleague. One of us. We'll do right by him, if we can."

"Yes, we will," said Jaap—saluting, this time.

ONE THINKS OF DYING HEROICALLY

BREMEN, ÖSTLICHE VORSTADT AND THE RIVER WESER: 24 MAY

The Resistance woman was called Anna. Her name was Hanna, but that sounded Jewish and made people look at you closely, note the dark hair and a certain—what?—*Mediterranean* quality about your features. But if you said Anna and put your hair in a knot, you reminded them of someone else, the singer in that movie, perhaps, or the pretty teacher at their children's *Grundschule*—someone, they just couldn't put their finger on it. But not a Jewess, and certainly not a cell leader in the Resistance living underground with false papers and a cyanide capsule disguised as a bead in your necklace.

So she was called Anna, and from here on, as an officer of the SOPADE, currently holding a loaded pistol, she was in charge. Let that be perfectly clear.

What was also clear to Oskar, an officer of the Wehrmacht on secondment to the Abwehr, was that he had a gun too, though he'd tucked it into his pocket. And he had a duty, a mission to complete. He studied Anna across the oil-polished expanse of Aunt Tilde's formal dining table and then looked past her to the old clock on the wall. Just past midnight: Tilde and Dr. Ruhmann had gone off to their rooms an hour ago, though Oskar doubted they were sleeping. As for the others . . . he moved his gaze around the table, wordlessly polling them. Lena seemed unimpressed, either by Anna or the pistol. She looked sick, exhausted. Clair had his head down, resting on folded arms—but his muscles were taut, his fingers twitchy.

Finally the prisoner, von Ewigholz, who didn't look or behave like one, despite being bandaged around the ribs and lashed to a dining chair with an electric cord (no one had been able to find a proper rope). His eyes were shut but he was obviously alert, taking in every word, sensing every movement around the table.

"All right," Oskar said to Anna. His cover identity, Stefan, the mildly political librarian, was wearing so thin he was tempted to shuck it. But maybe not just yet. "What will we do now? Where will we go?"

Anna stared at him—rather by default since no one else was looking back at her. Her gaze was fixed and hard, yet it struck Oskar as unfocused, or maybe focused on something beyond this room. She's lost, he thought. She had orders—a mission, like his own—and now everything's gone sideways. One of her comrades is dead, the other badly wounded. But worst of all—a nightmare, the thing she most dreaded—the SS has gotten involved.

Was Oskar reading her thoughts or was she reading his? Anna shook her head, as though to clear some obstruction, then swiveled her gun hand toward von Ewigholz and said, "First, we do away with *him*."

"No!" said Clair, lifting his head from the table. His face was flushed and his long hair matted. He might or might not have known the dark connotation of the verb *umbringen*, but a pointed gun spoke for itself. "You're not going to do anything else to him. He's been . . . very patient with me. Very kind, actually."

Anna made a dismissive sound, a little snort. *Kind? An SS man?*

"You already shot him," said Clair. "Isn't that enough? Just leave him here with me, and you all go on with your . . . whatever it is you're doing. Your little conspiracy. Go on! I won't tell anything to anyone, I promise. This is all so completely insane I wouldn't know where to start. I'm just here for a . . . a fucking *summer camp*."

Oskar couldn't tell if Anna understood. Enough, apparently.

"You will come with us," she told Clair.

"Well, in that case . . ."

Everyone—Lena, Clair, Anna, Oskar—was caught off guard. Von Ewigholz had opened his eyes but made no effort to move;

he addressed them calmly, reasonably, like an attorney explaining a point of law.

". . . I'm afraid you'll have to take me, too. I've pledged to accompany this young man and to protect him from harm until he reaches his destination, which is Ordensburg Vogelsang. I intend to fulfill that pledge—in fact, I cannot do otherwise; it's a matter of honor. So you may murder me, or leave me tied up here, but in that case you'll have to murder Mr. Townsend as well, or detain him indefinitely. Because when and if you ever do release him, he'll report your actions to his father, the senator, and that will bring, at the very least, discredit to your cause, as well as the wrath of the authorities upon everyone you've dragged into this criminal escapade. Aunt Tilde, do you want her to experience a Gestapo interrogation? Kindly Herr Doktor Ruhmann? So, you will take us both, me and Mr. Townsend, or you will kill us now. Go ahead, do it—just point the gun and shoot. Please aim better this time."

He stopped, finally, and sat looking smug, to the extent that he betrayed any emotion at all. Oskar felt one impulse to shoot the man himself and another to applaud him. Personally, he'd have been hard put to capture the full absurdity of this cock-up the SOPADE had made of a simple *Treff*, the most straightforward of operations. The SS man had summed it up pretty well.

"This does make a certain amount of sense," said Stefan Sinclair, the mild librarian. "But Lena and I—people are expecting us, you know. Maybe we should go it alone, and leave you"—looking at Anna now—"to manage the, ah, complications."

It was a delicate moment, and he hoped he'd judged it right. So many degrees of unknowing. He'd been blown as a Resistance operative but not, as far as he knew, as an Abwehr officer beneath that. If he could shake himself free of Anna, he could easily retreat to the Nest. Though his mission had failed, he had important information to pass along. There would be a second mission, and he would redeem himself.

Anna was staring at von Ewigholz, seeming at once grim and weary and tough. She had a mission as well. After what felt like a very long time, she shook her head. "I don't know what went wrong here. You brought the SS to a safe house—why do that? No, don't answer, I can't think now. Maybe there is a reason, maybe we were betrayed somewhere else along the line. We'll find out eventually. The first thing is to get somewhere safe. Away from here. Tonight. We'll leave Alex in Dr. Ruhmann's care. Everyone else will get on the boat."

The boat? Oskar felt the pocketed Walther in his hand, weighing it like a stone on some unfortunately literal scale of destiny.

He could walk out of here. God knows what he'd leave behind him, but no one could stop him if he decided to leave right now. He glanced at the people around the table and each one was another stone, piling up on the scale and tipping it in the other direction. He'd never gone along with Nietzsche, back in *Gymnasium*. There seemed to be so much more in life than the Will, the Self.

"Where's the boat, and how do we get there?" he said. "Is there room enough?" His cover was slipping again, but maybe no one would notice.

"We walk," Anna told him. "It's not far. There's room—I think. Would you like to give me that gun?"

"I would not," Oskar said.

She actually smiled. It was almost a nice smile; you could glimpse the pretty schoolteacher she liked to be mistaken for. But Anna's teacher was no more real than Oskar's librarian. "Do you know how to use it, at least?"

"I do."

A short while later—having gagged von Ewigholz, freed him from the chair and relashed his hands behind his back—they left through the back door, making for the river.

It was what the English would call a narrow boat: long and low and nearly symmetrical, stern and bow closing into wedges meant to punch through the reeds and water grasses and cast-off debris that congested slow-moving inland waterways. For hundreds of years, vessels quite like this one had hauled cargo and passengers between cities and towns throughout Europe. But over time the roads got better and safer, and the railways came in, and finally the high-speed motorways, so by now the notion of traveling by riverboat was, frankly, not a serious option. No, it was something you might persuade tourists to pay for—*Come see Old Germany as your ancestors did!*—but beyond that, what was the point? Even in the old river towns, people seldom gave these boats a second thought.

Which, of course, made this mode of travel perfect. Oskar was impressed. Not enough to change his opinion of the SOPADE as a bunch of hopeless amateurs, but you had to give them credit. They knew how to make themselves invisible. They'd done it in 1933, when Hitler got himself named chancellor and Germany held its breath, but the Socialists never took to the streets; indeed, they all but vanished from sight. *Abwarten ihrer Zeit* was the phrase you heard—"awaiting their time." And from what Oskar could tell, they still were, five years on. Perhaps their day would come, and perhaps there'd still be a Germany when it did.

There were two boatmen, evidently a father and son, the latter still school-aged though there was nothing of the classroom about him. Both were lumpen, coal-smeared, slow-moving types—a good match for this boat and for the Weser itself as it uncoiled from deep in the heartland. They emerged from the pilothouse at the stern as the passengers approached, standing by an open hatch that gave access by a steep ladder to the compartments below. Their faces, characteristically expressionless, grew alarmed when von Ewigholz came into the faint halo of the boat's kerosene lanterns, moving stiffly and favoring his wounded side. They'd removed his hat and covered his uniform with a cloak, but he nonetheless made a terrifying impression: chiseled alabaster features, white-blond hair, eyes both blue and red, like ice crystals floating in blood.

"It's all right," Anna told them. "This man is our prisoner."

Scarcely reassured, the boatmen drew back and, after the others had descended, left it to Oskar to wrestle von Ewigholz through the hatch and down the ladder into a cabin that apparently served for both dining and sleeping. It was lit by two more lanterns and, in a nod to domesticity, furnished with a pair of old-fashioned armchairs that were screwed to the floor near a small potbellied stove, on either side of a filthy Persian rug. When von Ewigholz had regained his balance, Oskar let him go, and they both stood for a moment looking up at the older boatman through the open hatch.

"What is your vessel called?" said von Ewigholz.

They were all surprised, except perhaps for the boatman, who smiled with pride or satisfaction or, possibly, appreciation of such good manners. He said, "She's called *Eulenspiegel*, and you're all—"

If he'd been about to add "welcome aboard," he thought better of it and drew back out of sight. They could hear him conferring quietly with his son before the hatch thumped down and a metal fitting clanked into place. Oskar felt a stab of claustrophobia, but on inspection this was an ordinary door latch, accessible from either side. If not quite trapped, they weren't really free—a feeling that by now was familiar.

Incredibly, it was possible to sleep. There were four bunks, two forward and two aft, in little compartments separated from the main cabin by sliding doors. Clair and von Ewigholz were assigned to one, Oskar to the other, while the two women took turns on watch so there would always be somebody guarding the prisoner. Oskar volunteered to stand a shift, but Anna explained that this was now a SOPADE operation and he would do as he was told, that he should be thankful they'd let him keep the Walther. And so he was. Though he suspected that, from their point of view, it would turn out to be a mistake.

The berthing compartment was efficiently arranged so as to be just large enough for its purpose with not an inch of wasted space. He admired the ingenious craftsmanship of its tiny closets, its wash-stand with a night pot on a sliding tray beneath, cabinets nested into the slanting side panels, bedside shelves with a finely worked railing to keep the books from sliding off. There was enough light through the open door to make out a few titles, and God help the psychoana-lyst hunting for an underlying pattern among Hegel's biography of Jesus, Twain's *Leben auf dem Mississippi*, *Baedeker Deutschland* (1913), *Der grosse Gatsby*, *Emil und die Detektive*, a collection of folk songs, a guide to Hannoverian cuisine, *Der Steppenwolf*, and *Till Eulenspiegel*, *der bekannteste Narr der Welt.* Oskar chose the starboard bunk and opened the small port to admit a puff of cool night air, the odors of brine and diesel, and the intermittent clang of a bell buoy. He hoped to doze off for an hour or two, until first light—maybe he'd see things more clearly then.

When he opened his eyes, it was midmorning and Lena was asleep in the neighboring bunk. The boat's engine throbbed somewhere beneath him. Lena lay on her side facing him, an elongated disk of sunlight lapping over her shoulder and gilding stray wisps of hair like new-spun filaments in a fairy tale. The loveliness ran through him as sharp and fast as an arrow. He almost gasped. Waking had never come as such a shock, even when it had been occasioned by bugles and accompanied by the shouts of a drill sergeant. He tried to sit up but had gotten tangled somehow in his own clothing—or no, it was a thin blanket someone, he supposed Lena, had drawn over him as he slept. He squirmed free, feeling stupid and confused. His body had doubled in weight, it seemed. The ceiling boards were high enough for a man of Oskar's height to stand upright, but he managed to knock his head, hard, against a narrow beam that ran down the center, amidships. He groaned and caught himself as the boat lurched to port, then stepped toward the doorway. Before leaving he took a final look at Lena, who hadn't stirred.

Out in the main cabin he found Anna and Clair occupying the two chairs—she with the gun in her lap, nestled there comfortingly like a skein of yarn, the boy twisted sideways with his legs over an armrest, looking peevish.

"She won't let me go out on deck," Clair said, as though he'd been waiting a long while for someone with whom to lodge this complaint. "It's a beautiful day, and I just have to *sit* here. What's the point? So what if somebody sees me? It's a *boat.* I'm a *passenger.* If anyone stares, I'll just *wave.* What could be more innocent?"

Anna gave Oskar a look that—as with all the rest, now that he thought about it—seemed to contain elements of both collusion and challenge. He reckoned that at some point he and Anna were going to have an interesting conversation, but this wasn't the time for it. He tried to think of how best to answer Clair, whose objections seemed reasonable enough. Could he explain to this young

American that, yes, it would seem entirely innocent, and that was exactly the problem? That innocence in Germany today was a rare and potentially fatal affliction? But that, lucky for Clair, he was surrounded by people who'd become immune to it?

"Just wait a while," he said. "There are some books in here you can read."

"I can't even *read* German."

Anna laughed. *"Das ist absolut nicht richtig von dir."*

"I don't speak German, either, but I know that wasn't nice."

"She does have a point, though," said Oskar, who suspected that Clair's incomprehension was at least partly tactical.

The boy gave him a funny sort of smile, not unlike a game player's: that move's clever, but you'll get nothing out of it.

Anna stood up. She'd had enough of this, and there was other business to get on with. She gestured toward the second berthing compartment, whose door had been left slightly ajar. "You need to look in on him," she said. "I'm worried something's the matter. With the wound or . . . I don't know. Just have a look."

Oskar had barely entered the other room before Clair elbowed past him. "What did she say? *Angst über* what?"

The compartment was dark but Oskar, obliged to look over Clair's interposed shoulder, could see sweat gleaming on von Ewigholz's forehead. The air was close and too warm, and there was a strange smell, sickly and unpleasant. He slid back the curtain on the opposite side and opened the window as far as it would go. When he turned around, the SS man had opened his eyes and was frowning up at Clair, who was hovering just out of reach, anxious as a cat.

"Let me—" Oskar pushed closer, kneeling close to the bunk. Somebody—Clair? surely not Anna—had untied von Ewigholz's arms and removed his uniform jacket. Blood had soaked through the bandages into the shirt, already torn and stained from the shooting, and Oskar could see now that it had also run down into the musty bedding. The wound must have reopened. He caught the man's eye—sharp as ever, though glazed, maybe feverish.

"What do you think?" von Ewigholz asked.

Oskar thought first that this was a remarkable question, not only for the absolutely calm voice but also for how it seemed to address

Oskar personally—not Stefan Sinclair or some anonymous enemy but a fellow German officer, a comrade even, who wouldn't lie to him under these circumstances.

His second thought, which he spoke aloud, was "I'll need to look under the bandage."

Von Ewigholz nodded and tried to shift his body to allow better access to the wound, grunting in what Oskar imagined must be considerable pain. The bandage was thick and had been skillfully applied; Oskar hated to mess with it. His training in battlefield medicine did not go very far.

He called out to Anna in the main compartment: "Go see if they've got rubbing alcohol, or any kind of liquor, and first-aid supplies. They must have." When she'd gone, he turned to Clair. Now distraught, nearly frantic, he needed a task: to be useful, to help. "What kind of clothing have you got?"

Clair stared back at him, his gaze so perplexed that Oskar wondered if he'd spoken in German by mistake. Then the boy seemed to get it—fresh bandages—and stood to open the closet where his bags were stored. Oskar ran a hand over the prisoner's forehead. Warm and wet, but not blazing as you'd expect if the wound had gone septic. Von Ewigholz was watching him closely, and for an instant Oskar had an uncanny feeling that the man was able to read his thoughts, or at least to track them by his changing expression. The two of them stayed like that, eyes locked, mutually calculating, until Anna came thumping down the ladder carrying bottles of various colors and shapes, the younger boatman trailing behind like an ominous, mumbling shadow.

"All right," Oskar said, "let's see what we've got."

The wound was less hideous than other bullet wounds Oskar had seen—but most of those had been in photographs, the sole exception being the result of an accidental discharge that had carried off the top of a cadet's head while he was cleaning a Mauser. This was really two wounds in one: the bullet had entered just under the lowest rib and exited a few inches away, to the rear and farther to the side. No vital organs were involved, and Dr. Ruhmann had done a good, workmanlike job with the closing and stitching. But the patient hadn't been allowed to keep still long enough for the tissue to seal, and Oskar could see, once he'd swabbed the blood away, where the sutures had been strained, and a couple had torn away completely. The surrounding flesh was bruised and swollen—but again, to Oskar's eye, not alarmingly so.

"How bad?" said von Ewigholz.

"Not so bad," said Oskar, "though it needs cleaning. And some of the stitches—"

Von Ewigholz nodded. "I'll do it myself, if you like."

Oskar shook his head. "Better let me. I expect it will hurt."

"Ha!" he said, with a grim, stoic smile.

The war-movie hero, thought Oskar. And his name is Hagen, after all. Chanting poetry while he bleeds to death.

Anna came closer, holding out a glass she'd half-filled with brownish liquid. "I don't know what this is, maybe rum," she said to the SS officer. "Don't sailors drink rum? Anyway, you better have it. I'm not sure this one knows what he's doing."

Von Ewigholz held the glass with both hands and, to avoid sitting up, poured the contents into his mouth. "None of you," he said, choking it down, "knows what you're doing."

Anna took the glass back, gave him a cursory glare and left the compartment. In her place loomed the young boatman, proffering a metal case whose scarlet cross sign had faded to the color of rust.

"Just put it there," said Oskar, pointing to a spot on the floor. "I'll call you if I need help. Now," he told von Ewigholz, "try to keep still."

The SS man nodded and watched with what seemed a detached sort of interest as Oskar sorted through the medical supplies, picking out a needle and suture thread that was stiffened with age. "Were you trained for this?"

"Not much," said Oskar.

"It's the same with us." Von Ewigholz lay back, staring reflectively at the overhead decking. "It's odd, but one doesn't think of getting hurt, not in our service. One thinks of dying heroically."

You may get your chance, Oskar thought. We all may. But not this morning.

THE VAMPIRE DID NOT DISAPPOINT

BERLIN, KREUZBERG: THAT EVENING

The Cabaret Trigilaw was already crowded, with an hour yet to go before midnight. Standartenführer Kohlwasser had chosen a table near the front but off to one side, allowing a close view of the stage and concealed from the prurient eyes of other patrons by a miniature jungle of potted palms and a climbing *Monstera deliciosa*—"delicious monster," a perfect emblem for this place. Kohlwasser, having given the matter some thought and changed his mind twice, had elected to come in civilian clothes: a suit of nappy beige linen, tailored in what he'd been assured was the au courant New York style, not the boring cut they wore in Washington. He shared few beliefs with the poison dwarf Goebbels, but he did agree about the power of conveying a message by using symbolism—and the message he wished to give his American guests was: Here is Berlin! Here is the new Rome, the seat of an empire that will rule from the Baltic to the Mediterranean, from the Pyrenees to the Carpathians and, who knows, maybe someday the Urals. And this, gentlemen, is how we enjoy ourselves in the new Rome, how we drink and dance and screw—as though there will be no regrets for the next thousand years.

Ordinarily, yes, you would wear the black tunic for that sort of thing. But with Americans, you just didn't know. How did they feel about uniforms with death's-heads and lightning runes? Did such things offend their Christian sensitivities or their admiration of the lone cowhand in his white hat? You couldn't be sure. But you did know that after a shoot-out and a mumbled prayer, they liked to visit the saloon. So here we are, gentlemen: I give you the Cabaret Trigilaw, the greatest saloon in the entire world!

His guests were late, but he'd expected that. And at last here they came, stumbling toward him, their eyes still adjusting—five of them, six if you counted the journalist Greimer. Kohlwasser sucked his tongue in distaste, but such was the business; you couldn't be too choosy about collaborators, usefulness being the only metric that mattered. Yes, over here, see what a good table I've reserved for you! The very best! The Americans were half-drunk already, perhaps a little more than half. Greimer nudged them along like an irascible hound put in charge of cloddish sheep. Catching Kohlwasser's eye, he signaled, by tipping his head, which of the new arrivals was of particular interest. Kohlwasser—on his feet now, arms extended, welcoming everyone, *yes, yes!*—gave a quick nod back, but as it happened, this tip was unnecessary. He'd recognized his man from the surveillance photographs, and at this range there was no mistaking the burly, rubicund Toby Lugan.

"So happy you could make it," Kohlwasser said once his guests had reached the table. He indicated a chair next to his own and Lugan accepted, dropping his full weight onto it with such force that Kohlwasser wondered if this was a test. Let's see what your German chairs are made of! In any case, the chair didn't splinter, the other Yanks distributed themselves and Greimer was left at the distant end alone, which appeared to suit him well enough. He could see everything from there and even scribble secret notes or make use of the miniature camera Kohlwasser had provided, to his boundless and childish delight. Here, see, it hides just beneath your lapel, the lens peeks through the buttonhole, you work the shutter by pressing your party pin. Incredible!

"Who's the singer?" Lugan said, louder than was required with his mouth so very close to the *Standartenführer's* ear.

A curious thing: until that moment, Kohlwasser hadn't been conscious of any singer or music or, indeed, anything at all outside the tunnel of his attention. It was a wonderful thing, his ability to focus, to stare down the tunnel at some perplexing object until it wilted under his gaze, laying bare whatever tawdry mysteries it had been concealing. But at times this gift was inconvenient.

"This singer, she's a nobody," he told Lugan. "The real talent comes on later. Look, here's a waiter, what shall we have to drink? Is anyone hungry? How about oysters and champagne? And maybe some company—why not have some girls sent over? What do you say?"

He looked at Lugan, but instead of boozy agreement he found . . . impatience? The jowls drawn tight in annoyance? Or was it only discomfort, the Irish Catholic (per his background file) feeling wrong-footed in a place like the Trigilaw? Too late to fret about that now. The game was on, the players fielded, the crowd already panting with excitement. And the music—now that he was hearing it, what a calamity it was, someone's idea of naughty wit: take a boyish ditty, a Pathfinders' hiking song, *Here we go up the mountain, tra-la-la,* and thrust it into the painted mouth of an all-but-naked chanteuse —what mountain could she be thinking of, *meine Herren*? Some of the Americans—petty salesmen, by the look of them, submanagers at a kitchen-appliance store—found this amusing indeed, but not Lugan. The minority counsel of the German Affairs Subcommittee had not crossed a fucking ocean for this. He looked annoyed, and no wonder.

Kohlwasser touched him lightly on a muscled forearm. When Lugan looked, he gave him a faint nod that meant *Watch this.* Then he raised his other hand, the index finger pointing at the ceiling, and made a little circle there, like he was stirring something upside down.

The owner materialized like the evil spirit he was. A short, oily man in expensive clothes, Glewitz smoothed an emerald cravat with one hand while resting the other on the back of Kohlwasser's chair. *"Herr Standartenführer,"* he purred, lowering his head reverently. "How can I make your visit more enjoyable?"

"You can strangle that singer, for a start. Who else have you got lined up for tonight? These gentlemen have come all the way from America."

"Ah, indeed?" Glewitz made a show of astonishment and switched to English, which was somehow more obscene than his German. "So very far, just to visit our little nightclub here? Well, we must show you something extraordinary! I wonder . . . but no, never—or perhaps? Oh my!" He screwed up his face as though striving to fend off an idea so diabolical he might die from uttering it aloud. Shifting his head to a spot midway between Kohlwasser and Lugan—whom he understood, by instinct, to be the object of tonight's courtship—he whispered, "Do you think . . . *der Vampir?*"

"Yes," said Kohlwasser. "I think that will do nicely."

Glewitz straightened, tugged at his cravat, muttered under his breath and finally—perhaps overdoing it—crossed himself. "I shall do it, then. I shall . . . awaken him. It may take some time." Turning crisply to face Lugan, his tone now solicitous, he said, "May I recommend, sir, something stronger than champagne. We have some very fine whiskeys, very long in the cask, that I might—"

Lugan surprised them by laughing, his head tossed back, his stomach quaking. They were putting on a show for him, and he was enjoying it. *"Sehr gut, mein kleiner Freund,"* he said, fluidly but with a Boston burr. *"Whiskey und Vampir. Geht's gut!"*

Glewitz pulled out a huge handkerchief—emerald to match the cravat—and wiped his oily brow, and it seemed to Kohlwasser this was not merely for effect. Then he scurried off to wake the vampire while the band launched into a medley of inoffensive dance tunes. A waiter arrived with Irish whiskey, or at least something approximately the right color in a bottle labeled Tullamore Dew. Lugan splashed it into a pair of glasses, one for himself and one for Kohlwasser. He drained it back and poured another, sliding his chair uncomfortably close.

"Tell me what you know," he said, "about a little shit named Erwin Kaspar."

Interrogation was in Kohlwasser's line of work, and he believed he was good at it. He prepared himself in advance, drew up a list of questions, made notes in anticipation of likely responses—the first would be a lie, followed by an effort at misdirection, followed by lies that grew progressively worse, desperate lies, lies that pleaded and bargained and wantonly sobbed for credence. And in the end, when there was nothing left: the truth.

But all that depended on a set of circumstances that, in the normal order of things, was easily arranged: that Kohlwasser would be the person asking the questions, not the one answering them.

He'd chosen tonight's venue on the assumption—a safe one, surely—that in a place like the Trigilaw, he'd enjoy a home-court advantage. He'd chosen Greimer to make the dangle on the even safer assumption that it would put Lugan at ease. People like Greimer, journalists of shaggy mien and adjustable ethics, starved for readership, ever scrabbling for the mythic Big Scoop—Lugan must encounter them every day. When a man like Greimer shows up dropping hints about a source in the Security Service, the holy Sicherheitsdienst, you don't necessarily believe him—not without some tangible proof, some scrap of paper with a red stamp on it, which Kohlwasser had provided—but neither do you think too hard about it. You don't suspect a trap. Men like Greimer don't lay traps; they lick at whatever's left in them when the trapping's done.

Why, then, did Kohlwasser find himself being asked a question like this, in a tone like this, before he'd managed to pose a single question of his own?

Well, all right. So here we are.

"Erwin Kaspar," he repeated. "Should I recognize this name? Is this someone you'd like me to check on for you? Here, let me write it down."

He made to reach for a notepad in his pocket, but Lugan stopped him with a large paw on his wrist.

"Have a drink, Helmut," the man said. "I think we have some talking to do."

It was fascinating, actually. How did Lugan know his first name? *Here is a man who knows things*—message received. Kohlwasser raised his glass cautiously; the whiskey might or might not have been Irish, but it wasn't so bad. When he took a second, more liberal swallow, Lugan looked satisfied. He eased off somewhat, settling back in his chair and showing a momentary interest in what the band was up to. American popular music, Kohlwasser guessed. Typical Glewitz pandering. He looks at a table of Yankee tourists and sees dollar signs in bad suits.

"This fellow Kaspar," Lugan said conversationally, "he comes up to me one evening a few months back. Right off the boat, or so I gathered. But here he is, smack in the middle of Embassy Row, sticking out like a debutante at a hookers' convention. Might as well've sewn a big *S* on his back. Cover story about a trade mission, pretty shabby work, not up to your usual standards of fine German spycraft."

Kohlwasser almost rose to this but demurred. This was good, the man was talking now; he understood that in this sort of business, there must be an exchange.

"Says to me he's got some information, but it's very sensitive. Can't hand it over to just anyone. Says he's hoping to contact *certain parties in our government.* Who the hell's he talking about? And what kind of information?"

"That would have been my question, Mr. Lugan. Precisely that. You must have asked him, I should imagine?"

"Didn't even have to ask him. He was dying to tell me how big this was. Only, I don't think he knew the answer himself. Not really. I think he was an errand boy. All they'd given him was a little teaser, a little something to whet my appetite. Something like—"

And in one big hand, like a magic trick, a sheet of paper appeared, the same paper Kohlwasser had slipped Greimer several hours earlier.

"I'll tell you the truth," Lugan said, letting it fall to the table, open and face-up, the header—BÜRO DES REICHSFÜHRERS-SS—blaring like a headline. "The truth is, you people are making me feel like I'm a hound dog or something. Toss a little red meat my way and expect I'll slaver all over it. And you know what—I hate to admit this, but it worked the first time. I snapped it right up and trotted over to a big shot's house with it, all proud of myself. And then what happened? I'll tell you: not a damn thing. There was no follow-up. Young Kaspar disappeared, and whatever he wanted to tell me, or give me, or club me over the head with, I never heard another peep about it. Tried to get back in touch, but it was funny: nobody'd seen him around. Must've gone back to Germany—sorry, sucker. I tell you, I felt like some kind of idiot. That doesn't happen to me very often, and I don't care much for it."

Lugan poured himself another drink but for a few moments only stared into it.

"How can I help you, Mr. Lugan?" Kohlwasser said. "What did you come here for tonight?"

"What did I come here for." The veins on the man's neck were as fat and lively as baby snakes. "I'll tell you what I came here for. I'd like to know what's going on with you people. It's my job, you understand that? I work for the Senate German Affairs Subcommittee, and this big shot I mentioned, he's the ranking member, if that means anything to you. It's our business to know what's happening over here and how that affects the relations between our two countries. And we're trying to do our jobs properly, but you people aren't making it easy. Leaking secret military documents—okay, fine, we'll take it, or we'll go steal it ourselves, but please, don't go drawing *us* into whatever little intrigues you've got going on over here. Left hand, right hand, we don't know what the fuck we're shaking. And now here you are tonight, with some new pot on the stove. I'm not interested, *Standartenführer.* And what the *hell* is in this bottle?"

Kohlwasser had made a decision, about halfway through Lugan's impassioned diatribe, and it was to let the man talk. He could sift the real message from all the attendant bluster later on. For now, he'd listen politely. He waited until he was fairly sure the man was finished, for the time being; then he said, "As it happens, Mr. Lugan, I'm eager to learn more about this young Kaspar myself. From what you've told me, and from what I've been able to pick up on my side, I believe he was likely an agent provocateur. What I'd like to know is, on whose behalf? Who sent him to Washington? What were they hoping to accomplish?"

Lugan stared at him. His eyes were bleary with drink, but Kohlwasser sensed that this was the man's normal operating condition. He was that dangerous creature, an intelligent brute. And sure enough, when he spoke again, he came right to the key point:

"What *you've* been able to pick up *on your side*?" Lugan's jaw moved as though he were tasting the words. "So you're looking for Kaspar yourselves."

"Myself, Mr. Lugan. In the singular. It seems we have, you and I, an interest in common. I believe this Kaspar, whoever he is, may lead us to something large and important—important to both our countries, possibly—and needless to say, I'll be happy to share with you whatever I'm able to discover. In consideration of our mutual interest. Between just the two of us. As I'm sure you'll do so as well, on your own part."

Lugan laughed. "That's a deal with the devil if I've ever heard one. I'm sorry to say, *Standartenführer*, I don't have a whole lot more to tell you. I just met him the one time. Then I saw him again on the boat."

Kohlwasser's heart, not usually a sensitive organ, missed a beat. "On the *boat*?"

"The boat, the ship—the *Robert Ley*. Wasn't sure it was him at first. There was something different, but the more I looked . . . it was our boy, all right. Had a couple of pals with him."

Kohlwasser couldn't help himself; the little notepad was already in his hands. "Did you recognize the other people? Had you seen them also before?"

"Look," said Lugan, "it's not my job to keep track of who rides around on German boats, is it? More in your line of work, I'd have thought."

"It is not in my—" Stopping too late, realizing Lugan was baiting him.

The American nearly smirked. "No, I expect you're above all that. Matters of state security and all. Well, as I say, that's all I've got for you."

"Perhaps, then," said Kohlwasser, pushing the point gently, but pushing it, "you might describe them for me, Mr. Lugan. Kaspar and his 'pals.' All the details you can remember."

The vampire did not disappoint. Kohlwasser had seen him in much better form, but the Americans weren't to know that. A remarkable thing about this performer was that his time in the concentration camp had, if anything, only sharpened the verisimilitude of his act. Whereas before he'd needed a thick layer of white caking to give him that fresh-from-the-casket look, now he came by it more naturally. His body lurched unnervingly across the stage or balanced perilously as though he might, at the faintest puff, collapse in a heap of bones and bloodless flesh. The only thing substantial about him was his floor-length black cloak, lined in crimson—and even that was decrepit.

He was a very good vampire. The best!

Glewitz was afraid of him. The little sneak avoided the stage while he was on, making a rare circuit of the rear tables, inquiring into the health of petty bureaucrats and uncouth party louts in their bulging uniforms and goggle-eyed out-of-towners enjoying a nibble of forbidden fruit—or not, what did Glewitz care; it was past midnight and the bouncers were turning people away.

Meanwhile, onstage, perspiring alone in the spotlight, safely out of his employer's line of vision, Stav the vampire had wrapped up his opening shtick, delivered a few ominous messages to random members of the audience and now stood trembling in an unfathomable inner crisis of self-loathing and opiate withdrawal, hoping against hope for inspiration. Not having expected to be called out so early, he hadn't had time to make his usual surreptitious survey of the crowd, so he was winging it—badly, he feared. So far it seemed no one had noticed—only the band and the whores working the tables—but Stav had a feeling, a terrible sick feeling, that some reckoning was at hand.

And there was another thing. Something at table 4, the one behind the palm trees, kept tugging at his attention. Like a fly buzzing there, at the corner of his vision. He kept batting it away—literally so, to his shame, swatting at the thin air with a trembling hand—and after a while, even a crowd as thick and drunk as this one would notice something like that. Now he swatted again, and a few people laughed. Again, and the laughter spread more widely. Stav smiled back. It wasn't what he was hoping for, but he could work with it. He raised his hand one more time, waggling his fingers playfully to titters from back in the room—and the world dropped out from underneath him.

Stav was buzzing now: he'd become the very fly he'd been batting away at. He looked down through clouds of cigarette smoke at table 4, which was refracted into thousands of tiny facets by his fly eyes. The people sitting at the table were surprisingly cowlike. One of them was a bull, and another was perhaps a goat or something goatish. Oh yes, Stav recognized that one; it wasn't a goat but a devil, the cause of all his personal torment. The others were just cows, and the noises they made were the ordinary mooing and farting. The bull was louder and larger and appeared somehow out of place. In fact, now that Stav looked more closely, trying to squeeze the thousand facets into a singular image, he was pretty certain the bull was Death himself. Evidently he put this realization into words, because suddenly other voices were repeating it—*the bull is death*, moo, fart, *what does he mean the bull is death?*—and at that Stav flew right off the stage and out of the Trigilaw, and if there is any more to tell of him, you will not find it here.

BE CAREFUL ABOUT BREATHING

Two hours past dawn on its third day out of Bremen, navigating a wide southward bend of the river, the *Eulenspiegel* passed through the small city of Hameln, where a festival was about to get under way. From the river, with the old city hulking in medieval slumber above, they watched the preparations along a cobbled waterfront promenade: horses being draped in colored ribbons, carts spilling over with cut flowers, a purple canopy being stretched between four tall poles, a bishop sipping coffee on a papier-mâché throne surrounded by acolytes, sleepy children in fancy spring clothes being spoiled with a tray of sweets, their faces smeared with jam, a quartet of horsemen dressed as knights smoking and laughing while grooms fussed over their mounts, painters adding the final curling adornments to opposite ends of a streetwide banner proclaiming HIMMELFAHRT 1938.

Ascension Day. Oskar's mental calendar clicked over. Spring was turning to summer. History was on the march, even if here, at the center of Germany, time seemed to have stopped or, rather, to be circling like the movements of a lovely Schwarzwald clock.

Oskar had been to Hameln before. Twice, in fact: first as a child on vacation with his family, a day's excursion to the home of the famous rat catcher. They'd admired the statue in the main square and heard the story recited, with musical accompaniment, by players on a balcony. Then they'd all toured the museum and Oskar had bought, with his own money, a little flute. Did he imagine himself playing it, dancing merrily through the streets, leading the other children on a delirious flight down old farm tracks into the mountains, the Weserbergland, where they would live without rules or lords or parents? He couldn't remember. He couldn't even recall whether, at that age, he'd understood that the story was meant to be a sad one.

The second visit he remembered more clearly. The summer after he'd started *Gymnasium*, he'd joined the dj.1.11—a very exclusive group; all his friends were envious—and Hameln was a dot on the map over which he pored night after night, preparing himself for his first Great Trek. The main destination was a mountain near Kassel, the Höhe Meissner, two days south of here by footpath: a legendary spot, all but sacred in the lore of the Movement, the site of a youth summit in 1913 and another planned for that year, 1929. It had been a magical time, not just for Oskar but—he was still pretty certain—for Germany itself, and for young people everywhere. The end of the Golden Twenties, the dawn of a brilliant future, a time of comradeship that crossed borders and languages, when everyone in Oskar's circle was quoting Rilke—stirring, if often murky, evocations of a *neue Seite*, which may have been a new leaf or a clean slate or a fresh direction but it was awfully alluring, whatever it was—and the impulse to wander, to plant your feet on new soil, had grown in everyone's mind to something like a holy beckoning. On that second visit, the story of the rat catcher turned upside down in Oskar's mind: now the children of Hameln were playing the tune and the grown-ups were dancing to it. Where would it lead them? No one seemed to worry about that. To someplace new—Rilke's *neue Seite*, a fresh page of history—and that was enough.

Strange to think of that now. Strange to be here, on a boat chugging slowly through Hameln on Ascension Day.

Clairborne was enthralled. The others had finally relented, to the extent of allowing the boy up on deck, even in daylight. It had become pretty clear that he wasn't going anywhere without von Ewigholz, and equally clear that the prisoner was going to need a doctor again, soon. The new stitches were holding, but the surrounding tissue was inflamed and a white discharge had appeared around the exit wound, his skin now hot to the touch. Oskar wanted to act sooner rather than later, but the SOPADE women, Lena and Anna, took no counsel and were intent on making it to some destination they didn't care to divulge. Not Hameln, evidently. And not Nienburg or Minden or Rintein or any of the promising-looking towns whose wharves the *Eulenspiegel* had all but brushed against on its long crawl upriver. Meanwhile the days were passing, Germany had entered its early summer glory and Oskar was growing mildly frantic. Clair, on the other hand, seemed to be enjoying himself.

"Did you see that? Look, there's a man on stilts, in raggedy clothes—he must be twelve feet tall! And he's chasing after that little guy dressed in red, like the devil."

Von Ewigholz lay beside him on the foredeck, his torso propped against the sloping bulkhead of the forward hold. Even from where Oskar stood, roughly amidships, he looked terrible. Clair either didn't notice or was laying on good cheer like a salve—ineffective though arguably touching, if one were susceptible to that. Oskar felt rather hard-hearted just now.

"That's the Trickster," von Ewigholz said, speaking in English—his voice as precise and modulated as ever, though quieter than usual. "He tempts fate but always eludes it. Parents don't approve of him. He teaches bad lessons, they say. He lies and steals and blames it always on someone else. But the people he steals from are greedy, and the people he lies to are liars themselves. Don't you have these stories in America?"

If he was in pain, which Oskar imagined he must be, he covered it well. Clair twitched beside him—anxious, helpless—but went on describing the scene along the waterfront as one might for the benefit of an elderly relative whose eyesight was in doubt.

"Now the band's tuning up. God, it's terrible! Do these people practice *at all*, or just come out when there's a parade or something? What are those things that look like little tubas? And yes"—he looked at von Ewigholz, the two of them sharing for that moment some mysterious sympathy—"we *do* have instruments like that in America. I just don't know what they're called."

Von Ewigholz laughed but then had to stop, pressing one hand against his wound, leaning on the other against the deck, as though he were trying to push himself back together.

Oskar turned away when Lena climbed partway out of the passenger cabin, holding a piece of paper on which someone had drawn, in charcoal, a rudimentary map. Oskar couldn't see it very well but it looked like a map of the river, with boxes to represent the town—some town, anyway—and lines crossing it to show bridges.

"Here," she said, reaching up to him.

Oskar took it and half-lifted her to the deck. She found footing there beside him, their faces closer than they'd been in days. Her skin was damp and pink from having been rubbed with water out of a small, zinc-coated tub that served their bathing needs, or mostly failed to. Her scent—of lard soap, kerosene, sweaty clothes, last night's cheese-and-onion soup, a splash of violet from a heart-shaped vial he'd seen in her bag—rose around her like a child's impression of a cloud, and Oskar indulged the fleeting illusion that they were alone in it. Lena indulged him too, for the instant until this peculiar intimacy faded. Then she took hold of a rail and pulled herself more upright and distant, braced against the gentle rocking of the *Eulenspiegel*, her hair loose in the May breeze.

Detached. That was the word he was looking for. Since coming back to Germany, she'd grown detached from him and also, he felt, from the previous editions of herself: the bright schoolgirl, the librarian, the suburban conspirator, the make-believe wife. In the latest edition she was Lena the revolutionary—a brave woman on a dangerous mission—and you could say this version was the best, the fullest expression of her character, the most exciting or revealing or rewarding. But the others had been pretty good, too. Oskar had been somewhat in love with one or more of them. Now he was unsure. *Live your cover*—he'd been trained in that, though it still gave him trouble. But *become your cover*—that was different. How did you invent a new persona and then somehow *be* that person?

"Come with me," Lena said. "We have to speak with the boatman. I'll need your help." She headed aft, running her hand along the railing.

So . . . was he afraid of her? Was it as simple as that? Oskar set off behind her, finding the boat's rocking gentle and predictable. He decided that, more likely, he and Lena had signed up for different causes and boarded different boats. Her journey was more adventurous, her footing less sure, so she needed to hang on. As for Oskar's journey, this wasn't even part of it, just an odd detour—a break, actually!—for as long as it took to see everyone safely to wherever they were going. Then back to the Nest, a new assignment, a new cover to live, real danger again. Anyway, what a beautiful day it was!

The older boatman waved Lena's map away. He'd planted himself on a tall stool bolted into the deck behind the ship's wheel, a large and apparently sensitive apparatus that he constantly adjusted with short, quick tugs one way or the other. "I need no map for this river," he said, in a sharp regional dialect that made his words sound clipped off—a good language, Oskar had always thought, for shouting in windstorms. It must have struck Lena as rude.

"But we should take the *right* bend in the river—look here, see where it divides? The *right*, not the *left*."

The boatman gave the wheel a jerk—to the left—that sent Oskar and Lena grabbing for support.

"It'll be fine," Oskar said. "Just leave the map with me. I'll stay back here—really, it'll be fine, don't worry."

Lena scowled but passed him the paper, crumpled now, and glanced toward the boatman, who was conspicuously ignoring them. "And Oskar, look here, there's a bridge, see? Someone will be waiting there. There may be a message. It could be in a package—something they'll drop over. This is very important. I need you to catch the package—can you do that?"

"They won't drop it," said the boatman, not bothering to look around. "It'll be on a rope and you just need to cut it loose. My boy can do it. Anybody could."

"I need you to catch it," Lena repeated, more loudly.

like that one," said the boatman, a while after she'd gone. "The other, well. I knew her dad."

"You knew her dad . . . from the SDP?"

"A good man, a brave man. Foolish. We're all fools, aren't we? Sailing head-on into this."

Oskar didn't think it wise, or necessary, to ask, *What?*

"That bridge is coming up soon," the boatman said. "You can take my knife. In fact, you'd better keep it."

Oskar weighed the knife in his hand: ugly but useful-looking, short and fat-handled, the blade whetted sharp as a razor. "Thanks," he said.

"Yes, sure."

Hameln fell behind them, the river widened, streets turned to tracks and then to cropland. The fields were plowed and sown and tended with such precision as to look like painted scenery. Even the hedgerows had been pruned to uniform dimensions, though they varied in texture and color: wild roses blooming in pendant white clusters with purple ladybells and yellow-eyed daisies peeking out from beneath them. The air was heavy with the smell of roses and manure and freshly cut hay. As the river neared a bend, the *Eulenspiegel* moved out into open water and then seemed to cut sharply to starboard to avoid an outcrop ahead—only now it entered a separate channel that Oskar hadn't noticed before, its opening masked by reeds and its narrow course squeezed from both sides by yellow-green sedges that squeaked against the old hull. The bridge came into view so suddenly it was almost overhead before he noticed it; there was no time to steer for the center or to maneuver at all. The figure on the bridge had to be waiting in just the right spot, and you had to have a knife ready in your hand, and the package had to be dangling *right there*, at the proper height for you to snag and cut it.

The fact that these circumstances coincided perfectly, leaving Oskar with a lump of black wool in his arms, was the single most impressive thing he'd experienced in his dealings with the SOPADE. It gave him the sort of breathless aesthetic pleasure he'd felt in watching a precise infantry operation reenacted with models on a miniature battlefield. You couldn't believe such a thing had actually happened, and yet it must have, because we were speaking German instead of French.

He was still breathing this heady air while Lena and then Anna, who appeared on deck just in time to snatch the parcel away, tore at the wool wrapping and started pulling out an odd assortment of things—A mask? And what's this, a stethoscope?—before discovering, at last, the document tucked in the center that made sense of it all.

Anna ran her eyes over it, blinked twice, then went through it again, more slowly. "We've got to get ready," she said. "There's trouble ahead."

"There always is," said the boatman.

About a dozen kilometers upstream, the Weser lost itself in marshland. There were dozens of islets, most only large enough to support a tangle of alders or a few birches with dull green leaves that snapped in the breeze like tiny pennants. Narrow channels ran between them, usually ending in bogs where runoff from the farms had mixed with rotting vegetation to create black, fertile and fetid soil that hosted a range of berries, brambles and fruit-bearing creepers with a ground cover of carnivorous sundews to feast on the insects they attracted. The main channel curled snakelike through this gurgling labyrinth; for a couple of hours, it felt like the boat was constantly turning in one direction or the other. The young boatman stood in the forepeak with a barge pole, though he seldom stuck it in, so apparently he was measuring the water depth or maybe just having fun. The sun grew hot and Oskar felt his nervousness blurring into lethargy—one turn after another, shadows sliding around over the deck like loose carpeting—until, in the middle of a slow, 180-degree swing to port, they came in sight of a village that seemed to be crouching there on the western bank, waiting to surprise them.

Down by the river was a little terminal that looked like a country railroad station. It had its own tidy wharf, a sign facing up- and downriver that read POLLE and a prominent flagstaff with an arm for running up signal pennants. Oskar guessed the stationkeeper was an old navy man; the two flags on display had been rigged smartly to catch the wind without wrapping around on themselves. From the main mast waved a bright red swastika, from the arm a four-squared black-and-yellow pennant that stood for the letter *L*.

L? It had been a couple of years since he'd had to memorize these things, but a few clung oddly to Oskar's mind, and *L*— or "Lima"— was one of them, because it meant *Stop your vessel immediately.*

That was bad enough, and to enforce the suggestion, two men emerged from the station house. One wore the uniform of a local policeman while the other, perhaps the old navy man Oskar had imagined, was dressed in proper *bürgerlich* fashion, all the way to a hat and waistcoat. They bade their time near the water's edge while the boatman throttled down and eased up to the wharf, his son at the bow snaring an eyebolt with the barge pole to drag the old vessel to a halt.

And so, without fanfare, the show was on. Oskar rose from his seat beside Lena on the quarterdeck—a pair of canvas chairs, rarely used, having been dragged out for stage dressing—and faced the two men on the shore with a half-smiling, half-impatient look he'd rehearsed in front of the polished nickel plate that passed for a mirror. "What's all this?" he demanded, drawing on all of Stefan Sinclair's meek imperiousness. (*Why is this book two weeks overdue?*) "I don't believe a stop was scheduled here. Already we're running late. We paid full fare, right through to Bad Karlshafen."

The policeman took this badly—a challenge to his authority— but the stationmaster just tipped his hat and said courteously, "Good morning, sir, good morning, *gnädige Frau.*" Casting a dark eye back toward the stern, he called, "Good morning, Herr Tiller."

The boatman muttered, his words unclear but his annoyance unmistakable.

Tiller, thought Oskar, seized by this irrelevance. *Till Eulenspiegel.* A boat named after a wise fool, a fairy-tale trickster.

"I'm afraid we need to search your vessel, Tiller," said the stationmaster. "There was some trouble in Bremen, the police are looking—"

Now the policeman interjected himself: "May I see your papers, please? And, Tiller, get all your crew and passengers on deck now. Everyone! This is no joke."

The old boatman strolled forward from the pilothouse, as though curiosity had overcome his aversion to authority. "No joke—well, I should hope it isn't. And what crew? It's just me and Josef, same as ever, you know that. As to the passengers, well . . ."

Oskar had never seen anyone who so obviously had something to hide. He lowered his cap, wiped his mustache, shuffled indecisively and finally declared, "There are no other passengers! What do you think I'm running here, a ferry service? There's Herr and Frau Sinclair, just back from America—they've paid the full fare, you heard him yourself! Now look at their papers and go back to polishing your paperweights. If you're searching for criminals, there's a coal merchant in Minden I can tell you about."

The policeman was having none of this. Summoning the dignity of his office, he charged the quarterdeck and brushed past Oskar and Lena, making straight for the hatch leading down to the main cabin. Oskar got the impression he'd had dealings before with old Tiller and wouldn't trust him to count the fingers on his own hand. The stationmaster followed, perhaps worried that he might miss something. Lena added her own bit to the confusion by tugging at the policeman's coat sleeve, waving her travel papers at him, insisting that he examine them immediately. The whole performance peaked naturally when the hatch opened of its own accord, a second before the policeman could yank it open himself—and there stood Anna, wearing a nurse's cap and a hospital face mask over what Oskar expected was the world's most affronted scowl.

She came slowly up the ladder, full of grim purpose—and, good Lord, he could see how she'd gotten away with this kind of thing for five solid years. The policeman backed off, making room for her. After reaching the deck, she closed the hatch softly but definitively, easing the latch into its cradle, dusting her hands on her sleeves, one at a time—and only then did she look from the policeman to the stationmaster and back again. Carefully she lowered the mask, leaving it resting under her chin, and calmly said, "Would someone please tell me what is going on?"

The two officials answered at once—a shooting in Bremen, eyewitness accounts, a manhunt under way, all boats being searched—and Anna nodded patiently. She'd heard enough, thank you.

"You'll need to see my papers, then," she said. "And, I suppose, the patient's as well. Shall I get them, or would you like to—?" She motioned toward the hatch.

The men looked at each other, and the policeman said, "What can you tell me about this patient?"

Anna sighed. "Of course until the doctor sees him, there's no official diagnosis—you understand that. But I must tell you: I fear it's consumption. Highly contagious at this stage. Naturally, we've taken every precaution. These people have been very kind. I'd never have chosen to bring him to the clinic by boat; but under the circumstances, a train seemed inadvisable, and when I inquired into hiring an automobile—"

"*Ach!*" said the policeman, now sympathetic. "Not with the *Himmelfahrt*! Everything's booked. You couldn't hire a tractor and a farm wagon."

The nurse wasn't a hard-hearted sort, after all. She knew this was a joke and played along with it. "Well, I don't think *that* would have been quite suitable either, *Herr Offizier.*"

"Aha! No, *Schwester*, perhaps not. Well, then."

They all stood there, crowded together, in a situation that Oskar recognized as straight out of Clausewitz. Between them on the narrow deck lay the *Schwerpunkt*, the invisible pivot on which every other thing—formations and alignments and concentrations of force—must turn. Here, a canny and well-timed move could decide the outcome of a battle or, indeed, make the battle unnecessary. Clausewitz was a great one for ducking actual combat. "Bloodshed in war," he'd written, "is like the occasional cash transaction in a business normally run on credit."

Anna might have studied the same text. She played it easily, almost carelessly. "If you wear this," she told the policeman, "you should be quite safe." From a pocket she drew a mask identical to her own. "The patient is isolated in the forward berthing compartment. I imagine you'll need to have a look at him, to confirm his identity. I'll fetch the papers from his luggage—don't worry, there's no chance of infection, I've kept everything quite clean. You just need to be careful"—now offering him the mask, holding this protective talisman reverently—"about breathing."

The policeman looked as though he had no wish even to touch

it. Still, he'd puffed himself up for the others' benefit—the nurse's especially; he would admit that. Now he wasn't sure what to do.

At this point, Anna turned almost brazen. "If you *don't* see the patient with your own eyes, and later your superiors ask about it, what will you tell them? Here, *mein mutiger Offizier,* I'll be right beside you."

The policeman sighed. He took the mask and held it to his face and, with a nod of the purest fatalism, disappeared into the cabin below, followed closely by Anna.

They were back in under two minutes. Oskar had no idea what had happened down there, what she'd done to make the prisoner presentable—drugged him into unconsciousness, he later suspected—or where she'd hidden Clairborne the whole time. It was just conceivable, in hindsight, that she hadn't bothered to hide him at all, that the boy was simply lounging in the other compartment with the door shut. It wouldn't have mattered. The moment of maximum danger came and went, an anticlimax. Clausewitz couldn't have done any better. Oskar wasn't fond of Anna, but he would never question her judgment again.

They stood awhile longer on deck, some dark energy having been discharged, as if a quick storm had blown through. The stationmaster took the opportunity to reprimand the boatman Tiller: He'd known in his heart the man was up to something, and now we see what! Taking on new passengers after all the berths have been paid for! A glance at the ship's log will tell a lively tale!

"Yes, sure," grumbled Tiller, "go on now, off my boat. These good people are in a hurry. It's a question of hygiene."

Oskar was back in his deck chair beside Lena when Tiller the younger nudged the *Eulenspiegel's* bow away from the wharf and the old man pumped up the engine and they nosed into the channel, pushing against the slow current. Oskar looked back at the village of Polle, watching the stationmaster lower the Lima flag and fold it neatly while the policeman stood nearby taking notes, until something by the building distracted him and he closed the notebook and walked over. The river resumed its long turn to port, and the little station was about to be swallowed by a bank overgrown with bilberries. Oskar could barely make out an automobile, smallish and black—an Opel, something like that—and two men in dark coats, inappropriate dress for this kind of weather. For a few seconds he studied the three tiny figures standing together in the sun, and then the village was gone and there was only the Weser, rolling in its ancient bed like a place in a storybook.

GOLDEN PHEASANTS

LAKE ALSTER AND THE RIVER HAVEL: 26 MAY

The Honorable Thomas DeWitt "Bull" Townsend, ranking member of the Senate German Affairs Subcommittee, was not happy.

Certainly not with his suite in the Atlantic, which his staff had assured him was the best place in Hamburg—built like a palace, with a breathtaking view of the water.

"It's called the *Atlantic*, damn it, so why am I looking at some pissant *lake*? And who do you have to fuck to get hot water in here?"

Nor was he happy with his schedule, which his staff had spent half the night revising, so as to give the senator more time for sightseeing.

"Who's this guy from the Interior Ministry? Why's he want to meet me *informally*? The hell's that mean—over a couple beers? At a bowling alley? Hiding behind some rosebushes? I can't even pronounce his name—*Jesus-voos?* Look here, tell me what this says."

Gisevius, with a hard G. Hans-Bernd Gisevius. Old aristocratic family, deep connections with the Prussian officer corps, friend of Lord Halifax, the British—

"I know who Lord Halifax is, you moron. So this *Geeza-voos* is a pal of his? Hmm. What's Toby say about this? Where the hell is Toby, anyway? All right, just—keep it short, okay? And no rosebushes—friends with the Brits, probably try to kiss me. What's next?"

Finally, he was not happy with the news about his son—more specifically, the absence of any.

"Long's it been now—two, three days? Should've got to that place by now, shouldn't they? Even if Clair's calling the shots. Even if they stopped to buy a whole new summer wardrobe. Boy can spend money faster than his mother. Least he doesn't drink, not that I know of. Look, you didn't hear that, okay? Mother's a fine woman, just—she's never taken to Washington, is all. Hell, *I've* never taken to Washington. Gotta do it, though. Slay the beast in his lair. What was that soldier's name? The one from the boat. Von something. Look, get somebody on the phone, see what you can find out. Call the school, the camp, whatever the fuck it is. Mother's gonna ask, next time I speak to her. All right—what's next? And where the hell's Toby?"

The sun smiled wanly over the river Havel, north and west of Berlin, like some irony-laden Nordic commentary on the theme of summer. Tobias Lugan had been rowing for a while—not really biting into it, just giving the oars a yank now and then for the sake of stirring up some waves—but now he stopped, let the oars ride high, and marveled at how little difference it made. The water was flat, and the current, if there was one, wasn't about to sweep them out to sea. The boat was on loan from the military attaché, along with, Toby supposed, the girl, whose name was Susan and who worked in something called Liaison, which he supposed entailed walking around with important documents like the one in her lap, bound in red imitation leather and blocking the sight line up her skirt.

"Pour me another drink, would you, doll?" he asked nicely.

Susan must have been glad to have a day out on the water—or else she found him an interesting change from the Ivy League pricks at the embassy—because she took out a new chilled glass from the cooler and filled it halfway to the top before tonging in ice cubes. She bent toward him with the imitation leather firmly in place and Toby leaned forward to meet her. The smile she offered him was on the same thermostatic level as the sunshine: if you liked sweating, you'd have to work at it.

He swallowed some of the liquid—nearly straight gin—and decided to kill time making conversation. "What's that?" he said.

He was looking at a body of land with a pointy tip that stuck out into the river. It was mostly woods, with wide patches of well-mown turf and an occasional glimpse of a house back among the heavier foliage. The houses looked big, but you couldn't see much from here.

"That's the Schwanenwerder," the girl said. Her voice was what it might be if she'd watched Billy Wilder movies and then decided to try that out on guys who hadn't seen their wives in a while.

"Yeah, I mean is it an island or—"

"I think technically it's an island, yes. But there's a causeway connecting it to the mainland. There has to be—a lot of party bigwigs own houses out there. *Golden pheasants*, the locals call them."

She used the *Deutsch* for that, and her German was more appealing than her English. Toby wondered if he'd misappraised her. Maybe this Susan was a bona fide operative. Worked the Bendlerstrasse circuit, teasing Foreign Ministry types out of their tuxedos and blackmailing them for spy gold—like leprechaun gold, only less fungible, in Toby's experience. It bore thinking about.

"I appreciate your doing this," he said.

He meant the big red book, and she seemed to understand that.

"It's not *really* all that sensitive," she said, handing it over.

The cover was blank, but inside was a title page of sorts, typed in capital letters.

GOVERNMENT OF THE THIRD REICH
PRINCIPAL STATE AND NSDAP DIVISIONS
INCLUDING AN APPRAISAL OF FUNCTIONS
AND RESPONSIBILITIES
(REV. 7 MARCH 1938)

"Basically, it's a lot of organizational charts," she said. "Mostly that's all it is. But you wouldn't believe what we had to— I mean, this stuff changes all the time. They're constantly pushing career people out and bringing political people in. But sometimes they leave the career person in place and just make up a new title for the party hack. *Or* sometimes they've got an old hack already in place— the ones with low party numbers, they're called the *alte Kämpfer*—

who they kind of surreptitiously replace with a career person, just so the work gets done. Sometimes they set up a whole new *Amt* to do what an existing *Amt* has been doing and then leave both in place. It's up to the office chiefs to fight it all out, which creates some really interesting incentives. And sometimes we can't figure out *what* the heck they're doing—there's just a designation on a chart and you have to make your best guess. I'll give you an example. What do you think the Reich Settlement Office does? The boss has a PhD in anthropology. This is part of the SS. *The SS.* I mean, *you* tell *me.*"

Lugan chucked appreciatively, to encourage her, though he couldn't care less what the Reich Settlement Office did. He flipped through some pages, and it was just as she said: chart after chart.

"I was kinda curious," he said as casually as possible, and the gin probably helped, not being a serious kind of drink, "about the intelligence part of it. Like we've got the FBI and the Customs Service and Treasury agents and whatnot—"

"Customs is actually part of Treasury."

Lugan smiled: how he loved a smart girl. Loved *and* loathed. "So I was wondering what *they've* got, exactly. I'll give *you* an example." Leaf out of her book, *ha.* "I was having drinks last night with a gentleman from the Sicherheitsdienst. I only know this because he gave me his card—he was in civilian clothes and this was an unofficial occasion, to say the least. But from the general, ah, tenor of our conversation, I got the idea he's hot under the collar about some rival agency or department or whatever it might be. Seems to think this other outfit's running an operation that he—being the SD—would like to squash. So I'm trying to get a feel for how these things work over here. Who are the players? How deep's the rivalry? How high up does it go? That kind of thing."

Girl Susan heard him out with what he took for a shrewd look in her eye. When he was done she said, imitating his tone with fair competence, "Who are the players." Then, in her own voice: "How long have you got?"

"I'm not sure—when does your boss need his boat back?"

"When does *your* boss need his errand boy back?"

"My boss is Uncle Sam," said Toby, liking this.

"So's mine."

They'd both watched too many movies. Toby didn't even like movies, but the few he'd seen had been too many. "I guess we've got all day, then."

He waited for her to say the next line, which he knew would include "all night"—but instead she said, "Take a look at Appendix 6. There's a breakdown of information-gathering and counter-intelligence responsibilities."

She waited, like a patient schoolteacher, for Toby to thumb through to the right place in the book. It was back toward the end, the sort of thing people have in mind when they say even the footnotes have footnotes.

"As you'll see, there's a great deal of overlap. We're not completely sure, but it's generally thought that this is another case of multiple agencies being tasked with the same general mission, so the bosses compete over every last thing. You do see this a lot, *but:* pay attention to the overlap between the military side and the civilian side. You'd think there'd be a clear separation, right? But from what we can tell, there's not. The SD is part of the SS, which is technically civilian but has military aspirations. The Abwehr works for the General Staff, which is military, but traditionally it's the fist inside the civilian chancellor's glove. What I'm saying is, neither side's happy with just part of the action. And if you bore down deeper"—now she was reaching over, turning the pages for him—"it gets even more Byzantine. You can't imagine. Well, you're from Washington, so maybe you can. Anyway, that's where I'd start. Since you've got all day."

She gave him a smile, the bitch.

There were happy shouts across the water—a family in a motor launch coming up from behind, kicking up spray. The sun felt marginally warmer. Toby felt marginally drunk. He looked around at the green inland shores of the Third Reich and wondered in passing what the hell he was doing here. A place just as strange as Washington, yet somehow even more convoluted. In DC, at least, the right hand knew it was the right hand and that its God-given task was to smash the left hand to a pulp. Here you had a guy like Kohlwasser who didn't even know who his enemies were—they might be his own fucking army. Lugan closed the book and ran a finger down its imitation leather spine, feeling no desire to learn more of these secrets just now. A sickening burden had been placed on him. Or maybe he'd taken it on himself. Or maybe it had just been lying in his path one damp March night and he hadn't had the sense to step around it.

"Pour me another drink, would you, doll?" he asked, not so nicely this time.

COUSIN PETER IS ILL

BAD KARLSHAFEN: LATE THAT AFTERNOON

Long white corridors. A gallery with French windows on three walls, all of them open, gauzy curtains fluffing their skirts in the irresolute breeze. A row of slender statues, classical figures mounted on square modernist plinths—Greeks and Romans and Teutons intermingled with careless promiscuity, but how many guests would notice a thing like that? A goddess is a goddess, and all of them looked so *healthy*, their poses so athletic, their gazes outward across the open grounds and the river so serene. They set the tone, for above all a spa is a place of healing, of restoration, of soothing and reinvigorating the senses, of tucking away your watch and opening your checkbook and accepting the care and nourishment and attention that are your due.

The spa at Bad Karlshafen was not the first place one would think of for treating a septic bullet wound. But business—which depended on the ancient thermal springs and the whims of a European leisure class that had been avoiding central Germany of late—was slow. The river Weser was at the door. A sympathetic physician was on the staff. And so the motor vessel *Eulenspiegel* called at the service wharf—normally used for the off-loading of food and medical supplies, occasionally for the on-loading of former patients whose cases had proved terminal, tucked discreetly into an inlet out of sight of the main grounds—and tarried there just long enough for the boatman to cure the most urgent of his many personal ills. Who says a visit to Karlshafen isn't good for you? Tiller felt lighter and more chipper than he had in months. He was moved to wave good-bye to his erstwhile passengers, who were still collecting themselves on the shore as the vessel made its escape to the waiting river.

"*Zum Wohl!*" he shouted to them happily. To your health.

Only Lena waved back. Von Ewigholz, barely conscious, was lying on a makeshift stretcher, Clairborne was hovering over him, Anna was engaged in bitter negotiations with the dock crew and Oskar was scanning the nearest side of the spa, which was old and grandiose and shadowy, slipping his fingers in and out of the trigger guard of the little Walther in his pocket. On the whole, he was glad to have his feet on solid German soil again. On the whole, so far, they'd been lucky.

An entire wing of this temple of healing stood empty. The size and absolute stillness of the place were unnerving—but what stuck in Oskar's mind, for some reason, was that all these well-lit spaces were free of dust, the floors buffed to a reflective sheen as though a cleaning crew had just made its rounds. He walked the whole length of the wing, peering in doorways, picking up magazines from the reading stands—there were foreign editions as well as familiar German ones, none more than a few months old—and trying not to mind the clomp and echo of his own footsteps. At the end of the hall, a set of wide glass doors opened into a greenhouse or conservatory, the glass ceiling supported by an ornate Wilhelmine armature that rose the full, three-story height of the building. It was drenched in sunlight and divided by clusters of tall potted plants into semiprivate alcoves, some of them with bathing pools. A sign mounted beside each of these indicated the water temperature: TEPID, VERY WARM and so forth, all the way up to WARNING: QUITE HOT, CARDIAC PATIENTS PLEASE AVOID. It was a strange place, jungly yet civilized. As with the other rooms he'd seen, there was no human presence apart from that phantom maintenance crew.

So it was true: they really did have the spa to themselves. They were *safe*—yet some part of Oskar refused to believe it.

Like a sentry on watch, he made a sharp Wehrmacht about-turn and marched the whole distance back, letting his footsteps echo, daring ghosts or spies or assassins to show themselves.

In the last suite on the right, he found his companions and the sympathetic doctor, whose name was Kleister. He'd been barred from practicing medicine on the grounds of being a *vollblütig* Jew; that term, now enshrined in German law, meant "full-blooded" and referred to persons who had at least three Jewish grandparents. This status came with a list of proscribed occupations, modes of attire and leisure activities. Kleister had managed to evade most of that—Oskar got this story from Anna, after a bit of prodding—on account of having treated a certain Nazi's delicate complaint. "I bet it's Riefenstahl," she'd hissed. Officially, he was now registered as a naturopathic therapist. In practice, he attended a select number of longtime clients of the spa, where his private apartment had a telephone and a balcony overlooking the river.

Dr. Kleister had a calm, reassuring bedside manner and a face like the Alps, all valleys and ridges. His smile made you feel you were seeing your own good fortune reflected there—his joy in your recovery—rather than any happiness of his own.

That smile was now shining down on the *Obersturmführer* when Oskar stepped inside. Von Ewigholz was sitting up in bed, his hospital gown open enough to display fresh white bandages. A thin rubber tube ran between his wrist and a bottle mounted on a rolling stand. He was awake yet somehow absent, in a kind of trance, his eyes on something outside the window. Clair stood on the other side of the bed at his customary distance, just out of reach.

The doctor turned at the sound of Oskar's entrance. "Ah, another friend." For sanitary reasons, perhaps, he didn't offer his hand.

"I'm Stefan Sinclair," Oskar said.

"Oh, indeed?" Kleister responded indifferently. At a certain point, a man has heard enough lies.

"The doctor says he's going to recover."

This was Lena, using her newest voice, much like Anna's. She was emerging from a white-tiled room with an unusual sort of bathtub set directly in the floor, big and deep enough to have a small ledge at one end, perhaps for sitting with the body only partly immersed.

Probably it was somehow tied into the hot springs, with water piped from room to room—but this was only a guess; Oskar had never seen a place like this before. Lena paused in the doorway, her light sweater bulging near the hip to serve notice that it was her turn to carry the pistol. The doctor couldn't have missed this, though perhaps he was used to such things or simply no longer cared. He shone a small light, no larger than a fountain pen, into the patient's eyes, then snapped it off, then on again. From where Oskar stood, it didn't seem to make any difference. Von Ewigholz continued to stare out the window. Clair continued to fret. And where was Anna?

"The doctor says," Lena went on, "that whoever made the sutures did a competent job, but the wound was never properly cleaned. He says all he needs now is a good rest. He'll be ready to move in a day or two."

Maybe so—but the doctor hadn't said any of this to Oskar, and a man might say almost anything to a lady with a gun. When Oskar caught Clair's attention, the boy gave him a quick, wild look of . . . panic? Warning? Nothing good.

Dr. Kleister, apparently done with his exam, clasped his bag shut and turned to face Oskar and Lena as though he were about to impart grave news. "It would be my honor," he said, "if you and your friends would join me for dinner tonight. Nothing at all formal—I could have some dishes prepared and sent up to my rooms. The desserts here are especially good. We can listen to music." He paused, and his eyes softened a bit. "It would be an honor *and* a pleasure. I don't have many visitors here. I understand, your visit doesn't come under normal circumstances. Still, since you'll be staying awhile . . ."

Oskar gave a slight, courteous bow, the kind they taught you at Lichterfelde. "That would be very nice, *Herr Doktor.* Thank you!"

Lena was a harder sell. "What about him? The patient?"

This was for Oskar, probably; Kleister must have sensed as much, but he answered anyway: "In my opinion, the patient would do better with some quiet. A bit of privacy. The healing process, you know, is quite demanding of one's vital energy. Too much company can be a distraction. Perhaps, to ease your mind, I can have a nurse—"

"No," said Lena.

"*Ich wird von ihm bleiben,*" said Clair, his rare German outburst catching everyone's attention. He went on in English: "Don't worry, I won't make trouble. You can all go and eat."

"Anna can stay," said Lena firmly. "It's her—" She bit it off.

Her turn on watch, thought Oskar. So that was how they'd organized it. Always one of them in the SS man's room, with the pistol.

Something about Clair seemed to rouse Kleister's sympathy. "I'd say you could use some rest yourself, my young gentleman. And a good meal too, I think. Do you drink wine back home? They bought cases upon cases here in the twenties, and now I'm afraid we'll never manage to drink it."

Whether from being young or American or too exhausted to listen carefully, Clair missed the dark implication—that a bottle of wine stood a better chance of surviving the Third Reich than anyone present, Kleister at the top of the list—and seemed to hear only an invitation to drink with the grown-ups. It made him smile.

Which the doctor returned. "Shall we say eight o'clock, then?"

The dinner proved to be excellent. In fact, it was too good to be merely praised, filling a void in Oskar nearer to the heart than to the stomach: *Faisandeau aux champignons des bois*, according to a card that had been lettered by hand in classical script, folded in thirds and placed on the serving platter along with a vase of fresh-cut flowers. The mushrooms too, Kleister assured them, had been gathered just that morning, the herbs snipped in the kitchen garden by the cook. Only the pheasant had been bagged yesterday, and hung overnight as per custom to properly cure. A precise method of doing so was recorded in etchings from centuries ago, the doctor explained; then he entertained them by impersonating a slain fowl, its wings pinned to the board just so. They laughed. They drank more wine.

His apartment was also nice—more sumptuous than "my rooms" had led Oskar to expect. The dining table stood at one end of a long chamber, bisected by an archway, whose other end held a piano and several chairs. You could have real dinner music here, given the means and the musicians, and Oskar wondered if Kleister had enjoyed such refinements in happier days. Something about the man's present, fallen state suggested he had. Tonight's music came from a phonograph connected by wires to a hidden loudspeaker; Grieg's *Lyric Pieces* seemed to emanate at a tasteful volume directly from the heavens, an illusion Oskar initially found startling but soon grew accustomed to. Why Grieg? he wondered. A Norseman but not a proper German. A Romantic but not in the thunderous Wagnerian mold, with no hint of the twentieth century in those plainspoken melodies. Maybe there was nothing to think about—pleasing music, something to enjoy over dinner—or maybe the doctor was trying to transport himself to another country, a more civilized time.

A third possibility didn't suggest itself until Clair exclaimed, "Oh, 'Wedding Day at Troldhaugen'! I *love* this piece. I could listen to it for *hours*."

The boy hadn't spoken much except to praise the food. Oskar supposed he was following a code he'd learned at the senator's house—mind your manners and leave the talking to your elders—but he'd been holding his own as new wine bottles were opened for each course, turning redder by degrees at the cheeks and nose, a change from his usual pallor, which until now had seemed comical. This new surge of vitality marked a return of the reckless spirit he'd shown aboard the *Robert Ley*. He leaned back in his chair, fingers tapping the air as the "Wedding Day" repeated its main theme in a march cadence.

"You have played this piece before?" Kleister asked him. His English, to Oskar's ear, was fluent but strictly Continental, a lingua franca spoken these days in places where German might be impolitic.

Clair looked surprised. "I have. Why do you ask?"

"I thought, already, you must be a musician. Your fingers, when they've nothing to do—you play your scarf."

Clair laughed uncertainly.

But the doctor continued in earnest: "And now, see, you've got even the fingering correct. You're a flautist, I think?"

"Well, not really." The boy was embarrassed. "I've been taking lessons, but— It's a hobby, I guess. I mean, I enjoy it, but my teacher says I need to practice more."

"I should say you practice all the time. Perhaps unwittingly, yet you can't seem to help it. You've brought your flute?"

"I—it's in my luggage somewhere." Clair looked gratified and faintly amazed by the doctor's interest. This must not happen much, Oskar guessed, at the senator's house. "Do you—shall I get it?"

Kleister gave him a broad alpine smile, the furrows deepening kindly. "That would be wonderful. I've got some transcriptions—let me have a look."

Clair rose quickly and Kleister more heavily; the boy left the room, and they heard the outer door open and close. The doctor strolled to the other end of the long chamber and stood looking at cabinets—a wall of them, hundreds of wide, shallow drawers designed for sheet music. Oskar and Lena, still at the table, found themselves alone in each other's company for the first time in—since returning to Germany? Each seemed to browse the other's face as though it were a stack of recent newspapers, scanning for who knew what: Items of shared interest? Recent stories they'd been wanting to talk about? A puzzle they'd half-solved but needed some help with? There was too much, and, strangely, there was also nothing.

Kleister brought the moment to a close by addressing them both from the far end of the room. "What possessed you," he said, still poking at drawers, flipping through sheets and tucking them away again, "to bring *him* into this?"

"We didn't *bring him* into anything," said Lena. She rose with her wine glass and advanced to the archway, much less menacing without the pistol at her hip. "They offered us a ride, and we took it. It was a convenient way of throwing off suspicion."

"Yes," the doctor said, distracted now; he'd found the music he was looking for. Satisfied, he turned to look at them. "Yes, I imagine it must have seemed inspired and daring to step into an automobile with an SS officer. And a what? This boy is American. So, he's a student, a vacationer? Or just someone who happened also to need a lift that afternoon? And none of this troubled you, at any time?"

"He's the son of a United States senator," said Lena. "The soldier is his escort. They came over on the ship together. And it looks like they've gotten to be friends. The boy won't—"

" 'Friends,' " repeated the doctor. He looked at Oskar as though seeking a second opinion.

Lena went on: "I know it's crazy, but these things happen. People make friends. I guess even in the SS. It's a complication, I know. But we're dealing with it."

The doctor nodded. "No doubt you are."

"Listen." Lena was angry now; Oskar could see her neck turning pink. "This could prove to be an advantage. This boy—we can *use* him, do you understand? A senator's son. People notice when someone like that goes missing. Even the government won't be able to hush this up."

"Use him?" Kleister came nearer, staring at Lena as if checking for signs of mental imbalance. "Use him as what, a hostage? A bargaining chip? Something to shame the Nazis with? These people don't shame easily, I can tell you."

Lena seemed troubled by this. Oskar guessed what they'd been hearing so far was mostly Anna's thinking. Anna weaving her plots, Clair another thread in them.

The outer door opened and they heard footsteps—almost running, then stopping, backtracking. The door closed with a bang.

By the time Clair entered the room, his face flushed, they were more or less composed to meet him.

"It was under the books," he said, "so it took me *forever.*" He laid the flute case softly on the dinner table and pulled the instrument out in pieces, which he then carefully twisted together. "I haven't played in ages. I know I'll be terrible."

The doctor came nearer, his presence a kind of encouragement. "There are no mistakes," he said, shaking a finger with mock sternness. "There are only variations from one performance to the next. In art, there is no 'correct'—only beauty."

Clair gave him a quizzical smile, his eyes somewhat glazed but sparkling. "My teacher said something like that once. My teacher's German, too."

"Then your teacher is very wise—especially to be teaching in America. Ha! Well, look, I've found some Grieg for you, and also some other things. Do you know Schoenberg?"

"The serialist."

"Much more than that. But yes. Come on, then—let's see how bad we are."

Kleister stepped with newfound energy to the piano. Lena chose a seat nearby, not too close, with a long view toward the entry-way. Oskar was about to join them, but Clair stepped into his path. "Something's up," he whispered, "back at the room. Anna was acting funny. I'm worried about Hagen."

Oskar put a hand on his shoulder. Just a bit of reassurance, mild case of nerves—that's what it should look like. "Afterward," he murmured, "we'll talk. Don't worry." Clapping the shoulder: *Turn around now, the show must go on.*

They began with the piece Clair already knew, though he'd learned it in a different and simpler arrangement, one that was graceful and easy to remember, where the flute took the melody while the piano stood in for a chamber ensemble. Clair stumbled at first, but then his determination seemed to burn through the alcohol and he dug into the tempo and stayed there, playing through his mistakes, getting it right the next time. When they reached the end, Clair was damp with sweat; strands of hair clung to his temple where he'd brushed them out of his eyes.

"That was *very* good," said the doctor. "Truly exceptional. Now we make it beautiful."

They played the piece again, at a tempo that sounded more natural to Oskar: loud, then soft, then very loud, the processional leading to the slow ceremonial interlude and finally the glorious, foot-thumping dance. When it was over, Clair stood beaming with tears in his eyes. The doctor rose and formally shook his hand.

"You are an artist," he said. "Never think you are not. No matter what else you may think you are."

Clair nodded.

"Let's have a rest now," the doctor said. "I've got something here to listen to. Something rather special and . . . delicate. Perhaps you'll like it. Though I must be honest: not many people do."

Kleister occupied himself, happily it seemed, removing the platter from the phonograph and easing another from its brown paper sleeve. Clair remained standing in a kind of transfixed state, holding his flute with a handkerchief to keep the sweat off it. Oskar slid a chair up behind him, and Lena handed him his wine glass.

"You were so good," she told him.

That seemed to pull him back into the present. He took the wine and said thank you, then sat down. He'd entered a new world, one where being invited for dinner and music was very serious business. The doctor was ready for the next act.

"*Das Buch der Hängenden Gärten,*" he announced, "by the German composer Arnold Schoenberg, now working, according to the latest news I've heard, in America. All of Schoenberg's work is banned in Germany, so we shall all be breaking the law in just a minute, which I find makes it easier to concentrate. What is it about these notes, this phrasing, that's so dangerous to the sanity of the German people? It cannot be *only* that the composer is Jewish. Schoenberg's student Webern has also been banned, despite having no Jewish grandparents at all, the lucky fellow! So the poison comes not from the blood but from the music itself. And in this case, we have not just poisonous notes but poisonous words to go with them—a setting of poems, rather scandalous poems, full of wild and unhealthy passion, by the poet Stefan George."

"George!" The name was out of Oskar's mouth before he knew he was going to say it, and the sound of his own voice—surprised, happy, childish—caused him a moment of shame that he saw, just as quickly, was ridiculous.

"You know George?" Kleister said, intrigued, reverting to German.

"I—we read him a lot, in the *Jugendbewegung*. Quoted him a lot, I should say. I found him . . . difficult."

"He speaks to certain readers more clearly than others, I think." The doctor looked from Oskar to Lena to Clair as though speculating which of them George would speak to most clearly. "So then, you have circled the flame!"

Oskar recognized this as a George quotation—*Wer je die flamme umschritt / Bleibe der flamme trabant!*—that everyone in the Movement knew, though not many outside it, which only made it better. He nodded.

Kleister nodded back. He understood. "Very good!" he declared, in English again. "We now have some music that seems quite simple, quite classical—a singer accompanied by a piano—yet manages to sound like nothing we've heard before. Something unworldly. The text is written here." He removed a few sheets of ordinary paper from the record sleeve and offered them to Oskar. A series of brief stanzas had been typed out, numbered 1 through 15. "Regrettably, there's no translation. I'll set the scene for you. We're in a garden, surrounded by walls—a place that seems beautiful at times, wild and even dangerous at others. The speaker—here, the singer—is an adolescent, in love for the first time. Over the course of the song cycle, this love drives him to intoxication, torment and finally release. The poet uses the garden to stand for the changing nature of young love, especially as it turns feral and seems to burst through the walls that contain it. The composer, in turn, uses the passion of the text to smash through the walls of musical convention. As the garden loses its flowers and fruits to wind and frost, so the music turns away from key and harmony and the sort of melody we're used to hearing—all the things that keep our feet on the ground while we listen—and we're tossed about like this poor young man in the magic and terror of his desire. Well—you can see why the Nazis will have none of that!"

Having prepared his audience, the doctor lowered the tone arm, and down from the hidden loudspeaker came Schoenberg.

It was an amateur recording. There was a background hiss and the rustle of sheets of music before the performance started: a line of solitary piano notes in the left hand, like tentative steps, and then the soprano, first at the upper end of the register and then dropping into lower regions that seemed to give the singer trouble. It was a difficult piece—to play, no doubt, but also to listen to. The character of each section was distinct, and hearing them strung together with only brief pauses in between had a jarring effect. At times Oskar would have said the music made sense, both words and feelings comprehensible. At others, the words seemed detached grammatically from one another, chosen for sensual effect and aimed at some part of you that was not the brain. Then there were spaces with no words at all, and spaces full of words but nothing identifiable as melody.

Holding the text, Oskar now and then glanced at it, trying to figure out where they were. But it was mainly a distraction. He'd get caught by some passage and then realize that he'd lost his place in the recording, so he stopped trying to read along.

The final section was longer than the rest, and unlike most of the others, he could think of how to describe it: as *elegiac*. By the very last line—*The night is clouded over and humid*—he found himself very much in the narrator's shoes, having weathered all the confusions of adolescence and returned to his senses, alone, in a place lacking any definite qualities. When the music stopped and there was only the hiss of the record, he glanced at Clair, who looked fascinated by the last thing he'd successfully taken in—and what would that have been? Oskar skimmed backward through the text and found

> *If today I do not touch your body*
> *The thread of my soul will be torn*

This seemed about right for an eighteen-year-old.

"And there," said the doctor, lifting the needle, "you have it! Poisonous music! I trust no one is feeling the ill effects. Shall we have dessert, then?"

It was very late by the time Kleister's pent-up social energy was spent. He and Clair had played more music—Grieg again—and they'd listened to another record—Stravinsky this time, *Le sacre du printemps*, so savage and magnificent!—and in the denouement they gathered in a smaller room, the doctor's private study, to watch a silent movie. It was another amateur production but an elaborate one, filmed at someone's home on a lake near Berlin. It was summer and the people in the movie were doing summer things, diving, sailing, playing croquet, dining alfresco, climbing out of an open motorcar that reminded Oskar of the old Horch. There was a young woman who appeared in almost every shot, and probably she was the reason Kleister had chosen this particular reel after an evening of passionate music—but maybe she was just the owner of the house or the person who'd hired the photographer. Perhaps this evening's motif had not been passion but escape—into art, into beauty, into a dreamtime when life had been good.

In the study there was a telephone. Oskar attempted to keep his eyes off the thing, but the doctor caught him looking and gave him a nod—like the earlier nod, a covert understanding. As they gathered themselves to leave, Oskar tried to think of a reason to tarry, to let the others go on without him. But then Clair was giving him an odd, insistent stare, and Oskar remembered promising the boy they'd talk afterward.

The guests exchanged formal good-nights with their host and set off down the long, empty hall toward the stairway. Aside from Kleister's apartment, most of the top floor was taken up by offices—apparently unused, with empty slots in the doors where nameplates would have gone—and finally one marked STAFF ONLY, with a bathroom symbol.

"If you'll excuse me," Oskar said. "All that wine . . ."

Clair quickly said, "Oh God, me too."

Lena gave them a scowl. "I'll see you downstairs. I need to check on Anna."

Oskar didn't bother groping for a light switch: the moon was nearly full, and the bathroom had two large windows. Clair walked over to look out onto a courtyard. On the other side, sixty or seventy meters away, stood a wing of the spa still in active use. Lights sparkled in several windows on the lower levels.

Oskar said, in a phrase he knew from American cartoons, "What's up?"

For an instant he feared Clair was about to cry. This intuition might well have been just the early onset of a hangover, for when the boy spoke, his voice was quiet and evenly pitched; he meant to be taken seriously.

"I really think," he said, "we need to get out of here."

"I agree," said Oskar—surprising himself, because until that moment he hadn't consciously decided. "But why?"

"I'm not sure. There's Anna, for one thing. I wanted to tell you, when I went down before to get the flute, that I didn't see her at first—I just saw that Hagen was all by himself and he seemed to be sleeping, so I didn't— Anyway, Anna showed up, but it was like she'd been up to something and I'd just missed catching her at it. She was— I'm not sure, but there might have been somebody else around; I kind of thought I'd heard voices, without really *hearing* them—does that make sense? But I got the feeling Hagen was in danger. God, that sounds so stupid and dramatic. But that's what it felt like, so I didn't want to leave. But Anna scares me. And I knew everyone was waiting, so—"

"You did the right thing," Oskar said. "Listen, if Anna's up to something, as you say, it's best that we leave her to get on with it. We'll make our own plans. We can start now. How about Lena?"

"What do you mean?"

"You've got, ah, this *feeling* about Anna. What about—"

"No," said Clair. "Maybe. I don't know, I think Lena's all right. I mean, they're both kind of mean to me. And Anna's fucking crazy. I'm sorry, but she is. Every time she looks at me, I feel like I'm a turkey and she's a Pilgrim. I guess that's an Americanism—sorry!"

Oskar got the general idea, and it was amusing, though he honestly felt too tired to smile. He could've fallen asleep right there, in the bathroom on his feet. He'd done it before, in training—bashed his head on a sink, spent a whole day in the infirmary.

"But it's not them," Clair said. "Not Anna and Lena. It's—"

Something woke in Oskar then, as if it had been curled up along his spine, waiting to be roused.

"There were these two men," said Clair, "back at the ship. Remember how me and Hagen didn't come ashore right away? That was Hagen's idea. Something about these two guys bothered him, and he said, 'Let's just wait, they'll go away.' So while we were killing time, I asked who they were, and he just muttered something in German. But, you know, I understand *some* German—nobody thinks I do, so I get to hear the most remarkable things. I mean, I know '*Arschlöcher*,' and *everybody* knows 'Gestapo.' But what he *did* say, in English, was that I shouldn't worry, that nobody would bother me while he's around. Only he's not really *around* anymore, is he? In that sense."

There may have been a note of despair in Clair's voice, but by force of will he suppressed it and added, "I've seen them since—I'm pretty sure—at least once. In Hameln, on shore. Near that man on stilts. And they saw me. *And* you. Because you guys were stupid and we were all sitting right up on deck. In broad daylight."

"I've seen them too," said Oskar. He hadn't registered it until now—as if a movie reel had been played too fast the first time through, and now he was watching it again at the correct speed. "In that village where we stopped. Polle. Just as we were pulling away. The same car. A black Opel. My God."

He stared at Clair, wanting more—more details, a fuller explanation, something the boy couldn't possibly give him. There was one thing, though.

"Back at the ship," he said, "the *Robert Ley*. When you stayed behind, you and Hagen, he told you the men would go away. But why would they do that? Why didn't they just wait for you? Or have the crew start searching?"

Clair looked back blankly, as though the question made no sense. Oskar felt like shaking him. Finally the boy said, almost meekly, "They didn't care about us—they weren't following us. They were following *you*."

The moon through the tall windows glared as harsh as a klieg light, revealing every flaw in Oskar's laboriously made yet erroneous modeling of the world. He must fix it all, right now. His body made a reflexive move of its own volition, to get on with this, but Clair stopped him with a hand on his forearm. The long fingers that had played a scarf—another detail Oskar simply hadn't noticed—drew him around until he was looking into the boy's intense, half-drunk yet harrowingly percipient eyes, inches from his own.

"That thing Dr. Kleister told me," said Clair, "when he said I was an artist? *No matter what else you may think you are.* He meant something by that, didn't he? You know what he meant."

"He meant—" Oskar felt like he'd been dropped into water, warm water, the spa's renowned thermal springs, and was floating there effortlessly. Any move on his part might upset the equilibrium. "I'll ask him," he said carefully. "I'm going to see him now. I need to use his telephone."

That must have sounded insane to Clair, as it did to Oskar. But the boy let go of his arm.

"Go make your phone call," he said. "I'll get Hagen. Then we can go."

———

Kleister had left his door unlatched, expecting Oskar to return. He was waiting in the semidarkness, the only light coming from the moon and a single lamp in the distant study.

"Thank you," Oskar murmured, slipping past him. "It should only take a minute, if I can get a line."

"The service here is usually excellent," the doctor said, trailing him through the apartment. "Our clientele—some of them are here to get away; others like to remain constantly in touch. We cater to all types."

As it happened, an operator came on quickly. Oskar asked for a line to Bremen, and she said, "Will that be the Altstadt or the Vorstadt?" The Old City, he told her, and recited the number he'd memorized months ago.

To his relief, the connection went through with no problem and was answered almost immediately at the other end. A bored-sounding voice said, "Brandt Insurance, here is the claims desk. What can I do for you?"

This was not the script as Oskar remembered it, nor the kind of voice he'd expected to hear. Seeing no alternative, he went on anyway: "I'm calling for Herr Braun, please."

Now there was silence on the line, a weird silence filled with warbles and scratches and mysterious sounds that he imagined to be disembodied voices, trapped in the wire. He could hear his own heartbeat, too, and was about to slam the handpiece down before the call could be traced when the bored voice came on again.

"I'm afraid Herr Braun is not available tonight. Is there anyone else who could help you?"

"No, I'm sorry—may I leave a message for when Herr Braun returns? If you could tell him, please, that his cousin Peter is ill and has been taken to the hospital. His condition is not critical, but the doctors are concerned. Have you got that?"

"I believe so," the bored voice said. "Is there a number at the hospital?"

Oskar hung up, his hand now trembling. He didn't know if he'd just violated some protocol. He couldn't guess what the consequences would be if the message failed to reach Jaap, his contact, or, for that matter, if it *was* delivered. They'd know he was alive, at least. That he was in Germany—otherwise the cousin would have been named Paul—and in some kind of trouble.

He turned to find Kleister standing very close behind him. Those eyes by lamplight seemed darker than ever. They contained so many emotions it was hard, if not impossible, to filter them and determine which one was currently operative. Maybe they all were, and perhaps this was what happened to doctors, the very best ones—feeling every single thing felt by every patient, until you became a walking compendium of human sensory afflictions. When Kleister spoke it was unnerving, because he sounded so ordinary: a weary man being kept from his bed in the middle of the night.

"What was your *Gruppe*?" he asked.

"My—"

"In the Movement. I was there in the beginning, at the first summit. My *Gruppe* was the Blau-Weiss, have you heard of that? A little pack of Zionists at the Höhe Meissner? It rather taxes the imagination, these days."

"I'm sorry, no." Was there a point to this? Had an evening with young people left Kleister feeling sentimental? But then Oskar recalled the circumstances under which he'd been recruited by the Abwehr. Jaap, too, had wanted to ascertain this. "I was in the dj.1.11," he said.

"Ah, indeed. Then I don't need to tell *you* anything, do I? You've read George, you know these things often end. But I would ask you to tell *me* something, if I may. You can't possibly be in the SOPADE."

It wasn't a question, so Oskar didn't trouble to deny it. He held his palms out: *I'm just what I seem to be.*

The doctor wasn't buying it. "But you *are* something, though, aren't you? You're in league with the underground. You make cryptic telephone calls. You carry a weapon."

Oskar reacted foolishly, slapping a hand to his jacket to make sure the gun was still there, that Kleister hadn't deftly removed it. The doctor gave him a sympathetic smile, and Oskar understood the rest: like Clair and his scarf, only with Oskar it must be some habitual gesture, like slipping a hand into his pocket and letting it rest there—something like that. Almost anyone would make a better spy than Oskar was.

It occurred to him—not a new thought, but now it caught fresh wind—that the doctor was putting himself at risk for all of them, including Oskar, and perhaps he owed him something for that. He let the hand slide down from his pocket and tried to think back through his various identities to the person who stood at the core of them, which might have been what Kleister was trying to discover with these questions about the Movement. That was possibly—for Oskar, for Jaap, for Kleister—the last time they'd been perfectly certain of where they stood, on account of who they were standing with.

"I'm not with the SOPADE," he said. "But I'm not with the Nazis, either. I'm not your enemy. I'm a German officer. My father was a German officer. I'm a patriot."

Kleister nodded. It was enough—probably more than he'd expected. "My father, too, was a German officer. I once considered myself a patriot. Now I don't know what the word means. Nor what 'German' means, even. Schoenberg is in America. Brecht is in Denmark. Beckmann is in Amsterdam. George died in Switzerland. Are *they* Germans? And if so, if they left but remain German, what does it mean that I'm still here?"

"Maybe," said Oskar, "it means you're braver than them. You've chosen to stay and fight."

"And you, my good officer. You too, you've chosen to stay and fight."

"I don't think—this isn't really what I'd call fighting."

"Oh, don't worry about that," the doctor said. "If you stay, you won't have to wait long. Your fight will come."

The walk down from Kleister's apartment to the empty wing of the spa seemed much longer than the walk up. Before, he'd had company and everyone had been tired and hungry but also wary; they weren't sure about this doctor or what he had in mind for them, and they were still getting used to these empty, immaculate corridors and the shadows and the silences that filled them. They were easily spooked and expected to be surprised—and when it turned out to be so pleasant, delicious food and plenty to drink and Clair playing his flute, that was a surprise in itself.

Oskar didn't expect anything this time. He'd had enough for one night. He welcomed the shadows because he was tired of seeing clearly. The silence was a reprieve. All he really wanted was a few hours sleep—no more than that, because whatever his next move was, he needed to make it quickly. Maybe it would come to him in a dream. Or possibly it was so obvious that everyone but him had already seen it.

Groggy with fatigue, he nearly tripped on the wide marble stairway leading down—he'd misjudged the height of the risers—so he took the remaining steps more slowly, one hand on the smooth spine of the banister. On the last step, he came to a halt.

At first he didn't understand why; he didn't see what was wrong. But then he did—and he'd seen it all along, as he'd seen those men in the Opel. The trouble wasn't his eyesight. Right in front of him in the hallway was a line of footprints. Here in this place where phantom janitors kept every surface clean enough to pass a white-glove inspection, a trail of muddy tracks ran from the main corridor into the depths of the empty wing. Maybe one of his companions had stepped outside—Anna, tired of watching an unconscious prisoner, or Clair sneaking out to relieve himself. These innocent explanations rang as hollow as such things generally did. Anyway, the tracks were so numerous they must've been made by at least two sets of feet. Oskar should have learned by now—perhaps he had, finally—that in his new line of work, the most outlandish and lethal theories had the greatest likelihood of being true.

How about this, then: trained assassins had come here to murder him.

The notion was too mad to think about, so Oskar chose not to. Instead, he slid the Walther out of his pocket and set off down the hall.

TRYING TO COUNT BULLETS

Someone had turned off all the lights. That was the first thing Oskar noticed. The second was that someone—maybe a different someone—had opened all the doors. Moonlight spilled from each room into the dark passage. The effect was eerie and even beautiful, a river of darkness with small islands of silver light every dozen paces or so. If you stayed close to a wall and kept away from doorways you'd be nearly invisible, except, of course, in silhouette. Oskar tested this principle by crouching low and staring ahead as he moved down to the last suite on the right, where his companions ought to be.

There was nothing, neither silhouettes nor sounds nor a flutter of moving air to suggest an open window or a doorway through which anyone might have escaped outside. He could see the tracks—clearly now *two* pairs of shoes—where they entered the nearest patch of light before fading into the shadows. He imagined those two men advancing like soldiers, a careful distance between them, each taking one side of the hall, opening doors as they went. And then what—a rapid glance inside, leading with the gun, sweeping the room with it? Would they bother to search every suite? Oskar guessed not: first a pass to check for signs of occupation, clearing the ground floor, moving to the next.

It wasn't much to stake your life on, but Oskar didn't feel at liberty to indulge in calculation. He rose with the Walther, in both hands, pointing across the floor ahead while he moved forward swiftly, crisscrossing the hall in long diagonals to make himself a more challenging target.

No bullets came ripping at him out of the black void at the end of the hall. He reached the last suite on the right and ducked inside, pressing himself to the wall, breathing hard and loud.

The room was empty. Moonlight poured onto the bed where von Ewigholz had been lying; its linens were disarranged, the intravenous tube dripping free from its mount, bits of Clair's luggage open and jumbled on the floor nearby. Drawing a breath and holding it, Oskar stepped toward the inner door to the bathroom. He'd taken four quiet strides when a noise came from behind him, and before he could turn to look a lithe shadow danced out of the shadows by the doorway and an awful burst of pain shot downward from the crown of his head. He understood that he'd been struck, not shot, but his muscles seemed to be spinning out of control, and he felt himself losing his balance as someone tried to tug the Walther out of his grip. He could have fired it, but his vision was too blurry to identify the target, and perhaps in some corner of his brain he detected something strangely familiar in all this, a recognizable pattern of screwing things up. He let go of the gun and bent over, fighting a wave of nausea.

"You betrayed us!" Anna hissed.

Oskar tried to tell her to be quiet, but his voice was slurred.

"*You* be quiet!" she said. "We trusted you, and you ratted us out."

Good Lord, was she actually shouting? When Oskar shook his head, it set loose a fresh wave of pain. He felt a hand moving along the back of his cranium, a touch that was almost gentle.

"Give him a minute," said Lena. "I think you might've cracked his skull. There's a lot of blood."

Oskar managed to bring his eyes into focus and found Lena's face in the vicinity of his own. Like a newly perceptive infant, he assembled the rest of her: the body leaning forward, one hand extended toward him, the other holding his gun. He took a couple of breaths before trying to speak again. "We've got to get out of here," he said, more coherently this time. "There are two guys—"

"We know about your little henchmen," said Anna. "Is that who you called on the doctor's phone? Oh yes, Clair told us about that—did you think he wouldn't? And what have you done with him? Is he your hostage now? You bastard."

None of this was making much sense, and Oskar feared she was going to hit him again. "Please," he whispered, "you've got to keep your voices down."

"Let him talk, Anna," said Lena. "Oskar—can you hear me? Do you understand?"

"Everyone can hear you. That's the—"

"Oskar, just listen. Clair came down and told us you were using the telephone. We—well, we got angry and went to look for you. But then we heard noises, people walking around—were there only two of them? So we hid and waited. Then we came back here, but Clair and Hagen were gone. Oskar, what have you done?"

"Shh!" He went on in a furious whisper: "I haven't— Look, we can talk about this somewhere else. It isn't safe here."

"Fine," said Anna, waving the ancient revolver at him. "Just get up! If you're going to vomit, then vomit. We'll all go up to the doctor's place and have a nice talk there. Give us any trouble and we'll shoot you. If we bump into your friends, do tell them that."

Oskar's mind had cleared to the extent that he was able to recognize this much: his only hope of keeping Anna quiet was to do exactly as she said. And so he raised an arm in surrender, and Lena pulled him to his feet. He wobbled for a moment but then was okay. He nodded.

Anna, momentarily satisfied, stuffed the old pistol into her belt. Oskar almost advised her to take it out again—she might need it—but as she wasn't shouting and he was likely the one who'd get shot, he kept his mouth shut. The three of them stepped together into the dark hallway.

Which wasn't empty any longer. Of course it wasn't. The man who stood waiting just outside, away from the moonlight, barely even a silhouette, was short but bulky, his apparent width exaggerated by a black leather coat that hung open so you could see something gleaming silver at his belt—some kind of badge, Oskar thought. It was strange that he had time for such a thought at this moment, but everything seemed to be happening more slowly than usual. The man's arm, for example, seemed to float upward like something rising through the water—and only the tip of his gun, the silencer screwed to the end of it, broke out of the shadow to glint softly, for just that instant, in the moonlight. Oskar thought he could see straight down the barrel, but the illusion was spoiled by Anna fumbling at his side, trying to free the pistol from her belt, only, of course, much too late.

The man fired at Anna as soon as he'd swung his arm up. The silencer dulled the explosion to a sort of harsh metallic cough. Then, while she continued to grapple for the old pistol, he took more careful aim and fired again—a smoker could have lit a cigar in between, so slowly did it play out for Oskar. There was enough time and barely enough light to see the man's eyes shift from Anna to Lena—the former wasting her final strength on a gun that wouldn't come out of her belt, the latter seeming to remember that she was already holding a gun herself. The man's arm moved sideways, time snapped back to its normal tempo and three things happened so nearly simultaneously that the exact sequence remains open to debate.

Anna managed to discharge the pistol, shooting herself to death through the lower abdomen, but she would have died in the next few seconds anyway, and the gun made the loudest noise ever likely heard in these rarefied hallways.

The Gestapo man went goggle-eyed, his eyes losing so much focus that he tried but failed to properly aim his weapon—a result either of the gun blast or the third thing that happened at more or less the same instant.

Which was Oskar slicing upward with the knife he'd gotten from the boatman Tiller, lodging the short blade in the man's windpipe. He yanked it out and slashed from right to left, severing a jugular vein and cutting halfway through the larynx.

The man was dead before he fell, and Oskar and Lena were left standing amid the gore and general moral calamity. His head seemed to swell with each throb of his pulse, as though it were being pumped up to some multiple of its normal size. He took Lena's hand and held it, more for his own sake than for hers.

"Okay," he said. "Now we've got to go."

She didn't move, which he could understand but not allow. He pulled her around, away from the bodies, and they set off up the hall toward the distant conservatory. They'd covered about half the distance when they heard footsteps behind them, out of the black void.

"Clair!" called Lena. "Hagen! It's us, we're—"

"No," breathed Oskar, yanking her off the spot, "*listen* to me this time."

The first bullet whipped by very close to where they'd just been standing. The fact that they could hear it probably meant the silencer was slowing the muzzle velocity. The shooter must have deduced this as well, because the next shots were louder.

"All *right*," whispered Lena. "I *will*."

And then they were running at full gallop, making gracelessly for the doors ahead. Glass shattered in front of them while the gunshots continued from behind; then everything fell quiet. The remaining Gestapo man must've decided to empty his clip, then reload and finish the job more methodically. They reached the doorway and stepped into the sunroom, which the night had transfigured into a weird moonlit jungle.

Oskar took a few steps in, trying to orient himself. He'd been here only once before, with the sun blazing then, and the world hadn't been spinning so noticeably. He recalled the room as being split into a series of alcoves by greenery, huge pots grouped in clusters. All he could see now were masses of black foliage. Step away from the wall, and your only point of reference was the elaborate armature supporting the glass roof three stories above. Beyond that, only the stars. The moon, though bright, was low in the sky and blocked off by the main building.

"Oskar." Lena's voice was barely a whisper. "What are we going to do?"

He didn't know but wasn't about to tell her that. He'd make this work, somehow. Lure the assassin into the maze and—

Already they'd wasted too much time. Hearing footsteps out in the corridor, crunching on glass, he touched Lena's arm and made a motion with his head. Even he wasn't sure what he was signaling— *move now*, something like that—but she seemed to understand. The two of them crept along the nearest wall of plants until an opening appeared, and they stepped through it into a long, roughly oval-shaped clearing with a pool in the center and wicker chairs at either end. The pool seemed to glow—and while the ambient light was silver and the plants were black, the water looked green, a pale and poisonous green. The Luxury Spa on Mars.

Lena took over now, leading him around the pool and into a kind of tunnel beneath tall cycads. Oskar recognized them by their family resemblance to plants he'd seen in a hothouse at the Tiergarten—like ancient fat-bellied ferns, their huge fronds curling out like a thousand grasping fingers. The footsteps sounded again, no longer behind them but seemingly from everywhere, echoing off tile and glass. She tugged at his sleeve and they were moving again, out of the tunnel and into another alcove, circling another pool.

There's a wall up ahead somewhere, Oskar thought. A wall, maybe a door. They'd make it to the door if his legs didn't collapse, and the evening air would revive him.

Then gunshots, like the footsteps, issued from all directions at once. Bullets ripped through the foliage around them with a sound like a wet rug being whipped with a carpet beater. More glass shattered, and Lena screamed.

Of course she'd scream, as anyone would; not many people are trained to keep quiet while being shot at. This was, however, what the gunman was hoping for. The next bullets were closer, and Lena did the next instinctive thing, something only a few people are trained *not* to do: she turned and pointed the Walther where the shooting seemed to be coming from and fired back, twice. The muzzle flashes briefly lit their hiding spot like matches being struck.

Oskar grabbed her hand and pulled it downward. She must have been holding the gun too tight, because it went off again—another explosion, another flash.

"Run," he whispered.

They were racing heedlessly now, batting leaves out of their faces, tearing through cover into other open spaces and then back into cover. Oskar taxed his memory, trying to count bullets. Three shots just now, how many before? How many times had von Ewigholz fired the weapon, back at Aunt Tilde's house? Twice, he thought. So, five shots in all. A Walther PPK clip holds six bullets. You can store a seventh in the chamber, but you wouldn't unless you planned to use it immediately. Would von Ewigholz have expected to use his weapon that day and slipped in an extra bullet before stepping ashore at Bremerhaven? Oskar didn't imagine so.

Therefore there was just one bullet left.

He knelt, panting, with Lena close by. They'd paused to rest in what looked for all the world like a bamboo grove, hundreds of canes a bit thicker than his thumb bearing thousands of narrow leaves. The shadows the plants cast by moonlight were like sand where a flock of plovers had been running about, then waves had washed over, then the plovers had gone running again—innumerable repetitions of the same basic pattern at every level of sharpness. Oskar guessed he had lost more blood than he'd hoped because his perceptions kept blurring, his thoughts losing focus, and now it was Lena whispering, *Come on, we've got to keep going.* Oskar just looked up at the sky; he was mildly surprised to see that it was divided into strips, forming an elaborate pattern that seemed to spell out a coded message.

"We're close to a wall," he said softly.

Or maybe only his lips moved. Lena stared at him in concern, but after a moment she nodded.

"There should be a door," he explained.

She tightened her lips, as if annoyed. Probably she'd already gotten that far. She gave his arm another pull and he was up now, they were walking, their feet following the path left by the flock of plovers. Around a corner, through a foliated archway—and there was the wall of glass, overlooking the grounds, as well as a tall man wearing a black uniform.

Lena raised the gun, but it was von Ewigholz. Pressed against him, partly supporting his weight, stood Clairborne.

"Thank God," the boy said, his voice a stage whisper. "I wanted to leave, then Hagen said to wait. He said you'd get here."

"We're not alone," said Oskar, who still felt he needed to explain things. While he was at it, he added, "There's only one bullet left."

Von Ewigholz looked him straight in the eye, one soldier to another. It felt to Oskar like a silent interrogation, and something he now realized had been going on for quite some time.

"Then we can't afford to miss," the SS man said, reaching out with the hand not draped around Clair. "Give me the weapon."

Tightening her grip, Lena looked ready to spend the final bullet shutting him up. "You're crazy," she said.

"Give him the gun," Oskar told her.

"You're crazy, too."

"Lena." He felt an odd sort of clarity, bordering on omniscience, and suspected that it was a prelude to passing out. "You said you'd listen to me. And we *can't* afford to miss. Give him the gun."

Von Ewigholz came forward, pulling free of Clair. "Everyone stay where you are," he said, taking the gun from Lena as though it were an afterthought. She gave it up like a wavering churchgoer letting go of her last shred of faith—and turning on Oskar a look that said as much. Von Ewigholz inspected the weapon, pulling back the firing pin to peer into the chamber. He didn't bother to check the magazine—either he accepted Oskar's math or he didn't want to make any more noise. Then he stepped to the nearest tangle of leaves and stood with his back to it, the gun at chest level and aimed at nothing Oskar could see.

"Over here, comrade!" he called. "I've caught them for you!"

Had he counted on Lena to add a note of credibility to this? She started yelling curses and lunged across the empty space and might have reached him had the Gestapo man not been so close by. The man stuck his head through an opening in the leaves and seemed to be trying to figure out what he was seeing: the angry woman, the man he'd been sent to murder, a wild-haired boy who looked frightened to death and a tall *Obersturmführer* who . . . and that would have been as far as the survey went before the bullet entered his frontal lobe.

Had he lived a second longer, he might have seen Oskar fall, too, and it seemed at first as though von Ewigholz had managed to shoot both people with a single bullet. That confusion got sorted out quickly enough, and Clair and Lena—being the only two fit to do so—lifted Oskar through a blown-out section of the glass wall and lugged him across the lawn to where the black Opel stood waiting in the driveway. Von Ewigholz was in good enough shape to keep up with them. When they reached the car, he insisted that only *he* should drive, and only he would talk in the event that anyone stopped them. He'd also taken the dead man's gun, his own now being empty. For once, no one was of a mind to quibble.

It was still dark and the car was jostling up a bad road when Oskar returned to consciousness. Lying with his head in Lena's lap in the narrow back seat, he could see Clair up front, his young face limned dimly in blue from the lights on the dashboard. He tried to sit up, but nausea swooped down to meet him, and the best he could do was turn his head so as not to vomit on Lena's clothing. He retched, though only a string of drool came of it. When the car hit a bump, it felt as though Oskar's skull were attached directly to the undercarriage; the pain was beyond imagining, though it faded, and Oskar felt himself fading again, too. A fresh bump woke him up. On the second try, he was able to pull himself up into something like a sitting position, his head propped against the seatback.

"Where are we?" he said.

The car windows were rolled down, but all he could see outside were trees everywhere, looming in the penumbra of the headlamps, stretching twisted limbs over the road and vanishing beside the car with a whoosh and a brief echo of engine noise.

"We're in the Reinhardswald," von Ewigholz said, sounding almost cheerful. The dim blue light suited the icy character of his skin, the hardness of his features. Compared to Oskar, he looked healthy, and he drove with the sort of intuitive carelessness one uses on familiar roads.

Oskar tried to think of something reasonable to say—to reassert his presence, or maybe to reestablish his mental competence—but all he could think of was "I've been to the Reinhardswald before." It sounded stupid right away.

"Yes!" von Ewigholz exclaimed. "The fairy-tale forest. *Die Brüder Grimm.* And it's now protected territory." He repeated this for Clair in English, adding, "Like one of your national parks. Only here, you know, it's not so much the wildness that's being protected, or the views, or what you call the natural resources. This place hasn't

actually been wild for a very, very long time. It was a private hunting ground for centuries, guarded by wardens, groomed by forest-
ers. Look at the trees, how huge they are. It's because the smaller
trees were cut to make room, and the unhealthy branches carefully
pruned out. No, what's protected here is the *magic*. The old legends.
The great myths of Germany."

They drove on for a while in silence, the road twisting relent-
lessly, always crawling up onto higher and higher ground. Oskar
could halfway remember a map—a map made for tourists, he
thought, meant to look older than it was—showing stylized trees
and mountains and rivers coursing like melted sapphire. And there
was a castle—

"We used to come hiking here," von Ewigholz said, speaking
German again, his voice quieter. "In the Weiss Ritter. Wonderful
days."

"Weiss Ritter!" Clair repeated, making a great thing of the *r*'s.
"The White Knights. How old were you?"

Von Ewigholz gave him a look, a curious one from Oskar's
back-seat perspective.

"I was the youngest of the group," he said. "Eleven, at the start.
But we came back each year. Then one year there was some trouble.
After that, I—"

There was some trouble. Oskar remembered the Weiss Ritter: a
right-wing bund that got itself banned from Movement gatherings
on account of its members' proclivity toward getting into fights.
There were boys who'd been badly injured—Jewish boys, or boys
who looked like they might be Jewish, or Socialists, or "friend-lovers"
(he'd never heard that Movement term elsewhere), or any number
of other things a White Knight could not abide. It seemed to Oskar
there were pieces here that fit and some that didn't, the largest of
these being that a former Weiss Ritter, now an SS officer, had lately
shot a Gestapo agent in the forehead.

The car was braking now. They'd pulled up onto level ground
and entered a clearing in which, between the headlamps and the
moon, Oskar could see what looked like an old-fashioned wood-
man's hut. There was a space to park out front, rolled flat, covered
in fine gravel, that showed signs of other vehicles having come and

gone. Von Ewigholz switched the lights off, set the hand brake and turned in the driver's seat so he could see everyone.

"This is the last place to stop," he said. "It's a public camp house. Hikers can use it, hunters, anyone. People leave things behind sometimes. Books and so forth. I was thinking that perhaps someone left a few pieces of clothing that might be useful for disguise. And also perhaps a hiking map."

This was smart, Oskar thought. Smart but peculiar, somehow counterintuitive, von Ewigholz thinking about disguise. Something that Oskar didn't really understand. It was like an experiment in science class where the results turned out . . . not wrong, exactly, but different from what you'd expected. You'd poured these ingredients into a container and stirred them together and they turned an unusual color that you couldn't find on the chart. But maybe it was the wrong chart, or you didn't follow the instructions properly, or one of the ingredients had been labeled incorrectly . . .

"Should we go in?" Clair said.

"No," said von Ewigholz. "Just one of us would be faster."

"I'll go," said Lena, reaching for the door handle.

"Wait!" Oskar's voice was loud in the car's close interior. "Somebody might already be in there. Which of us looks . . . least alarming?"

The four of them appraised one another. Lena had blood on her clothes. Von Ewigholz likewise. Oskar—well, he was probably the worst off. So it was down to Clair: disheveled but presentable.

"But what if they try to talk to me?" he said.

"Grab whatever you can and leave," Lena told him. "If you're confused, just say *entschuldigen.*"

"*Entschuldigen!*" Clair mimicked, making a great show of the *u,* and draped his scarf dramatically around his neck.

After less than a minute, he scampered back with a half-folded bit of paper flapping from one hand and an anorak from the other, breathless and giggling as he leapt into the car.

"God, there was a fat man *snoring* in there. And somebody else—I didn't want to look. Let's get out of here."

As befit a getaway driver, von Ewigholz already had the Opel in gear. He switched the lights on, and the car lurched back onto the forest road.

Lena took the crumpled paper and flattened it on her lap. "Does anyone have a match?" she asked.

A *Wandervogel* should always have matches, but Oskar did not. Von Ewigholz fished out a zinc lighter with the emblem of the SS Cavalry Regiment and handed it to Clair. The boy struck it merrily, his face glowing in the blue-and-orange flame that revealed this paper as a map, a finely detailed one showing topography and watersheds, with a few points of human interest added as though in afterthought. It was entitled *"Sababurg und Reinhardswald mit umliegendem Gebiet."*

Lena read the title aloud for the benefit of the front seat. "The 'surrounding territory' looks pretty empty," she said, running two fingers over it as though checking for land mines. "I don't know where we are on here. Was the spa called Bad—" Abruptly she squeezed her eyes shut. "Oh, Anna."

That name seemed to break the spell of electric, incredulous, half-frantic energy that had been running through them since their escape. Oskar hadn't especially noticed it until now, when the charge dropped and in its absence he found only dread and the smell of still-damp blood and a dark road away from the horror behind them to whatever doom lay ahead. His head started to hurt again.

Lena might have started crying. He felt an impulse to take her hand, to comfort her—but then the thought of Anna woke other things in him too.

"What was she doing back there?" He was looking at Clair. "You said you thought she was up to something. What did you mean?"

"I don't know." Looking bewildered, the boy snapped the lighter shut, extinguishing the flame. In the darkness, Oskar could hear him take a breath, letting the air out through his teeth as though the blank noise, the failure of speech, fairly represented his thoughts. But then he said, "I guess it was just an odd feeling. Just—how she was acting when I came down to get my flute."

"It's not fair to talk like this," Lena told them. "Either of you."

Oskar was ready to reply—and then they'd be arguing, and perhaps that would be healthy, airing out their suddenly dark and conflicted feelings—but von Ewigholz eased off the accelerator and glanced at Clair.

"It wasn't just a feeling," he said. "And you weren't wrong."

He let the car roll to a stop. His expression was all but impossible to read by the faint dashboard lights. He seemed to be frowning. He looked, perhaps, like someone who'd just been reminded of a trivial but vexing oversight—a book left on the table outside, a call he'd meant to return.

"She was making a plan," he said, in his ordinary flat timbre. "I don't know who she was making it with. Someone on the staff there, probably. Another member of the cell. Or of another cell, who knows how they work. I wasn't quite awake; the doctor had given me something. But I wasn't quite asleep either, and she didn't know that. I could hear them talking in the hall—"

"I *knew* it," Clair interrupted. "I *knew* somebody was there."

"You were right." Von Ewigholz's eyes remained expressionless, but in his voice there was a kind of insistence, as though he were not just speaking but declaring. "And from what I could hear, the plan seemed to be about you."

Clair stared back for a moment, confused, then gave a short, nervous laugh. "About *me*?"

"About you—and *this opportunity*. We can't waste this opportunity, she said. There was more, but that's all I could hear."

Oskar's head was throbbing, and it felt like a manifestation of his anger. He clenched his hand into a fist but couldn't see anything to punch.

"But what did she mean?" Clair said. "*What* opportunity?"

Von Ewigholz shook his head. "That's all I heard. I'm sorry."

Oskar had never once heard an SS man say he was sorry and couldn't imagine that such a thing was possible. Sorry for what? Lying there half-conscious recovering from a bullet wound, because some amateur guerrilla had screwed up a simple drop-off and gotten him shot? This thought made Oskar angrier still, and it was unsettling to realize that the anger was on behalf of von Ewigholz.

Then Lena said, "Oh, no."

Oskar looked up quickly, afraid that some terrible new thing had arisen. But Lena still had her eyes closed.

She was shaking her head. "Oh, Anna," she said. Her tone had changed.

"What do you mean?" von Ewigholz asked—and his voice was different too, sharper, more like an interrogation.

"I mean . . ." She opened her eyes, which shone large and clear in the dim blue light. "I mean about Clair—Anna's big plan. Her stupid plan, all the way back on the *Eulenspiegel*. What to do with him."

It was obvious that she had more to say, so everyone stayed quiet and let her get to it.

"It was to do with a manifesto. I don't know who wrote it, but it's a statement of SPD principles, 'A Message to All Germans.' It was published in *Neuer Vorwärts*—we read it in America. Anna's cell, though, wanted something bigger. They had the idea that they could pressure the big papers, the European papers, maybe even German ones, into printing it. Only no one knew how—and then somebody thought, What if we had a hostage? Of course it was crazy, but they never sat down to think *how* crazy it was, because there were no hostages in sight. And how would you even *get* one? And what Socialist would do that? But then, you know, suddenly we had Clair."

"You never *had Clair*," von Ewigholz said, with disconcerting force. "Do you think I would've let you—"

"You weren't in much of a position to stop us," Lena interrupted, bridling. "To stop *her*. I mean, I don't think she would've—"

"A fanatic is capable of anything," he said. "I would have stopped her. Or he would have."

He meant Oskar, signaling as much with a slight inclination of his head. Oskar was as surprised as anyone.

Clair snapped the lighter open again. "Well, *this* is exciting," he said drolly. "I've never been a hostage before."

Lena's eyes were down on the map again, but if she saw anything of interest there, she kept it to herself. Von Ewigholz put the car back in gear, and they resumed their bumpy progress along the forest road, which seemed to have gotten even rougher beyond the camping hut.

Oskar was brooding—a serious activity that required his complete awareness. He registered an occasional change of landscape or elevation without focus, like the music you don't really notice in a movie because you're concentrating on the characters and their improbable but arresting plight.

After a while he said, to no one in particular, "I think she saved our lives."

He was thinking of Anna struggling idiotically with the old revolver. Only not idiotically, he thought. She'd drawn the Gestapo man's attention away from Oskar, whom he'd been ready to kill. And in so doing, she'd given Oskar time to make good use of Tiller's knife. She hadn't thrown away those final seconds of her life—she'd given them to her comrades. She'd let Oskar be the hero, to rescue Lena and rejoin the others. Had she understood what she was doing? Or was it some noble instinct, activated in extremis?

One thinks of dying heroically—von Ewigholz had said that. Oskar had never given dying much thought at all—and now it seemed a miracle that he was alive, an unfathomable gift.

"Do you have a plan?" he asked von Ewigholz.

"This is my plan," he answered, gesturing around them— meaning, presumably, the old forest.

It seemed to Oskar as good a plan as any. He laid his head on the seatback and fell promptly asleep.

THE HIGH POINT OF THE SEASON

BERLIN, FASANENSTRASSE: 27 MAY

The Baroness von F—— read the morning papers that day with unusual avidity. In the afternoon, she summoned the young friend of an old diplomat to buy more. By three o'clock, she was taking little sips of her fourth cigarette from the meerschaum holder—the house girl having hidden herself away on the top floor instead of serving tea. The Baroness didn't seem to notice.

It was one of her "at home" days, those twice-every-week, rain-or-shine occasions when she opened the grand and gloomy flat to all comers. Attendance, after dropping over the winter, had picked up again as the famous *Berliner Luft* grew warm and redolent of lilacs, while the quickening pace of events in the Sudetenland—the "May crisis," the papers were calling it—gave everyone something fresh and horrid to talk about. The Baroness's old redoubt in the Fasanenstrasse was one of the few places in town where one could talk of such things openly, among like-minded people, while swallowing cocktails and enjoying, or enduring, whatever music was on offer. There were *so* many unemployed musicians these days, and many of them, poor dears, would play for pfennigs and a swipe at the hors d'oeuvres.

Sometimes there was dancing, and the Baroness hoped there'd be tonight. She hadn't danced in ages—and no, she didn't plan to make a spectacle of herself this evening, thank you. But she loved the *idea* of dancing and felt rather strongly that more people ought to be doing it. There was something, as the English said, "in the air."

And there was something in the papers.

In her newly restless state of mind, the Baroness amused herself for three-quarters of an hour arranging the latest editions on little tables around the Grand Salon. From one of them, the *Tageblatt* declared,

SON OF U.S. SENATOR HELD
BY SOCIALIST CRIME GANG

while from another, the normally sober *Allgemeine* all but shouted,

KIDNAPPED!!!
VISITING VIP FEARS
FOR SON'S LIFE

But pride of place—an antique easel standing adjacent to the buffet—went to the *Morgenpost*, exceptionally sordid today with a front-page splash by the all-but-dead-and-resurrected journalist Greimer, under the headline

DEAD OR ALIVE?
"I SAW THE YANKEE
KID ON A SLAB,"
EYEWITNESS CLAIMS

"*Ach*," said the Baroness, admiring her handiwork from a tactful distance. "What trash! Such a horrid little person." Then she remembered: "Where is my tea? Fräulein, where *are* you?"

The girl was nowhere to be found, but it was half five already. So the Baroness decided to have some cognac.

The gathering a few hours hence in the late Baron's library was more animated than usual—in the cartoonish fashion, with everyone's features and characteristics exaggerated to an almost ludicrous degree. Except no one was laughing tonight. Even Cissy, the White Russian princess, sat quietly on the edge of an old armchair, its leather interior having caved in some weeks ago after decades of honorable strain and rigor, her posture regally upright, one hand clutching a martini while the other worried a table napkin.

"I guess this is what you'd call a 'setback,' " said the old Brigadier. "I hope it suits you."

"Now, *Brigadegeneral*," said Guido, the art dealer. "You know Hans-Bernd had nothing to do with this."

"Well, who did, then? Don't tell me it's the damned Socialists. There *are* no Socialists in Germany. And if there are, they're hiding under a bed somewhere, praying to Engels's ghost to make all the bad people go away."

Hans-Bernd stood by the large globe, rotating it from east to west and then back again. One moment you saw Germany in green. The next, America in a pale, indeterminate blue-gray color. Then Germany again. Hans-Bernd was dressed casually, as though just back from motoring about in his flashy Mercedes or maybe playing a round of golf with his British pals. He displayed a sort of fatal calmness, but the skin above the neckline of his white cotton sweater was blood-red—to anyone who knew him, a frightening contrast. "It's a cock-up," he said. "And the timing could hardly be worse."

"You like to *time* your cock-ups, do you?" the Brigadier asked.

Hans-Bernd turned on him. Still, the same fatal calm. "Yes, actually. Whenever possible."

Cissy started to interject—perhaps simply to remind everyone that there was a lady in the room, in case bloodshed was being contemplated—but the old general cut her off.

"I thought you *wanted* something like this. A setback—you were always going on about that, weren't you? Something to embarrass the regime and embolden the army to act. Isn't this the sort of thing you had in mind?"

"Well, that would depend—"

This came from the naval officer, the one called Jaap. They turned to look at him. Such a reasonable fellow, you felt. He had that sailor's quality: steady in a storm, feet planted solidly on deck.

"That would depend," he said, "on the exact circumstances,

wouldn't it?" Using his fingers, he ticked off the various points. "Is the boy dead or alive. If he's alive, where, and who's holding him. If he's dead, who killed him. How will the father react. Who will the Americans hold responsible."

"Oh, but he can't be *dead*," said Cissy. There was a courteous silence, but she offered nothing to support this proposition. Perhaps it had been made on literary grounds.

"I doubt the Socialists would harm anyone," said Guido.

"There are *no damn*—"

"Who cares about Socialists?" said Hans-Bernd, flapping his arms like a querulous falcon. "Or even about this child? We're talking about the fate of nations." He thumped on the globe, wincingly hard. "Redrawing the map of Europe. Why should anyone give a damn about some pampered Yankee schoolboy?"

The Brigadier was thunderstruck, and Guido shook his head— even by the standards of the art world, this was pretty cold-blooded. Jaap didn't react, just kept watching Hans-Bernd as though anticipating a sequel.

At last Cissy broke the silence: "Because he's just a *Junge*, for heaven's sake."

"Exactly!" Hans-Bernd almost shouted. "Ten thousand honest citizens get locked up in concentration camps—twenty thousand, a hundred thousand, it doesn't matter—and we just get on with our business. But let the spoiled whelp of some foreigner no one's ever heard of get snatched and it's on every front page in Germany. Well—that's human nature, isn't it? Nothing good or bad about it, it's just the way we are. And that's why these cock-ups have to be *managed*. If there's going to be a scandal, it should be *our* scandal. The timing, the reaction, the outcome . . . we should have somebody *in there*, driving it, steering it. Instead we've got a total catastrophe. And you know, I'm scheduled to meet with the senator tomorrow afternoon."

"You are?" said Guido. "What—"

Hans-Bernd held up a warning hand. "Nothing to do with this. And more's the pity."

Jaap stood up. Something was bothering him, a loose wire dangling in his mind, a connection that continued to elude him. He'd been troubled all day—actually, since the middle of last night. A call had come through from Nest Bremen saying they'd received a signal but couldn't discuss it on the open line. Jaap had been obliged to leave his hotel in the Mitte and venture to the Tirpitzufer in order to place a secure call, wherein he was told that one of his operatives had surfaced after being out of contact for nearly three months. The message was garbled, unfortunately, Pfeiffer having changed the protocol a few weeks ago on the grounds of "heightened security." In so doing, he'd torn up the old plain-language code that had been in use since the invention of radio and brought in new people to use the rewritten code—also in plain language but somehow better, more scientific, in that it didn't *sound* like code, in case anyone was listening. Of course, that very possibility was why you talked in code in the first place, but no one had consulted Jaap. Nor had they asked him to sign off on hiring—could you believe it? — a theatrical coach to teach the duty officers how to speak naturally on the telephone, again for heightened security. The result of this hogwash was that the duty officer had scribbled down something about an agent being sick and then gone off watch. At least, thank God, Pfeiffer hadn't changed the nomenclature—Jaap was still Herr Braun—so the message was properly flagged for his attention and the agent in question correctly identified as [Opname] Erwin Kaspar, [Name] Oskar Langweil, [Ort] DE, [Status] *Unbekannt*.

So Ossi was alive, somewhere in Germany. And "sick," which Jaap took to mean having some kind of trouble. At least it would have signified that in the old code. Jaap supposed you'd been in the spy game too long if you caught yourself feeling nostalgic about some outdated code.

He began to pace. Hans-Bernd was talking, then the Brigadier, now Cissy, but Jaap was preoccupied, picking at this small but somehow important mental knot. He tried to, in the jargon, back-trace it: code, in-country, Ossi, Tirpitzufer, Bremen, midnight, meeting, senator, Socialists, boy, kidnapping, setback. Then he tried it sequentially, past to present. This time he remembered the broken chair, Hans-Bernd's sweater, the globe, the telephone, the theatrical coach.

The globe.

He stopped pacing. He looked at the globe, then turned away. It wasn't *this* globe he was thinking of; it was how he'd seen it a few minutes ago. Not focusing, just glancing. Hans-Bernd spinning it: green, blue-gray, green . . .

"When did this boy arrive in Germany?" he said.

They looked at him oddly. Well, they would, wouldn't they? Who knows what he'd interrupted. Whatever it was, he got the feeling they were happy to change the subject. Guido said, "I believe it was three or four days ago. I can check the newspapers, if you—"

"Do check, please," Jaap said. "Find out what ship he came on, if you can. Also, was the senator on the same ship? Anyone else? When was the boy last seen, and where? Wait, never mind, just— bring some papers here, would you? Thanks."

The evening had been a rousing success, a social triumph, the high point of the season in the glittering *Hauptstadt*. Its most vivid moment had *not* been, as everyone expected, the arrival of the born-again journalist Greimer with a lady from the Press Office on either arm—nor the moment shortly afterward when a beefy percussionist, lately employed at the Cabaret Trigilaw and acting upon instructions from the Baroness herself, had shown these ladies to the door, one in each hand. "We'll be having none of Goebbels's whores here," the Dame is said to have remarked, though no one could precisely remember hearing her say this.

The *moment* had come around eleven. A young man whom no one seemed to know—"strange," they said afterward, "underfed" or "discontent," dressed despite the heat in a long cloak and clutching a volume of poetry—had either leaned on or stumbled into or, best of all, been violently thrust against the aged balcony rail, which had splintered and sent the fellow plummeting into the orchestra below, smashing a purported Guarneri violin. Despite no mortal injuries resulting, everyone who was present and many who were not would be speaking of only two things for days to come: the kidnapping and the party. The "May crisis" would be temporarily forgotten. The Press Office would not be happy.

Among the last guests to leave that night were the handsome

Hans-Bernd from the Interior Ministry and a Kriegsmarine officer in the rumpled uniform of a *Kapitänleutnant*. They left together
but separated outside on Fasanenstrasse, the former carrying a nondescript leather case that held, had anyone looked, plans for the
German occupation of Czechoslovakia, the latter empty-handed
though his mind was filled to capacity. He'd arrived hours ago feeling disconsolate. Now he was exhilarated, frightened, impatient and
hyperalert.

He had plenty to think about. His agent. The war that was coming (or not). The senator's missing son. But foremost, his chat with
Hans-Bernd in the late Baron's sanctum sanctorum, the writing
room next to the library. Their main topic had of course been the
General Staff's planning documents, passed personally to Jaap that
afternoon by Admiral Canaris, commander of the Abwehr, to be
delivered to Senator Townsend: *proof certain*, in the admiral's own
words, *that this nation has no favorable intention toward the Czechs*.
Ponderous stuff indeed—but Jaap had yet one more thing on his
mind.

He'd waited until the *tête-à-tête* was drawing to a close, and then,
while Hans-Bernd was packing the documents away in his briefcase and—who knew?—trying on the idea that he held the fate of
Europe in his hands, Jaap said casually, "You know, back there you
were explaining why we need to keep matters under our control. To
drive them, you said. To *steer* them."

Hans-Bernd nodded. He was holding the leather case, feeling it,
weighing it.

"You said we need to have somebody *in there*," Jaap went on. "I'm
just curious—what did you mean, exactly?"

Hans-Bernd blinked at him, his attention slowly shifting.
"In there with the senator's boy, that's all. If there's going to be a
kidnapping—there never should've been, that's foolish and counter-
productive, but supposing there were—we should have something
to say about it. Even if we can't dictate the outcome absolutely, we
should at least be in a position to make sure the worst doesn't happen. The worst being, of course, the murder of the hostage."

Jaap nodded—yes, that was all perfectly reasonable. "And if we
did have somebody in there," he said, stepping as lightly as he could,

"if we *could* dictate the outcome, what would it be? Just as, well, a thought experiment."

Hans-Bernd frowned, seeming unsure of how much thought this experiment deserved. Picking up the briefcase, preparing to leave, he said, "There are two possibilities, aren't there? If the boy's dead, the blame has to fall on the government. And I don't mean passively—*Oh my, how could they let this happen?* Somebody's got to have blood on his hands. And if the boy's alive, the regime can't get any credit. We'd have to find somebody—a beat cop, a Good Samaritan, a Catholic fucking priest, it doesn't matter. This person saved the day, and as for the government," he said with a shrug, "*Oh my, how could they let this happen?* Either way, it won't make the papers. But that doesn't matter. Our audience is a tiny group of senior officers, and maybe it's only Ludwig Beck."

He took a step toward the door, then stopped. "Oh—and since we're playing this game, everything should happen by tomorrow morning; I'm meeting Townsend in the afternoon. We're playing *tennis.*" He paused, letting the word bounce. "The inspired thought being, when you play tennis, you carry a bag." He gave the leather case a shake. "Out of one bag, into another."

With that wisdom he departed, Jaap on his heels. They said good night on the sidewalk. Hans-Bernd went off to commit treason, Jaap to puzzle out whether or not his man really was *in there* and, if so, what he might do about it.

DO YOU TRULY WANT TO KNOW?

By dawn they'd left the Opel behind, having driven it deeply into a rough stand of young *Tannenbäume* and then backtracked, setting out along trails that were marked at intervals by notches cut into the bark of certain trees or by tiny, elegant cairns. Oskar's head throbbed for a while, but breathing the spring air seemed to ease it. The trails led generally southward, with bends and switchbacks taking them anywhere from southeast to due west. They were on high ground, though the trees enclosed them so completely that the only views were down forest naves so long that an arrow shot from a hunter's bow would fall to the ground before reaching the end, and the new daylight was admitted only sparingly by leaves so high overhead you couldn't identify them by shape.

Oskar had been in mountains like this before—had conceivably hiked this very path—but the paradox of ancient woods was that they were always changing. However many centuries they'd stood there, the mood and character and the feeling you got walking through them were never alike from one time to the next. Von Ewigholz had been right to call it magic; hardly a childish thought, it came from a deep understanding of place, and there was no better word for it. How many hundreds of stories had grown from this black soil, how many witches had stepped out of the dawn mist, how many Jacks had strode whistling through, how many blooded princes had come to grief? These were just stories, and no grown-up believed in them.

But then grown-ups had their own foolish and strange beliefs, far beyond the power of reason. Maybe such beliefs had driven these four companions here, maybe not; perhaps there was no good explanation.

Oskar felt differently that morning than he had felt at any other time in his life, but the closest points of reference, the ones that seemed most useful, were certain moments from his youth and particularly from his days in the *Jugendbewegung*, when he'd come with his comrades to a place like the Reinhardswald after a spell of struggle and confusion at home or in *Gymnasium* or with the world in general, days when he hadn't been sure who he was or might become, when life could not be endured and there must be an end to it, there simply must—and then he was here, among trees as old as Germany, with friends who would be his friends forever, and everything needful in life could be stowed efficiently in a rucksack, with room for a recorder and a songbook. If you could walk, the world belonged to you. If you could play a song on your recorder, the children of Hameln would follow you into the mountains.

Now Oskar was walking with a tune running through his head that he hadn't given much thought to; it was pleasant enough and had the right sort of rhythm for the pace they were making, unhurried yet resolute, repeating itself untiringly—until he caught himself whistling along. And he realized it had to stop.

It was the *Geheimeslied*—the Secret Anthem you learned when you were admitted to the dj.1.11, the song that could never be written down, the one you sang only at the start of meetings or around the holy campfire, with your comrades, your brothers. Never in public, nor even whistling or humming, nor even *thinking it in your head*. Oskar smiled. It seemed comical now but had been so serious then, and he supposed it still was, if for different reasons altogether. It was a kind of affirmation: who you were, who you stood with. Who had circled the fire with you. And so, by an inevitable chain of association, Oskar found himself thinking of Jaap Saxo—in the jargon of the trade, his controller. Where was Jaap now? Had he gotten Oskar's message? And if he had, how could he possibly respond?

That conundrum ran through Oskar's head like the Secret Anthem, cycling endlessly, and he felt just as helpless in trying to break out of it. The predicament seemed familiar—another ghostly remnant of his boyhood, reanimated now in these ancient woods—and he supposed it was rather like those moments when he'd felt just at the edge of understanding something huge and important, if only he could find the one missing piece, the link that would tie it all together. So many pieces were already in place, so many ideas and yearnings and dreams and plans and poems and wordless intimations were floating there, available but waiting to cohere. *Verdammt*. This was never going to end, was it?

They halted an hour short of midday in a glade between two overshadowing rises that were too small to count as hills. The grass was high enough to be cut for hay, with small white daisies on tall stems and cornflowers that looked blue from a distance but purple close up. Hagen spent one Gestapo bullet on a good-sized hare. They drank from a stream and used the water to wash their faces and scrub some of the blood from their clothes. Clair built a fire, then lay down in the warm grass to sleep. Lena chose her own spot some distance away. Oskar rigged a cooking spit while Hagen dressed the hare. Then the two men sat cross-legged at a distance and angle calibrated by masculine instinct, allowing them to stare at the fire while keeping the other in view, far enough apart to be safe from being leapt upon but close enough to speak quietly if anything needed to be said. Oskar had no idea how such matters worked themselves out. He'd read a bit of Jung and gotten the vague idea that his body was inhabited at times by some ageless archetypal being, probably not a very nice one. The Blond Beast—well, look at Hagen.

When he did look—because the thought was irresistible—he found the SS man staring back. It was as though he'd been waiting calmly, like a predator with time on his hands, for precisely this moment.

"You know what the problem is now," Hagen said, as straightforwardly as he said most everything. "The problem is that they can kill him. The SOPADE will be blamed. It's a tidy solution. No conflicting accounts, no inconvenient survivor to say, 'Really, they treated me quite well. We had a fine dinner one night when they let me drink wine.' Better just to kill him. That's what they'll think. Probably they're thinking it right now."

Oskar felt these ideas entering his consciousness like a series of soft blows, one after another. There seemed to be no gaps between them where a counterargument might be wedged in. But for the sake of discussion he said, "Who's *they*? I mean, specifically. And how can you be so sure?"

Hagen chose this of all moments to smile. It wasn't especially cheerful; rather, more commiserative—as though Oskar had inquired into some complicated family matter and the smile was by way of asking him, *Do you truly want to know?* Oskar waited for more, but apparently Hagen had said all he intended to. He turned his attention to the carcass on the spit, getting up on his knees so he could reach in and turn it. The movement caused him to flinch, and he ran a hand gingerly down his side.

"Here," said Oskar, moving closer, "let me have a look."

The other man paused and then slowly raised his arms, like a prisoner submitting to a pat-down.

There was no sign of bleeding. Oskar lifted an edge of the bandage, and from what he could see, the tissues seemed to be mending and the inflammation had gone down. "It looks better," he said.

"Yes, the doctor—he did a good job, I think."

For a Jew? Oskar wondered. But perhaps that was unfair. Who knew what this man thought about Jews, or about anything? He softly pressed the bandage back into place.

"And how is your head?" Hagen asked. He rose on his knees so he could look down at Oskar from slightly above. "Bend your neck, please. No, like this—"

Without warning he placed a hand on the back of Oskar's head and slowly but firmly pushed it forward. The moment was disconcerting but at the same time mundane, a pair of battered soldiers inspecting each other for damage.

"Not so bad" was the verdict.

"No?" said Oskar.

Hagen slapped him lightly on the shoulder. *"Immer weiter!"*

Ever onward. But to where?

"Do you have a new plan?" he asked.

Hagen was turning the hare and didn't answer right away. "Well, you know," he said finally, "in my service, we're not really trained to make plans. Those are made"—pointing the stick that was his cooking tool up at the sky—"by somebody high above. We're trained to act. And to be true and loyal at all times. Look, it's right here."

He turned sideways to display his large steel belt buckle, which featured an eagle clutching a swastika, encircled by lettering. Oskar knew what it said without bothering to read it. *Meine Ehre heisst Treue*, a slogan he'd always thought marginally incoherent. "My honor is called loyalty" certainly was more suited to a boys' hiking club like the Weiss Ritter than to the Black Knighthood of the SS. The obvious question was how Hagen squared this weighty concept of loyalty with what he was doing here and now. And Oskar supposed the most likely answer was that he saw no conflict at all—that he'd been given an assignment and was doing his best to carry it out. He was honor-bound to be Clair's protector, to keep the boy safe and trouble-free until he got to where he was going, and if that entailed incidentally getting entangled with the Resistance and having to shoot a Gestapo man—well, that was unfortunate, but it had no bearing on his one essential duty, his singular version of *Treue*.

That was only a theory, the best one Oskar had managed to date. The truth was, he found this man basically unfathomable. Maybe the rest of the SS were as well. Though he doubted it.

The hare was sizzling, and the two men sat watching it. The silence between them had grown weirdly comfortable. Oskar felt no impulse to break it and was surprised when Hagen picked up their conversation more or less where they'd left off.

"You're probably better at planning than I am. I imagine your training was quite different."

That was a probe, of course, but, all things considered, a gentle one. It might even have been a sporting challenge: *I got us this far, let's see if you can do any better.* Oskar could imagine Hagen saying that, the calibrated tone he would use, the hint of combativeness neutralized by his artful choice of pronouns, dropping the formal *Sie* for the more companionable *du*. In fact, now that Oskar thought about it, they'd been addressing each other as *du* for some time now. When had *that* started? And how long had he been thinking of the other man as Hagen? Be careful who you circle the fire with, he told himself.

"I wouldn't know where to start," he said.

"Well, we do have a map."

And so they did. Oskar went to fetch it, slipping it out of a pocket in Lena's jacket while she slept. He stood for a few moments watching her chest rise and fall, the copper hair tumbled across her face, mouth slightly open, one arm outstretched as though reaching for something in her dream. Oskar felt a powerful and helpless sense of longing—not so much for Lena, perhaps, as for something he'd seen in her, or through her, a prospect so dazzling he'd drawn back from it. He yearned to return there. But first he needed to get out of here, to get everyone out. Away from this dangerous meadow in a fairy-tale forest, where beauty always signified a trap.

By the time Lena and Clair awoke, Oskar and Hagan had, if not a plan, at least a tentative outline. Hagen laid it out while the others ate, given his gift for speaking plainly and the lesser probability that he, as opposed to Oskar, would provoke Lena to object. The two of them had agreed on that.

"Here is Sababurg," Hagen said, pointing to a spot near the center of the map, which was spread over trampled grass and weighted with little stones. The place in question was identified by an icon—two turrets with a gate between them—that was easy enough to interpret, but Hagen explained it anyway. "This is a castle. A famous castle actually, the Dornröschenschloss. You'll know it, Clair, from the story of Snow White. Those thorn roses are real, or at least were. The thicket ran five kilometers across, a means of holding up attacking armies. Today it's mostly a ruin, but also an attraction that's very popular at this time of year. There's a beer garden and craftsmen selling, oh, many things, clothing and fake weapons and items you might hang up in your home, all very traditional. We loved to go there, those in my group. The younger boys would buy shields and wooden swords, the older ones real hunting knives."

"That's very nice," Lena said through a mouthful of gamy meat. "But what—"

"It sounds boring," said Clair.

"What's it got to do with us?" she continued.

"The point is," Hagen told them, "it's a lively place and one that's difficult to monitor. Supposing we're under surveillance, which we must assume. And while it looks very old, it's been brought up-to-date for the convenience of visitors—telephones and modern plumbing and so forth. In short, it has most of the things we need right now: food and a means of both changing our appearance and sending a message."

"So you propose," Lena said, swallowing, "that we just march in there, do a little shopping, sit down in the beer garden—and then what? Sing patriotic songs to throw off suspicion?"

Now here, thought Oskar, is where he'd have made some intemperate remark and wrecked everything.

But Hagen just went on in his blandly factual manner: "No, of course not. You're quite right: we can't all go marching in there at once. That could be fatal. Far better if just one person goes in. To buy bits of clothing for everyone—shirts and hats, that kind of thing—and a bag to carry the food in. And while that's being prepared, there should be time for another telephone call."

"A telephone call," Lena repeated, as if she needed to say the words to gauge their absurdity. "Who, exactly, are you planning to call?"

"I should probably get in touch with my father," Clair interrupted. "On the off chance he's noticed I've disappeared."

Oskar and Hagen traded glances. They hadn't considered this.

"That might be a good idea," Hagen said carefully, "or it might not. It could bring a kind of attention we don't care for just now. Or put you at greater risk. Perhaps it's wiser to wait until you can call from somewhere absolutely safe. That would ease his mind. If you called right now, you'd have to tell him, Hello, Papa, it's Clairborne and I'm in a horrible fix."

The boy started laughing. He couldn't stop—this imagined conversation with his father seeming to have cracked some barrier between the conceivable and the absurd. "Believe me," he managed to say at last, "I'd *love* to make that phone call."

"Well, you can't," Lena said, but this dose of laughter had lightened everyone's mood. "So who's the lucky person, then? Who gets to see Snow White's castle?"

Hagen was not to be hurried. "Here are the things to consider. We believe Oskar was singled out for attention as far back as the *Robert Ley;* his description has presumably been circulated. Later, when the boat stopped at Polle, the authorities met a Herr and Frau Sinclair and inspected their papers. So now they'll be looking not just for Oskar but for a couple traveling together. We don't know whether Clair has been reported missing, but it's certainly possible, and in any case, his limited German doesn't recommend him for a trip to Sababurg alone. That leaves me, but look—my uniform has bullet holes in it, and here are some mysterious stains, my shoes badly scuffed. An SS officer doesn't go around looking like this."

"It sounds like you've ruled out everybody, then," Lena said.

"Perhaps not. We've ruled out Oskar, a couple traveling together, Clair, and myself. We haven't ruled out a woman traveling alone."

Lena had already prepared an objection: "They've *seen* me."

"*Someone* has, but only wearing a certain outfit, with a certain bearing, playing the role of a new middle-class wife. If we substitute a few bits of clothing, adjust your demeanor and get rid of the husband, they'll never make the connection. Remember, those men who boarded the boat weren't concerned about you; they weren't paying very close attention. Whatever description they've given, it wouldn't be much to go on."

Pensive, Lena bit her lip. "Look," she said, "it's not that I'm afraid to do this. I'm not. But what if they've questioned Tilde? And old Dr. Ruhmann. Or, dear God, poor Kleister."

Hagen held her gaze for a moment. "There's a risk," he conceded. "Whoever does this, there will be a risk." He seemed ready to say more but left it at that.

And maybe that was all she wanted—for the personal danger to be acknowledged. She nodded slightly, then again, more resolutely. "All right. Dress me up. Tell me *exactly* what I'm supposed to do. Let's get going."

They made a survey of the wardrobe on hand. The main problem was bloodstains, but by judicious selection and some rough tailoring with Tiller's knife, they managed to outfit Lena in the somewhat dated style of a jaunty *Wandervogelin*. Clair sacrificed his trousers to make hiking shorts—not being German, he was embarrassed about undressing in public, so Hagen lent him his own battle-stained uniform slacks, which fit like a tent, to the boy's seemingly boundless delight. They tried on the anorak but decided it was better left off, this being wrong for the weather. As a final touch they added Clair's scarf, which was long enough to wrap around twice, effectively eliminating her neck.

Lena waded into the stream, bending over to get a look at herself. "I look like a frog," she said.

"Careful, then!" said Clair. "Somebody might kiss you and change you back."

She'd already turned to leave when Oskar caught her arm and handed her a scrap of paper torn from a corner of the map. She held it close to her face, squinting at the minuscule writing.

"That's a number in Bremen," he said quietly. "Reverse the charges. Don't worry, they'll accept it. And this is a message for Herr Braun. He probably won't be available, so just leave this message— exactly these words."

Lena flicked an eye at him, quizzical and shrewd. Then she read it aloud with exaggerated precision: " 'Cousin Peter is feeling better. Please drop by for a Scotch on the rocks.' That's stupid, Oskar. If you saw this in a movie, you'd say the same thing. Is this really how spies talk?"

Oskar tried on the von Ewigholz smile: *Do you truly want to know?* Then he watched her walk away until the trail turned and she was out of sight.

CHRIST ON A ROCKING HORSE

BERLIN, MITTE AND KREUZBERG: EARLIER THAT MORNING

"What the hell kind of country is this?"

Bull Townsend could not sit down. The third breakfast of the morning lay steaming on a silver tray, two previous servings having been sent back to the kitchen because by the time the senator got around to spearing a cube of *Schinken* he declared it too cold to digest.

"Why hasn't the goddamn ambassador called? And where the hell is the *Polizeikommissar*—wasn't he supposed to be here an hour ago? If these Germans are so damn punctual, why can't they even keep an appointment when a person's life is at stake?"

The senator's progress about the room, too erratic to be called pacing, had taken him to a pair of enormous windows looking out over the Pariser Platz with a clear view of the Brandenburg Gate.

"The hell's a father supposed to do in a situation like this?" he said, seeming to address the city at large. "Just tell me that."

He turned from the window to face the grandly appointed hotel room. He looked terrible. In the opinion of Toby Lugan, who'd seen him at his best and at his worst, he looked *defeated*—and men like Bull should never look like that. They were, for all their human flaws, the mythic beasts that carried Toby's whole world around on their backs. He depended on them to keep standing, to go on bellowing their slogans and glad-handing their donors and gut-punching their political enemies for as long as the voters saw fit to keep them in office. If a man like Bull had to go down, it shouldn't happen like this. It should be out on the hustings, fighting to the final bell, going for the knockout even in a hopeless match.

"Tell me that," Townsend repeated, sounding almost pitiful. Or as if he really wanted an answer, which was so rarely the case.

"You're doing everything you can," Toby assured him, from his seat at a round Empire table big enough to play poker on. Before him, scattered in a fit of temper, lay police reports and newspaper clippings and embassy memos and one fuzzy picture of the missing Clairborne, blown up from a snapshot Bull carried in his wallet, outdated by a couple of years and showing the boy in his Sunday best and smiling obediently but, even so, with that look in his eyes, the silvery glint of insurrection. Where did that come from, Toby wondered—the mother? He barely knew Townsend's wife. But if she'd ever had a glint like that, three decades of booze had dulled the shine of it, and Bull had surely added a little abrasion. No, wait, Toby didn't mean . . . it was just that Bull wasn't likely an easy man to live with, was all.

Jesus H. Christ, thought Toby. Now I'm running damage control on my own brain.

"I'm not doing squat," said the senator from across the room.

"You've done everything the *Polizeikommissar* recommended," Toby said, incidentally correcting Bull's pronunciation. "You've been right out front, dictating the message, setting the tone of communication."

"*Setting the tone of—*" Townsend moved closer surprisingly fast, practically charging across the floor. "Listen to yourself, Toby. The hell's that even mean? I'm talking about my *son* here, and you're talking about dictating some goddamn message. I want to dictate anything, I've got a secretary for that. What I want is to find whoever's got my boy and wring their scrawny kraut necks. Now, who's going to help me do that? You? Mr. Ambassador fucking Wilson? Herr Adolf kiss-my-ass Hitler? Whoever it is, that's who I want to be talking to. And I tell you what, I'll put the fear of God in him."

Under the circumstances, Toby thought it best to let Bull blow himself out. For something to do in the meantime, he poked into the nearest stack of paper and extracted a copy of the senator's schedule—not the most current one, most of the engagements having been crossed through by someone in blue pencil. The only entries left untouched seemed to be related in one way or another to the kidnapping. This was not a picture Toby wanted to see.

"You know what, Senator," he said, addressing Bull by his proper title in hopes of brightening his mood. "It occurs to me that maybe we're letting the criminals have the upper hand here."

Townsend came to stand by the table, still glowering. "What in the *hell* you talking about?"

"I was just thinking . . . you know, we've kind of let them put you on the defensive. Everything we've been doing, your appearances, your press statements, even your private, off-the-record activities—it's all been coming in reaction to what these thugs are up to. And we don't even know what that really is. So I'm thinking, it's *you* who ought to be calling the plays here. You go where you want, see whoever you feel like talking to—you don't sit waiting for the phone to ring, if you know what I'm saying."

Townsend stared at him as if they'd been introduced just now and he was impatient for this stranger to explain himself. In a rather frightening tone, he said, "Go on. Whatever you're trying to say, do it in plain damn English."

"All right, let's take a look here. Ten a.m.: tour of the Krupp arms works. No point in that, we make fine weapons right at home. One o'clock: rally for Friends of the New Germany. I'd say at this point, the New Germany needs to *earn* your friendship, wouldn't you?"

Townsend grunted. So he was listening.

"But look here—four o'clock. Tennis with Herr Hans-Bernd Gisevius of the Interior Ministry. Let's think about this one."

"Interior runs the police, don't they?"

Toby rolled his eyes, then hoped the senator hadn't noticed. "It's complicated. They run *some* of the police. This country has more kinds of police than Carter has Little Liver Pills. But yes. But what's also good is this venue could be very effective. Private club in the Grunewald—that's on the west side of the city, a bunch of muckety-mucks have houses out there—so you go out in public for a little while, show the world you're not holed up at the Adlon, then you drive out to this club and disappear again. The press are told you're in conference with a high-ranking official from Interior. What's all that about? Who else is in there? We aren't saying. The Germans aren't saying. For all anyone knows, you're playing tennis. Then you come out and tell the reporters, 'No comment,' and drive back to the city and, let's see—how about seven o'clock, prayer service at the Gedächtniskirche? With chamber music. That might set a nice tone."

"Damn it, Toby, I told you. I don't give a rat's ass about any fucking *tone.*"

But his anger had dissipated. His mind was somewhere else now, away from a problematic son who for all anyone knew—for all Toby knew, anyhow—had staged his own disappearing act to get back at his dad for making him waste the summer at some Hitler Youth camp. Toby frankly wouldn't have put it past him. Nor would he even blame Clair, especially, except for the fact that, stunt or no stunt, it was making Toby's own lot temporarily wretched.

"Tennis doesn't sound so bad," Townsend was saying. "Get the old heart pumping."

He stood at the center of the room rehearsing an imaginary volley, switching from forehand to backhand with little grace but much exertion, making the game look actually *violent.* Though Toby had never seen him play; maybe there was a row of secret graves at the Army and Navy Club where his opponents were laid to rest.

This was the Bull Toby loved, and the one he—and America— needed. It was good to have him back.

You could say that Berlin agreed with Toby Lugan on the whole. Strolling from the Mitte to the Kreuzberg evoked in him a series of graduated emotions that ran along pretty much the same scale as an equivalent journey from Beacon Hill down to Southie. The shirts around the Tiergarten appeared to be stuffed with the same custom blend of pomposity and rectitude and moral shiftiness as those around the Boston Common. A few blocks out, you got into a purgatorial realm of strivers and worriers and clock watchers and butt sniffers, a cleanly and aspirational but fundamentally haunted world where people were afraid of losing the things they already had while still yearning painfully for more of the same, but better, newer, fancier; they aspired to graduate from middle-class anxiety to full-blown upper-class terror, to live in barricaded fortresses and send their children under guard to the very best schools to get their vowels straightened and their noses and chins reset to a proper inclination.

And then the Kreuzberg. Ah, this bloody, teeming, pug-ugly netherworld of deeply shadowed "backcourts" whose streets ran the wrong way and addresses were merely hopeful suggestions, whose open windows broadcast a running melodrama of laughter and curses and sobs and the occasional gunshot, whose clocks were right only twice a day, at quitting time and last call, whose walls were out of plumb but stood regardless, gravity could go stuff itself, building inspectors too, and Toby loved all of it just as he loved Southie. These were his people, and the sight of them in the streets—moving or going nowhere, perplexed, out of breath, dyspeptic, smiling insensibly, lost in thought, plotting their next caper, dreaming of a good meal, fearful of being recognized, fired with lust for that girl in the shop window, gutted with regret over things that should never have been said—made Toby's heart swell with universal sympathy and his fist clench with a strange and jealous anger. He didn't know where this anger came from or at whom he should direct it. He thought there was something right about this world and wrong about the other one, where he was forced to live. He felt someone ought to be made to *pay* for this discordance. And he also knew that feeling like this was crazy.

His meeting with Standartenführer Kohlwasser had been set for eleven at something called the Black Shoe. Now it was eleven-sixteen, according to his Timex. If such a place actually existed, it apparently did so without benefit of a sign. Not above asking for directions, Toby accosted the nearest passerby, who turned out to be a boy no older than twelve, dressed in clothes passed down, you had to presume, from a much larger brother. The boy knew just where Toby meant and pointed down the block, but this was mostly one anonymous shopfront after another, so in the end he led Toby in person to the proper address and waited courteously for whatever reward might be offered. The minority counsel of the Senate German Affairs Subcommittee knew many facts about exchange rates and monetary policy and balance-of-payments schedules but had no idea how much to tip an urchin who'd done him a kindness. The smallest bill in his pocket was a five-mark note, but what the hell, there but for the grace. The boy looked as though he'd just gotten enough money to bail his dad out, and Toby felt better about himself.

The Black Shoe was much the same inside as out, which was piss-poor. It was half full, which seemed slightly odd, since by conventional reckoning it was well past breakfast and too early for lunch. Toby expected to find Kohlwasser sitting by himself at a table in the back, probably facing the door, and was right on both accounts. As before, at the Trigilaw, he was wearing civilian clothes, a tasteful gray suit with a tie striped English-style in green and brown. Neither of them wasted time on social niceties; Toby took the only other chair, and Kohlwasser snapped his fingers to summon a waitress. She popped right over, looking tired but a little frantic, as if she'd been at it since dawn. She awaited their order incuriously—two whiskeys, water on the side—and when she turned away, Toby got the impression that she'd already forgotten them, if she'd seen them at all. Two whiskeys back table, that's all she needed or wanted to know. A pair of gentlemen in expensive clothes, one of them possibly foreign, would seem less real to her than the phantoms dancing at the edges of her vision.

On the table in front of Kohlwasser was a manila envelope fastened with a string. He let it sit there without comment, leaving Toby to wonder whether he should ask about it or pretend not to have noticed. His companion waited until the drinks came and then for a while longer, meanwhile striking up a bit of a conversation. Toby played along, though he guessed they were just warming up, volleying back and forth. The real game was in the envelope, and it would open when they actually started playing. The drive to the Grunewald was hours away.

"Have you any news," Kohlwasser began, "about our mutual friend Herr Kaspar?"

Toby was surprised, having expected he'd lead with Clairborne—out of common decency, if nothing else. Express his concern, best wishes, *Let me know if there's anything* . . . "How would I know anything new about Kaspar?"

"Well." Kohlwasser lifted his glass, swirling the contents as though to check for impurities. "He contacted you previously, in Washington. As you described it, he sought you out. Perhaps he might've done so again."

"Sorry. Haven't heard from him."

"Or perhaps you've been contacted by someone else."

"Who would that be?"

"I couldn't say. We don't know who Kaspar was working for, do we? I think it's safe to assume he was reporting to someone. Whoever it may have been, there's every reason to suppose they'll try again. With a different messenger, this time. Someone more . . . persuasive than Kaspar, who sounds like something of an idiot. Again, judging from your own description."

Toby took a sip of whiskey, or whatever it was. It didn't taste like poison, which was all he cared about. "Maybe not an idiot. An amateur, I'd say. But if you don't mind my asking, *Standartenführer*: what are you worried about, exactly? You say these people, whoever they are, will try again. Try *what* again? Talking to me? Hell, I'll talk to anybody. That's what I'm doing on a fact-finding mission. Can't find many facts if I don't listen to what people have to say."

Kohlwasser seemed mightily annoyed by this, which gratified the hell out of Toby. There was just something about this smug bastard in his prep-school tie—

"The people we're talking about," Kohlwasser said, his voice hard as a sidewalk, "are cold-blooded murderers. And this should concern you, Mr. Lugan, because it seems likely that these same people are involved in the kidnapping of your senator's son."

Toby felt sweat gathering on his forehead. He said, "Tell me what you know. Not what's *likely*."

"Very well," said Kohlwasser, who at least had the courtesy not to seem pleased by having shaken Toby's composure. He was all business now, leaning forward in his chair. "We know this: Our so-called Erwin Kaspar, at the time you saw him on the ship, was traveling under the name Stefan Sinclair with a woman, slightly older, purportedly his wife. After leaving the ship, they joined two other people and departed from Bremerhaven in a motorcar. One of the passengers was Clairborne Townsend. The other was a German officer—from the SS, it amazes me to say—and these four traveled together at least as far as Bremen. There, we believe, they made contact with a Resistance cell, and in the struggle that ensued one person was killed and at least one wounded. We don't know precisely what happened; the interrogations are ongoing. Now, from this point, I'm afraid, we lose a bit of clarity. We have a sighting two days later in the town of Hameln—Kaspar, the woman and young Townsend, aboard a riverboat and to all appearances enjoying themselves."

"On a fucking boat?" Toby said.

"And enjoying themselves. This is something to think about."

"It damn well is."

"The next sighting—and the last, I'm afraid—is some distance upriver, in a village called Polle. There the boat was halted for a routine inspection. The papers of Herr and Frau Sinclair were verified and—"

"Wait," Toby said. "You're claiming your people had them and let them go?"

Kohlwasser shook his head. "At this point, the boy hadn't been reported missing. The crime in Bremen was being investigated, but no suspects had been identified. And here's another thing: there was no sighting this time, at Polle, of the Townsend boy. There *were* two other passengers, a nurse and her patient, their true names unknown. We also have, if you're counting, Mr. Lugan, two missing police officers along with their automobile. Clearly these outlaws are violent and determined people. You can be sure we've mounted a considerable effort to capture them. There's no doubt we'll succeed, and soon. But now I hope you can understand why I need to know *anything* you can tell me, especially about unusual approaches from any quarter. We simply don't know what's happening here, or who may be at the root of it."

"But it's the Socialists, isn't it? That's what it says in the papers."

"There are Socialists involved, yes. One of them was killed in Bremen. But this raises more questions than it answers, when you think about it. I'm afraid the situation remains murky."

Toby wiped his forehead with his sleeve. Kohlwasser snapped his fingers for more whiskey, calling after the waitress, "And some napkins, please."

"Now, tell me if I've got this straight," Toby said. "Clairborne was last seen—"

"In Hameln."

"Right. Then poof—he vanishes. And your SS man, he's vanished too. So you're thinking—just tell me, there's no need to be namby-pamby—they're dead? Maybe *both*, or one dead but not the other? Go on, I'd rather hear it from you. I've got to figure—"

And now at last, the manila envelope came into play.

Jesus H. Christ, thought Toby, watching Kohlwasser's fingers as they unwound the string from the closure. How many damn times can you wind one string around a button like that? And what now?

"Now here, I'm afraid," said Kohlwasser, "is where the situation becomes even murkier. Let's go back to the ship. Not the riverboat—the *Robert Ley*, crossing the Atlantic."

Go back to the *what*? Toby stared impassively as Kohlwasser pinched one corner and then lifted the envelope, spilling the contents onto the table. Now he was looking at a pile of photographs, some blurry and others sharp, most black and white but a few in the vivid, unreal colors of modern film, reds that glowed like lacquer and blues that seemed to be laid on with burnished metal. One of the latter caught Toby's eye and made him wonder what the hell he was meant to see here. Three middle-aged women in bathing suits, poorly focused and off-center? The swimming pool tilting behind them?

"In this kind of investigation," said Kohlwasser, "where we have difficulty identifying key suspects and establishing a motive, we start casting our net more widely. We go outward, we go backward, we scoop up bits and pieces of anything that *might* be evidence, because we don't know in this instance what real evidence will look like. Sometimes we find things that are interesting in themselves but have no bearing on the case. Sometimes we hit on something that makes the situation immediately clear. And other times, Mr. Lugan, we find things that make the whole business more complicated."

Toby guessed he was referring to the photographs. But if so, he seemed happy for now to let the images speak for themselves. Kohlwasser sat sipping his whiskey and, God damn him, straightening his tie, leaving Toby to make of them what he could. Was this some kind of puzzle—let's see if your eyes are as sharp as ours? To hell with that.

"All right," said Toby, taking no care to hide his exasperation, "so we've got some pictures somebody took on the boat. Not a professional, obviously. Here we are by the pool, smiling for the camera. Here's hubby playing badminton: see, he's missed the shot and looks so mad—the kids'll love this one. And here we are out on deck at night, you could probably even see something if I could get this flashbulb to work. Tell me what I'm looking at, Helmut. I don't have time for this."

"Ah!" From Kohlwasser's expression, you'd have thought Toby was being clever. "But that's just the point, Mr. Lugan. It's not what you're looking at—I should say, it's not what the photographer was looking at. It's what the lens captured inadvertently. Remember, we're on an ocean liner, the ship is crowded, it's hard to find time to oneself, there are always other people about."

"I was there," said Toby testily.

"Indeed you were. And you'll find yourself in some of these photos. Not because you posed for any—you probably weren't aware a picture was being taken—and not because the camera was aimed at you on purpose. Rather, because on a ship with many people and many cameras, such accidents are unavoidable. Now if you will, Mr. Lugan, look at the photos again."

He started with the color shot by the swimming pool, tilted at a crazy angle, as though the ship had just heeled hard to starboard. Here were the three women, behind them a kid running with a big inflated ball—you shouldn't run on deck, your ma should've told you that—and in the pool near the edge of the frame were two pallid figures, young men, apparently horsing around, one trying to drag the other under the water.

"Ah," said Toby. "Okay, there's Clairborne. Who's the other guy?"

"That would be SS-Obersturmführer von Ewigholz, assigned to accompany young Townsend on the voyage. I believe Clairborne calls him Hagen. I'd imagine you two must have met."

"Hagen. Right." Toby halfway remembered a pro forma introduction, one of a great many. Truth be told, Clair and Toby tended to keep out of each other's path, but there was no sense in going into that with Kohlwasser.

He moved on to badminton. Fat man whiffing the birdie, onlookers laughing or trying their level best not to. Give the guy points for trying, was Toby's view. It was easy to spot Clair this time, though the boy had drawn a hand across his mouth, probably to mask a shit-eating grin. Let's see you pick up a racket, wiseass. The German stood there with an arm around his shoulders. Good buddies, or at least making out to be. Toby personally doubted Clair had ever been buddies with anyone in his life.

"Look, Helmut," he said. "I see you've got quite a few pictures of Clairborne, and that's fine, the one we've got is hardly what I'd call a good likeness. But could you just maybe give me some, you know, captions here? I already know the boy was on the damn boat."

Kohlwasser's sigh reminded Toby of teachers he'd had, the ones who liked to say, *There's no such thing as a stupid question* until you provided an exception.

"In gathering possible evidence," Kohlwasser said, "we naturally conducted a number of interviews. Most of the passengers were American, and for now we're treating them as off-limits. So this left us with the crew and the Labor Front volunteers—especially the latter, whose job, after all, was to mingle with the passengers and keep tabs on their activities. And indeed they proved to be a fruitful source of information."

He paused; Toby would have sworn it was to heighten a certain kind of effect, the chill that falls on a room when a high-ranking Nazi utters a phrase like that one. Unable to restrain himself, he laughed—at the banality of the idea and because he wanted to take the piss out of Kohlwasser. Maybe he was trying for an effect of his own.

"We were naturally interested," Kohlwasser went on icily, "in any contacts young Townsend might have made during the voyage.

Secondarily in anyone who might have shown a particular interest in him, a suspicious interest. The Sinclair couple was mentioned, especially the wife. She and Clairborne seem to have struck up a casual friendship. Nothing remarkable: a few drinks, a stroll on deck. Our friend Kaspar figures in these accounts as something of a bystander. But the overriding theme, which we kept hearing over and over again, in one way or another, was that young Townsend and his military escort kept to themselves for the most part."

"In other words, you got nothing. And a whole table full of pictures that prove it."

"We kept hearing this," Kohlwasser repeated, drumming a finger now, "over and over again. In one way or another. But some of these accounts were distinct. Noteworthy. The informants themselves found them to be. One DAF man observed—" He slipped his hand into a pocket and pulled out a little notebook.

Toby interrupted: "DAF, that's the—"

"The Labor Front, I'm sorry. Very sharp eyes, the DAF. This fellow reports 'an unusual attachment' between Townsend and the officer, von Ewigholz. Another uses the word 'intense.' Still another says, 'Their affection seemed more than comradely,' and goes on to describe—"

"All right," said Toby, grimacing, waving a hand as though to fan these ideas away. "I see where you're going. But two things, *Standartenführer*. One, who the fuck are these people to be saying things like this? And two, I've known Clairborne most of his life—hell, I know his family, I've watched him grow up—and yeah, he's not exactly what I'd call manly, but he's not some damn degenerate. If you guys picked some goose-stepping pervert to watch over him, hold his little hand so he doesn't fall overboard—well, that's hardly his fault."

Kohlwasser took this in without comment, but when Toby was finished he rested a fingertip on one of the pictures—an underexposed image captured by someone out on deck—and slid it toward him across the table until it nearly tipped into his lap. "The window, Mr. Lugan," he said. "Look in the window."

Toby raised the photograph to peer at it closely, even though he already had a premonition of what he might see there. This fell so shockingly short of the mark that he lowered the picture to the table.

"Christ on a rocking horse," he said, picking up a napkin to dab his brow but then regarding it abstractedly, as if unsure what it was doing there. "This would kill Bull. I'm not lying to you, it would kill him. Not even to mention the scandal involved. Jesus."

Kohlwasser was gracious in victory. Whatever sick game he was playing, he'd won the round and now efficiently gathered up the photographs and slipped them back into the envelope.

No matter how many times you wrap that string around the button, thought Toby, it isn't enough. "Who's seen these pictures?" he asked quietly.

"No one who will ever speak of it. You can trust me, Mr. Lugan. As I trust you. This is the nature of our partnership."

So now it was a partnership. The minority counsel of the Senate German Affairs Subcommittee and a senior intelligence officer of the Third Reich had conceived it in a cabaret with a tame vampire and now it had sprung from the womb as ugly as sin, christened with cheap whiskey, bawling for the life's blood of Bull Townsend himself, Toby's friend and a pillar of his universe.

"Not a word to the press," he said.

"Nor to anyone else," Kohlwasser promised.

They stood up to leave, but Toby paused and grabbed Kohlwasser's arm, pulling him close. "You're telling me everything, aren't you? You really don't know where they are?"

Kohlwasser didn't blink, not even slightly. "We'll know very soon. We have a good idea where the policemen went missing. We'll locate the car. It won't be long. We have men on the ground."

Toby let go. "Men on the ground. Men in the air, men in the water—this just needs to be over. And out of the papers. And . . ." He hesitated. "I'm grateful for your discretion, *Standartenführer.*"

Kohlwasser's smile made Toby wish he hadn't smiled at all.

"Don't worry, Mr. Lugan. In a day or two it will all be over. We'll deal with the culprits in a very quiet, very final way. And we'll make sure Clairborne returns home safely."

Toby didn't say, *It might almost be better* . . . He would never have said it, and didn't dare to finish the thought. Make that: He never started the thought. He walked out of the Black Shoe into the sunlight and took a deep breath of *Berliner Luft* heavy with brown coal dust, wishing he were back on Beacon Hill or, hell, Capitol Hill. Someplace where you could tell your friends and your enemies apart.

WHEN WARS START

BERLIN, GRUNEWALD: LATE THAT AFTERNOON

It had been years since Jaap Saxo had held a tennis racket. He'd never played on a court like this one at the Rot-Weiss Club and was loath to do so this afternoon. His misgivings centered chiefly on the prospect, imminent now, of staring down the court at an opponent like Cissy—not because he knew her to be insuperably good or shamefully awful, only because in her pleated skirt she looked exactly like what, in genealogical fact, she was: a White Russian princess. How did you—a commissioned naval officer—conduct yourself in a game like that? Would sending her nothing but high, easy shots amount to insubordination? Or, conversely, would smashing the ball straight back at her constitute a physical threat? Like many career servicemen, Jaap did not lack confidence or composure, yet social nuances often eluded him.

But *die Pflicht ruft, meine Herren.* Duty calls. The point of Jaap's being here, which had taken some doing, was to run a modest surveillance operation on Hans-Bernd's meeting with the American senator, which would happen—if it actually was going to— in the next few minutes. He wasn't worried about the tough and wily Hans-Bernd, who'd scrabbled up through the party hierarchy before growing disillusioned and switching sides. As for the senator, Jaap didn't care one way or the other; he was simply a target of opportunity, a man in a key position "over there" who, at present, was standing on German soil. The fact remained that this was a sensitive encounter: high-level secrets were involved, and people could end up getting shot. Jaap would be among the first to fall, but by the time the scandal ran its course there might be a bullet left for Admiral Canaris himself. And that would be the end of the Abwehr.

The admiral knew it, and was backing Jaap's gambit to the extent of loaning him his private car: a Mercedes so ludicrously long you could play darts in the back seat. Canaris had had it custom-built with full armor plating and a secure radio-telephone system, not because he needed such a thing—he walked to work at the Tirpitz-ufer or, when he was in a hurry, rode a horse—but because Admiral Sir Hugh Sinclair, chief of the British Secret Intelligence Service, had had a similar automobile built for him by Rolls-Royce. It was Jaap's opinion that the spy business would run more efficiently if such men could focus instead on exactly what kind of war they were fighting, but as usual no one had sought his advice. He was happy about the radio-telephone, however. He had an agent on the loose and was hoping to get in touch.

It was three minutes to four and Cissy was ready to volley, shifting restively near the baseline. Jaap indulged himself by watching her for a few moments: a princess bouncing a white ball on copper-red clay with the Grunewald at her back, a million leaves turned golden green by the afternoon sunlight of northern Germany. Such a vision could break your heart, and delude you into thinking there was imperishable beauty in this world, a pure and Platonic ideal beauty that wouldn't be snuffed out in one second by a well-aimed bomb. The Luftwaffe had a one-thousand-kilogram bomb they called the Hermann. The Brits were reportedly working on something bigger. And if the Yanks got involved . . .

"They're coming," said a short gentleman sitting nearby on a bench, mostly hidden by a newspaper. Guido, the art dealer, the other member of the classic three-person surveillance team. They were backed up by a driver–cum–radio technician–cum–sharpshooter whose presence the admiral had stipulated as a condition of loan-ing the car. A fresh-faced ensign, he was sitting somewhere behind Jaap's back in a service drive with a K98k sniper rifle on his lap. The admiral trusted navy men, as Jaap did fallen aristocrats, jaded social-ites and former members of the dj.1.11.

Cissy hit the ball, so excited that the shot came in low and fast, far too wide for Jaap to reach. She fished out a second ball and this time lobbed a gentle shot that bounced in Jaap's forehand territory, and now they had a volley going. Cissy moved around the court with an effortless grace that made it hard to tell if she was an experienced player or a quick study or just adept at sports in general. Whichever it was, this gave Jaap plenty of opportunity to glance over at the adjacent court, where Hans-Bernd was unscrewing the brace from his racket and, across the net, a large and boisterous-looking man was jogging in place and pumping his arms as though preparing to leap into a boxing ring. Jaap barely recognized Senator Townsend, who looked quite different in this context than he did in the newspapers. A third man stood off-court in the fluttery shade of an ash tree, where Jaap couldn't get a real look at him without turning to stare. Such things are done deliberately by professionals, but Jaap hoped—and dared to believe—that this wasn't the case here. He glimpsed the man wiping his brow and guessed he was merely hot and had sought out the shade for that reason, and this just happened to fall in Jaap's blind spot—nothing sinister about it.

Anyway, it didn't matter. Guido, from his bench, could see everything. The ensign had checked the important sight lines. And Jaap was pretty sure who this other American was. His name was Toby Lugan, and he was no stranger to Berlin; he'd worked at the U.S. embassy for a while and was said to be a friend of Colonel Truman Smith, the military attaché and a friend, in turn, of Hermann Göring, namesake of the bomb. This tidy web of connections had once upon a time led Jaap to dispatch an agent to approach Lugan in America—a misbegotten adventure whose consequences were still playing out. But as much as he'd love to get Lugan in a room and question him about that, he couldn't let himself be distracted. What mattered right now was the leather case in Hans-Bernd's tennis bag, lying in plain sight beside the post from which the net was strung. He was staring at the bag while Cissy's shot flew past his ear.

"Let's play!" she called.

Jaap nodded and moved himself into position to receive her serve. Toby Lugan was now behind him. Jaap glanced at Guido, who fluttered his newspaper. Cissy threw the ball straight up, and for an instant Jaap imagined it was just hanging there. But then it dropped and she smashed it and it caught the outside corner of the box. Jaap nearly fell on his face trying to stretch for it. Cissy squealed in triumph. The game was on.

Anyone who doubts that sport is a proxy for armed combat should consider this: nothing seemed to be happening for a long time; then too many things happened all at once. Cissy and Jaap were into their third set, the princess having won the first 6–3 and the second 7–5—Jaap having finally overcome his class consciousness and started scrapping in earnest—while on the other court Hans-Bernd was trouncing the senator, who seemed indifferent to the score and possibly unaware of it. His sole interest appeared to lie in pounding the ball as hard as humanly possible. In the course of one especially savage stroke, his legs got tangled up and he fell to the court and lay there rocking on his back, clutching a knee and bellowing curses that were beyond Jaap's powers of translation. Hans-Bernd leapt over the net and the third man, Lugan, came quickly to kneel at the injured man's side—and at that moment the ensign appeared with his fresh face flushed with urgency to tell the *Kapitänleutnant* he'd gotten a phone call.

Jaap looked at Guido, who nodded and cocked his head to the side: *It's all right, go.* The ensign led Jaap through the trees to the waiting Mercedes, bounding ahead to open a massive passenger door. Jaap climbed aboard and seated himself before an elaborate console with many colored lights, picking up an oversized handset that weighed as much as a bowling ball.

"Yes, Saxo here," he said loudly. "Who's calling, please?"

From the handset came a squall of static and then a bored-sounding male voice: "I'm sorry, this call was meant for Herr Braun."

Jaap squeezed his eyes shut, though it didn't help much. He still felt like an Abwehr officer and not an insurance claims adjuster, and his mind was still mostly wrapped around that leather case on the tennis court. Still, one must try.

"Braun here," he said, in what he hoped was a natural-sounding voice, though there was surely nothing natural about the way it tumbled and echoed through whatever secret contraption the handset was wired to.

At the other end, the world-weary man said, "All right, then. *Meine Dame*, I have Herr Braun on the phone for you. Go ahead, please."

Jaap waited until finally a quavering but distinctly female voice said, "Herr Braun? Hello, Herr Braun? If you're there, I've got some news about your cousin Peter."

There was silence then; Jaap feared the connection had been lost. "Yes, I'm here!" he said. "I can hear you! About Cousin Peter, you say? Well, I hope the news is good!"

"The news is good! Cousin Peter says—"

There was some problem on the line—the woman's voice seemed to break up; you'd almost think she was laughing. Then it came back clearly again.

"Cousin Peter is feeling better! He would like you to please drop by for a Scotch on the rocks!"

Now the distortion returned, much the same as before. Jaap tapped the handset a couple of times. "Did you say Scotch on the rocks?"

"That's what he said. Well—that's all, I guess. It was nice to talk to you, Herr Braun."

"Wait!" Jaap's mind was swirling, the lights on the console seeming to flash sympathetically. "Don't hang up, please. Just a . . ."

It was right there, he knew—whatever simple message Oskar was trying to send him. He tried the back-to-front trick: rocks, Scotch, better, Peter. Nothing. Then straight through again: Peter, better, Scotch, rocks. And there it was.

"Tell Peter," he began excitedly. "*Meine Dame*, are you there?"

"I'm still here, yes."

Thank God. "Tell Peter there's plenty of Scotch where the tchaj came from. Have you got that?"

"I don't know. Could you spell it, please?"

For a second or two Jaap's memory failed—it was one of those words you never wrote down because it always looked wrong. "Just tell him 'that weird drink'—all right? The place where that came from. And—one more thing, *meine Dame*—tell him to bring the whole family, there's plenty for everyone."

"You people are very odd," said the woman on the telephone. "But I'll tell him. I'm hanging up now."

The tennis courts had changed hands by the time he made it back. New players were warming up; Cissy and Guido had been relegated to a bench near the dressing rooms.

"They took the bag!" Cissy blurted.

"Tell me slowly," said Jaap, who felt as though he were undergoing a mental process akin to depressurization.

"Some medical people were here," said Guido. "They showed up almost right away, so I imagine they were on the club staff. They examined the senator, and after a couple of minutes they carried him out on a stretcher. While that was going on, Hans-Bernd transferred the case to the senator's bag. Then the other man picked up the bag and left with it."

"The *other* man." Jaap needed to be absolutely certain. "Not the senator."

"No, the senator was on the stretcher. And making quite a fuss."

"Did the other man look in the bag?"

"He did!" said Cissy. "I saw him."

"Had he noticed Hans-Bernd putting the case in the senator's bag?"

Cissy shook her head.

Guido shrugged. "Not that I could tell. But would that matter? When he finds the package, he'll be able to guess where it came from."

Jaap smiled at the two of them. "Thank you—that was really well done. I'm sorry I had to—"

Cissy laughed. "Anything to avoid getting beaten by a woman."

"It's funny you should say that." Jaap winked at her. "You know, something interesting's come up. Do you fancy a bit of travel? It would mean taking tomorrow off—can you manage that?"

"She couldn't get today off," Guido said. "But she doesn't care, she came anyway. What do you have in mind?"

"I was thinking," said Jaap, though in truth he hadn't really started to, not in earnest. There'd be long hours of that ahead; for now he was running on instinct. "How about a drive in the country? Germany in summertime! What do you say?"

"Germany in summertime." Cissy had instincts of her own. "That's when wars start, isn't it."

THE NAÏVETÉ OF YOUTH

REINHARDSWALD: THE SAME AFTERNOON

Now Oskar knew how it felt to have an agent out in the field. He hadn't been worried about Lena until she vanished from sight. And even then, some period of time passed during which he imagined her marching along in her *Wandervogelin* disguise—her stride bounding and confident, her chin set, her eyes sharp—through the old forest and over the stream and into the clearing once planted with dangerous thorn roses, to the castle of Dornröschen and a public telephone.

But as the minutes crept by and the sun edged westward, his thoughts began to darken as though a shadow were moving over them. Hagen stretched out in the tall grass and fell into the abrupt, efficient sleep of a soldier. Clair strolled along the streambed plucking wild marsh marigolds and placing them carefully in the water like tiny boats, watching them swirl and bob and occasionally succumb to the swift current. He had to keep hitching up the baggy SS trousers. Oskar watched him until he, too, was out of sight, and by that time the shadow had overtaken a large region of his consciousness.

He started considering how things might go wrong. At the beginning, his thoughts were constrained by probability: circumstances that could foreseeably arise and how Lena would conceivably deal with them. Say, a routine identity check. May we see your papers, madam? So you are Frau Lena Sinclair, this is correct? Just a moment, please, I must check this list. Wait—Frau Sinclair, where are you going? *Offizier*, stop this woman!

At that stage, Oskar found such thoughts troubling yet manageable, yielding to rational analysis. He could posit some dire event and ask himself how likely it was that this might happen, how serious the ramifications would be. But with the next stage came a less reasonable kind of worry, and he began thinking about not just things that might happen but also those that already had. Why had Hagen left the car in that particular stand of fir trees, then led them to this meadow where they might be seen by anyone standing on that bluff? Or by an airplane flown out to search for them? What had Anna really been up to that night at the spa? And she and Lena— what had they been planning before Oskar stepped in? Was Lena still carrying out some secret SOPADE mission? And those Gestapo men—why only two of them? Surely there must be a pack out there, talking to everyone, sniffing at every trail, sifting the tiniest grains of evidence—and they had bloodhounds, rifles, radios . . . Lena was walking into a trap! Oskar had sent her there, armed with nothing but a telephone number on a scrap of paper!

But even that wasn't the worst. Yet another stage awaited, a sort of *deutsche Romantik* maze in which you found yourself chasing your own sanity up blind paths that grew narrower and darker still. Who was Oskar to imagine he could outwit the collective malevolent intelligence of the Third Reich? Who had ever strayed into the ancient German forest and come whistling out the other side? Only the truly innocent, the simple Jacks, the immaculate Hansels and Gretels—and Oskar was no innocent; he had blood on his hands. He'd sliced a man's throat in half. He'd betrayed his country, putting others at risk by doing so. He'd botched his first and only mission. He'd slept with another man's wife. He'd strayed from the path like a lost sheep, and now the wolves were circling around him.

At a certain point, it became unbearable to sustain these thoughts, and he yelled, "I'm going after her!" Oskar didn't know if anybody heard him; he just set off down the trail.

———

Clair heard Oskar call out; he didn't catch all the words but recognized a form of "to go," and that was more than enough. It meant that he and Hagen were alone, and this thing that had been crawling thrillingly, agonizingly inside him could be let out again. He'd almost shouted in relief, though at the exact same moment he also imagined himself shouting like a crazy person there in the meadow, looking ridiculous. This constant self-reflection was a terrible thing that was always happening, he couldn't help it—watching himself as if he were living in front of a mirror, evaluating every minute of his life, and it was never quite right, there was always something a little off, a little fake, like he was putting it on for the mirror, which of course he was, because the mirror wouldn't ever go away. This was deeply troubling, but it was so much a part of Clair that he didn't think about it very often—only on rare occasions like this, when the immensity of everything inside him burst through all his steadfast efforts to contain it.

And now he *did* shout, loud and wild, and he *did* feel like a crazy person, and deep in his mind the never-sleeping observer realized that this was what *ecstasy* meant, and what they meant by *love*. He ran through the meadow letting the too-large trousers slip down his skinny frame, kicking them away. He found Hagen where he'd been sleeping until Clair shouted, and partly fell but mostly threw himself on top of him, pulling the anorak away so their naked legs could intertwine, burrowing into his strong, warm chest, pressing his head into the sculpted null space between neck and shoulder, wrapping his arms around every part of Hagen he could reach. He wiggled pleasurably and then lay still.

For now—for the next two or three minutes, if recent history was any guide—this was all Clair wanted. It was more, in fact, than he'd *ever* wanted, because it was more than he'd been able to conceive. Such conceptions as he'd managed to form had been fleeting, furtive, embarrassing and inaccurate. Worse than that, they'd been unworthy—unworthy of *this*. And of Clair. And what could possibly be worthy of Hagen?

Hagen was sleepy but slowly waking up. The perfect, magical body stirred beneath him—that was a word he'd never appreciated before, *stirred*, a simple and rather boring string of letters Clair had dutifully learned in another, childish world that meant something altogether new and extraordinary in this one. *Hagen stirred.* And for Clair the earth seemed to shift on its axis and a thousand electric synapses to fire at once, from his optic nerve down to his groin. He was not one for stirring, himself, but other words had taken on secret new meanings just for him. Clair *sprang*, he *pressed*, he *ground*. He *shuddered*. At times it was downright alarming; until a week ago, the idea of sex had lain inside him like an odd, misshapen, imponderable lump seemingly medical in nature, producing symptoms like discomfort and swelling and the occasional low-grade fever. But generally speaking, it hadn't troubled him and he'd more or less trained himself not to think about it.

Now he could think of nothing else. At least not for very long. His body, as it turned out, was designed exclusively for sex, and its capacity for sustained and repeated exertion was astonishing. Not much stimulation was required—the first time, his first gasping and throbbing revelation, had been provoked by nothing more than Hagen's arms around him, both of them fully clothed and standing in the middle of a ship's passageway late one night. That wasn't to say that his body didn't crave stimulation or that he could ever get enough of it. He'd spent himself during Hagen's kisses, his caresses, the *other* kind of kisses, the embrace of their naked bodies, and soon it became evident that there were other kinds of embraces too, an apparently infinite number of ways to address this constant, pressing and urgent need he'd only lately discovered.

"God, is there something *wrong* with me?" he'd asked once.

Hagen had laughed, wearily, as they lay together with cool air floating off the sea through the stateroom window. "*Achtzehn*," he'd said finally. Eighteen.

"Well, *fünf-und-zwanzig* isn't exactly over the hill," Clair told him.

"*Danken Sie Gott.* There is nothing wrong with you. You are beautiful. You are perfect."

And Clair accepted it all—well, maybe not *perfect*—because his lover had said so. He believed he was beautiful to Hagen. And he knew there was nothing wrong with him. If there ever had been, he was cured of it now. He'd been cured by *this*.

Hagen was staring up at him. Those bottomless eyes—Clair felt sometimes like he was tumbling into them, weightless, detached from his body. Then his body would move on its own, and he'd be back inside it, straining, yearning, breathing in short gasps, the whole swirling ballet of physical consummation.

"What's going to happen to us?" he asked Hagen, their mouths very close, breathing each other's words.

The blue eyes clouded, but even the clouds were marvelous, making the sky look touchable, and Clair ran a finger along Hagen's cheekbone.

"Nothing bad will happen to you," Hagen whispered. "I will die to prevent that."

"You won't die. Not ever."

The eyes closed. Clair felt a chill and pressed himself harder into Hagen's warmth, comforted by the omnipotent strength there, the unassailable protection. He lay motionless for an unusually long time. Finally he was distracted by a persistent buzz that might have been a hovering dragonfly but turned out to be a tiny aircraft, high above, flying slowly across the sky. It hardly seemed to be a real part of the world, and soon it was gone.

Oskar cursed himself for not bringing the map. Lena had studied it before she left, tracing out the twisty route to Sababurg and committing it to memory. Oskar hadn't even glanced at it, too busy composing his message to "Herr Braun," using insipid code words that would probably mean nothing to Jaap Saxo. He had a vague idea where the trails led and some vestigial instincts, mostly dormant now, from his *Jugendbewegung* days. He recalled with chagrin how he'd stood in a small remnant woodland in Washington imagining that someone might be following him and almost wishing this were the case—he'd been a proud Abwehr officer then, chosen for his disregard of danger and entrusted with a vital, delicate assignment. Which he'd woefully failed to complete. And his disregard of danger had amounted, in the end, to a willingness to jump off a bridge rather than fight it out with two men who'd just stepped out of a motorcar. Now he *was* being followed, by a number of men that was, in effect, beyond calculation, and his regard for danger had never been higher.

He'd paused at a fork in the trail, trying to invoke whatever instinct or thoughtful choice or lucky guess might get him closer to Sababurg, when he heard an aircraft overhead. He couldn't see it at first, but then it appeared in a gap through the trees, a small biplane with a dark gray hull and the black cross of the Luftwaffe outlined in white on the underside of its wings. This was hardly the inspiration he'd hoped for, yet it sufficed to send him scurrying onto the right-hand path, which ran down a hill into deeper cover than offered by the one on the left. He halted under a giant fir whose trunk was black and scabrous with age and stood there panting while the noise of the engine grew louder and then changed in timbre, as though the plane was turning or maybe dropping to a lower altitude. Whatever it was doing was happening slowly, because for several minutes the noise went from louder to softer to louder again, at one point seeming to pass directly overhead. He resisted the urge to duck.

His first worry was for Lena, for whom he felt responsible, but he quickly realized that the greatest danger was to the other two back in the meadow. Would they have the sense to take cover? Yes—or at least Hagen would. *We're trained to act*, he'd said. So then act, by God, thought Oskar. But then he remembered that at his last sighting Hagen had been soundly asleep and Clair had been playing like a kid by the stream—and now Oskar felt a kind of dread that seemed to rise from his stomach. Should he turn back? Warn the others, grab the map and hightail it for Sababurg?

As before, the choice was made for him. The sound of the aircraft faded at last and the woods grew quieter, if not really silent. In the woods, there's always some crackling or scurrying to keep you on your toes; the air is never so motionless that it doesn't stir a few leaves; you leap at the tiniest thing when your nervous state is precarious. And the noise that was coming from somewhere down the hillside was not tiny. It was recurrent, it was steady and it was getting louder.

It was footsteps. Oskar edged around the fir tree, pressing himself into the trunk. Thankfully, the ground was soft with fallen needles and mounds of moss. He squatted behind a tall clump of ferns where he judged he'd be hidden well enough to risk glancing out once the footsteps had passed. The proper moment was a long time arriving, the steps growing louder and louder—only one set of them, but so close he could hear the hiker breathing—and when he raised his head above the ferns, he saw it was Lena.

He cried out, much too loudly, and if she'd been armed she probably would have shot him. Then she laughed and he stepped back onto the trail, where she surprised him by throwing her arms around his shoulders. It wasn't so much a hug as a kind of proof that they were both really here and their plan had somehow worked. Lena was lugging a satchel loaded with fried bread and roasted pheasant legs and colorful bits of clothing already stained by the grease.

"And I've got a message for you," she said.

"Not now," he told her. "We've got to get back. Did you hear the plane?"

She nodded, shrugged off the satchel and handed it over. It must have been heavy, but Oskar was too preoccupied to notice.

B ack in the meadow, they found Clair and Hagen sitting together by the stream, looking flushed and a little bit wet. Perhaps they'd been swimming.

"Time to move on!" Oskar announced, trying to make it sound like good news—some rollicking excursion, not a desperate run for their lives.

Clair sprang up readily. Hagen rose more slowly but seemed to have recovered most of his strength. His expression was cautious and combative, as though he sensed danger close by and was prepared to deal with it.

"Where are we going?" Clair asked.

The boy seemed strangely happy, which Oskar put down to the naïveté of youth. He started to answer, but Lena cut him off.

"I've got a *message* for you—don't you ever listen?" And she gave it to him as she'd gotten it from Herr Braun: the weird drink, the place where it came from, bring the whole family.

"That's all?" said Oskar.

"You want more? 'Uncle Kurt is slicing the cheese'? You people really are ridiculous."

"Well," he said, "I guess there's a change in plan."

"I'm glad," Hagen said, "to hear there *is* a plan."

"Please check the map," Oskar told Lena. "We're looking for the Gasthaus Schwalbenthal. At the edge of the nature preserve."

"Oh, they're expecting us?" she said archly, pulling the map out. "Herr Braun made reservations?"

Oskar didn't know what Herr Braun had done or what he had in mind. Something, anyway—that was enough for now.

"Is this the place?" said Lena, pointing at a spot near the bottom of the map, barely a thumb's width from the southeast corner. "That looks pretty far."

"The moon is just past full," said Hagen. "We'll be there in time for breakfast."

Lena looked doubtful. Oskar felt tired already.

Clair swung his arms, impatient to get started. "I *love* moonlight," he said.

WHAT HERR BOAR HAS TO SAY

While Helmut Kohlwasser prided himself on being a cultivated man, he had no taste for Wagner. Was he missing something? He knew full well, as everyone did, that this was the favored composer of the national leadership (though not of the army, whose commanders were said to be Bruckner enthusiasts). But to Kohlwasser it all just sounded so . . . obvious. And things that were obvious were generally also, in his professional experience, incorrect, or at least incomplete. The great Ring cycle, for example, he found lacking in proportion, subtlety, finesse—and, maybe worst of all, in any flavor of genuine human experience. For life is lived, is it not, on a less than godly plane. One's actions and motives are seldom purely noble or diabolical. One's understanding is always imperfect, one's feelings ambivalent. We do the best we can under the circumstances, knowing so very little.

And thus in the cement-gray light of dusk Kohlwasser found himself standing before his window at the Reich Security Main Office listening to a jolly, tuneless, politically offensive yet quite funny piece of musical theater by the banned composer Hanns Eisler, in the company of Berlin's—perhaps the world's—most tiresome and unpersuasive Faust, the journalist Greimer. History, he was pretty sure, would not judge Greimer kindly. The man was peddling a dubious commodity and demanding a high price for it. What he—along with half the German press—wanted now was exclusive access to the big story of the day: the missing American boy and the breathless hunt for his kidnappers. What he offered in return was little more than parlor gossip.

Ach, but such a parlor. The salon of the Baroness von F—— was one of the very few places in Berlin to which Kohlwasser had never managed to gain access by his own devices. The grand apartment in the Fasanenstrasse was, by some accounts, the apogee of the city's social arc; according to others, it was the last redoubt of the old, pre-Nazi order. In the SD's official reckoning, it was a sinister, hermetic lodge where the tottering aristocracy, the Prussian officer corps, foreigners, Bohemians, "cosmopolitans," modernist painters and playwrights and antisocial elements of every stripe—not omitting the odd Jew—engaged in a ritual commingling so vile as to threaten the health of the German *Volk*.

In Kohlwasser's view all these notions were, like Wagner, a tad too obvious. He strongly suspected that the famous salon was simply a flat like many others in this old, once-fashionable district. That its most sacrosanct ritual involved playing waltzes and getting drunk. And that its shadowy denizens were not so much dangerous as out-of-date—the sort of people for whom there was no place in the New Germany. Political primitives. Cave dwellers. No one to worry about.

But every rule has its exceptions. There were moments of brilliance in Wagner, and troublesome personalities among the Fasanenstrasse set. Some kind of conspiracy was being woven there, and Kohlwasser had turned up a corner of it. He couldn't judge the scale or design of the offense, not just yet. He knew it involved the little sneak known as Erwin Kaspar; but beyond that, precious little. If Greimer could provide so much as a couple of real names to link with Kaspar's false one, or a snatch of overheard conversation, or a glimpse of a document left carelessly on a table—well, then an hour of his ghastly company might prove endurable.

"Take me through it again." Kohlwasser turned from the window and peered down at the journalist, who sat hunched on the leather sofa, holding a large snifter protectively. He felt like a director trying to coax a credible performance from a singularly untalented player. "Not the chap falling off the balcony. Before that, the gathering in the back room. Who was involved there? Be as precise as you can."

"Not exactly a back room," Greimer said, picking at some bit of food caught in his teeth. "Quite a nice window in there, actually. East-facing. Looks right down the Landwehrkanal, if the Baroness would open the damn drapes."

Kohlwasser's jaw clenched reflexively. He couldn't tell if the man's obtuseness was, so to speak, innate or affected. He suspected the latter when Greimer raised one bristled eyebrow to glance up slyly, as if checking for a reaction. Such insolence. Yet Kohlwasser was resolved to bear it: informants were like children, precious though frequently exasperating, and Greimer might be more than that—a precocious only child. "*Who*," he prodded, "was in this room with the splendid view?"

"Well, let me think." Swirling brandy, sniffing at it. "There was the old Brigadier. Or there probably was. He's a regular. And I reckon Cissy was there too."

"You *reckon*. I'd prefer it if you actually *knew*."

Greimer, having evidently teased the glass sufficiently, drained it in a gulp. "It might help me remember," he said, his throat audibly venting hot fumes, "if I knew what I was remembering *for*. Why don't you just tell me what this is all about? That would really help."

That, Kohlwasser thought, could help this buffoon stitch together some fantastic story, cut to order. "What it's about," he said placidly, "depends on how well you remember what actually happened that night. You tell *me*, and then maybe I can help *you*. There might be a scoop here that will make your career. So try hard now. Leave nothing out. For instance, who is Cissy?"

"You don't know Cissy?" Greimer's tone changed from petulance to near delight. "But everybody knows Cissy. She's a princess, I think. If not, she really ought to be. Ukrainian, Belorussian, something like that. But speaks better German than I do. And she sings—if you get enough champagne in her! Knows all the lyrics, voice like an angel. Yes, I'm sure she was there; Cissy never misses a party."

"That's wonderful. Who else?"

Now that Greimer had started, he seemed happy to go on talking. "Well, you know that fellow Gisevius from the Interior Ministry—he's the only one I recognized. Used to be high up in the party, didn't he? Started having doubts, they say, and got shoved aside. Probably bitter about it—that would explain the pickle up his ass."

"So this Gisevius, you've heard him voice his doubts? Or openly criticize the leadership?"

Greimer gave him a canny smile. "*Oh* no. He's much too clever for that. Keeps his own counsel, he does. It's more, you know, the look about him. Anyway, he was there that night. One of the last to leave, in fact. Disappeared into the library and was never seen again. Rather like the old Baron, eh?"

Kohlwasser pulled a chair from beside his desk and turned it to face Greimer across the wide coffee table. He sensed that they were approaching something big and wanted to come at it directly. Seating himself, he reached for the decanter and said, "More brandy?"

"Since you're offering."

Kohlwasser tipped in a generous slug and watched the look of pleasure spread across the other slug's face. "I've heard those soirées can run quite late. Were you there the whole time?"

"Me? No. Till about midnight, I guess."

"How many people were still there when you left?"

"Only . . . not many. I can't recall exactly."

"But this man Gisevius, he was one of them."

"Right."

"But who could he have found to talk to, so late?"

"Beats me. The Brigadier was long gone by then. Cissy left with Ricky and Dodo. There would've only been the navy fellow."

"Yes, of course—the navy fellow." Kohlwasser trusted that his excitement—barely expressed in the involuntary fluttering of an eyelid—would be lost on Greimer. "This would be the person you didn't recognize."

"Excuse me?"

"You mentioned before, while speaking of Gisevius: *He's the only one I recognized.* So there was someone—"

"Oh, right. Yeah, there was this navy man. Seen him before, once or twice. Never properly introduced."

"He's been to the flat on other occasions, then? And he's spoken with Gisevius each time?"

"Hardly spoken to anyone, from what I've seen. The Baroness, she seems to know him. And the Brigadier, I think. Once there was a younger guy. But he was army, not navy. Struck me as odd, now that I remember it. Don't usually mix well, the Wehrmacht and the Kriegsmarine. But here you have a brand-new *Leutnant* in full dinner dress and an old sea dog—a two-and-a-half striper, whatever that's called—and they're huddled together like a pair of bandits. How do you figure?"

Kohlwasser had barely started to figure anything. He felt like someone who'd been squinting through a chink in the paneling when suddenly the whole wall collapsed, revealing many things all at once. But at that moment he was interrupted by a loud and seemingly urgent knock on the office door.

"Come in, for God's sake," he snapped.

The door swung inward and a slim man in a black uniform advanced holding a sheet of yellow paper, then came to attention. "As you requested, *Herr Standartenführer*—the report of aerial surveillance."

The report was brief, and Kohlwasser quickly found what he was looking for. He glanced up at the uniformed man—the SS equivalent of a sergeant—and said, "I need to speak to the senior police officer in this district. Whoever that is."

The sergeant clicked his heels together. "That would be the chief watchmaster of Kaufungen," he said. "I'll place the call immediately."

As the door closed, Kohlwasser turned to Greimer, toward whom he felt a sudden, irrational surge of warmth. "I'm eager to hear more about this young army officer you've mentioned. Perhaps you could describe him to me, as best you can remember. But first let's raise a glass together."

Greimer straightened on the sofa, his reporter's instinct aroused. "Are we celebrating something?"

"Not quite celebrating. Not quite yet. Let's say we're *anticipating*." He poured two fingers of brandy into a glass, then lifted it to clink against Greimer's. "The net is drawing tight. Tomorrow, we'll close it."

It had been a slow season at the Gasthaus Schwalbenthal. Otherwise, Frau Müller would have resented being dragged out of bed after eleven at night to check in the couple from Hamburg. And what an unlikely couple they were: she as slender and pale as a blanched asparagus shoot, he as compact and swarthy as a coal miner, though to her surprise his voice—as he spoke for the two of them—was refined and his manners impeccable, a nice change from what often came around here, but we'll say no more about that.

They registered as Hr. & Fr. Max Grundeis. In the space provided for "Purpose of Visit"—required by new laws that Frau Müller felt were pointless—the little man wrote in a tidy, bookkeeper's hand, *Dying for good country air, the city is unbearable!* This gave Frau Müller a laugh, and as a reward she handed them the key to her very best room, away from the public road, with a lovely view up the valley.

"Poor dears, you must've had a long drive," she said, leading them up the creaking staircase. "All the way from Hamburg!"

The young woman groaned comically. "Five hours!" she said, her voice melodic and faintly accented—it couldn't be Czech, surely? "In this one's tiny sport car."

She was only poking fun, Frau Müller was sure, yet her swarthy companion gave her such a look. Well, well—perhaps they *were* married.

She was turning in at last, having shoved old Müller aside to make a space for herself, when—wonder upon wonders—the bell was rung again by some other late-arriving guest. This one was a fresh-faced lad in sturdy hiking attire, carrying what was unmistakably a rifle bag. He signed in as Samiel Weber. Purpose of Visit: boar hunting.

"You'll be wanting an early start, I suppose," Frau Müller said. "We don't usually serve breakfast before seven. But I *suppose*—"

"Oh, don't worry about that. I'll be off before dawn."

Mind you go quietly, then, Frau Müller was about to say, but then he began counting out money, evidently meaning to pay in advance, and her heart softened. "I'll leave out some biscuits. You won't want your stomach growling and scaring off the boar!"

He gave her a smile, and Frau Müller found it hard to imagine that he was actually a hunter—until he marched upstairs like a soldier the night before a battle, fearless and cocksure. Well, she thought, we'll see what Herr Boar has to say about that.

FOOLISH AND DANGEROUS

NATURPARK MEISSNER-KAUFUNGER WALD: 28 MAY

Hagen was almost right: they *could* have made it to Schwalbenthal in time for breakfast. But two things happened.

A little past midnight, on a flat and easy farm road, with open pastures on one side and woodland on the other, they nearly collided with an armed foot patrol coming from the opposite direction. What saved them was a single faint noise—like the buckle on a rifle strap clicking against the barrel—that only Oskar heard. He stopped in his tracks, and when Lena turned beside him he held a finger up to his lips. Clair and Hagen, a few paces back, seemed to get the message, wordlessly closing the gap until the four of them stood together, their breathing slowed to a minimum, listening.

Moon shadows slid over the road as a southerly breeze agitated the tree boughs overhead, and they strained for any sign of what lay out there in that shifty darkness. Oskar could imagine an enemy formation rising black against the pale backdrop of the pasture. To his heightened senses, every twitching branch was a weapon being raised, every sigh of the wind a whispered conversation. Then the clinking sounded once more, closer now, and again a few seconds later.

"Get off the road," Hagen murmured. "There, in the bushes. Keep low."

The four of them slipped into a gap between trees where a surge of brambles strained outward, creating a dark and prickly pocket underneath. Oskar found himself pinned against a bracket of stems, his back punctured by countless thorns, unable to move without tangling with dozens more. Hagen crouched beside him, holding the pistol taken from the dead Gestapo agent. The clinking was close now, and Oskar could hear boots clomping as well. How many were there? It was hard to judge, because they were falling in unison. He fought a childish urge to squeeze his eyes shut. But then with no forewarning, their enemies stepped into view and weren't so frightening at all.

Two men—an older one with a notable bulge around the midsection and a younger one who rose a head taller, his arms swinging carelessly, jostling the rifle at his shoulder—marched out of the darkness and then, after several strides, back in again, as they continued unhurriedly up the road. They remained in view for no longer than a few seconds, but in that time Oskar managed to form a general impression, and he was eager to share it, especially with von Ewigholz.

Waiting for the footsteps to fade—then for a while longer, to be safe—was even harder than awaiting their approach. At last Hagen, by some very small movement, broke the enchantment that held them all paralyzed, and they began painfully extracting themselves from the bramble patch.

"Those uniforms," Oskar said, "what *were* they? They weren't SS or Wehrmacht. They looked . . . maybe green? I couldn't tell in this light."

Hagen was dabbing blood from where a thorn had raked across one temple. "Green would be Ordnungspolizei. Local police. Which is strange."

"How do you mean?" Lena asked. "As in *odd*? Or strange as in a Fritz Lang movie where everybody dies?"

"Well . . . it's probably not a good sign. It would suggest they've broadened the search, that it's now an all-out effort." He caught Oskar's eye. "And perhaps something more as well."

Oskar frowned. "They've guessed where we're heading, you mean? I don't see how—"

Lena threw her arms wide. "What does it matter how? The woods are full of cops in the middle of the night. This is hopeless. We're walking into a trap."

"I don't think so."

That was Clairborne, and it caught them by surprise. The boy's tone was measured and reasonable—a bright student in the class-room, politely challenging his professor. "If they knew where we were going, they wouldn't bother searching the trails. They'd just wait for us out there. They've called in reinforcements because they're getting, you know . . . a little frantic. My father must be raising holy hell. It's becoming an *international incident.* Nobody likes that. So while they're running around yelling at each other, we stroll calmly into this guesthouse under their noses. It's brilliant." He shrugged in his insouciant way, flashing them a smile. "I'm not saying it will work, mind you. But it's brilliant. And we've got no other tricks in the bag, do we?"

"We don't," said Hagen, who seemed to be making an effort to sound agreeable.

"It *will* work," Oskar said.

Lena said nothing, just stepped far enough out into the pasture to get a look at the moon. In that flat, silvery light her face looked stiff and pale, like driftwood, her expression containing no emotion that Oskar could name.

Perhaps he should have thought harder about this.

The sky was turning blue with a smear of pink at the horizon when they came to the edge of the forest. There the landscape changed so suddenly and completely that they stopped walking, all four of them, without conferring, and for half a minute stood taking in the view and undergoing a sort of psychic recalibration.

They were facing roughly east. The moon had fallen low behind them and only brushed the tips of a million stalks of unripe barley that rippled outward like a landlocked sea. Some distance off—about three kilometers, according to the map—those waves broke against a low wall of trees, and behind that, majestic, scarcely credible in this flat terrain, rose the Höhe Meissner, its two great humps and broad wooded flanks filling up so much of the vista you could scarcely register it all at once; your eyes needed to pick out bits of it and then stitch them together. The moon struck it face-on, the brightening sky cast it in silhouette, the windbreak of trees concealed its base—the effect was to make the mountain appear disconnected from the land around it, like a titanic floating island that had come to rest in the center of Germany but might take off again at any minute.

"Let's go," said Oskar. "We've got to make it around to the south slope—that's where Schwalbenthal is. It used to be a mining village. Now it's just—"

"Hold on," said Lena.

Something about her tone, a hint of slyness. The others turned to look at her.

"Shouldn't we make ourselves look a little more *Wandervogelisch*? Look, I've got some stuff here—odds and ends I picked up in Sababurg, remember? We might as well change now, before it gets light. Here, you'll love this."

She shrugged off her sack and loosened its drawstring. They all bent over to inspect the contents as she tugged them out one at a time. First came a floppy cap, dipping to a point at the front, its long plume snapped. Two oversized muslin shirts. A pair of Ottoman breeches. A wide loop of shiny blue cloth that she hung around Oskar's neck, declaring, "Lyric poet's sash!" Another cap, Wilhelm Tell–style. Lastly a pair of sandals with laces that ran up the calves, sized for Lena herself.

"You should have the pants," she told Clair.

He held them at arm's length, dubious. But, like a good American, he trooped off dutifully toward the nearest hedgerow. The rest of them fell to trying out costume bits in varying combinations, laughing at the results, passing them back and forth. Oskar took a liking to the archer's cap, Hagen to a peasant shirt whose length he nevertheless seemed puzzled by.

"Try tucking it in," Lena suggested. "Then let the bottom puff out. No, here, let me show you. First we'll get *this* out of the way." She tugged the handgun from where he'd jammed it under his belt. Then she stretched her arms around him, adjusting the hang of the cloth. "That's not bad. What do you think?"

"Maybe a little jaunty," said Oskar. "For a peasant."

Hagen gave him a sour look; then Clair called from the bushes.

"Come over, I'm not sure I'm doing this right."

Hagen's expression changed to something closer to amusement. He'd taken a few steps in Clair's direction when Lena said, with a new kind of sharpness, "I think that's far enough."

She was gripping the handgun in both hands, tipping it back and forth between Hagen and Oskar. "The two of you, sit down. And Clair! Come out here right now, I don't care if you're naked. We're all going to have a talk. Finally."

Oskar felt as though his mind had just split into halves—one that saw clearly what was happening and understood with fair precision the events that had led up to it, another that refused to accept it. "Not now! For Christ's sake, don't do this now. Look!" He waved an arm at the Höhe Meissner, looming closer and more solid than ever in the waxing daylight. "It's *right there*—the place we're trying to get to! We've only got to stay together a little longer, please. Give Hagen the gun back. Or just . . . you keep the gun, that's fine. But let's keep moving."

Lena seemed deaf to it all. Clair stepped out meekly from his hiding place and she wagged the gun at him, apparently a signal to come nearer.

"What's going on?" said Clair.

"Lena wants to have a talk," Hagen said without turning to look. "So we're going to have a talk."

His voice was so perfectly calm it gave Oskar a chill. It might have been the voice of someone who didn't intend to die here, or who didn't give a damn. He pointed to a spot beside the road. "So," he told Clair, "sit there." The boy obeyed, and Hagen sat down where he could quickly interpose himself between Clair and the gun. "Now let's talk," he said.

Lena bit her lip. "Okay," she said, taking a seat and laying the gun on her crossed legs, one finger still resting on the trigger.

Oskar felt too agitated to sit, but it felt odd to keep standing. He wondered if Lena knew anything about safety catches. Then he reflected that if he had time to wonder such a thing, the pace of events must have slowed, and the situation was likely controllable. So he sat down facing Lena and said, "What is it?"

"All right." She shifted her posture, getting more comfortable. Settling in. "First of all, *you* need to tell us what's going on here. You haven't explained anything, but you expect us to keep traipsing along after you, just because you say so. Why are you so dead set on us getting to this *Gasthaus*? And what was that crazy phone call about, with the stupid code and Cousin Peter and all that? Just—start at the beginning." She lifted the gun and waved it in his approximate direction. "Go."

Oskar drew a breath. The beginning. He glanced at Hagen, who gave him a slight nod that could have meant anything, then at Clair, who looked politely curious. "I guess the beginning," he said, "would be the Movement. So it's going to be hard to *explain* anything, because to be honest, I'm not sure how much of it makes sense now. Especially to outsiders. And I don't mean anything insulting by that. You can ask *him*."

Hagen said, without inflection, "You had to be there."

"See? So you're right, this plan is crazy, but not exactly the way you mean, and the craziness is why it might work. It *will* work."

"You're not explaining this very well," Lena said. "Try it in words even outsiders can understand."

Oskar sighed, feeling helpless. But he did try. The whole shebang, as Leo would say. Höhe Meissner, the magic mountain. The yearly climb to its summit, almost a holy pilgrimage. Stopping at the *Gasthaus* before the final leg—the last place to buy food and drink and matches and toilet paper, whatever you wanted to have up there but hadn't already squeezed into your rucksack. For the dj.1.11, this meant tchaj—a mysterious and potent beverage whose ingredients might not have been as secret as the *Geheimeslied*, though nobody seemed to know what they were. The proprietor of the *Gasthaus*—Müller, or Just Plain Müller, because that's what he asked to be called—brewed up vats of the stuff when he knew a Movement gathering was coming, or when he felt in his hostelkeeper's bones that the dj.1.11 might be about to arrive, or maybe because he'd grown to enjoy it, though Oskar considered this unlikely. Oskar personally thought it tasted horrible. As far as he knew, everyone else thought so too. Still, it was a group tradition, it marked special occasions and therefore made minor occasions feel special, it was red and murky yet if you sprinkled some on the fire it turned the flames clear blue, it felt daring and forbidden and it made your head spin. All these things the boys had liked, so they drank it. The taste was probably God's way of making sure they didn't like it too much.

And now we telescope from that misty past into the glaring present—when somehow, almost telepathically, his friend Herr Braun had gotten to tchaj from "Scotch on the rocks," a code phrase of Oskar's own creation, meant to trigger certain mutual associations. "Scotch" meant Scotland, where Oskar had traveled with members of the group and they'd been detained by local authorities. (No charges were brought; the boys were released on the recognizance of their *Sippenleiter*.) Herr Braun knew that story, he'd mentioned it at their first meeting, and Oskar hoped he'd make the connection now. "Rocks" was likewise a pointer, this time to a landform not far from where they sat: a promontory of silver-gray rock that was the group's habitual camping ground. This had been Oskar's attempt to suggest a rendezvous point. He knew it was a stretch, but maybe Herr Braun would understand.

And so he had, apparently. He'd caught at least the gist of Oskar's message and responded in kind, with a revised destination. The companions were to proceed to *the place where the weird drink comes from*—which was just up there, look, a bit to the right, halfway up the slope. Now, if they could only get moving . . .

"What then?" said Lena. "What happens when we get there, assuming we make it that far? We're trapped on a mountain instead of being trapped in the woods? Herr Braun swoops down out of the sky and plucks us up?"

A good question, Oskar had to admit. He could only hope Jaap had something in mind. "I really don't know."

Lena nodded. She'd been toying with the handgun, passing it from hand to hand, and now she gave it a spin on one finger like you saw in the movies. This trick must have been harder than it looked, because the gun made one full rotation before twirling off her fingertip and landing with a thud an arm's reach away with its barrel pointed straight at Clair.

He sat staring at the gun for a couple of seconds until Lena snatched it back up. Then he said, in evident amazement: "You could've killed me."

"The safety was on." She looked shame-faced yet stubborn. "Do you think I'm an idiot?"

Clair laughed now—shakily, a hand to his heart, miming relief.

"Yes," said Oskar. "If you make us sit here all morning, then yes, you're an idiot."

Lena twisted her mouth but did not immediately reply. At a guess, she was thinking that some sort of criticism might be warranted, though not of this exact nature. Still, the ground had shifted.

"I'm keeping the gun," she said, looking from Oskar to Hagen. "And you two can go first. Clair and I will hang back a little."

"Good," said Hagen. He placed the floppy cap on his head and stood up, looking at once foolish and dangerous.

The others stood as well. For a few moments they examined one another in the new day's light, in their eccentric clothing, before a landscape more breathtaking than any work of art, and it felt as though one of them ought to say something. They were the most wanted people in the Third Reich. The next step any of them took would likely begin their final journey. Maybe it was too much.

Oskar walked out onto the road. "*Hu hüpf!*" he said—a hiker's call, it meant nothing in particular. And they set off for the Höhe Meissner.

ON THE ROAD WITH THE BARONESS VON F——

BERLIN, HÖHE MEISSNER AND KAUFUNGEN: THE SAME MORNING

The admiral's custom-built Mercedes swung onto Fasanenstrasse a few minutes before seven a.m. The chauffeur, unfamiliar with the oversized vehicle, took the turn too wide and nearly sideswiped a dairy cart on its morning round. The skidding of tires and the milkman's curses were barely audible through the armor plating and reinforced glass.

"Steady on," murmured Jaap Saxo from the forward passenger seat.

Beside him though some distance away, the driver, a beefy gentleman lately employed as a percussionist by the Baroness von F——, flexed his boxer's paws at the wheel. He wore formal evening attire and a black cap with a narrow brim he'd borrowed from a mate who worked on a river tug. It was perhaps the least odd thing about him. But the regular driver was out of town—dispatched last night on confidential business by Jaap himself.

"It'll be fine," Jaap said, not to the driver, particularly, nor to himself. To the gods, maybe. He held no unconventional beliefs in that regard, but if he recognized any patron it would be Odin, a devious fellow who'd given an eye to acquire secret knowledge—in Jaap's view, an early-career blunder—though generally he kept to the background, sending a pair of clever birds out to spy for him.

Between Jaap and the driver on the wide front seat rested a foil-covered box of the type used for Swiss chocolates, tied with a bright red bow. There was a card attached, with a name inscribed in a light, possibly feminine hand; it barely quivered as the great motorcar eased to a halt before number 88. The beefy gentleman leapt out with surprising alacrity and fairly pranced up the steps of the grand Schinkel portico. Jaap stepped onto the sidewalk, glanced up and down the *Strasse*—all but deserted at this hour—and put on what he thought of as his battle face.

At seven o'clock exactly, the beefy gentleman drew open the door and the Baroness von F—— breezed through it, followed closely by the elderly Brigadier. The grande dame descended the half dozen steps to street level without breaking stride, only then pausing to favor Jaap with a courtly nod. She was dressed in an outfit that must have been à la mode among the motoring set a couple of decades ago, before the advent of the car roof: a long coat of soot-brown leather tailored trimly and secured with straps, a streamlined hat probably anchored with pins somewhere, a pair of study gloves and a flamboyant, sky-blue scarf designed to billow. Jaap wondered if she'd omitted the goggles on purpose or just forgotten them.

"*Allez. Dépêchez-vous alors!*" she called—not, as it first appeared, to the bewildered driver still lingering at the door but to the Brigadier, who was negotiating the steps with an abundance of caution. He'd done himself up splendidly as well, in full parade dress, the Iron Cross at his neck and so many medals on his chest it was a wonder he could bear the weight. And having stood, could he walk? The uniform was a relic of leaner times, and the old man looked decidedly pinched. Though also magnificent, and rather singularly so. Those battle decorations had not come cheap. Jaap looked on with a complicated mixture of feelings as the Brigadier joined the Baroness, one arm gallantly extended to help her into the car. Should he be worried about them? Too late now.

"*Bon courage, Votre Excellence,*" Jaap told her. "Lives may depend on your success."

"Yes, yes," the Brigadier said, shooing him off, "we know all that. Out of the way now. Capable hands. You keep to your post, await my call. Radio works in this thing, does it?"

"The radio is . . . complicated. The driver can handle it; he's been fully instructed."

"Has he?" The Brigadier cast a stern eye at the man in question, now lumbering down from the portico, circling the flank of the car, muscles bulging under his tuxedo jacket. "Yes, I expect he'll do. Well, then."

Seized by an impulse, and despite his rumpled civilian attire, Jaap took a step backward on the sidewalk, came to attention and gave the Brigadier a formal salute. The old soldier returned it in kind, then turned stiffly on his heel and boarded the Mercedes, joining the Baroness on the commodious rear bench. Jaap shut the door and watched as the chauffeur eased the old car away from the curb like a barge drifting off the wharf.

All his forces were deployed now. The ravens were in flight. He allowed himself to enjoy a moment of exhilaration—a glorious moment in which nothing yet had gone wrong.

There were two main approaches to the Höhe Meissner, the mountain sacred to generations of German youth—the first one bold, steep and direct, hence favored by more adventurous elements of the Movement; the second longer, easier and more scenic, looping through a low spot called the Kasseler Kuppe, skirting a lake and a site of mythico-historic interest known as Frau Holle's Well, then curling south and rising unhurriedly to a stony shoulder, the Schwalbenthal. The spot enjoyed modest and mainly local fame for its views, its calamitous history (including the 1907 landslide that carried most of it away) and its public inn, politely mentioned in Baedeker on the strength of a menu showcasing local game and a *Biergarten* perched thrillingly at the brink of a cliff. There were half a dozen tables out there, ranged beside a low stone wall that was broken in places, whole sections gone missing as though the mountain had shrugged them off. The footing was rough, and the tables needed shimming to keep them level. Even so, the inn was fantastic, the air crisp and the May sunlight gentle, and by midmorning four of the tables were occupied.

Frau Müller could scarcely remember a time when the *Gasthaus* had been this busy. Well, no, in fact she could—but that was many years ago. Right through the twenties and into the present decade, business had been so brisk that she and old Müller couldn't manage it on their own; they'd taken on extra help, made new guest rooms up in the attic and even thought of modernizing the plumbing. But since 1933 . . . well, things had changed, hadn't they? The young people no longer came around so often on their hiking trips, and to Frau Müller it felt as though the life had gone right out of the place.

She would never have said as much to her husband—a great supporter of the new government, as was she, of course—but some of the changes were not so much to her liking. *Ja, ja*, she understood— you don't need to tell her again!—that all Germany must move forward as one, that young people need proper values instilled in them and the Hitlerjugend was far more wholesome than the old rabble of motley bands with no adequate supervision. And yet . . . in a secret chamber of her heart, Frau Müller missed those days, those packs of rascals and vagabonds that used to tramp around back then. Birds of passage, wandering bacchants, self-taught troubadours with guitars strapped to their backs. Boys who tried to pay for their meals by writing poetry on a *Reisekarte*. Girls who asked Frau Müller to hold still, please, while they sketched her for their travel books.

Hold still! There'd been no time to keep up with her chores back then, even going full tilt. Stopping to rest for half an hour would have meant the chickens not getting fed or someone sleeping on dirty sheets that night, with her good man with that back of his already busy hauling a sack of potatoes up from the cellar.

Well—country life had never been easy, so you count your blessings. There were eight paying guests today, at the start of summer, when there ought to be twenty. But eight, as old Müller would remind her, was better than none; the world at least was saying, Yes, we know you're there. And who could tell? Maybe business would pick up again. The Czechs might finally learn to behave, and this talk of war would die down and life will get back to normal.

Ach, but such idle thoughts—when there was plenty of work to do in the here and now! Eight paying guests—minus the lad who'd set off hours ago with his rifle—waiting at their tables outside and a tray of biscuits steaming from the oven and her good man malingering God alone knew where. Frau Müller parceled the biscuits into linen-swaddled bowls and bustled out the kitchen door, down the steps and out to the terrace—a journey of no great distance, yet at every step she felt herself nagged by something, maybe an uncompleted thought, a twinge of intuition. She went from one table to the next setting the bowls out distractedly: one for the pair of stout gentlemen in lederhosen; one for the older couple from Munich, regular guests; one for the middle-aged woman sitting alone with her historical novel; and one for the well-dressed couple from Hamburg, last night's late arrivals—he looking bright-eyed this morning, she looking . . . what would you call it, anxious? Impatient? But whatever was nagging Frau Müller, it didn't seem to be out here on the terrace.

No: it was coming up the road.

She saw them at last—four of them—and for an uncanny moment she felt as though they were stepping out of the past. They were young; they were gotten up in hobs and fobs; they didn't look quite respectable. But you could tell—with an innkeeper's eye you certainly could—that they'd chosen to look like that and were just trying to make an impression. Their stride was heavy, as though they'd been walking for a long while. Their faces were either cast down in weariness or raised in nervous expectancy. She took them at a glance for two young men followed by two young women—but no, that was wrong, one of the latter was a boy with long hair, something you never saw these days. Never. In fact, you never saw anything like this little pack of make-believe Gypsies. The sight of them tugged at Frau Müller's heart from two very different directions. Part of her wanted to rejoice at what seemed a visitation out of the happy and prosperous twenties. Another part was afraid, because things you never saw these days were generally things you ought not to see. Improper, even dangerous things. But what could be dangerous about this little troupe of wanderers? Even her shrewd eye couldn't tell her that. Which only made it worse.

Where had her husband gotten to? Old Müller wasn't the quickest man in the world, but he had a good head on him and no shortage of opinions. He'd surely have something to say about this.

———

For a good part of that final push up the mountain, Oskar had kept himself from worrying about such things as his swollen feet and the Ordnungspolizei and Lena several paces behind him with a nine-millimeter pistol in her bag by trying to conjure a scenario wherein he opened his eyes tomorrow to find himself lying on a soft bed somewhere, not locked in a cell in Prinz-Albrecht-Strasse. While his imagination had not thus far proved up to the task, it was the attempt, not the outcome, that made this a useful distraction. Then, after a few kilometers, they reached a fork in the trail—left to Schwalbenthal, right to the lake—and a fresh distraction arose, one that required no effort on his part. He was not the only one who felt the pull of it.

"We used to go swimming in that lake," Hagen said beside him.

They didn't break stride—only stared together up the right-hand path as they turned onto the other one, bearing north, the road twisting back on itself in conformance with the terrain.

"So did we," said Oskar.

"It seems like a long time ago."

Oskar did not enjoy sharing thoughts with an SS man, even this one. Some accident of history had made them companions; that was all right, such things happened. But the troubling thought arose—it had done so already, and now it came again—that the two of them had much in common. They were German officers. They were Movement veterans. They were bound by oaths to the Fatherland. They were being swept along by the torrent of events. And now, without conscious intent, they'd fallen into lockstep on this mountain road that each had traveled many times before.

That was distraction enough, but the land itself eventually overwhelmed it. The trail turned east and gained altitude; the Upper Hessian plain spread itself out below them; the nearest peak of the Meissner, known for some reason as the Calf, came into view on their right; the sun inched higher into a huge and empty summer sky. Oskar began to feel warm and wondered what had become of the Wilhelm Tell cap, which he must've left somewhere. They passed a marker and a side trail leading down to Frau Holle's Well— ancient and by legend bottomless, a shaft plunging straight to the

Underworld, though Oskar preferred a variant he'd heard along the Movement's mystical fringe: the well as *omphalos*, the holy navel of Germany. Had Hagen heard that one too? Oskar willed himself not to ask.

The final turn was to the south, and by now it was midmorning. No sign announced the Gasthaus Schwalbenthal—you came upon it offhandedly while thinking of something else, gazing off in the wrong direction. You'd just trudged over a rise, winded, then ducked around a bend overhung with oak limbs—and there it was a hundred meters ahead of you, an assertive and unlikely presence in this wild landscape, three stories tall, half-timbered, with too many windows to count. The timbers were stained ochre red to match the roof tiles; the stucco had once gleamed white but the paint had milked down to an ashen gray—or maybe the white was only an artifact of Oskar's memory.

His eye ran from the building to the terrace to the row of tables. He was close enough now to see the people out there pretty clearly, and none of them was Jaap Saxo. Though Oskar hadn't been consciously holding his breath, he exhaled in disappointment anyway.

Weariness overcame him. Hope had been holding it off—a phantasmal hope he hadn't dared acknowledge—but that figment vanished in the mountain air, and the weight of exhaustion came down so heavily that he almost sagged beneath it. He thought of stopping, of sitting down right here in the road and waiting for destiny to run him over. But then something kicked in—stubbornness or curiosity or army discipline, or maybe simple thirst—and whatever it was made him actually quicken his step, pulling ahead of the others, first to tag the old gatepost where guests had once tethered their horses.

While his companions straggled up behind him, Oskar had a quick look around, recording small changes, appraising the motorcars in the courtyard—one caught his eye, a small Bugatti whose license plates bore the letter code for Berlin—and finally spotting the landlady standing by a small door that led, he remembered, into the kitchen. He waved at her, swinging his whole arm. She might have smiled back—hard to tell, from thirty paces off—but her arms were filled with tableware, which she carried inside.

"Okay," said Lena, close behind Oskar and more loudly than necessary, as if she wanted to share her skepticism with the valley below. "So now what?"

"Now we sit down," said Clair cheerfully. "Or lie down!" The thought seemed to please him. "How long are we staying? Can we get a room? Do they have room service?" He aimed these questions at Hagen like a series of playful jabs.

Wearing his usual *Übermensch* mask, Hagen affected to be oblivious, though Oskar was pretty sure he was acutely attentive to everything and perhaps to Clair most of all. He stared at Oskar like a sentry waiting for the watchword.

"Let's get a table," Oskar said.

Maybe that was the watchword, or so obvious as to require no deliberation. They trooped over to the nearest empty one, squeezing between a matronly woman, who lowered her book to stare at them, and a well-dressed pair of urbanites, whom Oskar immediately placed in the folder marked "Bugatti." These two made a point of not regarding the newcomers as they knocked chairs aside and thumped themselves down with groans of relief.

Clair said, "Are we going to get some food?"

"Are we?" Lena aimed this at Oskar, a challenge of sorts. "Do we have time? Isn't your friend Herr Braun—"

Hagen cut her off by the expedient of shifting his chair on the flagstones, fractionally narrowing the angle at which he faced her across the table. It was odd how his inexpressive features could be read as placid or stern or even menacing, depending on factors Oskar had yet to work out. Lena swung her head away and now appeared to be scanning the horizon for hostile forces.

"Well, *I'm* hungry," said Clair. "Isn't there a waiter?"

Oskar wondered about that. He knew the landlady had seen them arrive, but she hadn't reappeared from the kitchen, and as the moments stretched out, her absence seemed to become a new and possibly meaningful element of the scene. *Stop staring at the damned door,* he told himself, and in so doing his gaze happened to brush against another set of eyes at the adjacent table—belonging to the female half of the well-dressed Bugattis. So, she'd deigned to glance over and he'd caught her at it, but now she gave him the tiniest of smiles. Her eyes were a startling bright amber and her skin was preternaturally pale, and Oskar got a discomfiting feeling he'd seen her before. Though where could he have seen a person like that? She looked away, and Oskar's eyes lingered a while longer, first on the woman in profile and then on her male companion, who was short enough to be almost completely hidden behind his newspaper. The last detail Oskar noted was the name of the paper, the *Hamburger Abendblatt*. Yet the license plate was from Berlin.

Maybe it meant nothing, like the landlady's protracted absence. He'd simply guessed wrong about who owned the car. His brain was overtaxed by exhaustion and fear. He took a breath and turned back to his companions and willed himself to relax, to behave naturally. A mountain inn, a breathtaking view, a welcome and restorative respite. He tried to smile but sensed it wasn't working—something was out of place here. Something was wrong.

"Should I go and get somebody?" Clair said. "What should I say? *Können Sie mir helfen, ich habe Angst, dass ich—*"

But then the side door opened and out came the landlord himself—Just Plain Müller, pausing on the stoop to peer this way and that, checking every feature of his environment as if worried that some guest might have clogged the mountain stream or knocked a few ancient trees over. In time he surveyed the terrace, where at last he found something that needed his attention. He came at them cat-like, not quite directly and not quite looking.

"The same as ever," said Hagen, the audible trace of a smile in his voice.

It was true: Müller looked no older and no slower and no surlier than he ever had. Oskar would have found it hard to describe the man if pressed on it. He was neither tall nor short, dark nor fair, handsome nor ugly. He might have been the product of a generations-long breeding program whose goal was the elimination of all distinctive traits. When he reached the terrace, he visited each table according to some inscrutable hierarchy that placed the elderly couple first, then the men in lederhosen, the matron with her book, the Bugattis. Oskar tried to guess the pattern and hoped it wasn't what it appeared to be: that Müller was closing in on the new arrivals by degrees, getting a look at them from every possible angle.

At the next table over, the pale woman motioned for the landlord to draw closer, into whispering range, and leaned toward him as if about to broach some delicate topic—but if that was her intention, her voice undermined it to an almost comical degree: it was too clear, too musical, with an accent that made you think of old cities and lamplit streets and chambers hung with tapestries.

"Tell me, *mein lieber Herr*," she said, "what is that extraordinary drink you have here, the one people always talk about?"

Müller looked startled for a moment. His smile came hesitantly but grew warmer as the effusion of charm took effect. "I . . . I'm not sure I know what you mean."

"Oh yes, you must! I know—I've *heard*—it's a specialty of the house, your own secret recipe. I won't tell anyone, I promise! But please, you must let me try it. My husband as well."

Her companion lowered his paper at last and looked up at Müller, his dark eyes full of sympathy. And Oskar knew—he was sure this time—he'd seen those eyes before.

"I'm afraid we have no choice, my friend," the little man said. "She sets her mind to something and . . . well. So, this mysterious beverage—I trust you can guess what she's talking about?"

Müller straightened his shoulders. "I believe, sir, she means the tchaj."

As performances go, it wasn't awfully convincing. But the realization that it *was* a performance—therefore scripted for a certain audience that, given *the tchaj*, could only be Oskar—ran through him like an electric current. He felt as though the pale young woman had very discreetly, and unnoticed by anyone else, dropped a live wire in his lap. Now he was obliged to sit there as though nothing extraordinary was happening—carry on with the pointless niceties of ordering food and drink, chuckle at old Müller's banter about their being late for breakfast (they'd have to call it lunch now; the menu was the same but the prices were double), while ignoring the couple at the next table as steadfastly as they were ignoring him. Buckle down, breathe normally, be a good operative. *Live your cover.*

He tried to focus on the table, his dining companions, ordinary things. Lena removed her sandals to inspect the blisters on her heels. Clair was studying the view, trying to match up sights with their corresponding symbols on the hiking map. Hagen seemed to be lost in contemplation, but that might have been a pretense, like Oskar's, because when the woman flipped a page of her novel, with a sound like a dry leaf rasping in the woods, he visibly twitched and gave her an irritated look. The woman frowned back. Oskar glanced at her book; he could just make out the author's name, Werner Beumelburg, and enough of the cover to surmise that this was a "front experience" novel, another volume in the approved genre celebrating the glories of life during wartime. The woman noticed his interest, and he gave her what he hoped was a suitably patriotic nod.

What was the plan now? Oskar assumed there must be one, because there'd been a signal and a messenger, *two* messengers, to deliver it. Jaap must have sent them. It couldn't mean nothing.

Both Müllers, Herr and Frau, emerged from the *Gasthaus* weighted with serving trays. Accorded the lesser task of delivering food and coffee to the newcomers, she performed it to a minimal standard of professional competence while mumbling to herself, indistinctly, on the general topic of life's unfairness. Just Plain Müller carried a smaller tray with an earthenware jug and two glasses, which he set out with modest ceremony before the charming young lady and her undeserving spouse.

"You'll note the clarity," he said, pouring three fingers of alarmingly red liquid into one of the glasses. "This comes only with proper aging in special casks."

Oskar turned away—it was somehow vaguely embarrassing—and stared at the bloody-looking sausage and puffy rolls on his plate, trying to decide if he had any appetite. He remembered feeling hungry during the climb, but now it seemed that communication between his stomach and his brain had ceased, the sight of food triggering no response at all. Clair and Lena were meanwhile tucking in with evident pleasure. Hagen, toying with his knife, met Oskar's eye and gave him a wry, comradely half-smile.

At the next table, the couple whom he took to be his secret allies were waving their glasses of tchaj around, deeply engaged in a lively conversation about nothing important. Oskar caught the names Ricky and Dodo, mention of a cabaret "down in the slums," a sardonic allusion to an event identified only as "the incident"—the empty chatter of socialites. He was all but grinding his teeth. When were they going to make their move?

Then it occurred to him that maybe they were making it already.

He'd been watching them for a while; there was no reason not to, since they were so fully self-absorbed that people at other tables were looking too. He reflected that in all this time he'd seen a lot of tchaj being splashed around, tipped from glasses, replenished from the pitcher and waved gaily in the sunshine, but not much actually being drunk. Yet the couple—the woman especially—seemed well along toward intoxication.

Now she drew herself upright and looked around brightly—she had an idea, an inspiration!—then bent down to peer under the table, searching for something, where had she put it, around here somewhere . . . aha, there it is! She came up holding a large black box, leather-covered, its corners reinforced with brass, and laid it heavily on the table. That's right, thought Oskar, leave it there for a couple of seconds, let the suspense build. As before, she overplayed it—how hard can it be to open a simple spring latch; you just press the damn button—but she did it with such conviction that even Oskar was dying to know what was in there.

Give them a mystery to solve. He recalled that precept now, one of the hundred nuggets of fieldcraft compressed into his weeks of training at Bremerhaven. The best course is to make yourself unnoticeable. But if you can't do that—if people are going to be looking, thinking, wondering—then create some trivial mystery and, next, provide its solution. The textbook example was the bulge in a jacket pocket that turns out to be a fat detective novel. *But it can be anything,* they told him. *Be original.*

The young woman opened the black box, and inside was what looked like a very nice camera, a Rolleiflex, with a neck strap and a shiny attachment for flashbulbs. She pulled it out carelessly and held it wrong. He worried that she might drop it.

"Darling, we must have pictures! Such a marvelous backdrop!"

She rose and spun around to face the cliff's edge, a scant two paces away, making a conspicuous effort to keep from wobbling. This part was so convincing that Hagen stood quickly and reached

her in one easy bound, taking her by the elbow and sliding his other
hand around in case he needed to catch a falling camera.

She turned her face toward his with a look of surprise and grati-
tude and only maybe a dash of flirtation. "Such a gentleman!" she
said. "And what quick reflexes!" She stepped back for a better look
at him. "Well, since you've come to join us, would you mind taking
our picture? Here, it's quite easy . . ."

The putative little husband stepped in now. "*Liebchen*, don't
bother these good people. I'm sorry, sir, it's the altitude that affects
her. Come away, *Liebchen*."

"I don't mind," said Hagen. He took the camera and examined
it respectfully. "This is a fine instrument. German-made, isn't it?"

"Indeed. And the lens is by Zeiss, also of impeccable Aryan pedigree."

Hagen looked at him sharply, unamused, but before anyone could
stray further down that path the pale woman grabbed her partner
by the wrist and maneuvered him into position to be photographed.
Hagen popped open the viewfinder and took his time arranging
the composition. "To the left, please . . . yes, hold it there . . . now
smile"—a familiar ritual that on this spot must have been enacted a
thousand times. They ran through it in various iterations, lining up
different aspects of the backdrop, and then the young woman had a
fresh thought.

"You've been so kind—why don't I take *your* picture now? You
and your friends! It will be lovely, you all look so . . . *authentic*. And
we'll have copies made for everyone. Darling, don't you agree?" She
turned to her partner. "Wouldn't it make a lovely, a lovely"—here
her excellent German seemed to abandon her—"*podarok na pamyat*."

"Keepsake," the little man said quickly. "Yes, *Liebchen*, it would
make a lovely keepsake. There, there, don't fret."

Oskar wondered at this new twist in the performance; he had
no doubt it was calculated, but toward what end? Then he saw that
the two fellows in lederhosen at the farthermost table had paused
in their conversation and were looking toward them. A glance over
his shoulder—yes, the matron had lowered her novel. Evidently a
young lady speaking Russian in the heart of Germany was something one couldn't ignore.

"*Kommen Sie dann!*" The lady was on point again, this awkward moment behind her. She motioned to the three of them still at the table like a choir director—everyone rise, *bitte*. "Yes, good. Stand over here, please. How wonderful you all look! Proper *Wandervögel!*"

What was she up to? Oskar watched her grappling with the Rolleiflex, which looked quite large in her hands. She glanced up once and caught his eye—half a second at most, enough to verify that he was paying attention. In that instant, he experienced an intuitive flash: She's going to have trouble with the camera. She's going to need help.

And so he was ready. The companions lined up with their backs to the panoramic view. The little man stood by the table with a glass of tchaj in his hand. The woman assumed an awkward stance with her feet spread well apart and the Rolleiflex dangling low on its strap, staring down at the viewfinder and steadying the camera with one hand while groping with the other for the focus knob. She was muttering quietly, as if coaxing the balky creature to be a nice Rollei and take a pretty picture.

"Oh," she said, looking up, chagrined and exasperated, "I just can't get this thing to work!"

Hagen moved to help, but Oskar was a step ahead, drawing up close.

The woman didn't meet his eyes, just kept fussing with the knob. "I think it's stuck," she said. "I can't make it turn. Could you have a look?"

He bent forward, staring down, his head nearly touching her shoulder.

"You're Ossi, yes?" she said, sotto voce, in the same breathy tone with which she'd been muttering to herself. Even he could barely catch it, just inches away. "There's a way out—but only one. You'll be leaving in police custody. Now, show me how the focus works."

She shoved the camera into Oskar's hands, which had the effect of pushing him slightly away.

He felt his awareness rotating as slowly as a kaleidoscope, making strange patterns out of familiar objects, even the camera. He clutched it and pulled it out of that swirl, staring hard until it coalesced again into a solid, single-faceted object. "You just touch it lightly," he said. "Look, you can do it with one fingertip. See how the focus changes?"

The woman leaned in again, allowing Oskar to guide her finger onto the knob. "Draw attention to yourselves," she murmured. "To *him*, especially. He needs to be recognized. Do it quickly." Taking back the camera, she swung it around, showing off her new skill. "It works now! It's easy! Thank you so much, *mein Herr*—but look, you've dropped something."

At her feet, just where Oskar had been standing, lay a small packet, evidently a letter—the envelope crumpled, the address blurry as though the ink had run. He snatched it up, nodding his thanks, and stuffed it into his pocket.

He needn't have worried; no one was watching, everyone's eyes on the giddy young woman and her fancy camera.

"Now look happy!" she commanded. "It's a lovely day, the swallows are singing—everyone smile!"

There had been a time not so long ago when Chief Watchmaster Hans Diehl could have—and surely would've—chosen not to take this phone call. *Who?* he would have said. *Kohlwasser, what sort of name is that? He's a what—Standartenführer? A banner leader? Like a drum major, that kind of thing? Calling from where? Well, look—tell him I'm sure there are plenty of marching bands in Berlin that would welcome his services. We have no need of him here in Kaufungen.*

You can bet your hat, he'd have said it right to this pompous desk warrior's face. And until the year before last, he would've been safely within his rights to do so.

The chief had served proudly and without a single red mark against his name for thirty-two years. He'd risen from assistant village constable to the mounted Gendarmerie, from there to the municipal Schutzpolizei, back to the Gendarmerie as a senior watchmaster, and for almost a decade now he'd been top man for the entire *Bezirk* of Kaufungen, the largest and most physically challenging territory in northern Hesse. He'd run every sort of case you could imagine, from murder to missing livestock, arson, blackmail, poaching, rape, breaking in, drunken mayhem, violent assault, the whole mad rainbow of domestic eruptions—and yes, kidnapping as well. He knew this job from top to bottom; no one was better at it, no one more professional or discreet.

Yet none of that mattered any longer. Years of experience, local knowledge, the respect of the community he served—all of it counted for less than a single sheet of paper signed in 1936 by none other than Heinrich Himmler, erstwhile poultry farmer and now apparently the world's second greatest authority on everything under the sun. And by the magic of that pen stroke, centuries of German law and custom had been overturned, the thoughtful apportionment of police authority among nation, state, district and municipality flattened like a child's paper castle into something unrecognizable. Everything belonged to the SS now—that was the nut of it. The whole intricate machinery of law enforcement, built and fine-tuned over generations, had been reduced to a single cog in a crude apparatus called the Security Service.

They'd given that cog a vulgar name: the Order Police. Whatever you'd been before—beat cop, fraud investigator, fire warden, dogcatcher—today you were Ordnungspolizei. There was even a new uniform, the same for every last man! Green, cut in military style, it made you look like a scoutmaster playing war games. For a couple of months, the chief had refused to put the damn thing on—he had a perfectly good uniform already, with years of use left in it—but then *word had come down*. And that was the new system in its purest form: words, a multitude of words, all moving in the same direction. They traveled by every medium of conveyance, typed out in directives, murmured in your ear, published in *The Black Corps*—an incredible thing, the official SS organ, at once vile and sanctimonious—and, worst of all, shouted through the static on that lamentable invention, the telephone.

The chief held the handpiece a few inches from his ear so the voice of the ill-mannered *Standartenführer*—a sort of colonel; he'd looked it up—rang tinny and hollow throughout his office in a tidy building in the heart of Kaufungen, a small and law-abiding town.

His sergeant, the only man on the force with as many years of service as Diehl himself, shook his head sympathetically.

"Excuse me, *Herr Standartenführer*!" Diehl shouted back at arbitrary moments, interrupting the diatribe at the other end. "I'm afraid the connection is faulty, I missed that last bit! Could you speak more plainly, please?"

This was the second call from Berlin just this morning, following one last night during an already delayed supper. Aside from getting his blood up, they served no purpose Diehl could see. He didn't need to be told it was serious business, the missing son of a foreign VIP. *Grosser Gott*, he'd had the whole force out for hours, as well as some auxiliaries he'd called up, plus some extra patrolmen on loan from the larger force at Kassel—and that had been a bitter pill, a question of local pride. Nor did he welcome hints about a "political dimension." Politics and policing didn't mix, in the chief's view; a law was a law, and the same ones applied to everybody.

Above all, he could not abide rudeness. And this blustery little colonel, this Kohlwasser, was as rude as any SS man Diehl had ever crossed lances with—which was saying a mouthful, as to a man and a dog they were an ill-bred lot. He pursed his lips and held the philosophic gaze of his adjunct for a few moments longer. Finally he nodded—*enough for now*—and the sergeant switched on the old radio, an antique model long retired from active use but kept around for emergencies such as this, when it served as a convincing simulator of telephone line noise, starting off quiet but rising in volume and pitch as the tubes warmed up. Diehl let it build until it drowned out the clamor from the distant *Reichskapital.* Then he dropped the handpiece into its cradle. If only it could always be so easy.

"What was he saying," he asked, "just before the end there?"

The sergeant shook his head. "Didn't catch it all, sir, I'm afraid. But I believe he said, *I'm coming down.*"

The chief watchmaster nodded. That's what he'd thought too. Well, let the fellow come, then, and get some cow shit on his parade boots.

Believe this?" said Bull Townsend from his bed at the Hotel Adlon. "This so-called doctor telling me to stay off my feet for two days? Two days! Some tendon came loose, I guess. Hurts like hell, I don't mind saying. Then he tries to give me a shot but I tell him to get that damn needle away from me, I've got things I need to see to and the world don't stop because my knee's hurting. My boy's out there, dead for all I know. And when his mother calls, I'll sound like I'm half in the bag? Well, forget it, Herr Doktor Arschloch."

Toby Lugan approached the bed cautiously. It was large enough to sleep three and looked as though an explosion had occurred among the many pillows and blankets that lay around Bull like twisted wreckage. The senator sat propped at an angle apparently chosen to provide an optimal flow of air from his diaphragm to his vocal cords. Toby didn't like his own chances of a getting a word in edgewise, though there were words that needed saying, one wise or another. "Listen, Bull—"

"And the goddamn embassy, those pricks! I ask for a situation update, they send over some girl looks like Margaret Hamilton at the wrong time of the month. Wants me to sign papers. Authorize her to act in loco. Promise to let her know the instant, the *instant*, we hear a goddamn thing. I told her, Ma'am, I'll promise you anything. Slide a paper in front of me, I'll sign it. Hand me a spark plug, I'll piss on it. All I want is to get my boy back."

"Bull, that's what I—"

"People you want to hear from, they've forgotten your number. Must've wrote it down on toilet paper, I guess. People you don't want to hear from—I'm talking about reporters—they're calling every other minute, had to tell the switchboard I'm sick and tired of this, take a message and then burn it. One of them got through anyway. Barely understand him, couldn't tell if his English was that bad or he was snockered. But he got me laughing, said he was on to a big scoop, something about Clairborne, wouldn't say what, needed me to give him an 'ex-klu-*seev*.' Finally had to hang up on the son of a bitch, he would've kept me up all—"

"Damn it, Bull, shut up."

The expression on the senator's face was worth Toby's career, should it come to that.

"It's Clairborne I came to talk to you about. And . . . one other thing, but that can wait, probably. I've just gotten a call from, ah, someone in the Security Service. They've got some reports, aerial surveillance and whatnot—it's nothing definite, there's only local people on the ground right now—but they think they've spotted Clairborne. Out in the country, east of Kassel. And there's some physical evidence—a hat on a trail, trampled grass, stuff like that— suggesting he might be with a few other people. They *might* be the kidnappers, my contact doesn't know; he's heading down there now, invited me to join him. Your personal representative, that type of thing."

"Well, damn it, Toby! Let me sit here blabbing when you've got news like this, what's wrong with you? How far away is it, this fucking place?"

"I'm told it's a four-hour drive."

"Four goddamn hours." Townsend struggled to rise, but the injured tendon wouldn't allow it. He emitted a low, prolonged bellow, then said, through gritted teeth, "Don't they have airplanes in this country?"

"I'm pretty sure they do, yes."

"So get on that phone and find one, then get on it and go find Clairborne. You might want to take that embassy gal along. I promised her . . . hell, I don't know what all I promised. Anyway, she'll probably know how to talk to them. Left her card there on the table."

Talk to whom? Toby wondered. Germans? Kidnappers? He picked up the card and read SUSAN DURST, SPECIAL LIAISON.

"The hell you waiting for?" said Bull. "Got something more important on your mind?"

Toby hadn't consciously been waiting for anything, but now he became aware once more of the leather case in his hand. It seemed to be getting heavier the longer he carried it around. And yes: though he wouldn't have put the matter so crudely, it probably was *incalculably* more important than the senator's missing son. Toby had spent a few hours last night absorbing its contents, which were written in a clench-jawed Prussian dialect that must have been taught at General Staff College, fully intelligible only to its graduates. But Toby understood enough to realize what a bombshell he was holding. So *this*, he thought, is how a major European power goes about the business of invading a smaller neighbor. Well, why not? They've had centuries of practice, gotten the thing down to a science. So that part wasn't surprising, from a Realpolitik point of view.

But it *was* surprising, number one, that somebody from the Interior Ministry had made off with these documents and, number two, that he'd slipped them easy as pie into Bull Townsend's tennis bag. Where, owing to an untimely confluence of cussedness and gravity, they were discovered not by His Honor but by a humble political spear-carrier. Who'd been toting this thing around since yesterday, and it was a mighty spear indeed.

"Is there some damn thing you're not telling me?" said Bull. "Something about Clairborne?"

"No," said Toby. "No, it's—it's something else. It can wait." He picked up the hotel phone, and when the switchboard answered, he said, *"Wie erreiche ich ein Flugzeug?"*

Like great hotels all over the world, the Adlon was well practiced at meeting the exacting requirements of its guests. Toby was in a taxi bound for Tempelhof in under ten minutes. Should he swing by the embassy en route to pick up Girl Susan? Better not—Toby could act in loco parentis himself, should it be necessary or advisable. Who knows what kind of tawdry mess he was going to find down there? Or how badly Bull might be hurt, should the whole thing get out? Maybe Toby's uncomfortable partnership with Helmut Kohlwasser would prove useful after all.

As for the leather case . . . well, we'll have to see, won't we? Maybe he'd burn it up, along with its sensational contents. Or just toss it out of the plane. Or maybe he'd wrap it up and send it to Czechoslovakia, let those poor bastards know what was coming.

It only made sense, Oskar supposed, that after months of living under cover, then in hiding, then under a new cover, discarding names as facilely as changing suits, he should now have trouble letting go of old habits, abandoning caution and allowing himself to get caught.

Yet that was what he'd been ordered to do. He could hardly believe it, though the message was clear. The messengers were people he'd seen that first night, when he'd been recruited; he didn't know their names but assumed Jaap had counted on him to remember their faces, a double-safe measure, along with the tchaj, to confirm where the order was coming from.

Then there was the matter of the envelope.

He'd tried to open it furtively while the picture taking was in progress, though he'd been obliged to stand dumbly and to smile on command and to strike a series of cheerful poses until the Bugatti woman decided the little game had served its purpose. She and her partner went back to their table and resumed their vacuous nattering. The four companions sat down over the remains of a late breakfast with, it seemed to Oskar, a new tension between them. They'd had a distraction, which was over now, and nothing had changed. Should he tell them otherwise? First he'd see what was in that envelope.

"I don't like this place," said Lena. "I think we should get out of here."

His first impulse was to flinch—she was speaking too loudly, and in English—but then he remembered: *Draw attention to yourselves. Do it quickly.*

"And go where?" said Hagen, not unkindly, a real question. "We've just come from"—sweeping a hand—"out there." He lowered his voice. "Here at least we can sit for a while."

Oskar drew the envelope out of his pocket. It had been opened already, the flap torn in such a way that he could glimpse a wrinkled document inside, seemingly an ordinary letter. And something else, bulkier. He gave the envelope a little shake and a little booklet with a stiff paper cover came sliding into view. A passport. And not a German passport, as the cover was cherry red, faded from exposure. What am I now? he wondered. He forced the opening a little wider. He was Swiss.

"For how long, though?" said Clair. "All day? If we're going to be here that long, I'd want to be *doing* something. Not just sitting around."

Oskar began to feel hopeful. That things were slipping out of his hands came, to his surprise, as a relief. He settled back and tried to focus on Clair: *He needs to be recognized*, the young woman had said. Well, here you are, then: a long-haired teenager talking not just in

English but distinctly *American* English. That must be almost as bad as Russian. He glanced at the lady with her novel—but no joy there: she seemed engrossed in the predictable story line.

"What would you like to do?" Hagen asked.

"*I* don't know." The boy sounded bored and petulant. "Let's see, what are the choices? Get a room, call a taxi, jump off the cliff. It's a tough decision."

Lena smirked. "We can probably narrow it down. I guarantee there's no telephone in this place—so, no taxi for you."

Clair laughed, changing in an instant back to the innocent off on an adventure, impervious, carefree.

Oskar tugged at this thought like a string, *draw attention, to* him *especially,* and it led him back to the last time he'd felt anything like carefree himself, and Clair had been the center of attention then, too.

"It's a shame," said Oskar, hearing something strange in his own voice but pushing on with it, "you didn't bring your flute."

Clair scowled. "Yeah, well. We had to leave in kind of a hurry."

"Can you sing?"

The others looked at him oddly. Hagen seemed to be trying to read his thoughts, and for all Oskar could tell, he might have succeeded.

"Of course he can sing!" Hagen said. "Like an angel, I bet."

Clair blushed. But he was smiling.

"Angels don't sing, do they?" Lena asked. "I thought they just stood around with their harps."

"You know nothing about angels," said Hagen. "Didn't your parents . . . well, perhaps not."

"I'll have you know," said Clair, "I was the soloist for *three years running* at Easter Mass. They kept thinking my voice would *have* to change by the next year, but it kept on *not* changing. And I kept getting better, so they *had* to keep me as soloist. The third year, they made a recording. My father bought a million copies as Christmas presents. I don't believe he's actually *played* it, but he gave a copy to anyone he ever met."

Was there a wistful tone in his voice? Perhaps so, since Hagen laid a hand on his shoulder.

"What can you sing?" said Oskar.

"I can sing anything. What I *know* is the standard repertory for boys' choir. And a little Cole Porter, especially the racy parts. And 'Gloomy Sunday,' but I can't sing that. 'Gloomy Sunday' makes me cry."

He said this so simply that Oskar knew it was a glimpse of the boy's heart. Momentarily blinded by the pure flash of it, he felt amazed that Clair, at eighteen, could still say such a thing out loud. He couldn't recall having ever been quite so innocent or, at any rate, so unguarded—but in Germany you learned from an early age, mostly by observing those around you, that speech was like dancing, a studied act. You could do it gracefully and even take pleasure in it, but only after you'd mastered the rules, the careful footwork. Clair hadn't ever heard about that; he still believed it was all right to be who you were and say what you thought.

Keep believing, Oskar thought, at least a few minutes longer. "Sing something, then," he told him—trying to make it sound like a friendly challenge, not a desperate entreaty.

Clair looked back at him, poised on some inner threshold. What was going on here? Some joke he wasn't in on, something weird and German that he didn't understand?

"I'd like to hear you sing," said Hagen quietly.

That pushed him across. He rose to his feet, maybe from habit, and began to sing in a strong countertenor, clear as the May sky:

> *And did those feet in ancient time*
> *Walk upon England's mountains green?*
> *And was the holy Lamb of God,*
> *On England's pleasant pastures seen?*

Lena was clapping in delight, Hagen looking on with taut attentiveness. Oskar barely took notice; he was busy scanning the terrace, tracking the reactions of the bystanders, which so far looked gratifying. No one could possibly ignore a thing like this.

"More, more!" called little Herr Bugatti.

His partner overbid him: "On the chair! Stand on the chair!"

Clair was beaming, and as Hagen steadied the chair, he climbed up and delivered the next verse with greater conviction:

> *Bring me my Bow of burning gold;*
> *Bring me my Arrows of desire:*
> *Bring me my Spear: O clouds unfold!*
> *Bring me my Chariot of fire!*

It was a strange song anyway, but in the present context, it seemed to Oskar downright surreal. Was there more of it? The two men in lederhosen were conferring earnestly, glaring in disapproval. The elderly couple looked slightly confused. Herr Bugatti, a helpful sort, had laid his newspaper on the table, folded so as to display a photograph, blown up and grainy but still faithful enough to the young subject that you could pick out notable characteristics: the hair, the nose, a faintly insolent smile . . .

And yes, there was more:

> *I will not cease from Mental Fight,*
> *Nor shall my Sword sleep in my hand:*
> *Till we have built Jerusalem,*
> *In England's green & pleasant Land.*

And now he was finished. Oskar and Lena and Hagen rose to their feet, clapping loudly and laughing as Clair took a long stage bow and stepped down, beaming and perspiring, from the chair—which wobbled dangerously, causing him to yelp in alarm, until Hagen reached up and, with a strong hand under each armpit, lowered him easily to the ground. Clair looked back at him in such a way that Oskar finally understood what had been happening all along, right in plain sight; the two of them hadn't even bothered much to hide it. But that was the piece he'd been missing, and now everything made sense. Why Hagen had refused to leave them, starting back in Bremen and ever since. Why he'd shot a Gestapo man in the forehead. Why he'd allied himself with Socialists and outlaws. In the end, it was pretty simple—if anything could be simple at a time like this.

The two men in lederhosen were coming over. They'd struck Oskar before as slightly ridiculous: office workers, he'd guessed, gotten up in *völkisch* style for an outing to the countryside, the real Germany, away from the crowds and dirt and decadence of city life. Yet here, what do they find on this mountain where everything ought to be clean and decent and racially pure? They find "cosmopolitans" singing in English and speaking in Russian and behaving like degenerates. They didn't look ridiculous anymore. Red-faced, their fists clenched, they came down the terrace with a slow, angry swagger. They looked like proper Nazis now. One of them snatched the newspaper from Herr Bugatti and shook it open, waving it in front of himself like a battle flag.

They halted a stride away, within punching distance. They looked at the newspaper and then at Clair, at Clair's companions, then at the newspaper again. For a few seconds, Oskar wondered if they were so dumbfounded or so stupid that they were in fact unable to speak.

That was when the one holding the paper said, "What's this, then?"

And his companion, slightly taller and more sunburned, said, "Who are you people? What do you think you're doing?"

"*Nun lassen Sie mich denken,*" Clair said blithely, his forehead beaded with sweat. *Well, let me think.* His German was pretty good when he wanted it to be. "I seem to remember we were *singing.*"

The tall man tightened his mouth and drew a fist back like an archer slotting a fat arrow. Hagen made a very small movement—shifting his weight, loosening his arms—barely enough to notice, yet it caught Oskar's attention, and the other man must have seen it as well; he lowered his fist but looked even angrier than before.

"We know who you are," the first man said, brandishing the newspaper. "The game is up." He turned his head. "Landlord! Get out here! Bring your shotgun!"

Lena bent to pick up her hiking bag, which held the pistol she'd taken from Hagen, who'd taken it from a dead Gestapo agent. Oskar shook his head energetically, but she paid no attention.

"*The game is up,*" Clair repeated, shaking his head. "So people actually say that."

The matron with the war novel was on her feet now, keen to see what was in the paper. Then she looked up at Clair, biting her lip, her eyes excited and a little wild. The men in lederhosen closed ranks; they seemed to be sizing up von Ewigholz, calculating the odds. Behind them, the Bugattis were gathering their belongings, evidently preparing a timely exit.

There were too many things to follow but Oskar chose to concentrate on Lena, her hand now dipping into the bag, and he edged toward her. On the opposite side of the table, she glared at him— thinking what? That he wanted to grab the gun himself? The last thing she'd imagine was that he wanted them to surrender without a fight. There was no way to explain, no chance to even try.

Just Plain Müller emerged from the *Gasthaus*'s front door, which gave him an elevated vantage from which to consider the situation on the terrace. He paused there, leaning on the stock of a long, bolt-action hunting rifle.

Lena must have noticed him in that same moment. Oskar watched helplessly as a series of inevitable actions began to unfold. He'd felt it coming but had not guessed the correct sequence. He hadn't foreseen that in trying to extract the pistol from the bag, Lena would manage to entangle it with the discarded clothing, so that for several awkward seconds she was brandishing the entire bag as a weapon. Still, the outcome was more or less foreordained, the main question being who would get shot before old Müller took her down.

"No! Stop!" Oskar was shouting, and everyone but Lena turned to look at him. Hagen seemed to read the warning in his eyes and followed them to Lena and down her arm to the bag. And then for the longest time, nothing happened. It was one of those moments.

Oskar had experienced a moment like this on a bridge in Washington, another in a hallway in a haunted spa. Though the details were different, these moments had a common texture, a sort of viscosity through which events slid very slowly around you, and if you tried in just the right way, you could nudge them as they went by. The effort involved was so subtle it barely registered as an intention.

Oskar blinked and Hagen was turning away from him, launching himself toward Lena with gymnastic precision—no movement wasted, no gap into which she might have squeezed a reaction. His arm fell onto her wrist above the gun, forcing it downward against her body; he reached in with the opposite hand to grab the bag and in that instant of physical shock wrenched it cleanly away. His arm straightened and the bag went flying over the low stone wall, past the face of the cliff, then down and down, spinning like a slain bird.

"The evidence!" shouted the fiction lover. "They're getting rid of the evidence!"

The sunburned man went over to the cliff's edge and looked down gravely, then shrugged. What evidence, what does it matter, nothing we can do now—the bag had vanished. Old Müller hurried down from the stoop but couldn't seem to decide whom to point his rifle at. He arrived just in time to watch the Bugatti spin out of the courtyard and sputter off southward.

Now a fresh distraction arose: a steady percussive beat coming from down in the valley that Oskar in his excited state took for distant gunshots. But the sounds grew louder and more distinct, approaching from the roadway just past the nearest bend—hollow, rhythmic, unhurried. They were hoofbeats.

The two horses—Haflingers, long-maned and burly, bred for the mountains—sauntered over the rise looking unfazed by the rigors of the terrain. Not so their riders, a pair of weary policemen whose sage-green uniforms appeared to have been slept in. The nearest one, spotting the small crowd in front of the *Gasthaus*, raised a hand in greeting; they came on at a saunter, rifles still in their scabbards. Only when they reached the gatepost did certain aspects of the scene before them—old Müller standing with a gun in his hands, guests clustered near the cliff's edge as though they'd been interrupted in mid-brawl—rouse them to alertness. The lead policeman reached for his weapon, and that signaled an end to the stalemate on the terrace.

"Look!" shouted the sunburned man. "Look here, it's the outlaws, the ones in the newspapers!"

"That one there," said the novel reader, pointing at Clair, "that's the American boy who was kidnapped. *Allegedly* kidnapped. And those three are his so-called kidnappers. But look at them—they're all four as thick as thieves."

"*Ich war . . . ich wurde nie entführt,*" Clair protested, losing some indignation in his struggle with the verb.

"You've got to arrest them," said the shorter lederhosen man. "Don't worry—my friend and I will help you keep them in check until reinforcements arrive."

"Arrest us for what?" demanded Lena, stinging from the loss of the gun. "You heard him yourself: he was never kidnapped."

Hagen looked at Oskar as though seeking some wordless form of guidance. Oskar gave him a slight nod, unsure himself of what he was trying to convey: *Let it play out,* maybe something like that.

The nearest police officer—a loping man with a mournful demeanor and two stripes on his sleeve—approached with his rifle at the ready while his partner tethered the horses to the gatepost. He looked them over carefully, pausing at last before Clair, studying the boy's features one at a time, perhaps ticking them off against a list he'd committed to memory.

"You are the senator's son?" he asked in passable classroom English.

Clair nodded. "And these are my friends. They haven't done anything wrong. None of us has."

Give or take a couple Gestapo corpses, thought Oskar. And traveling under false identities. Lying to the authorities. Stealing a government motorcar. Enough to hang the lot of them—though Clair would probably be spared on public relations grounds. Or maybe not: the phrase *killed while trying to escape* had slipped into common parlance. It never rang true, and Oskar supposed it wasn't meant to; you were meant to understand that they could do what they liked with you.

Did this policeman know about all that, the string of crimes trailing behind them? If so, he wasn't letting on; his manner was correct and dispassionate, the soul of German civic order. He acknowledged Clair's statement with a nod, then addressed himself to everyone present, glancing at Müller over his shoulder in order to include him as well.

"It is required that you all remain here for the time being. You four are hereby taken into police custody, pursuant to an ongoing investigation. You are not under arrest, but it is a crime to attempt to flee. You others are needed as witnesses. I will be interviewing you shortly. In the meantime, my colleague will ride to the park headquarters to use the telephone there. Now, landlord—Herr . . ."

"Müller. Just plain Müller."

"Herr Müller, you will please provide a room where the detainees may be temporarily concentrated."

As he was being led away, into the *Gasthaus* and up the creaking stairway to a chamber on the top floor, Oskar wondered if this was really where the whole strange journey would end, on the slopes of the Höhe Meissner. It would be fitting, actually—so many journeys had ended here before.

But no: *You'll be leaving,* the woman had said. *There's a way out, but only one.*

It was hard to believe that this was what she had in mind.

The landing field in Kassel lay adjacent to a cow pasture, and Toby guessed it had been used for that purpose until a short while ago, as its grass was not much shorter and its surface not much smoother than some pastures Toby had seen. The little four-seater bumped along for a while with trees and cows and fenceposts scooting by, until the pilot executed a smart left turn and taxied over to a fanciful Hessian contribution to a new architectural genre: Municipal Airport. The terminal had been built with an eye toward the main local tourist draw, a scenic drive called the Märchenstrasse, or Fairy-Tale Road, linking various destinations made famous by the likes of the Brothers Grimm. Though tiny, it sported a wide pitched roof and mullioned windows, and Toby wouldn't have been surprised to find seven small baggage handlers ready to greet him. But then, not much about the New Germany would have surprised Toby at this point.

He was welcomed, in fact, by SS-Standartenführer Kohlwasser, waiting antsily beside a gray staff car with a tall chauffeur or adjutant or whatever the fuck, who appeared to have been washed in starch and then ironed in an industrial laundry press. Kohlwasser offered Toby a cheerless smile as he deplaned. The adjutant hastened to open a rear door.

"What's happening, Helmut?" Toby said, approaching warily. "Am I late? Is Clairborne, ah . . ." He'd intended to say *safe*. But he guessed he could speak a little more freely, now that he was truly off the reservation. "Have you caught him yet?"

The man just gave him a tight-lipped stare and motioned him into the car. So, thought Toby, we're not going to speak while the pesky dwarfs might be listening.

"I don't know what's happening," Kohlwasser said at last, as the adjutant put the car in gear and they jerked forward, wheels spinning in the dirt. "And I don't know where the boy is. I've spoken to the local police commander, but he seems to be having problems with his telephone. We're going there now. These country policemen are thick-headed brutes, but we'll have him thinking straight soon enough. Either that or we'll find someone more reliable. It's a pattern we've seen all too often, I'm afraid: the old guard clinging to their outmoded habits. What's that you have in your briefcase?"

Toby smiled. Though he couldn't bring himself to like Kohlwasser, he enjoyed his deviousness and agility, his little tricks for catching you wrong-footed. He might have done well in an American courtroom. The problem being, if the tricks don't work, you can wind up on the wrong foot yourself.

"Don't tell me you've lost him," Toby said. "Please don't tell me I've flown down here for nothing."

Kohlwasser held him in a chilly glare for a few seconds, then seemed to decide he was wasting his animosity. "We'll find him. We have a good idea where the criminals were headed. It's a wild area, with only a few places to go and limited trails to get there. We're setting up checkpoints, and soon enough they'll walk into one. *Unless* . . . it's possible they're trying to meet up with an underground cell in the mountains somewhere. But that's unlikely. You can't have an underground without local support, and this is a law-abiding region."

"The heartland," said Toby.

Kohlwasser gave him a thoughtful look, as though checking for signs of irony. Finding none, he said, "Just so. And the wellspring of our support. We won a majority here even in '32. So don't worry:

we'll have young Mr. Townsend in our hands before long. The question then becomes . . ." He paused, maybe to be sure he had Toby's full attention. "What shall we do with him?"

What indeed. Toby was glad he didn't have to think about that right now. He could stash it in a mental locker marked "When the Time Comes," along with the leather case, with "Erwin Kaspar," with a whole stack of private obsessions and unsettled scores, all of which he would get around to eventually, some later and others probably very soon.

Kohlwasser didn't press the point. He settled back in his seat and they rode in silence through woods and fields, along roads that wound and climbed and threatened to drop them into marshy swales. It was beautiful country—as beautiful and frightening as the old fairy tales. Toby wasn't frightened but felt an unusual sense of foreboding, and he was unreasonably glad when the staff car pulled into Kaufungen, a medium-sized burg upon which the present century had not made a deep impression.

The police station was easily located—near the *Rathaus*, across the street from a beer garden overhung with hop vines, their big drooping leaves a voluptuous contrast to the prevailing asceticism. The adjutant didn't bother to park, just brought the car to a halt smack in the main roadway, an impertinence that would have been more glaring had there been any traffic. Kohlwasser was out before the hand brake had been set. Toby followed in no particular hurry, the inside of a Nazi police station not ranking high on his list of sights to take in on this fact-finding tour. By the time he ambled through the door, Kohlwasser was already in a heated discussion with an older man whom Toby took to be the desk sergeant, and whom he judged to be getting the better of this contest, if only by virtue of his grave, phlegmatic calm in the face of the SS man's badgering.

Toby's command of *Deutsch* sufficed to let him skim a few points off the top: that the American boy had been located, that the chief had left the building, and that no, *Standartenführer*, we did not think it necessary to apprise you of these developments. There was a mention of standard police procedure and of disciplinary measures and of *Lager*, which might be a beer or a camp. The upshot was finally the unfolding of a map: Naturpark Meissner-Kaufunger Wald, rendered in the fine topographic detail required by artillery officers, probably also useful to mountaineers and search parties. The sergeant conjured a pencil from behind one ear to make a few careful marks: X for the destination, a little box to signify the police station, a bold meandering line for the suggested route between them.

"There must be a shorter way," said Kohlwasser, making it sound like a direct order, as though by force of will he could overcome mere geography.

Well, perhaps he could. The sergeant looked at him thoughtfully. "You can go straight up the mountain," he said, running the pencil lightly over the map, leaving a ghostly trail behind. "But that's meant for hikers. And for horses. Is this something you would like me to arrange?"

Toby couldn't tell if the old man was enjoying a private joke, the country bumpkin gulling the city slicker. If so, he was playing it damn close to his chest.

"I think we can manage well enough," said Kohlwasser, snatching the map and roughly folding it up.

They drove on with an altered seating arrangement: Kohlwasser up front with the driver, clutching the map and barking directions, Toby alone in the back seat hugging the leather case in his lap like a pet he'd grown grudgingly fond of. They left town at speed but were obliged before long to slow down as each turn took them onto roads that became—as any fool could have predicted—successively narrower, steeper and less fastidiously maintained. Kohlwasser pointed and cursed; the adjutant fought manfully with the wheel and the pedals and the gearbox. Toby felt a curious sort of intellectual detachment; he imagined a curve plotted on graph paper, asymptotically approaching the axis labeled I for *impassible*. He figured the old sergeant must be chuckling by now.

And yet they lurched onward against all odds, slowly gaining altitude and momentum. The staff car panted finally onto a sort of ridge where the road, if no better, was at least reasonably level and gave them a generous view of the countryside. So maybe there was something to this *Triumph des Willens* business after all.

"Schwalbenthal should be just ahead," Kohlwasser told the driver. "Around this next bend. Have your weapon ready."

"*Jawohl, Herr Standartenführer!*" He moved a hand from the shift lever to his sidearm, a large weapon that until now Toby hadn't paid much mind to; it had seemed just a piece of the overall package, a nifty accessory. Now the man did something to it that produced a sharp, well-lubricated click.

This was, Toby reflected, the first time he'd heard the adjutant actually speak—and what was it about that voice that gave him a little frisson? It might have been the note of happy excitement, as if he'd been waiting for years, since his first days in training and maybe before that, his boyhood in the Hitler Youth, for the moment when a man like Kohlwasser would give him an order like this. Kohlwasser, for his part, looked pretty eager too. Good-bye, intellectual detachment—Toby was beset by a stupid memory of a Laurel and Hardy flick, *Babes in Toyland*, where all appears lost until one of the hapless heroes gets the bright idea of activating an army of life-sized wooden soldiers. And these ludicrous festive storm troopers come marching out of the toy shop to stomp the furry stuffing out of the bogeymen. The point of connection being, he supposed, that this stiff-assed army had been waiting there, ready for someone to flip the switch, and believe it or not, folks, those toy weapons turned out to be pretty effective.

He shifted he leather case on his lap. It seemed to have gotten heavier.

And then something happened—he'd have to run it through again later to figure out exactly what; it seemed there was a popping noise and the staff car made a dangerous lurch toward the drop-off at the edge of the road. Then another pop and the whole front end seemed to slump. The adjutant stomped on the brake and the car skidded to a crooked halt, the engine revving down with a clatter of overworked pistons. Now Toby could hear a hissing sound, air escaping from somewhere—maybe they'd just had a blowout. But two blowouts, nearly at once?

"*Herr Standartenführer!*" The adjutant was breathing hard, his voice pitched high with excitement. "I thought for a moment . . . were we just receiving fire?"

Kohlwasser gave him an angry frown, opened the passenger door and stepped out onto the rocky shoulder, scanning for a full minute the high ground rising jaggedly on the north side of the road. The adjutant meanwhile made a circuit of the car—both tires on the driver's side were indeed flat, and the front one showed a clean hole through the sidewall. He reported these facts to the *Standartenführer*, who listened impassively.

"Got any spares?" said Toby, aiming for gung-ho but falling short, landing somewhere in what-the-hell territory.

"Only one," said the adjutant. "But we have a repair kit."

Kohlwasser continued to stare at the mountainside as though it were enemy territory. But if somebody *had* been up there shooting at them, and might be lurking still, keeping them in his sights, the notion didn't seem to bother him. In fact, he looked strangely unruffled, contemplative, almost serene. All right, an unseen opponent had just made a clever move. What should he do to counter it?

This would be the very man, considered Toby, to handle a sticky situation involving scandal at the higher levels of a neutral government, should that prove necessary or advisable. And if he required any sort of compensation, Toby was holding a pretty fungible currency right in his hands.

C hief Watchmaster Hans Diehl concluded his tour of the *Gasthaus* terrace and paused to reflect on what he had learned. Not as much as he would have liked. He was inclined to treat the place as a crime scene—seal it off, assign some men to search the mountainside below for a mysterious parcel that might contain notional "evidence"—only it was far from clear that a crime had actually been committed here. So cross that off. Move on.

"You've collected witness statements?" he asked the officer waiting nearby—one of his own, thank God; the fellows from Kassel had no concept of procedure. "They're all in good order?"

"They are, sir," the man said, then stepped closer to speak in confidence. He wore a mournful expression that Diehl recognized: the look of a man who'd seen many bad things but had not yet acquired the knack of detachment. "Old Müller, the landlord—he keeps wanting to amend his statement, to make additions. Now he says he was highly suspicious of the couple from Hamburg right from the start. The female especially. And he says their motorcar was *not* French. It was English."

"Better leave it there," Diehl told him, "before it becomes American. All right—you can let the witnesses go. Then we'll take a look at the documents. And then I'll go meet the . . ." He caught himself: not *prisoners*. "The detainees."

The next phase of the walk-through brought no greater satisfaction. The chief stood in the front hall by a table that made do for a reception desk, where the following items were laid out: One hotel guestbook, latest entry 2350 hours, 28 May. One U.S. passport issued to Mr. Clairborne Townsend. One SS identity card issued to Obersturmführer Hagen von Ewigholz. One Swiss passport issued to Herr Stian Fogel. One letter addressed to the same Herr Fogel, penned in a florid hand, postmarked Berlin and signed "Your old loving Auntie"—subject of letter: forthcoming visit to Germany, thoughts and advices thereon, greetings to "a certain Fräulein whom we cannot wait to meet!"

The chief took the letter carefully and held it before his nose. There was a faint smell of something . . . attar of rose, could it be? Who kept attar of rose anymore? "This Fräulein," he said, "do we think . . ."

"It may be the female in custody, the one without papers. But that's only a supposition. Her name is Gretel Bücher. So she says."

"And the missing papers?"

"Dropped inadvertently off the cliff, according to her statement. Thrown over deliberately, according to witnesses."

The chief nodded. He turned his attention to the guestbook. "Now these last names here . . . at 2307 we get the couple from Hamburg. But then at 2350, who's this? One Samiel Weber, boar hunter. Where's he?"

"Gone before daybreak, says the landlady. She left biscuits out for him, and they were gone when she came down. And so was the young man, who has not returned."

"Ah—so he's a *young* man, is he?"

"A boy, almost, says the landlady." The officer hesitated. "The name's unusual, sir, isn't it? Samiel?"

Diehl took a breath. Remain calm. "It's the name of a character in *Der Freischütz*. Samiel, the black hunter. And Weber's the name of the composer. What do they teach you in school nowadays?"

The officer looked startled and seemed to be trying to frame a reply. The chief raised a hand, forestalling it. Honestly, he'd prefer not to know.

Was there a clue here? Maybe so. Or maybe just a young man on holiday from the better sort of university, having a snooty laugh. File for later consideration. Move on.

"All right," he said. "Where are you keeping the, ah . . ."

"Detainees? This way, sir."

They ascended a stairway to the top floor, formerly an attic. The chief could remember how it had been and when it had changed, and now it seemed to be changing again, reverting. The air up here was pungent with must. The Müllers were getting old; they were letting things go. At the end of the hallway, the officer opened a small door; the chief stooped under the lintel and straightened again to find himself in a wide room tucked into the hipped roof. The ceiling slanted down on three sides; a row of windows ran along the far wall at about waist height. And here they were, in semi-silhouette: the four objects of a manhunt that had overexcited the press, strained police resources and drawn unwelcome attention from the Gestapo. Truth be told, they didn't look worth the candle.

The American boy was easy to pick out. He sat nervously at the edge of a hostel-style cot with his legs tightly crossed, toying with a scarf no sensible person would be wearing in this weather. The other three—his kidnappers or accomplices or innocent companions, believe what you will—were likewise distinct types. A tall athletic male, the very model of a modern *Obersturmführer*, stood near the center of the room, awkwardly posed, as though he'd been pacing. The lone female, with flashing eyes above Slavic cheekbones, sat on a different cot along with the third male—this would be the Swiss—of medium build and medium everything else. These last two were inches apart yet facing in quite different directions; the chief got the strong impression that as soon as he left the room, they'd pop up and move to opposite corners.

A feature of police work—sometimes a help but often a hazard—is that one tends to slot people rather quickly into familiar categories.

The chief caught himself doing it now: the SS man was a bully, the boy was annoying but meant no harm, the woman had a temper and bore watching, while the other man, the Swiss . . . well, here was the problem, if indeed a problem existed, for this one was simply blank, to a degree that made Diehl suspect that the man was making himself purposefully opaque. And there was a slot for that, too.

It had been his intention to sit down and interview these people together on an informal basis—just a friendly chat, with an officer in the background discreetly taking notes. Invite them to tell their story in their own way, decide whether or not it rang true and proceed accordingly. But now he was having second thoughts. Something here felt just a little off. The search had ended successfully, yet the chief wasn't sure what he had found. Four individuals who seemed to have nothing in common. What were they doing together? Why were they doing it here? He felt as though he'd stepped in on a stage play with plausible characters but no plot.

And then one of the characters—the Bully, stage center—stepped closer until he was staring at the chief eye to eye but from a slightly superior height. If there'd been any doubts about whether Diehl had slotted this one correctly, the *Obersturmführer* now dispelled them.

"I demand that you release us at once. This young man is an honored guest of the Reich. I am an officer duly assigned to protect him. These are our hiking companions. You have no authority to detain us."

Hans Diehl felt himself smiling, though he hadn't meant to. At last, here was some clarity. He hadn't enjoyed being bullied by a colonel on the telephone from Berlin. He cared even less for the same sort of treatment from a first lieutenant, right here on his own patch. He turned summarily and exited the room, then stood at the head of the staircase, waiting for the sad-looking fellow to catch up.

"We'll be taking them to the station," he said. "Round up a couple men to help bring them down. Put the big one in cuffs. Mind you go gently with the Yankee boy."

A minute later, having scooped up the documents from the reception desk, the chief watchmaster stepped out of the *Gasthaus* feeling pleasantly invigorated. One at a time, he thought. We'll have a go at them one at a time, and we'll save the Swiss for last. Let's see how long it takes for that mask to crack.

To his surprise, the terrace was fully occupied. None of the witnesses had departed, despite being given leave to, and a few newcomers had shown up in the meantime. Well, no surprise; it was perfect mountain weather. The Müllers were out there as well, chatting up the guests, pouring that awful red stuff for everyone. They were all waiting, he supposed, to see what would happen next. So let them watch. Give them a taste of proper police work.

He barely noticed when, a short while later, as the detainees were being led to the car, the dull clap of a rifle sounded from not far away, followed quickly by another.

"What was that?" said the woman clutching her war novel.

"No cause for alarm," Diehl assured her. "Just a hunter, I expect."

The White Russian princess could not keep still. She'd climbed out of the little car half an hour ago, complaining that her legs were cramped. She'd paced a bit, walking repeatedly to an old larch tree—one of several nearly identical specimens, but this one seemed to attract her—and then back to the car. She'd lit three cigarettes, taken a few puffs of each and discarded it, wrinkling her nose as if discovering anew that she couldn't abide tobacco. Now she was standing pensively by a traditional split-rail fence erected by park authorities to mark the limit of automobile access to Frau-Holle-Teich. There was a gate nearby, but she seemed disinclined either to walk through it or to step away and stop looking so damn conspicuous. A group of hikers had passed by a little while ago, greeting her cheerfully, and she'd just stared back at them, as though this time she truly *was* having trouble with the language. But Cissy had been chirping *auf Deutsch* from her cradle in Minsk, Guido was fairly certain. Was there a name for stage fright that came on after the show was over? He thought not. But this show wasn't over, was it? They were in a pause between scenes.

"Come back here, please," he called to her. "Look, it's a beautiful spot, why don't you take some pictures? I'll put a new roll in."

"Oh, pictures!" She threw her arms up. "What a stupid idea that was! How does Jaapi expect . . . and where's our friend? He should've been here ages ago."

But she was walking back to the car, so that was good.

"You're doing wonderfully," he told her. "Everything will be fine."

"*Fine?* This is what men say when they mean 'Well, it could be worse. I'm sorry, old chap, both your legs have been blown off, but cheer up, you'll be fine.'"

Guido laughed. Cissy slipped out of character just for an instant, long enough to let a smile escape.

He glanced at his pocket watch. "It's still early. We'll give it a while longer. I'm sure he's all right."

"*All right?* My God, that's much worse than *fine*. That means nearly hopeless."

But it was all right, after all. The young ensign appeared twenty minutes later at the head of the trail with his rifle bag strung tightly at his shoulder, red-faced and running with sweat from the hasty descent. His clothing was torn, and his whole left side showed minor abrasions—he must have stumbled and fallen—but he was otherwise intact and beaming, exhilarated.

"There were three of them," he said between rapid breaths. "An officer. A driver. And a civilian."

A civilian . . . was that something to worry about? No time, Guido decided. "You'd better change your clothes. Then we need to get going. Places to be. Roadblocks to avoid."

"People to shoot?" said Cissy. "Because if not, perhaps we should get rid of . . ." She was pointing at the rifle bag, propped now against a fender of the Bugatti.

The two men traded looks. She had a point; and yet . . .

"Better hang on to it," Guido said.

Months ago in Washington, Oskar had seen a travel poster captioned, "Motoring in the New Germany." And here he was, enjoying that experience in its most quintessential form, in the back seat of a police car.

He sat jammed between Lena and Hagen, the latter in hand-cuffs. The mournful policeman was at the wheel with a colleague half-turned in the passenger seat, keeping an eye on them. Clair rode in another car, just ahead, with the officer in charge, the district *Hauptwachtmeister.* The little motorcade was taking its time on the mountain roads, pausing at forks, riding the brakes down the inclines, easing over the ridges as though allowing the prisoners a last good look at the Fatherland, in what might prove to be its last peaceful summer.

Just past the turnoff for Frau Holle's Well, at a spot where the road narrowed to bridge a stream, they encountered a roadblock. Even from his disadvantaged viewpoint, Oskar could see that this was no ordinary police setup. A black Opel sat parked by the bridge at such an angle as to impede traffic. Two men in leather coats stood beside it, one of them cradling an MP-38, a new and remark-ably ugly weapon that had not existed when Oskar was training at Lichterfelde. He'd fired one at the Abwehr school in Bremen and remembered two things about it: the touchy trigger and the mess it made of the target. The army was said to be buying them as fast as they could be stamped out, but as usual, the SS had gotten there first and begun issuing them on a priority basis to the Gestapo. And now one of them was pointed in the general direction of Clair in the car ahead as it rolled to a halt. The Gestapo men came up along both sides of it, peering through the windows. The fact that it was a police vehicle, clearly marked, seemed not to concern them.

The mournful officer had his window down—it was summer, the car was hot—and now he stuck his head out, trying to hear what was going on. Lena rolled hers down as well; no one stopped her, since the policemen now had other things to worry about. Oskar could make out two voices that sounded confrontational. But no shouting, not yet. And the Gestapo men looked calm enough, their bearing a sort of arrogant nonchalance. Still, they were blocking the road, the only way out.

"Do something, damn it," muttered Hagen.

Who was he talking to? What could he possibly have in mind?

A door of the car ahead opened slowly, and for a few long moments that was all; no one stepped out, and the nearest Gestapo man came around to peer in quizzically. When a hand emerged, apparently seeking assistance, he hesitated but finally gave it a helpful pull. Out behind it came the chief watchmaster, holding an assortment of papers, a few of which fluttered loose and blew across the roadway. The Gestapo man chased them down while his partner stepped around the car and exchanged a few words with the chief, seemingly humorous. The two of them shook hands. The first man returned with the errant papers and acknowledged the chief's thank-you with a shrug. Somehow, the standoff had become a collegial roadside conference. This *Hauptwachtmeister*, Oskar decided, was a genius.

Now the chief began a long-winded disquisition with frequent reference to the papers in his hand. He presented these one at a time—Oskar recognized the red Swiss passport when its turn came—and turned at certain moments to point at one of the cars and once to gesture more generally toward the Höhe Meissner, as though drawing that into his story line. The Gestapo men nodded and dutifully tried to follow, but after a while it seemed they'd heard enough, the complications of high-level police work wearing them down. Things were simpler in the Gestapo, and you could thank the Führer for that. One of them fetched an official-looking document from the Opel and handed this to the chief. Oskar guessed it was a *Passierschein*, a magical piece of paper conferring freedom of travel. Since there might be other checkpoints ahead, this would save everyone a lot of bother.

Alles in Ordnung, then. The meeting ended, and the police convoy crossed the stream. Now onward to the town of Kaufungen. Where, in a tidy building across the street from a *Biergarten*, by order of the *Hauptwachtmeister*, the four companions—minus Clair, who was ushered into an interview room—were separated, led to small holding cells and locked away.

Standartenführer Kohlwasser was of two minds. Three, possibly. The tire repair was taking too long—the fool of an adjutant proving unequal to a simple bullet hole—so he strolled ahead with Mr. Toby Lugan to the Gasthaus Schwalbenthal, which, as he'd rightly estimated, lay only a few hundred meters up the road.

Someone—and he had an idea who—had gone to considerable lengths to prevent him from getting here. Yet here he was, and he wasted no time apprising himself as to how things stood.

The senator's boy had come and gone before him. So had his confederates, three in number, their descriptions tallying to an acceptable degree with previous sighting reports going right back to Bremerhaven. The little gang had been apprehended by the Ordnungspolizei, detained for a short time and then transported from the scene, leaving scarcely a quarter hour ago. So much the *Standartenführer* gleaned from various bystanders, including the landlord, who struck him as a shifty type; it might be well to pull him in on suspicion of collusion, but that could wait. For the present, he felt it safe to infer that the prisoners were en route to the local Gendarmerie, where their disposition would fall to the pigheaded local cop who'd been so unhelpful on the telephone. He doubted they'd make it that far—the Gestapo should have roadblocks up by now—but in any case, they were temporarily out of his grasp. Although that might be to the good—and here was where his two- or three-mindedness came in.

It shouldn't take long, the state of his staff car notwithstanding, to locate the criminals and arrest them on his own authority. Whisk them away, charge them with murder and drop them in a hole somewhere. The problem there was the American boy, over whom a political storm would surely arise, and whom the SS would be obliged at some point to release. Which would not quell the storm and might even intensify it, as God knew what sort of lies the boy would spout. And so a different course recommended itself.

As long as the criminals were in the custody of the Ordnungspolizei, responsibility for their safety and well-being resided there as well. Should anything unfortunate happen—say, a party of aggrieved citizens, driven to violence, storming the station house and taking justice into their own hands—the SS would be blameless. Such an event could be arranged.

But there was a third possibility—or, really, a refinement of the second. It depended on Toby Lugan, who had indicated a certain ambivalence about the prospect of returning young Clairborne Townsend to his father. Could he be pressed to make his misgivings a little more explicit? Because if so, and if Kohlwasser could resolve the problem in a satisfactory manner . . . well, the minority counsel would be in his debt, would he not? And the debt would be enforceable under pain of blackmail, should it come to that.

This was almost too good to dwell on right now. And it came on top of another imminent triumph, the exposure of a conspiracy that began with the so-called Erwin Kaspar but extended, if his suspicions were correct, to the senior ranks of the rival service and might even reach Canaris himself.

But first things first. Kohlwasser was stuck on this accursed mountain. He looked around for Toby—and there he was, standing with one leg hitched up on a chair and a glass of red beverage in his hand, holding forth to an elderly couple who appeared to find him entertaining, though it was doubtful they understood what he was going on about.

Toby saw Kohlwasser and saluted him by hoisting his glass. "For want of a tire, eh, Helmut? Come try some of this. I can feel my hair growing back."

The admiral's giant Mercedes seemed to fill the main street of Kaufungen from curb to curb. The beefy chauffeur had gotten the feel of the motorcar by now, after a long morning on the road. He piloted smoothly around such obstructions as presented themselves—farm wagons, dogs, a flower vendor whose wares posed a colorful menace, a small pack of pedestrians committing the un-German crime of jaywalking (on which grounds he judged them to be tourists).

It would have been nice, he thought, to have some processional music to accompany their stately passage through town. Your first thought naturally would be Elgar—but that might strike some listeners as unpatriotic. Handel would get you halfway there, something from the *Royal Fireworks*. But to be really safe you couldn't do better than Beethoven: Symphony 7, Movement II, the Allegretto. He'd have to downshift for that and purr through Kaufungen at a walker's pace, timing their arrival to coincide with the big dynamic surge around 6:50—the strings build to *forte*, the Mercedes rolls to a halt, the percussion kicks in, the passenger door opens, the winds restate the main theme in a triumphal timbre and out steps the Baroness. *Bravissima!*

Well, he would do the best he could.

Oskar tried pacing in his cell, but there was no room for it. He'd expected bars; in the movies there were always bars, which you could clutch in despair or stare through with forlorn yet heroic resolve: you would get out of here somehow, no jail could hold you for long. This cell, however, had only a door, like other doors except for the small viewing hatch. He didn't see much point in staring out of that. He scoured what remained of his inner strength, hoping to scrape up a spoonful of heroic resolve, but what he got instead was an absurd and tragic recollection: Leo Gandelmann trying to pace in his tiny apartment, flapping his scarecrow arms, a clatter of cheap cookware, a ridiculous foil box. Zoo animals bellowing faintly in the background. Oskar professing his love for Germany. Leo's condescending smile. *Let's have dinner after the war.*

The loud voices coming from somewhere down the hall seemed at first to be connected to that memory; he imagined an impressive primate grunting in dissatisfaction, Leo the stoic zookeeper responding with a patient lecture about regulations. It took a few moments for that cheerful delusion to fade and something more dire, therefore more believable, to replace it.

So far, it had been possible to expect that however bad things looked, they were proceeding according to some kind of plan. Which plan had required that Oskar and his companions be taken in by the police—a seemingly fatal development that turned out to be lifesaving, for how else could they have slipped through the Gestapo cordon around the Höhe Meissner? And this, by extension, had given Oskar hope, even a fragile confidence. Jaap Saxo, he imagined, was busy in the wings, masterfully stage-managing events as they unfolded. He'd foreseen every eventuality, placed operatives at critical locations, hacked a path through the deadly thorn roses, and now Oskar needed only to follow it.

But how long, really, could you sustain that sort of wishful thinking? There had been one way out, and this is where it had led them: a police station at the heart of a police state. Where they were locked in separate rooms, unable to communicate or carry on with their foolish conspiracy. And what hit Oskar hardest now was that Jaap had laid it out so plainly, right from the start. That very first night in the Baron's library, he'd told Oskar exactly how it would go. *You'll have absolutely no one to back you up if things turn out badly.* And look: the man was as good as his word. There was nothing left but waiting, and that might soon be over too.

The voices down the hall were getting louder. Who would it be, he wondered—the *Hauptwachtmeister* again? Or was it time for the SS to take over? How long would a hastily fabricated Swiss passport protect him? Would he be tortured? Would he break down, betray his allies? How far would it go, how many names would he give up? (Even Leo's? No, please, not that.) And what about his friends? What awful things would they do to Lena? And Hagen . . . well, at least he was a soldier. One of their own. They might show him the kindness of a quick bullet.

The footsteps, when they came at last, fell with the weight of inevitability. A key clanked in the lock of Oskar's door. It opened just a few inches and the footsteps moved onward; he could hear other doors being opened in turn. Well, why drag it out? Oskar stepped into the hall. Hagen and Lena came out after him. They stood there looking at once fatalistic, puzzled and expectant, but what could they be expecting at this point? The old desk sergeant gestured to the three of them—*Come on, get moving*—and there was nothing to do but trudge after him, past the booking desk, on to the anteroom.

But the scene out there was not what Oskar expected.

C hief Watchmaster Hans Diehl had seen a bit of everything over the course of thirty-two years as a policeman. He'd seen his fellow human beings at their worst and at their most exalted. He'd witnessed acts of breathtaking heroism and of unspeakable depravity. He'd parlayed with thieves and rubbed shoulders with the high and mighty and consoled grieving parents and endured the smirks of criminals his evidence had failed to convict.

Yet here was something new: a specimen of humanity he'd never encountered before, a rare sort of creature that, had it ever existed, must be long extinct by now—or so Hans Diehl had thought.

Here was the Baroness von F——.

Though not large in stature, she seemed to occupy the entire anteroom, leaving just enough space for her male companion, an elderly general who, from the decorations on his chest, must have participated in every action from the Battle of Sedan to the spring '18 offensive. The lady herself looked as though she might have been a pioneering aviatrix, then gone on to become a silent film star, then gone on to marry the wealthiest man in the movie business, then poisoned him. Her gaze was intent, conveying a fervent and heartfelt interest, as if the chief were among the most fascinating people she'd ever met. He felt a powerful need to do something for her—open a door, light a cigarette, lay his coat down over a puddle. It was sorcery. There was danger here. The lady was an aged enchantress, a figure out of Gothic myth.

"Est là quelque part," she said, which he took to be the start of a fatal incantation. *"Nous pouvons parler?"*

The old general cleared his throat, like a rumble of distant artillery. "She wants to know if there's someplace we can talk."

Accede to this at your peril, an inner voice warned. And yet in the next moment the chief watched himself spring forward to release the latch securing the half door that led beyond the sergeant's desk. He stepped aside, motioning toward his private office. At least he didn't bow, thank God, as the Baroness swept past him. He caught the gaze of his sergeant, who was giving him a look he didn't care to interpret, it was so impertinent. Well, damn him. Hans Diehl would handle this. Whatever it was.

They'd barely gotten seated and he was still composing his first question—would "How may I help you?" sound too eager, too subservient?—when the Baroness surprised him by drawing a handkerchief and dabbing her eyes.

"Pardonnez-moi, monsieur," she said, regaining her composure only, it appeared, by an act of considerable will. "You must forgive an old woman. The truth is, I've become so worried about my nephew. If you might be able to help me, I should be grateful beyond words."

Her German was almost as thorny as her French, tangled up in subjunctives and conditionals, a living answer to why the chief had never gotten far with Goethe. He thought it remarkable that someone still talked like this.

"Tell me about this nephew, then."

"He's my great-nephew, actually. Or is it my great-great? These relationships can be so confusing. His mother, you see . . ."

The chief didn't try to follow it. He'd always pictured aristocratic families as being like fancy spiders, stringing their spangled webs all over Europe, crossing back and forth to mate and spawn and devour one another's young. The lady's drawn-out explanation comported pretty well with that. The only part that concerned him was the final bit: this great-great thrice-removed relative having come to Germany a couple of weeks ago and then fallen out of contact. Last known destination, the Naturpark Meissner-Kaufunger Wald.

All right, then—here were a couple of points the chief could latch onto. "You say he came to Germany. Came from where? And what's his name, this nephew of yours?"

"Stian. His name is Stian Fogel. He has come from Switzerland."

The chief sat back in his chair. He hadn't consciously been leaning forward, but there you are: the spell of the enchantress had rendered him uncharacteristically solicitous. That spell lifted now, and in its place was incredulity. Was he to believe that the young detainee just down the hall—the one notable for his extraordinary blankness—was a blood relative of the Baroness's? And that, by some happenstance yet to be explained, he'd fallen in with the missing son of a U.S. senator, target of a nationwide manhunt? The chief hadn't gotten far with mathematics, either, but he reckoned the probability of this must be on a par with stepping into the street only to be trampled by a runaway rhinoceros.

And yet . . . there *was* evidence in support of it. There was the letter, smelling faintly of attar of rose. That florid handwriting. *Your old loving Auntie.*

"Could you tell me," he asked the Baroness—and, damn it, he was leaning forward again—"was your nephew traveling alone?"

The grande dame gave him a sly, rather coquettish smile. "Oh no, *mein Herr,* I should say he was *not*. There is a lady friend. We have not met her. We have not yet even been allowed to know her name. *Il est tout un grand secret!*"

The chief sighed. Of course, he thought, all the pieces *would* fit. If you were going to make up a story as outlandish as this one, you wouldn't skimp on the details. But who in God's name would attempt such a thing, and why would someone like the Baroness—not to mention this *Brigadegeneral*, holder of the Iron Cross—go along with it? Each theory was as implausible as the other.

The obvious course was to draw no premature conclusion, take a formal statement from the Baroness, roll it in with the others, keep his nose to the ground and go on with his investigation.

A knock came at the door. He could tell it was his sergeant and that it was urgent by the pattern of raps, a code they'd been using for years. The door opened just enough for the old fellow to stick his head in.

"There's a call on the radio," he said. "It's that SS officer, the one from Berlin. He's driving here now. Something to do with the, ah, guests down the hall."

And now *this*, thought the chief, on top of everything else. "How did he sound?" he asked, ignoring the rather blatant curiosity being shown by the Brigadier. "Did he sound angry?"

The sergeant's head extended a little farther into the room. "He sounded . . . actually he sounded pretty excited."

Excited. Well, why not? There was a prize to be had. Honor and glory for the desk warrior from Berlin. The missing Yankee boy had been run to ground by good old-fashioned police work—no thanks to any goons in leather jackets blocking the roads and waving their guns around. But try telling that to anyone. Everything belonged to the SS now—including the credit that rightfully should go to someone else. Thirty-two years of hard plodding, and Hans Diehl had no say over who went and who stayed in his own damn lockup. Well, we'll just see about that.

"My lady," he said, rising from his chair, "I have the pleasure to inform you that I believe we have your nephew here, just up the hall. My sergeant will go fetch him for you. *And* his lady friend."

The sergeant raised an eyebrow; he was asking something, the chief couldn't tell what. Ah.

"Yes," he said, "bring all of them. And their belongings. Don't leave a thing. We'll show our friend from Prinz-Albrecht-Strasse a clean house."

"*Vous faites la bonne décision,*" the Baroness said with conviction.

It didn't sound like a profession of thanks. The chief wasn't sure what it was.

The old general stood and clapped a firm hand on his shoulder. "Good call," he said quietly. "We'll take it from here."

Toby Lugan found the *Standartenführer* an interesting character to observe, a case study in some psychological condition he didn't have a name for—call it reflective malevolence. Reflective in the sense of having been considered, weighed against other options, settled upon rationally. For example: he could be chatting away quite amiably, as he'd been doing with Toby on the drive down from the mountain (a cautious drive, the adjutant mistrusting his own repair work), then cheerfully and with no change in demeanor move on to the topic of torturing a confession out of someone. Should it be done secretly or in front of witnesses, so as to make a more telling impression? Should the guilty parties be executed on the spot or consigned to a camp to die more gradually? And how should one deal with the press? Issue a general statement or leak the story to a tame reporter and reward the fellow with a scoop?

"I have a man," he confided, "at the *Morgenpost.* He's been helpful recently. The only worry is, will he be sober enough to get the tone right? The . . . the *regret,* you know. That these souls were so misguided as to bring this fate on themselves. And the *hope* that others may learn from their example."

There was nothing personal about it, nothing emotional—that was the point. He reminded Toby in a roundabout fashion of the Honorable Theodore Bilbo of Mississippi, an entertaining fellow who'd recently taken to the Senate floor to oppose an anti-lynching bill, *for the Negroes' own good.* He'd given the matter a lot of thought. There was not a hateful bone in his body; he personally bore no ill will toward anyone. He'd just come to the reasoned conclusion that it was best for the Negroes, all things considered, if now and then a few of them got lynched.

These thoughts were rolling around in Toby's head as the staff car pulled at last into Kaufungen, retracing the hectic journey they'd made earlier in the day. As before, the adjutant pulled up in front of the police station and stopped the car in the middle of the road. As before, Kohlwasser jumped out straightaway—maybe a tad more zestfully this time around—while Toby took his own sweet time about it, pausing on the sidewalk to stare wistfully at the little crowd enjoying lunch in the *Biergarten* across the street. There was a fine-looking woman at a table there, thin as a chopstick and so pale that if you stripped off her clothes she'd probably glow in the dark. She was laughing with two fellows who didn't deserve her—one short and dark like a dago, the other resembling a baboon stuffed into an evening suit. Master race, my bonny Irish ass.

Toby might have strolled over—here was a case for American intervention if ever he'd seen one—but some kind of ruckus had erupted inside the station. It didn't seem unreasonable to theorize that Kohlwasser was murdering someone. Toby exchanged glances with the adjutant and got the impression that he was thinking along similar lines. They'd better go have a look.

Inside, things were better and worse than Toby had imagined. Better in that no one was lying dead on the floor. Worse in that Kohlwasser was so hopping mad his face had turned a color unknown to modern cosmetology, a bruise purple with crimson highlights and black webbing that might have been exploded veins. He was shouting, and Toby thought himself lucky that his *Deutsch* derived from a Catholic education and he understood almost none of it. The *Standartenführer*'s wrath was directed mainly at a senior police officer, whose career, Toby thought he heard, was *vernichtet*. Or possibly everyone present was *vernichtet*. The whole town of Kaufungen, *vernichtet*. Whatever had happened here was so awful that no one could live to speak of it. Toby had an idea what that might have been.

He caught the eye of the desk sergeant, the phlegmatic chap he recalled from his previous visit. "The American boy," he said, just loud enough to make himself heard. "He's gone, is he?"

"Left ten minutes ago," the man said, his tone studiously bland.

"Just . . . set loose? Free as a bird?"

"Along with his companions. Four of them altogether."

"On their own?"

"A great lady took them in her automobile. A Baroness."

Toby chewed this over. He couldn't tell if it was good news or bad. "Listen, was there a big German fellow, a military type—blond and blue-eyed, that sort?"

"Obersturmführer von Ewigholz."

"Right. And would you say . . . did he and the American boy strike you as . . ."

The sergeant raised his chin a notch. Toby divined that the man understood what he was asking but it was something a German policeman was not going to talk about.

"Well, thanks," said Toby.

He turned to see that Kohlwasser had apparently run through his list of threats and calumnies and dire guarantees as to the fate of everyone involved. Now he was turning to leave.

"Come!" he ordered the adjutant. "It's not too late, we can overtake them."

Back in the staff car, they made an unusual discovery: on the back seat lay a box about the size of, say, a cookbook, wrapped in gold foil and tied with a bright red bow.

"What the hell is this?" said Toby. "Chocolates? Is this a joke? Look, it's got your name here on the tag."

Kohlwasser's reaction was as peculiar as the box itself. He stared at it with an expression that seemed partly disbelieving and partly delighted, like a kid who'd found a present under the Christmas tree and was afraid to believe it was what he thought it was, the thing he'd been dreaming about, that he wanted more than anything else. He reached out gingerly, inch by inch—then he hesitated, drew his hand back.

"Later," he said. "We'll open it later. This kind of thing needs to be done very carefully. There's evidence here, and we must be careful to preserve it."

The change in him was remarkable. Toby tried to think of something to say but couldn't tell what was appropriate under the circumstances. Nor did he understand what the circumstances were, exactly.

Kohlwasser sensed his confusion. "He's gone too far now," he said, as if this was any sort of explanation. "He thinks I can't touch him. Now he even dares to taunt me! Well, I knew this would happen. He can't stop himself—he's so arrogant, he insists on leaving a signature. *This*"—passing his hand over the box, a hierophantic blessing—"is as good as a . . . what do you say, *Fingerabdruck.*"

"Fingerprint."

"Yes! But better, really. He reveals his thinking here. This is a mind-print."

Toby might have asked whose mind-print this was, but he didn't care. His own mind was on Clairborne, that smart-ass simperer, and his special Aryan friend. Wreaking holy havoc everywhere he went. Causing Bull no end of anguish, with untold anguish still to come. And even worse: scandal, public embarrassment, political ground-shifting. A contagion that would spread to Toby—that would seek him out like a radio homing device—and fuck him over royally as well. Odious little Clairborne, doing all this and getting away with it. Sashaying along on his merry way. And why? Just because. No reason. No justification. No right or wrong.

Maybe these Nazi fellows had the right idea. Cleanse the world with fire and steel. Crush the feeble, the sick, the corrupt, the degenerate. *Rette sich wer kann.*

Toby became aware again—funny how you could forget a thing like this—of the leather case he'd been carrying since yesterday. That was a sort of mind-print too; it had to be. If you knew how to read it, you could deduce who had stolen these war plans and why they'd been dropped in a United States senator's tennis bag. It was out of Toby's league—and for that he was thankful. From where he stood now, the matter of the leather case seemed curiously of a piece with that of Clairborne: another despicable betrayal, another symptom of some grave national malignancy, a tumor in the body politic. He was sick of carrying the thing around.

"Here, Helmut," he said, speaking hurriedly, not giving himself a chance for second thoughts, "here's another little gift for you. Sorry I didn't get around to wrapping it. But I think you'll—"

Step back now. The Baroness is just entering the police station, the beefy gentleman holding the door for her. The job is almost done, and she will either succeed or fail. Meanwhile, these last few steps require an exquisite sense of timing, and who has better timing than a percussionist?

Instead of returning to the Mercedes, the beefy gentleman remained on the sidewalk for more than a minute, enjoying the sunshine, scanning the block for any sign of the opposition. He saw nothing out of order. Shouldering his travel bag, he crossed the road at a leisured pace, making for the *Biergarten* and ignoring the stares of a couple of upright and unimaginative pedestrians. He didn't mind, knowing full well what sort of impression he made; he'd come to regard it as a positive attribute. People glance at you and see one thing, and it satisfies them; they don't go looking for anything deeper.

His contacts had chosen a table near the road. There were three of them: a happy sign. Everyone had made it. As he approached, the ensign-cum-sharpshooter stood up to trade places.

The beefy man removed his cap and held it out ceremonially. "You'll need petrol. There's a place near Kassel, just before the autobahn."

The ensign nodded, donned the cap and hurried across the street, taking his position by the huge Mercedes. And now we wait.

"Relax," said Guido. "Order something. Just three friends enjoying the weather, eating and drinking. Everything normal."

The beefy gentleman scowled—he knew how it was done. He eased the travel bag off his shoulder and set it down by his feet.

"What do you think?" said Cissy. "Shall we have champagne?" She waved for a waiter.

"It's a bit early," said Guido, consulting his watch. "But yes, why not?"

Only there was no champagne on offer. This was a *Biergarten* in a small town in Hesse. The waiter gave them a look that made his feelings about city folk stridently clear.

Just as well: things began to happen rather quickly. The door of the police station flew open and out breezed the Baroness with the chief watchmaster close behind, eyeing her with almost canine attentiveness. The grande dame wore a beneficent smile but her manner was brisk, her stride rapid and purposeful. Disregarding the ensign waiting to help her into the car, she stood there anxiously while the others emerged from the station, one by one. First the Yankee boy with a tall blond friend. Then a woman, fair-skinned, mid-twenties. Then the young Abwehr officer, called Fogel now. Lastly the Brigadier. There was confusion about who should sit where, but the old general barked at them and they got settled. The ensign pushed the Mercedes into gear and they were safely off, *danken Sie Gott*.

And with little time to spare. A second car, long and gray and menacing, drew up a few minutes later.

"There's three of them," said the beefy man. It was a question, basically.

Guido fielded it. "Yes, we know. It's all right—no change of plan."

They watched the *Standartenführer* exit the car and storm into the building. The other two—the driver and the third man, a civilian—lingered outside for a while. This wasn't good, it was a deviation from the script, and soon it got worse: the civilian was staring over *precisely*, not at just the *Biergarten* but at this table in particular. Had he recognized one of them? Did he sense something? The beefy gentleman began considering the available recourses—none of them attractive—but then things got noisy at the police station and the man turned away from them, he and the driver disappearing inside.

"I know who that was!" said Cissy. "I just got it. Remember yesterday, at the tennis—"

"Not now," Guido said.

The beefy gentleman grabbed his travel bag from under the table and hustled across the road with it. He opened the back door of the staff car, removed a brightly colored item from the bag and laid it gently on the rear seat. He was back at the table a few seconds later.

"*That* was the one," said Cissy, resuming exactly where she'd left off, "who picked up the tennis bag. With the other thing in it."

The beefy man had no idea what she was talking about. Guido's expression changed by degrees from doubtful to alarmed.

"And *now*," said Cissy, "he's with that horrible SS man. What does it mean?"

They might have gone on fretting about that, but time was pressing and too many pieces were in play. The *Standartenführer* appeared at the door of the station in an agitated state, the other two soon afterward. They climbed into the staff car and sped off in pursuit of the big, lumbering Mercedes.

"It doesn't matter now," said Guido.

"No," said Cissy, "but we should still tell Jaapi. When we get home."

The beefy gentleman said nothing. He looked up at the sky and began to hum.

The others didn't notice at first. Cissy was fidgeting, toying with her necklace, one of the few possessions she hadn't sold off; Guido was making a painful effort not to pull out his pocket watch. But the humming grew louder and, even worse, the man accompanied himself by thumping periodically on the table.

"Would you stop that?" Guido finally said.

The beefy gentleman ignored him. The humming was a technique of his own invention, a means of keeping track of the time. He'd played with many orchestras under many conductors, and so, being a percussionist, he'd counted off hundreds of thousands of rests. After a while he'd realized that with certain conductors, every performance was the same; you didn't need to count rests, since you could do as well setting a stopwatch. So the reverse must also be true: counting off certain performances from memory was as accurate as any timepiece. Which came in handy if, say, you moonlighted as a cabaret bouncer, working in places where the light was too poor to read a watch. When the owner told you to get him at such-and-such a time, you just chose a piece of the proper duration and played it in your head.

Last night with Herr Saxo it had been "Give them five minutes. Long enough to get clear of the town—assuming he can restrain himself that long. If not, well . . ."

Five minutes. That was easy. Any number of pieces would have fit, but for this occasion he'd chosen a personal favorite: *Turandot*, Act I, "Ah! per l'ultima volta!"

Oh, for the last time! Though the beefy gentleman hoped it wasn't the last; he rather enjoyed this kind of work. At the start of the climactic quatrain, he reached for his travel bag and pulled out an odd sort of instrument, a tin box with a handle on top and a wire serving as an antenna. Gamely he raced through the frenetic tenor line, recalling the last performance he'd played in, at the Staatsoper: a rainy autumn night, the week's pay barely covering his gambling debts. As the imaginary trumpets faded, he eased the plunger down.

On the road north of Kaufungen, the *Standartenführer*'s staff car expanded to cover an egg-shaped area with chunks of gray shell surrounding a charred, bloody yolk. The contents of the leather case were consumed by the fireball, except for a few half-legible tatters that would puzzle the chief watchmaster for days to come. He would make no sense of them.

But what sense could you make of anything, nowadays? This was Germany in the sixth year of the Millennial Reich. Unbelievable things were happening everywhere. Soon the story of the senator's missing son, rescued by hikers after some vague calamity in a *Naturpark*, faded from the newspapers. Now Czechoslovakia was back again: atrocities suffered by ethnic Germans in the Sudetenland, vows to restore national honor, a conference to be held in Munich, the last chance for peace. You shuddered to think of it; you couldn't keep your mind on anything else. It was a magnificent and a terrible moment to be alive. And yet somehow life ran on—you couldn't stop it, any of it. There would never be a last time.

EPILOGUE

SEVERAL LIFETIMES LATER

LÜBECK, BRITISH OCCUPATION ZONE: APRIL 1948

The field had been planted over in apple trees. The earth was black from having been cratered in a bombing run, then regraded and plowed and sown with wild rye in the autumn after the war by the Corps of Royal Engineers. The rye had stood for two seasons before being turned under and the field resown with grass. And now the apple trees, no more than saplings, really, were blooming this spring for the first time. The blossoms were brilliantly white above the soft green grass, and their stamens picked up the yellow light of afternoon—a stirring vision. But this was ten kilometers from the Baltic Sea and frost was expected by morning. Likely there'd be no apples this year.

Jaap Saxo, director of the Michael Group and, for official eyes only, a special adviser to the Control Commission for Germany, British Element, turned from the window and tossed his hat toward the rack by the office door, scoring a perfect ringer: one thing he'd gotten right today. He hung up his jacket, a nondescript item that marked him as nobody in particular, and went down the row of portraits on the wall, straightening as required: Clement Attlee, Kurt Schumacher, an American classical musician (autographed), the late Admiral Wilhelm Canaris and a man known as Tusk, founder of the dj.1.11.

Saxo had just returned from a funeral in Berlin. He rarely visited Berlin these days—he rarely went anywhere, especially outside the

British Zone. The Soviet sector was impossible; people vanished there. The French were punctilious about identification, and Saxo had too many identities for their liking. And the American Zone was crawling with Gehlen people, several of whom he'd tried to kill. He even avoided Bremen, because the Yanks ran the port there, and wherever the Yanks went, their trusted and thoroughly de-Nazified German helpers went with them. Nonetheless, Saxo had broken his habit and gone to this funeral because . . . it was hard to explain why, even to himself, but something demanded it. Not honor—that was the curse of Germany. Not loyalty, either; in this business, the notion of loyalty was too fraught. Truth, then: the absolute value of getting the story right. This funeral was the last chapter of a story that had begun, as it now seemed, several lifetimes ago.

But that was Berlin; this was Lübeck. Saxo had work to do, a meeting tomorrow with his SIS contact, frost or no frost, to prepare for. The contact—like Saxo, a former navy man; it was odd how these fraternities persisted—was flying out from London. He would bring many questions, and Saxo could offer precious few answers. But perhaps that would change. He had an operative coming in today, a man he'd worked with before the war and right through it, a man he liked and trusted. Saxo employed a number of such people, his own little network, paying them from an account the Brits had set up for him, a nominal shipping concern. A few had been in the Abwehr before the SD finally broke that up. Most of them he'd just fallen in with—exiles, artists, bons vivants, people you happened to meet along the way. The Americans had no use for them, nor for Saxo himself; they had their thousand de-Nazified specialists. But the Brits had been sympathetic. They couldn't fund an operation on the scale of the Gehlen Org, but they could afford Saxo and his closetful of eccentrics. Why they'd named it the Michael Group, he had no idea. Maybe someone at Century House had lost his boy Mike in the war.

The man he was waiting for came in shortly after six. Like Saxo, he was dressed in the sort of clothing nobody remembers. He hooked his jacket on the rack and spent a minute or so looking at the photographs, as Saxo had expected. Poor Canaris! They'd gotten him in the end, held him at Flossenbürg for a while and then hanged him a few days before the U.S. Third Army arrived. The newcomer paused before the photo of the musician. When at last he turned to face Saxo, he was smiling.

"That's a wonderful picture of Clair. Have you seen him?"

"In Hamburg. February. Haydn's Flute Concerto in D and something by Telemann, I can't remember. I've got the program in a file somewhere. 'Finished casework,' probably." He motioned for Oskar, who was currently known as something else, to have a seat. "That's one good thing we did, anyway."

"I think we did a number of good things," Oskar said. "But Clair—how *was* he? Did you have a chance—"

"Reception after the concert. He doesn't remember *me*, of course, but I dropped *your* name, and then he was happy to talk. Eager, actually. Lots of questions about everyone. I told him what I could."

Oskar raised an eyebrow. "What did you say about—"

"Exactly what I've told you: I simply don't know. It's not the easiest thing, tracing a particular SS officer. In this case, the trail leads east—an *Einsatzgruppe*, then regular combat, then anti-partisan duty—and there it vanishes. I'd say the strong likelihood is that our friend von Ewigholz met a grisly end, and that he richly deserved it. But we'll never know."

Oskar nodded: another story, more unanswered questions, nothing to dwell on. He sat quietly for a while—he'd developed a certain talent for that—and Saxo guessed he was adjusting as people did when they came in, getting the feel of his own identity, slipping into himself as you would into an old, comfortable pair of shoes.

"How was the funeral?" Oskar asked finally.

The question, which Saxo had been dreading, came almost as a relief. "It was quiet. Orderly. Proper. She would've hated it. But also approved of it—you know what I mean? The music was lovely, though. You know they've left the Gedächtniskirche standing, what's left of it. They're building new wings on either side. The acoustics are odd—wooden scaffolding everywhere. Everything in Berlin is just being propped up somehow. Where does all that wood come from? Someone in Norway must be getting rich off this."

Oskar smiled; he'd become a patient listener. "But how *was* the funeral, really? Who was there? What were people talking about? What was it like, going back?"

"It was damned awful, is how it really was. Who was there . . . well, who's left? Guido was there—and you know what, she left him a painting. Something from up in the attic. He thinks she probably meant it as a joke, but it's worth a small fortune; he's planning to sell it and open a gallery in Munich, cater to the Yankee trade. What people were talking about—what does anybody ever talk about? Not the war, anything but that. And nobody's sure what to make of the present, so it's either the future or the past, the distant past. In this case, mostly the past. It was maudlin. The stories were funny, a lot of them, but the whole atmosphere was maudlin. Maybe that's just Berlin."

He felt himself growing agitated—this was why he'd feared the question in the first place. He stood up and walked to the window. Dusk was gathering. Out in the newborn orchard, apple blossoms glowed like paper stars.

"And you *can't* go back. That world doesn't exist anymore. She was the last of it, and now it's over. She outlived Hitler! She outlived everyone. Even us, I sometimes think. But now there's none of her sort of wit left in the world. Or that sort of kindness and strength. And no, I'm not being a tortured Romantic. I understand we've got our own sort of strength, that we're building something new here. Look, have you seen the apple trees?"

Oskar ambled over to join him by the window. "Very nice," he said. "How about Cissy?"

Saxo almost laughed. So it was good to talk, after all. He followed, in general, the rule that operatives should not be "mutually conscious," but in this case, he'd make an exception. "Cissy's doing well. She sends her love. She's taken a job as a nurse in Vienna."

"A nurse?"

"Private clinic, very select clientele. People come from all over. From the East Bloc, especially. They share their troubles with the understanding nurse. She has many interesting stories to tell."

Oskar smiled. It was probably time to get down to business, but the two men stood there awhile longer, looking out over the field in the fading light. It felt as though there was something in the room between them—neither had put a word to it; maybe no such word existed—and as soon as one of them spoke, it would be gone.

"The apples were a mistake," said Saxo, closing the book on all that. "They'll never bear fruit. Not in this climate."

"Yes, they will," said Oskar. "You're just feeling gloomy. You're missing the Baroness."

"Am I?"

Saxo wondered about this. Oskar wouldn't lie to him, he supposed. "Tomorrow," he said quietly, thinking of the frost. "We'll wait and see. Maybe it will turn out all right."

A Note About the Author

Richard Grant was born in Norfolk in 1952, attended the University of Virginia, and served in the U.S. Coast Guard. He lives in Rockport, Maine, where he has been a contributing editor of *Down East* magazine, chaired the literature panel of the Maine Arts Commission and won a New England Press Award for his column in *The Camden Herald*.

A Note on the Type

This book was set in Janson, a typeface named for the Dutchman Anton Janson, but is actually the work of Nicholas Kis (1650–1702). The type is an excellent example of the influential and sturdy Dutch types that prevailed in England up to the time William Caslon (1692–1766) developed his own incomparable designs from them.

Typeset by North Market Street Graphics,
Lancaster, Pennsylvania

Printed and bound by Berryville Graphics,
Berryville, Virginia

Designed by Betty Lew